THE FORMATION OF A BEAST

COME OUT OF HER MY PEOPLE - LAST CALL

THE FORMATION OF A BEAST

COME OUT OF HER MY PEOPLE - LAST CALL

NANCY LORRAINE WHITE

CITIOFBOOKS, INC.
3736 Eubank NE Suite A1
Albuquerque, NM 87111-3579
www.citiofbooks.com

Hotline: 1 (877) 389-2759
Fax: 1 (505) 930-7244

Ordering Information:

Quantity sales. Special discounts are available on quantity purchases by corporations, associations, and others. For details, contact the publisher at the address above.

Printed in the United States of America.

ISBN-13:   Softcover   979-8-89391-280-7
              eBook   979-8-89391-281-4
              Hardback   979-8-89391-349-1

Library of Congress Control Number: 2024916995

TABLE OF CONTENTS

Dedication and Thanks

I first would like to thank the Lord, who spoke to my heart concerning the need for this book and who has directed me through its pages. To him be all glory and honor forever. I further would like to thank the men, although some have gone on to be with the Lord, who have opened the eyes of many, myself included, for the need to search out and embrace the truth: William Sowders, Cornelius Mears, and Martin Baxter. Also, those men and women who have requested anonymity yet have supported me with their abilities and knowledge through this work.

I especially want to thank my family, who have continuously supported and encouraged me. My father and mother Frank and Audrey White, My sister and her husband, Kathy and Jack Albert. My son and his wife, Dennis and Glynda Clark and my daughter and her husband Michelle and John Harper. My older brother, Frank White, and younger brother and his wife, Phillip and Lynn White. My dear uncle and aunt Hue and Nancy Spratley. Good friends such as Ginger Neison, and Bonita Hunter have been very influential with their love for the Lord. My dedication is to them, as they continue to seek truth and righteousness in Christ alone. My love and gratitude to each one of you. Without all of you, I could not have accomplished this.

"Therefore, putting away lying, let each one of you speak truth with his neighbor: for we are members one of another" (Eph. 4:25).

THE FORMATION OF A BEAST
INTRODUCTION

The contents of this book are not meant to slander, offend, or be insolent and disrespectful to the persons of any Christian denomination, nor any other religion. Rather, it is my sincere intent and desire to present facts as they have been written, recorded, then hidden and forgotten through the ages, in order to shed understanding to the reader. My hope is that the Beast and Mystery Babylon in the book of Revelation is exposed with enough clarity that it will be understood, identified, and avoided.

Please be aware that portions of the contents may be unpleasant to read and acknowledge and may be offensive to some; however, I ask that if you, dear reader, want truth, to remain honest with yourself and remember that the truth, though sometimes difficult to accept will indeed set you free.

The Bible is one book made up of ancient books collected and compiled together. Although the ancient cultures have long passed, the contents have remained consistent and reliable. The Old Testament language has come to us with very little re-copy of its original. But the New Testament has been re-copied from Greek and Latin books down through the centuries and therefore the original manuscripts must be researched for better clarity, more so than the Old Testament manuscripts. It is possible to read and understand the Bible with very little knowledge of the world from which it was written, but for a fuller and complete understanding we need to take our minds back in time. Regardless, the Bible is a timeless book with a message from our creator to all. It does not contain abstract ideas about God but rather it reveals his mind and his character.

Because of the King James Bible history, and for the ease of the reader, I have taken all biblical quotes from the NKJV Bible. For the Hebrew and Greek word definitions, I have used the *Strong's Concordance* and Hebrew etymology.

THE FORMATION OF A BEAST

Chapter 1

Awareness in Mankind

The awareness of a power greater than man is revealed through the world around us. In nature's miracles and through the balance of the universe, it becomes apparent that a higher intellect was and is at work. Within the core of man is a longing to unite himself with his creator. Throughout the centuries there has been differing and multiple cultural societies, religions, doctrine with creeds, rituals, and ideologies which have penetrated the thoughts and subconscious minds of man, leaving him in a state of confusion, uncertainties, doubts and fears. Mankind, in groping for truth, has turned to false gods and teachings, seeking out its maker, the life and the peace that the world can never bring.

Today the appearing of our Lord is nearer than we think, and many times we find our hearts longing for a closeness in our relationship with God that we are not getting from the assemblies we've attached ourselves to. Around the globe today, believers have become unsettled in their faith, hungering for knowledge and a deeper understanding of God's Word.

For years, we've been sitting in church pews as if sitting in theater seats watching an orchestrated message delivered in performance, and then we return to our homes feeling empty and unfed. Prompted to look further, beyond the confines of the churches, believers are gathering in homes to seek out the deeper things of God and to gain insight of the times we are in. There, they are able to thresh out the Word of God, peel off the layers and turn the stones over to discover the truths buried in the traditions and doctrines of men over the last two thousand years of Christianity. There we are removed from the influence of so-called church doctrine and manmade religions that prevent us from growing up and maturing in the Word and Spirit of God.

Like Abraham, we long "for the city which has foundations, whose builder and maker is God" (Heb. 11:10).

Our Heavenly Father made a call to his people, to those who hear his voice, "And I heard another voice from heaven saying, 'Come out of her my people, lest you share in her sins, and lest you receive of her plagues'" (Rev. 18:4).

This call first came to the church in warnings from the apostles before the fall of the church. The call during the Protestant Reformation years went forth announcing that this call was being implemented. The cry to come out has continued down through the centuries, and today, with the Gentile church age about to end, the call is growing intensely and desperately louder. Believers want to answer that call but don't understand what it is they should come out of. Most look outside their own house of faith thinking it can't possibly pertain to the religion they've chosen to serve and so they justify themselves in staying. Many are not interested in examining their faith because they are comfortable there and don't want to disturb the waters or leave the friends and acquaintances they've made.

Few believers understand the revelation or unveiling Christ gave his servants because the majority refuse to look where they themselves sit. Yet the majority sit in the midst of "her," completely unaware, without knowledge or understanding of what they are a part of, lulled into a sleep and a false security that as long as we remain faithful to the organization, we will be given our ticket to eternal life.

Most of us have been convinced that to leave the church, or actually the organization, means to lose your way, to fall from grace, or worse yet, become a heretic, condemned to an eternity of a burning hellfire. This may be a good tactic to hold people; however, it is through fear that people who sincerely are seeking out the Lord will remain. But the fear and doubt of one's own judgment is a result of not having enough knowledge to exercise confidence of choice.

The Lord had a controversy with Israel, "Hear the word of the Lord, ye children of Israel: for the Lord hath a controversy with the inhabitants of the land, because there is no truth, nor mercy, nor knowledge of God in the land

My people are destroyed for lack of knowledge: because you have rejected knowledge, I also will reject you from being priest for me: because you have forgotten the law of your God, I also will forget your children" (Hosea 4:1, 6).

We need to have knowledge and we should seek out knowledge with the Holy Spirit as our guide. Therefore, if we want to know truth and desire understanding, then we have to be willing to accept the knowledge of truth and thus acquire the understanding of things that are past, things that are present, and the things to come. If we lack this knowledge, then we find ourselves susceptible to being gullible and easily intrigued. Remaining ignorant is a dangerous thing. People quote an old cliché, "What you don't know won't hurt you." That in itself is a lie. What you don't know can **Kill** you . . . if you don't know there is poison in the drink and you drink it....

Sometimes gaining knowledge can be just as frightening or painful as it can be rewarding. Some things can be hard to accept, and it requires one to, "Trust in the Lord with all your heart; and lean not on your own understanding" (Prov. 3:5).

Knowledge can be strong meat, hard to digest. "For everyone who partakes only of milk is unskilled in the word of righteousness: for he is a babe. But solid food belongs to those who are of full age, that is, those who by reason of use have their senses exercised to discern both good and evil" (Heb. 5:13, 14).

To exercise our senses, a walk-through history is needed in order to examine the paths that were laid out before us that brought us to our present faith. The church of today actually has its beginning in Genesis, where the plan of redemption is first introduced. Through the old books of the Bible, we can trace the plan of God. And through Israel, the people God chose for this redemptive purpose, we have received the gospel of our salvation. Without God's word, a knowledge of the history of religions, and without understanding Israel (Jews) and the church, we remain ignorant, lacking in both knowledge and understanding. We cannot discern both good and evil.

Few Christians are aware of how the faith they practice came about. They don't understand the Jewish roots of Christianity because they, the majority being Gentile, have forgotten that Jesus went to the lost sheep of the house of Israel only. He did not go to the Gentiles. He did, however, raise up apostles who were Jews for that purpose. Somehow the church received from the Jews the gospel of Yeshua (Jesus), and then presented that gospel as though it were a gentile gospel and the gentiles the inheritance. Yet the gentiles are "grafted into" the inheritance. Scriptures such as "there is neither Greek (Gentile) nor Jew" have lost meaning. The walls of separation that were being torn down were swiftly re-constructed, however, our salvation began with the Jews and by all indication will end with the Jews.

"You worship what you do not know; we know what we worship: for salvation is of the Jews" (John 4:22).

We need to know what we worship, why we are climbing up a denominational ladder to reach Christ and receive his gift of eternal life. Is there really any one church that can claim they are the only way? Didn't Christ inform us differently?

"Most assuredly, I say to you, he who does not enter the sheepfold by the door, but climbs up some other way, the same is a thief and a robber, but he who enters by the door is the shepherd of the sheep. To him the doorkeeper opens; and the sheep hear his voice: and he calls his own sheep by name, and leads them out. And when he brings out his own sheep, he goes before them, and the sheep follow him: for they know his voice. Yet they will by no means follow a stranger, but will flee from him: for they do not know the voice of strangers (John 10:1–5).

Then said Jesus to them again, "Most assuredly, I say to you, I am the door of the sheep" (John 10:1–5, 7).

"I am the way, the truth, and the life: no man comes to the Father, except through Me" (John 14:6).

There are many roads to choose and many ways to follow.

"A foolish woman is clamorous; she is simple, and knows nothing, for she sits at the door of her house, on a seat by the highest places of the city, to call to those who pass by, who go straight on their way: 'Whoever is simple, let him turn in here: And as for him who lacks understanding, she says to him, 'Stolen water is sweet, and bread eaten in secret is pleasant.'

But he does not know that the dead are there; that her guests are in the depths of hell" (Prov. 9:13–18).

A woman in the Bible represents a church. She is boisterous, and appeals to the naive. She doesn't give them understanding. She is hypnotic in her approach. The word *stolen* here leans toward the definition of not only to thieve but to deceive, and her spiritual food is a mystery (hidden or secret). Her members are spiritually dead. She is death, sheol, the grave, like Gehenna in the New Testament, the very depths of hell. The majority of the women (churches) who are in the world today are like this woman. They soothe the soul with their tone of music, eloquent sermons, mystic rituals, high ceilings and artifacts to imitate a spiritualism and awe. The impressionable are impressed, drawn in, and fall asleep in the comfort of her arms.

There is an ancient source or starting point, a way leading to death and the grave, which is paved out through history and engraved in every religion. And every church and every faith-based organization existing today has its roots going directly back to that source. In order to recognize how the roots of every religion lead back to this source and how every religion has been influenced, we need to have a foundation of understanding. A brief summary and walk through the history of biblical events, the church, and the societies of men can give us that foundation.

<h1 style="text-align:center">CHAPTER 2</h1>

In the Beginning

The "beast" of Revelation has its beginning with the fall of mankind in the Garden of Eden when Adam and Eve challenged their heavenly Father's authority through their disobedience. Through the centuries it has crept throughout the world disguised and hidden in men's traditional religions, politics, and customs. Its tentacles reach to the furthest points of the globe, wrapping its control over Earth's inhabitants.

In the book of Genesis, we read the beginning of the creation of all things: the world, the universe, vegetation, animals, and lastly the creation of mankind. The account is a short summary of how the human race came into existence. The time frame is not disclosed because that is not the purpose of the record given. The purpose of the record is to lay a foundation, to enlighten us in understanding that the human family was created by God and created in his image, and was created to be his light in the world. Adam was favored above everything he created. He was created to be in fellowship with our heavenly Father but not by force as some mechanical robot without a will or choice; he was given a will and freedom of choice, however, the choice that he willed to make, plunged us into darkness. It was ignited by the lust of the eyes, the lust of the flesh and the pride of life. It was a self-will choice to gratify and exalt the desires of the flesh. Every person born since has inherited Adam's nature and his sin.

In Genesis we are also introduced to God's plan to redeem us and enter into the loving fellowship with him that we were created for. The account given, "In the beginning God created the heavens and the earth," denotes no space of time (Gen. 1:1). This could have been thousands of years; we don't know. The following verse states, "And the earth was without form, and void; and darkness was on the face of the deep. And the Spirit of God was hovering over the face of the waters" (Gen. 1:2).

With a little research, we learn that the word *was* should have been translated, *became*. The word from the Hebrew *tohuw* means to lie waste or a desolation. The word *void* is the Hebrew *bohuw*, which means a vacuity, empty or undistinguishable ruin. Thus, the world was created but came to be in ruins and vacant of life.

"Then God said, 'Let there be light'; and there was light" (Gen. 1:3). This was not the creation of the sun as the sun and other heavenly lights came later. Then God said, "Let there be lights in the firmament of the heavens to divide the day from the night; and let them be for signs, and seasons, and for days, and years (Gen. 1:14). "Then God made two great lights; the greater light to rule the day, and the lesser light to rule the night; He made the stars also" (Gen 1:16). In between these two events was the separation of the waters from the earth, the forming of the oceans and seas and the bringing forth of vegetation; grass, trees, fruit, herbs and such.

When God created the light in Genesis 1: 2, and called the light day and the night darkness, it was a term of light as life and darkness as death. The light here is the creation of the enlightenment of Christ, it is truth, righteousness and understanding. "In the beginning was the Word, and the Word was with God, and the Word was God. He was in the beginning with God. All things were made through him; and without him nothing was made that was made. In him was life; and the life was the light of men" (John 1:1–4). The darkness denotes being without the light or without life. "Those who sat in darkness and in the shadow of death, bound in affliction and irons" (Ps. 107:10). "And the light shines in the darkness; and the darkness did not comprehend it" (John 1:5).

I think it is worth noting that our vegetation produces oxygen for our breathing, and animal life was not brought forth until the vegetation was first brought forth. Also, until the first light, there was no life at all as every scientist or biologist knows that there has to be a source of light in order to bring forth life on Earth. Therefore when

Christ said He is the light of the world and also, He is truth and He is life it takes us back to creation.

The first man created to fellowship with God he named Adam. A name denotes a nature and this name denotes two things: the word *adam* is of the Hebrew word *adamah,* which means ground. He came from the earth thus he was earthly; Adam means "ruddy or red, to show blood in the face, fleshly."

The first woman, who was named Eve, was formed by God within the man before God removed her.

"And Adam said: 'This is now bone of my bones and flesh of my fles; she shall be called woman, because she was taken out of man. "(Genesis 2: 23)

Therefore, she was of the man or the same as the man in chemical makeup and nature; earthly and fleshly. This does not mean they looked like dirt, nor does the term *ruddy* or *red* mean they were colored like a ruby. What we are looking at is what all of mankind is: earthly and fleshly. In *Strong's Concordance, adam* is also used to insinuate one of low degree.

"And God made the beast of the earth according to its kind, cattle according to its kind and everything that creeps on the earth according to its kind: and God saw that it was good."

"Then God said, "Let us make man in Our image, according to Our likeness: let them have dominion over the fish of the sea, over the birds of the air, and over the cattle, over all the earth, and every creeping thing that creeps on the earth."

"So God created man in his own image, in the image of God he created him; male and female he created them" (Gen. 1:25, 27).

"Then God saw everything that he had made, and indeed it was very good. So the evening and the morning were the sixth day" (Gen. 1:31).

Sometimes people forget that the beasts or animals were created in the same day Adam and Eve were created. Both were created on the sixth day. "And the Lord God formed man of the dust of the ground, and breathed into his nostrils the breath of life; and man became a living being" (Gen. 2:7). God breathed his Spirit into Adam. There is nowhere written that he breathed into the other beasts of the field.

Man was created in the image of God, after his likeness. He was created in the form of God. He was created divine and was as a *shining light* upon the earth that fell into darkness and brought darkness into the world. In Matthew 5:14, Jesus says, "You are the light of the world," and in Matthew 5:16, Jesus told his disciples "Let your light so shine before men." In Matthew 13:43, he says, "Then the righteous will shine forth as the sun in the kingdom of their father." and in Daniel 12:3, Gabriel, speaking of the future says, "Those who are wise shall shine like the brightness of the firmament, and those who turn many to righteousness like the stars for ever and ever." This is just a few examples of how, when we are walking with God that we are not just walking in light, but we are light and the children of light.

We are familiar with the story about God telling Adam not to eat of the tree of *knowledge* of good and evil and how Eve was deceived and they both partook of the *fruit* of the tree. It is important to note that it wasn't the tree itself but the *fruit* of *knowledge* it produced.

I think it should be clarified that Adam's disobedience was not as simple as it reads. Adam partook of the "fruit of knowledge" of good and evil. In this passage the word *knowledge* comes from the word *da'ath* which means cunning, aware. His awareness of good and evil was cunningly devised.

In Genesis 3, we are introduced to Satan, in the form of a serpent. Verse 1 begins his deceptive conversation with Eve. "Now the serpent was more cunning than any *beast* of the field which the Lord God had made. And he said to the woman, 'Has God indeed said, "Ye shall not eat of every tree of the garden?"'" The Hebrew word for serpent is *nachash* and also means "shiny one" and "a whisperer." Note: The word *beast* is not some kind of red-eyed, sharp-toothed monster, but is defined as a living creature or thing. It is simply an animal.

Eve responds to his query with what she knows God commanded and expounds on the seriousness of staying far from it: "We may eat the fruit of the trees of the garden; but of the fruit of the tree which is in the midst of the garden, God has said, 'Ye shall not eat it, nor shall you touch it, lest ye die.'"

"Then the serpent said to the woman, 'You shall not surely die.'" For God knows that in the day you eat of it, your eyes will be opened, and you will be like God, knowing good and evil."

"So when the woman saw that the tree was good for food, that it was pleasant to the eyes, and a tree desirable to make one wise, she took of its fruit, and ate, she also gave to her husband with her, and he ate" (Gen. 3:2–6). These verses are metaphors and allegories, or types and shadows—that is, they compare the natural things or events with the spiritual things or events. The tree of life and the tree of knowledge of good and evil are not literal trees. The tree of the knowledge of good and evil is a type of man's own mind where knowledge is held and where imaginations are formed. The roots go down into the earth or the ground man was formed from. Adam himself was the tree of knowledge of good and evil and was in the midst of the garden. He was walking in light and through disobedience fell into darkness.

The tree of life is a type of Jesus, where the Spirit of God resides and life runs through it. Its roots go up into heaven unto God.

The serpent was not a literal serpent that could speak, but a living beast with a serpent nature, earthly and low. These types are brought out in the Gospels when John the Baptist refers to the religious leaders as vipers, and also when he uses trees as a metaphor for man saying in Matthew 3:10, "And even now the axe is laid to the root of the trees." God has always used natural things to represent the spiritual, and Jesus in his teachings did as well.

God had made man in his image and had given man dominion over every beast of the field. Yet they wanted to be exalted like gods, and through their disobedience they chose to bow down to self and a lowly serpentine nature. We see here the lust of the eyes, the desires of the flesh, and the pride of life.

In this dialogue, we also see the first lie, which set the course and the nature of the world and all of mankind. As the apostle James notes in his epistle, "And the tongue is a fire a world of iniquity. The tongue is so set among our members, that it defiles the whole body, and sets on fire the course of nature; and it is set on fire by hell" (James 3:6).

It is important to understand what transpired between Adam, Eve, and the serpent because it is where the seed of the beast of Revelations was planted and where it was germinated. Note in Rev. 12:9 how it reads: "So the great dragon was cast out, that serpent of old, called the Devil and Satan, who deceives the whole world;" Also in Rev. 20:2, "He laid hold of the dragon, that serpent of old, who is the Devil and Satan, and bound him a thousand years."

God finds them hiding from him and addresses them on what they did, and Adam blames Eve and God (the woman whom *you* gave), and Eve blames deception from the serpent. The serpent has no one to blame.

"So the Lord God said to the serpent: "Because you have done this, you are cursed more than all cattle, and more than every beast of the field; on your belly you shall go, and you shall eat dust all the days of your life."

"And I will put enmity between you and the woman, and between your seed and her Seed; He shall bruise your head and you shall bruise His heel" (Gen. 3:14, 15). Her seed refers to Jesus. This is the first prophecy of Christ.

From here on in the Bible, we often find mankind referred to as beasts, vipers, snakes, and other animals, depending on what part of the nature is being depicted. God gives an example of Christ's sacrifice for our sins and that of the world by slaying an animal and making coats of skin for Adam and Eve as a covering, which became the first animal sacrifice and shedding of blood for sin. What a beautiful picture for us; this was the first atonement enacted by God himself. After this Adam and Eve were sent from the Garden of Eden.

Soon after leaving the Garden, two sons are born to Adam and Eve. Cain and Abel illustrate two different attitudes of spirit and approaches to God. Cain, a tiller of the ground, brought a sacrifice to God from the fruit of the ground, but Abel kept sheep and gave the firstlings of his flock.

God had respect for Abel's offering but not for Cain's. This is because Cain was probably insincere with his offering and apparently had a sense of pride, presenting the work of his hands, the fruit of the ground. Abel's offering was a humble sacrifice to God and was most likely following the example given to Adam and Eve by God when he sacrificed an animal to clothe them with coats of skin.

Cain's nature comes forth and in his envy he kills Abel. He is cursed from the earth by God, then sent away, and travels to the land of Nod where he takes a wife and has children who share his sinful nature. The story of Cain and Abel illustrates the first rivalry towards the approach and worship of God.

Seth is born to Adam and Eve, beginning the righteous lineage line that leads to Jesus (Luke 3:23–38). In Cain's lineage there is no attention given to times and years.

As the earth became more inhabited, it became more inhabited with the sinful nature of man and full of corruption. The world increased in wickedness and, "Then the LORD saw that the wickedness of man was great in the earth, and that every intent of the thoughts of his heart was only evil continually" (Gen. 6:5).

God determined to destroy the Earth by means of a flood in order to cleanse it from this wickedness. But Noah, who was a descendent of Seth, found grace in God's eyes and was called upon by God to build an ark for himself and his family to be sheltered in. He was also to include a pair of every living creature God would bring to the ark.

After the flood, the Bible records the genealogy of Noah's sons and how they separated themselves into their own lands. Noah's son Ham, had a son named Cush, who in turn had a son named Nimrod. This same Nimrod was responsible for building a civilization which became the cradle of the "Beast."

THE FIRST CIVIL-RELIGIOUS STRUCTURE

The first civil-religious structure was developed in the land of Shinar, which encompassed northern and southern Babylonia. After the Flood, the people began to multiply and all were of the same language. The people had come to Shinar from the east and settled there, building a city for themselves. The kings of the east were god-kings considered to be a divinity. They were dictators and tyrants having complete authority over a state.

Everyone spoke the same language and were *all of the same speech*. This is important because it denotes that they were all likeminded, or in agreement together. They agreed to build a tower that would reach the heavens. That is, it would be a tall monumental structure reaching up into the sky. They agreed together to make a "name" for themselves.

The Lord saw the city and the tower that was being built and said "Indeed the people are one, and they have all one language; and this is what they begin to do: and now nothing that they propose to do will be withheld from them" (Gen. 11:6).

The Tower of Babel was a ziggurat (meaning to raise up or to elevate); temple tower which would reach the sky. These towers had a large base and were only three to seven stories high. According to the book of Jasher, the base of Nimrod's tower was in circumference, a three-day walk (Jasher 9:38). It was not a tall structure for us, but quite tall for the times. This particular ziggurat was identified with the tower of Ezida, the temple god of Nebo. However, later, with the discovery of the Babylonian temple Marduk, it has been thought that it was identified with a ziggurat called Etemenaki (house of the foundations of heaven and earth), which had two sanctuaries and stood about 300 feet tall. Whatever the identification, it is clearly evident that it was an object of enormous pride and rooted steep into idolatry.

The king of Babel was Nimrod, as previously mentioned, born to Cush, Noah's grandson. He was called "a mighty one before the Lord" (Gen. 10:8, 9). The Hebrew word translated for mighty came from the word, meaning "powerful, warrior, tyrant." Nimrod built four cities, Babel, Erech, Accad, and Calneh, all in the land of Shinar (Gen. 10:8–10). He was highly esteemed and he lived on through the stories of all those scattered throughout the world. After his death, many myths concerning how he died were told, written, and made into false pagan religions.

In one story, Nimrod was married to a woman named Semiramis. After Nimrod's death, Semiramis became pregnant and had a son whom she named Horus. She claimed that Nimrod had ascended to the heavens and impregnated her by the rays of the sun. She and Horus later became objects of mother and son worship.

The Egyptians adopted Nimrod as one of their gods and named him Osiris. They constructed a memorial, which we know today as an obelisk to represent his genitalia. The obelisk was an object of worship, which by representation was to declare that through the seed of Osiris the world would be civilized. Semiramis was also adopted by the Egyptians and they named her Isis. Isis is also known as Ashtoreth or Ishtar from which the word Easter is derived and Horus became known as Tammuz.

Varying stories and religions have since developed and have been spread throughout the entire world. Every religion of the world has been influenced and practices some sort of sun worship, mother and child worship, and even the idea of a tri-god from these three pagan deities

To prevent the people from continuing the building of their tower, God, confounded their language. They left off building the tower and the people dispersed throughout the land, becoming individual nations and carrying with them the same spirit and building of pagan systems for worship. This short story lays the groundwork of the civil-religious systems that govern our world today.

It is important to note that every nation that came up against Israel and every nation that ruled over Israel had a civil-religious system of idolatry, usually having many gods and coupled with a political system that was contrary to the government God had given Israel. Every one of those nations with their religious beliefs and practices originated from the dispersion following the Tower of Babel. In fact, when examined, every nation's politics and religions are steeped deeply in Nimrod's Babylon. Nimrod, determined to make himself a king of the Earth, placed himself between God and his people. He instituted the first civil-religious system which grew to be the "great, fiery red dragon" of Rev. 12:3.

CHAPTER 3

God Makes a Covenant

Abram (Abraham) was the first to be called out of an idolatrous civil-religious system. He'd left Ur of the Chaldees with his father, Terah, his wife, Sarai, and his nephew, Lot, to settle in the land of Haran. While there, God told Abram, "Get out of your country, from your family, and from your father's house, to a land that I will show you" (Gen. 11:31, 12:1). Abram was dwelling in a land of idolatry when God called him out. The book of Joshua records; "your fathers, including Terah, and the father of Nahor, dwelt on the other side of the River in old times, and they served other gods" (Joshua 24:2). Abram heard God, and, trusting, left all to journey with God. Later, in Genesis 17:5, God promised him a son by Sarai his wife and that he'd be the father of many nations and inherit the land he'd been brought into.

There were many events during the time that Abram first received the call to separate himself and was given this covenant. One of the more important was the "battle of the kings. When Abram and Lot separated. Lot went into the land of Sodom to dwell and Abram dwelt in Canaan. Abram learned of his nephew Lot, whom he referred to as a brother, being taken captive by kings who came against those of Sodom and Gomorrah. He fought against them and was victorious in bringing Lot back (Gen. 14:13).

Upon returning, he was met by Melchizedek. "Then Melchizedek king of Salem brought forth bread and wine; he was the priest of God Most High." And he blessed him and said: "Blessed be Abram of God Most High, possessor of heaven and earth: And blessed be God Most High, who has delivered your enemies into your hand. And he gave have him a tithe of all" (Gen. 14:18–20). Abram was so moved by him that "he gave him a tithe of all" the spoils he'd just risked his life for, "Now consider how great this man was, to whom even the patriarch Abraham gave the tenth of the spoils" (Heb. 7:4).

Later in Genesis 18 and 19, we read that the land of Sodom and Gomorrah became so corrupt that God decided to remove them from the Earth. Sodom and Gomorrah are a profound example of how nations plunged into depravity by conforming to the manner of Babel.

The Lord appeared unto Abraham and informed him of this and Abraham interceded for Lot. The Lord then sent two angels to Lot and they spared him with his wife and his two daughters. They gave them instructions to leave and not look back; however, his wife did look back (this wasn't just looking back with her eyes, but she looked back with her heart) and was turned into a pillar of salt. Probably she was covered with the salt rained down with the fire and brimstone. Afterward, Lot's daughters in fear of not ever marrying and having children, intoxicate Lot in order to lay with him and become pregnant. The result was creating the nations of Moab and Ammon, known to be adversaries to God and Israel and heavy into Baal worship.

Before Isaac was born, Abram fathered Ishmael by Hagar, his wife's Sarai's handmaid at Sarai's request because she was barren and feared not having any offspring. When Ishmael was thirteen years old, God made the covenant of circumcision with him and Abram circumcised Ishmael and every one of his men servants and himself also when he was ninety-nine years old. This covenant separated them from the nations.

But God had told Abram he'd have a son by Sarai and he was to call his name Isaac. At this point his name was changed from Abram to Abraham, because he'd become a father of many nations, and Sarai's was changed to Sarah. When Isaac was born, he circumcised him according to the commandment of God at 8 days old. When Abraham had Isaac he was 100 years of age and Sarah was ninety years of age.

For Abraham to leave his home land and family to journey in a strange land, not knowing where he was going and to trust God for an offspring of nations when already old and had no offspring, displays an exceptional amount of faith. But God made a covenant with Abraham and he believed God and it was "accounted to him for righteousness" (Gen. 15:6).

Abraham would have to let Ishmael go, at Sarah's request and God's command, because in Isaac his seed would be reckoned. This was grievous to Abraham and a test of his faith, but he believed God, and therefore sent Hagar and Ishmael away (Gen. 21:12). History tells us that Ishmael became the father of the Arabian nation.

Abraham's faith toward God was again tested, but in the most difficult way a person could be tested. He was told by God to sacrifice his son Isaac, "and he that had received the promises, offered up his only begotten son" (Heb. 11:17–19). He followed through with all the preparations, but just before he actually applied his blade to sacrifice him, God intervened and supplied a ram whose horns were caught in a thicket (Gen 22: 9–12). We see here Isaac as a type of Christ, being our sacrifice, and Abraham a type of God the Father. Jesus (Yeshua) in fact, was crucified on that same Mount Moriah. He had a crown of thorns placed on his head much like the ram also had.

The Israelites were and are commonly called Hebrews. This originated with Abraham because he had passed over from the other side of the flood from the Mesopotamia area. The word Hebrew comes from the root *abar*, meaning to pass over or through. Abram had come from the other side of the river (most likely the Euphrates).

Isaac became the father of Jacob, who was renamed Israel. He fathered twelve sons who became the twelve tribes of Israel, and a Hebrew nation (a nation that passed over). They were brought to Egypt by way of Israel's eleventh-born son, Joseph, who had been sold to by his brothers and taken to Egypt (Gen. 37:25–28). While there, Joseph, after a series of events, became Pharaoh's, right-hand man. He was admired and respected by both Pharaoh and all of Egypt and prospered well. Through a famine in which his family turned to Egypt for help, he became known to his brethren, and Joseph brought them and their father, including all they had, to Egypt to dwell in safety (Gen. 48).

They grew and multiplied there, but when a Pharaoh was raised up that "knew not Joseph," they were taken as slaves to the Egyptians and suffered great oppression. The Hebrews grew in numbers until eventually Pharaoh became concerned about the large number (Exod.1:8, 9). Pharaoh set task masters over the Hebrews and heavily burdened them, yet, they continued to grow in number. Finally, he determined to have every son born to a Hebrew woman killed. But God had a plan to raise up a man called Moses to deliver his people, the children of Israel.

Moses was born to a Levite man and woman. His mother hid him until she no longer could. Then to save him from being slain, she made an ark of bulrushes daubed with slime and pitch and placed him in it, then placed him in the Nile, concealed with the reeds or flags by the river's bank. He was discovered and drawn out by Pharaoh's daughter who reared him; however, his mother was chosen to be nursemaid to him and she, Moses' own mother, began his upbringing (Exod. 2:1–10).

The generations of Israel's sons are given us in Exodus 6:14–20 and lead us to Moses and Aaron, who descended from Levi, Israel's third son, which tribe would be chosen to be priests for Israel. Moses would become called out and separated with Aaron his brother to not only deliver the Hebrews but to teach them his laws and establish his covenant.

Let My People Go

Moses became mighty in Egypt, and one day decided to visit his brethren the Hebrews. Seeing an Egyptian striking one of his brethren, he was deeply troubled and killed the Egyptian. The next day he went out again and saw two Hebrews fighting and asked the one striking the other why he was hitting this man, "And he said; 'Who made you a prince and judge over us? Do you intend to kill me, as you killed the Egyptian?" Moses then realized the incident was known. Pharaoh also had heard and was going to kill Moses, so he fled to Midian (Exod. 2:11–15).

After forty years in exile, God called Moses out from Midian to return to Egypt and deliver the Israelites from bondage. To cause Pharaoh to allow the Israelites to be released, God unleashed various plagues upon the Egyptians where his power and authority were manifested. With each plague, Pharaoh would consent to let the people go, and then each time change his mind. Finally, with the tenth plague, which took the lives of every firstborn person and animal in Egypt, Pharaoh relented.

These plagues were more than just to trouble the Egyptians. They were orchestrated by God in opposition to the many Egyptian gods. For example, God sent frogs over the land and the Egyptians had Hapi as their god of the frogs. When he sent a myriad of flies into Egypt it was in opposition to Uatchit, the fly god. Every plague had a counterfeit deity that God buffeted.

The Israelites were called out from a place of bondage and a place of idolatry where other gods were worshiped, prayed to, and sacrificed to. They were enslaved and in bondage by a civil-religious nation. Egypt's government was developed and incorporated into their civil rule in accordance to the belief and worship of their various gods. But, the Israelites were led out by the mighty hand of God on a journey to the land promised to Abraham and his offspring where they would be free to worship the one true God of Abraham, Isaac, and Jacob (Gen. 12:7).

Pharaoh's heart again turned, and he and his army set out in pursuit of the Israelites. The Israelites escaped from Egypt had brought them to the Red Sea (or, as some call it, the Reed Sea) where they seemingly were trapped. God intervened and brought a thick cloud between Pharaoh and the children of Israel. Pharaoh was unable to continue until the cloud was lifted because they were unable to see through the thickness.

While Pharaoh and his army were detained, the Lord parted the sea, allowing Israel to pass through. When the cloud lifted, Pharaoh continued in his pursuit into the parted waters which God then released, covering Pharaoh and his army, and there they perished.

Israel's journey took them to the region of Mount Horeb, considered to be the back side of Mount Sinai, where they would have a fearful encounter with God. He came down upon the mountain with thunder and lightning and the sound of a trumpet which grew louder and louder. God spoke to them the Ten Commandments and the people feared the thundering and presence of God and stood far off. Moses drew near to the mountain and entered into a thick cloud where he met with the Lord. God spoke to Moses and all of Israel the laws concerning the Ten Commandments and the three appointed feasts of the Lord.

God instructed Moses to come up on the mountain where he would give him two tablets of stone written by the finger of God, the Ten Commandments. Moses ascended there and was with the Lord for forty days, communing with him. There he received from God the instructions on building the ark with all the articles and instruments for service. Instructions for the tabernacle and all the furnishings were also given. The consecration of Aaron as high priest and his two sons as priests were initiated there, and the order of sacrifice was given. The instruction on how Aaron's priestly garments were to be made were given to Moses. Also the instructions regarding the Sabbath was given (Exod. 19–31).

It was here at Mount Sinai that Israel received the "living oracles" of God. These oracles, known as the Ten Commandments, would be placed in the ark by themselves and remain there. They are the foundational instructions for all believers and the principles all believers stand on and profess to others. "This is he (Moses), who was in the congregation in the wilderness with the Angel who spoke to him on Mount Sinai, and with our fathers: the one who received the living oracles to give us" (Acts 7:38).

Moses seemed to the Israelites to tarry too long and they became restless. They turned to Egypt in their hearts and in order to appease themselves, they had, with the assistance of Aaron, constructed a golden calf which they made with what they'd brought with them from Egypt (Exod. 32:1–4). When Moses came down from the mountain, he discovered the Israelites had turned from their God and were worshiping the calf and turning back to the practices of the Egyptians. Moses had brought with him the Ten Commandments, which were inscribed by the hand of God on two tablets of stone.

In his anger, he threw the tablets down and broke them. He also broke up and ground to powder the golden calf. With all this disappointment and anger, he still loved his brethren, So Moses approached God at Mount Sinai so that he might make atonement for the sin of his brethren (Exod. 32:30).

Moses had received from God instructions for the building of the tabernacle, which he was told to build exactly like the pattern given to him. Moses pitched the tabernacle outside the camp and there met with the Lord. The two tablets were re-created, and the children of Israel were called to the work of the tabernacle. Many were called who had craft and spinning abilities, and had a willing heart for offering the materials and the work. "Then everyone came whose heart was stirred, and every one whose spirit was willing. They came, both men and women, as many as had a willing heart, and brought earrings and nose rings, rings and necklaces, all jewelry of gold" (Exod. 35:21, 22). I cannot help but note here the passage from Matt. 22:14, "For many are called but few are chosen." There were numerous Israelites who were called to help in building the tabernacle but didn't respond to the call because their hearts were not willing.

The children of Israel continued to journey through the wilderness, and although the Lord met their needs and led them with a cloud by day and a pillar of fire by night they still grumbled against God and against Moses saying they'd been brought out to the wilderness to die. Because of their constant speaking against God and Moses, the Lord sent fiery serpents among them. Many were bitten and died. The people went to Moses confessing their sin and pleading that he would intercede for them to the Lord. So Moses prayed to the Lord and the Lord told Moses to make a fiery serpent and put it upon a pole so everyone who was bitten should look upon it and not die.

This was a prophecy of Christ's crucifixion. "And as Moses lifted up the serpent in the wilderness, even so must the son of man be lifted up" (John 3:14). Jesus was not a serpent, but he had come and taken on the serpent nature of man through Mary, in order to overcome and conquer so that through his sacrifice we might be saved. "So Moses made a bronze serpent, and put it on a pole; and so it was, that if a serpent had bitten anyone, when he looked at the serpent of brass, he lived" (Num. 21:9).

Moses is referred to as a picture and type of Christ. Deuteronomy18:15 reads, "The Lord your God will raise up for you a Prophet like me from your midst, from your brethren, Him you shall hear." He interceded for the children of Israel, praying and making atonement of their sins. He led them from Egypt, a picture of false religion and bondage. He led them through a wilderness to a promised land. He instructed them in the building of the tabernacle exactly by the instructions and the pattern God gave him, as it was after God's heavenly pattern.

After Moses' death, the Hebrew children were led by Joshua whom God had separated to finish leading the people into the land promised to Abraham for their inheritance (Josh. 1:1, 2).

Chapter 4

In the Promised Land

In the book of Joshua, we begin to see the idolatrous nations formed by man and the impact they had on Israel. The first is the record of the fall of Jericho. Rahab, a woman who lived in Jericho, was spared with her family because she acknowledged the God of Abraham and assisted the Hebrews by hiding them when they came to spy out the city and assisted them in leaving unnoticed. When Israel marched around Jericho, bringing its walls down, she was spared with her family, was removed to safety and there after she with her family, resided with the Hebrews (Joshua 6).

Rahab came out of a civil-religious land of people who were worshipers of the moon-god Yerach, a male god who was the chief god of the pantheon and the sun-god Shamash, his female cohort. Later these names changed to Baal and Ashteroth. Because of the moon-god worship Jericho is referred to as the "Moon City." Upon defeating Jericho and entering into the city, Achan, a member of the tribe of Judah, took of "the accursed thing" (idolatrous items) which brought defeat to the Israelites in their battle with Ai. Joshua rent his clothes and prayed to the Lord, expressing his distress and concern of the other nations learning they'd been defeated and considering them weak would drive them from the land. The story is told in Joshua 7:10–15.

"So the Lord said to Joshua, get up! why do you lie thus on your face?"

"Israel has sinned, and they have also transgressed My covenant which I commanded them: for they have even taken some of the accursed things, and have both stolen and deceived; also, and they have also put it among their own stuff."

"Therefore the children of Israel could not stand before their enemies, but turned their backs before their enemies, because they have become doomed to destruction, neither will I be with you any more, unless you destroy the accursed from among you."

"Get up, sanctify the people, and say, sanctify yourselves for tomorrow, because thus says the Lord God of Israel, there is an accursed thing in your midst, O Israel: you cannot stand before your enemies, until you take away the accursed thing from among you."

"In the morning therefore you shall be brought according to your tribes. And it shall be, that the tribe which the Lord takes shall come according to families; and the family which the Lord takes shall come by households; and the household which the Lord takes shall come man by man."

"Then it shall be, that he that is taken with the accursed thing shall be burnt with fire, he and all that he has, because he has transgressed the covenant of the Lord, and because he has done a disgraceful thing in Israel"

So Joshua did as the Lord said and brought each tribe and the tribe of Judah was taken. He then brought them individually until it narrowed down to Achan being the culprit. Joshua told Achan to confess and not hide it. Achan replied that he had sinned in taking a "goodly Babylonish garment," two hundred shekels of silver and a wedge of gold that weighed fifty shekels. He said after he saw them he coveted them, and he buried them in his tent. The items were found with the silver under them and Achan, his family and all he owned along with what he'd stolen were taken to the valley of Achor and there they were all stoned then burned.

A Babylonish garment was literally a robe of Shinar. It was considered of great value, which is why Achan called it a goodly Babylonish garment. What we see in this story is how the Lord detests Babylon for all it represents, because it sprang up right out of Nimrod, and He will not except even a garment, or anything of value from Babylon to exist among His people. We see in Achan a display of the lust of the eyes, the desires of the flesh and the pride of life, which is coveting or idolatry. Also, as long as Israel had this among them they could not stand before their enemies. This is applicable to us today.

With Joshua overseeing the children of Israel, they received their appointed lots. They were able to conquer the territory's given them but they never completely rid themselves of the idolatrous nations as was commanded and this would be to their detriment. After Joshua's death, Judah was appointed to go up against the Canaanites and fight. They took Jerusalem, which at that time was called, Jebus being a city of the Jebusites. They were able to gain much of the land that was promised them however, they did not completely cleanse the land from idolatry, they didn't over throw the altars, nor the inhabitants and in some cases made a league with them. They forsook the Lord and served Balaam and provoked God to anger and they served Baal and Ashteroth, but God raised up judges to deliver them, yet they would not obey the judges (Judges 2:11–17).

The Israelites, as a result, became severely oppressed by the nations about them and cried out to the Lord in their distress. God, being merciful, would raise up men such as Gideon who would fight the inhabitants, have victory, and turn the people back to God. However, the continual turning back to serving the gods of the nations around them became a pattern.

In Judges 13 through 16, we see Israel, because of their backsliding, delivered into the hands of the Philistines to rule over them. One of the judges, Samson, was born to Manoah, a Danite man whose wife was barren, she was visited by an angel of the Lord who told her she would bare a son who was to be raised up as a Nazarite. A Nazarite never cut their hair and abstained from hard drink and wine. They were dedicated and separated unto the Lord. Samson was separated for the purpose of defeating the Philistines and although naturally strong, when the Spirit of the Lord was upon him, he was endowed with tremendous strength and abilities.

After Samson became a man, he was attracted to a woman of Timnath, a daughter of the Philistines and became betrothed to her but she was given to his companion. Samson went on as judge of Israel for twenty years. He then met a woman named Delilah, from the valley of Sorek, whom he fell in love with. Delilah was pressed by the Philistine authority to learn the secret of Samson's strength as he had defeated them in many combats and displayed great strength which they found intimidating. They therefore wanted to take him captive. Delilah began continually pressing him to reveal the secret of his strength but he kept it to himself. Yet by her continually asking and pressing on him he gave in and told her his strength came from his hair. She had Samson sleep on her lap and while lying there, she cut off his hair. This was for him like removing his covering from God. Samson lost his strength and was taken captive and put in fetters. The Philistines put his eyes out and assigned him to the grind at the mill.

Samson's hair began to grow, but he was still in captivity. A day came when the Philistines were having a sacrifice in the temple unto their god, Dagon, and decided to make a sport of Samson so had him placed in the court center where two pillars were holding up the roof. A young man still a youth, was there holding Samson's hand and Samson asked him to lead him to the pillars. Samson took hold of the pillars and prayed to God for strength to bring the pillars down and avenge for his eyes that were put out. God gave him the strength needed, so he leaned forward, holding onto the pillars, knocking them off their base, and the entire temple was weakened and collapsed.

This is a beautiful picture for us of how Samson (Israel's Leadership), though blinded, God still is with them and will enable them to bring down the pillars of their civil and religious enemies.

There has been much speculation on whether a man such as Samson could accomplish such a feat, regardless of his strength. However, excavation of a Philistine temple dating back to Samson's time by the Bar Ilan University of Archeologists, shows the architecture the Philistine's used and how probable it would be to collapse the entire structure by forcing the pillars off their base. The pillars were placed only seven feet apart. Once removed coupled with the weight of the people, the structure would have weakened and would ultimately collapse. Today this excavation belongs to an Israeli Antiquity Museum.

In the book of Ruth, Ruth is a Moabite woman, who was called out and separated from a false religious civilization unto the true God and his people. An Israelite, an Ephrathite of Bethlehem Judah, named Elimelech married a woman named Naomi of the same tribe. He left Israel during a time of famine with his wife Naomi and his two sons,

Mahlon and Chilion, and went to the land of Moab in order to better prosper.

While in Moab, Elimelech died and his sons married two Moabite women, one named Orpah, which means to turn the neck (turn your back on). and one named Ruth, which means friend. Both sons died, leaving Naomi and her two daughters-in-law alone. Naomi, hearing that there was now bread in Judah, set out with Ruth and Orpah to return to the land of Judah.

During the journey, Naomi had a change of heart and instructed the women to return to their homes where they could re-marry and she herself, would return to Judah. Both women grieved, but Orpah turned back to her home in Moab while Ruth would not leave Naomi and said to her: "Entreat me not to leave you, or to turn back from following after you; for wherever you go, I will go; and wherever you lodge, I will lodge: your people shall be my people, and your God my God" (Ruth 1:16).

After arriving in Judah, Ruth set out to glean behind the workers of one of the fields and the field that was appointed to her happened to be that of a near kinsman, Boaz. Boaz took notice of Ruth and showed favor to her by commanding his workers to deliberately leave behind ears of corn for her to gather. She reported her good fortune to Naomi who knew that Boaz was a near kinsman and therefore a redeemer.

Naomi instructed Ruth to go to the threshing floor at night where Boaz would be sleeping and not make herself known but to quietly go in, uncover his feet and lie down. She did as instructed; and when Boaz woke and inquired who she was, she then revealed her identity and proposed to him. "And he said, Who art you? So she answered, I am Ruth, your maidservant. Take your maidservant under your wing, for you are a close relative" (Ruth 3:9). To take under your wing, meant to marry.

Boaz announced Ruth's position in order that another rightful kinsman had opportunity to make claim for Ruth, but the only other kinsman was beyond his years so Boaz married Ruth and through her first born son, Obed, she became the great grandmother of David and the lineage to Christ was carried out (Matt. 1:5).

History tells us that Moab was an idolatrous nation, worshiping and sacrificing to a god they called Chemosh. Even the sacrificing of infants by stoking a fire around Chemosh and getting him red hot. They then placed the infant in his red hot arms and burnt it to death for sacrifice.

But Ruth had a call on her life and was separated to come out and she answered that call leaving her home land, family and religion to become a child of Abraham, marrying a Judean and committing herself to the one true God of Abraham, Isaac and Jacob, she was the great grandmother of king David and ultimately became a great grandmother of our Lord and savior Jesus (Yeshua).

The significance of this story is that Orpah and Ruth are a type of the early Gentile church where a portion would turn their back from following after the true God but another portion would become a servant and friend to the true God of Abraham and his descendants. Also a beautiful picture of the Gentile's receiving the word of God, beginning with Acts 10, is shown with Ruth harvesting in the field of Boaz, her redeemer, and later her husband. Boaz was also a type of Christ our redeemer.

One of the commandments that God had given to the Israelites was to leave, during the harvest, the corners of the fields untouched for the harvesting of the stranger's (Gentiles). "When you reap the harvest of your land, you shall not wholly reap the corners of your field when you reap, nor shall you gather any gleaning from your harvest. You shall leave them for the poor, and for the stranger: I am the LORD your God (Lev. 23:22).

In this we can see that God has always made provisions for the people of other nations. This was manifested when the gospel was delivered to the Gentiles first by Peter, as he had the key to open the door, and then Paul who had been commissioned by the Lord.

The children of Israel were in the promised land, yet would experience many ups and downs in their relationship with God. They would fall into the ways and practices of the nations around them in going after other gods and sacrificing unto them. Once in the land they became determined to have a king to rule their land like those of the nations around them. God had not given Israel a king to rule over them because he wanted their rule and their guide to come from him. He'd already designed their government while bringing them through the wilderness and had set in place priests and judges and his pattern of government hadn't included a king or someone in an authoritative position. He was to be the final authority. However, because of their intent to have a king, Saul was made Israel's first king. "But you have today rejected your God, who Himself saved you from all your adversities and your tribulations; and you have said to Him, No, set a king over us!" (1 Sam. 10:19) "So all the people went to Gilgal, and there they made Saul king before the Lord in Gilgal" (1 Sam. 11:15).

Saul failed as a king, and the Lord called out David from the tribe of Judah to be king in his place (1 Sam. 16). Samuel, a prophet whom God commissioned to anoint a king for Israel, was sent to Jesse, a man residing in Bethlehem. He was instructed by God to call Jesse to a sacrifice in order that he could show him of which one of Jesse's sons he'd choose to be king. So he sanctified Jesse and his son's, to prepare them for the sacrifice and called them to come.

When they arrived he first noticed Jesse's son, Eliab, because of his stature and thought surely he was the one chosen. However, God told Samuel to not look at his appearance or at his physical stature, He told him: "for the LORD does not see as man sees; for man looks on the outward appearance, but the LORD looks at the heart." Seven of Jesse's sons passed before Samuel and none were chosen so he asked Jesse if all his sons had come and Jesse told him there was yet the youngest who kept the sheep, David. Samuel requested he send for him and when he came the Lord told Samuel to anoint him as king. Samuel then anointed him king in the presence of his brothers, and the Spirit of the Lord came upon David and remained with him. But the Spirit of the Lord departed from Saul.

Another beautiful picture is that of David and Goliath. The Philistines had gathered against Israel and among them was a champion who was a giant. He stood six cubits and a span high. The measure of a cubit equaled the measure of a forearm and the span was across the hand. A forearm today would be approximately 18 to 22 inches, which would have made him approximately 9 feet tall.

He had on him a helmet of brass and a coat of mail (plates of metal) and greaves (shin piece of armor) on his legs. He had a spear with a staff like a weaver's beam, meaning it was sturdy and long, as much as six feet according to ancient designs. The head of his spear weighed six hundred shekels of iron, which was fifteen to eighteen pounds. He also had a shield-bearer who went before him and was thus well protected and confident in his size and in his image.

Goliath bellowed out a threatening challenge to Israel's army which struck fear in them but they went to the battle. Three of David's brothers followed Saul into the battle but David had gone to feed his father's sheep. For forty days the Philistine, Goliath, challenged them morning and evening. (David is seen as a type of Christ in this picture)

Jesse, David's father, sent David to the battle with a supply of food for his brothers and to see how they were fairing. After arriving to the battle area, he ran up to greet his brothers and while talking with them Goliath again approached bellowing out the same challenge, causing Israel's soldiers to flee with fear. "Then David spoke to the men that stood by him, saying, What shall be done for the man who kills this Philistine, and takes away the reproach from Israel? For who is this uncircumcised Philistine, that he should defy the armies of the living God?" (1Sam. 17:26)

His brothers didn't appreciate his brazen remark and accused him of leaving off minding the sheep so he could come to watch the battle. They then reported to Saul what David had said. "Then David said to Saul, 'Let no man's heart fail because of him; your servant will go and fight with this Philistine." (1 Sam. 17:32)

David was still considered a youth and not experienced in battle when he volunteered himself to stand up against Goliath, who had been a man of war from his youth. But David persuaded him by declaring his victory over a lion and a bear threatening the flock.

Saul armed David with his armor and he put a helmet of brass and a coat of mail and David girded his sword on but refrained from going because he'd not tested it. He told Saul he could not go with those items because he'd not proved them and he took them off. He then took his shepherd's bag and took five smooth stones out of the brook and placed them in his bag and went off with his sling and approached Goliath.

When Goliath saw this young inexperienced man, he was disdained, thinking David was beneath him. "So the Philistine said to David, Am I a dog, that you come to me with sticks? And the Philistine cursed David by his gods."

"And the Philistine said to David, come to me, and I will give your flesh to the birds of the air, and to the beasts of the field!"

"Then David said to the Philistine, 'You come to me with a sword, with a spear, and with a javelin: But I come to you in the name of the Lord of hosts, the God of the armies of Israel, whom you have defied."

"This day the Lord will deliver you into my hand; and I will strike you, and take your head from you; and this day I will give the carcasses of the camp of the Philistines to the birds of the air, and the wild beasts of the earth; that all the earth may know that there is a God in Israel."

"Then all this assembly shall know that the Lord does not save with sword and spear; for the battle is the Lord's and He will give you into our hands." (I Sam 17:43-47)

David then drew out a stone and sling it, striking Goliath in the forehead, and the stone sunk into his forehead and brought him down. David ran and stood upon him and with Goliath's own sword he killed him and cut off his head. When the rest of the Philistines saw this they turned and fled.

There are many views on this story. Some say that David is a picture of Christ's true body of people which will come up against the giant Babylon of false religion represented by Goliath, and bring it down with the truth, being the smooth stone which is a part of God's five-fold ministry after all the rough edges have been washed away. This sounds very plausible however, and although I don't dispute this view I would like to present another thought. David is an Israelite of the tribe of Judah. He is a youth just as Israel is a young nation today. Goliath had four brothers of great stature and David knew this so he prepared to meet all five. (2 Sam. 15–21)

The stones were smooth because, as anyone who is familiar with stone slinging knows that you should propel a smooth stone for velocity and accuracy. David had removed the armor of Saul because he'd put on the armor of God when he picked up the five smooth stones, placed them in his bag and carried his sling in his hand. "Stand therefore, having girded your waist with truth, having put on the breastplate of righteousness; and having shod your feet with the preparation of the gospel of peace; above all, taking the shield of faith, with which you will be able to quench all the fiery darts of the wicked one. And take the helmet of salvation, and the sword of the Spirit, which is the word of God" (Eph. 6:14–17).

David found favor in the eyes of the people He had slain Goliath and won various battles becoming honored and respected by the people. His popularity became a thorn in Saul's side.

He was soon officially made king of Israel by the people in Hebron (2 Sam. 5:3). David had a heart after God to worship and serve him thus the children of Israel served God and so prospered.

He desired to build a house for the Lord but because he'd been in many battles, the Lord told him that his son would build the house because he wanted it to be a man of peace, not of war. This reflects back to Melchizedek, the king of Salem or peace. It was necessary for David to engage in the wars because he was establishing Israel and Judah however, the Lord's house required a man of peace to build it and because of David the land had come into a peace time. David had developed the plans for the house of God and had all the furnishings. Everything for the building was assembled by David and he gave these instructions to his son Solomon along with his words of encouragement (1Chron. 28, 29).

Solomon succeeded him (1Kings 2:12) and built the temple of God popularly known as Solomon's Temple. He placed the ark of the covenant in the temple and appointed the priests for their order. They made their offerings unto the Lord as instructed by Moses and Israel continued in strength and prosperity under Solomon's rule.

Solomon married women from the nations around him who served other gods. Because of this his heart was turned from the God of his fathers and to the gods of his wives. "But King Solomon loved many foreign women, as well as the daughter of Pharaoh; women of the Moabites, Ammonites, Edomites, Zidonians, and Hittites." From the nations of whom the Lord had said to the children of Israel, you shall not intermarry with them, nor they with you: Surely they will turn away your hearts after their gods: Solomon clung to these in love. And he had seven hundred wives, princesses, and three hundred concubines: and his wives turned away his heart" (1 Kings 11:1–3).

"So the Lord became angry with Solomon, because his heart had turned from the Lord God of Israel, who had appeared to him twice, and had commanded him concerning this thing, that he should not go after other gods: but he kept not that which the Lord commanded." (1 Kings 11:9, 10)

Solomon was serving the gods of his wives, Ashtoreth and Chemosh. The Lord told Solomon that because of this: "I will surely tear the kingdom away from you, and will give it to your servant" (1 Kings 11:11).

The Lord told Solomon that he would not take the whole kingdom but would leave one for his father, David's sake and for Jerusalem's sake which he'd chosen. The Lord stirred up Hadad, an Edomite, against Solomon. He then stirred up Rezon of Damascus. Even Jeroboam, who was an Eprathite, whom Solomon had made a ruler over the house of Joseph, became an adversary to Solomon.

His son, Rehoboam, succeeded him; however, at this time the kingdom became divided in fulfillment of what God told Solomon would happen when he turned his heart from Israel's God by serving false god's. (1 Kings 11:11–13)

Rehoboam was hard on the people, saying, "And now whereas my father put a heavy yoke on you, I will add to your yoke; my father chastised you with whips, but I will chastise you with scourges!" (1 Kings 12:11) Scourges were whips that had metal nuts grouped and threaded at the end.

Because of this, ten tribes followed Jeroboam making him their king and Judah with Benjamin remained with Rehoboam. This divided the kingdom; one part of Israel with Samaria as its capital and the other, the Judaen part, with Jerusalem as its capital.

The Israelites would go to the temple in Jerusalem to worship during the feasts. This intimidated Jeroboam. so he made gods of two golden calves declaring that these were their god's which brought them out of Egypt. (1Kings 12:27, 28) The people were led into idolatry and continued with the succeeding kings worshiping their false gods.

The following dates may be different than those most of us have learned which came from Ptolemy's reckoning of time. However, since then there has been much study to Bible Chronology and the dates of Ptolemy have been shown to be erroneous. The dates referenced in this text are from *The Wonders of Bible Chronology* by Phillip Mauro.

In approximately 656 BC Ahaz, king of Judah died and Hezekiah, his son, reigned in his stead. Hezekiah turned back to the God of Israel and broke up all the idols throughout Judea. He even broke up the brazen serpent on the pole which Moses had made for them in the wilderness because they had made it an idol and were burning incense unto it. He re-captured Philistia and formed an alliance with Ashkelon and Egypt. He refused to pay tribute to Sennacherib which resulted in Sennachrib attacking and laying siege to Jerusalem in approximately 640 BC.

Sennacherib, king of Assyria, attacked the fortified cities of Judah and laid siege on Jerusalem. (2 Kings 18) This was a failed attempt, and is the only city known to be besieged by him. But he captured Samaria to the north, Israel's capital, and carried away the people into captivity. Judah to the south was left fending for itself from the Near East Kingdoms.

Hezekiah cut off the water supply to Sennacherib's armies by blocking the springs. He dug out a tunnel to the spring Gihon supplying water to Jerusalem. Today this tunnel still exists and can be visited. Since its discovery, many truths regarding the actual location of where the temple stood, Mt. Zion and The City of David have been revealed as well as the history of the Wailing Wall's actual construction.

While Sennacherib was besieging Lachesh, Hezekiah sent a message to him offering to pay tribute if he would withdraw from Jerusalem. Hezekiah was forced to empty the temple, the royal treasury and even stripped the gold from the door post of Solomon's temple in order to pay. (2 Kings 18:13–16) However, Sennacherib still marched on Jerusalem with a great army. Hezekiah humbled himself before God clothed in sackcloth. Because he humbled himself and sought the Lord, during the night an angel of the Lord killed 185,000 of Sennacherib's army and Sennacherib withdrew to Nineveh. (2 Kings 19:35

CHAPTER 5

THE BABYLONIAN CAPTIVITY

Around 617 BC, Hezekiah died and the Judean kingdom continued to fall into idolatry. They were easily enticed by the nations around them and their own kings who followed after other gods. They modeled themselves after the civil-religious government systems of the nations and sacrificed to their gods. Many prophets were sent by the Lord to warn them to repent from following after other gods and also warned them of the consequences. On different occasions, a king would repent and turn the hearts of the people back to their God as Hezekiah had done, but they never completely eradicated idolatry out of their land.

In spite of the prophet's warnings they continued in their sin and did not keep their Sabbaths nor did they refrain from following the ways of the heathen. Thus God raised up Nebuchadnezzar, king of Babylon, to lay siege on Jerusalem. In the fourth year of Nebuchadnezzar's reign, about 526 BC, he besieged Jerusalem and again a tribute was set in place.

Jehoiachin ruled Judah at this time and he refused to pay the tribute. The prophet Jeremiah warned him of the impending outcome yet was ignored. The outcome of this refusal resulted in his death during the seventh year of Nebuchadnezzar's reign and many of Jehoiachin's court were exiled to Babylon. In Nebuchadnezzar's nineteenth year, many again were exiled and later in the twenty-third year of his reign, around 494 BC, there was a great deportation of the Jews. They remained captive in Babylon seventy years. (2 Chron. 36:20, 21)

The prophet Daniel records some events under the direction of God for our learning. King Nebuchadnezzar had carried off to Shinar to the house of his God, vessels and treasures from the temple and, Jehoiachin, king of Judah. He spoke to the master of his eunuchs, Ashpenaz, to bring children from Judah who were full of wisdom, and had knowledge of science and had no defects and well favored so that they could be taught the Babylonian language and stand in the king's palace. He then had them prepared for their position and they were educated, fed and nourished for three years in order to stand before him.

There were four of the children of Judah whose names were Daniel, Hananiah, Mishael and Azariah. They were renamed with Babylonian names. Daniel was named Belteshazzar, Hananiah was named Shadrach, Mishael was named Meshach and Azariah was named Abednego.

Daniel had determined not to defile himself with the king's food and wine and requested to be excused from the chief of the eunuchs. The eunuch favored Daniel but feared the king and told Daniel that if he was lacking in a well-fed and kept appearance such as the others would have he'd be in danger of execution. So Daniel said to Melzar, who had been placed in charge of himself, Hananiah, Mishael and Azariah to prove them for ten days, feeding them pulse (a vegetable or legume mix) and water. "Then let our appearance be examined before you, and the appearance of the young men who eat the portion of the king's delicacies; and as you see fit, so deal with your servants" (Dan. 1:13).

He consented and gave them the ten days requested, and after the ten days they appeared much healthier than those who ate at the king's table. So Melzar took away the food of the king and gave them their pulse and water. Babylon's table could not sustain them, but their sustenance came from the Lord. "As for these four young men, God gave them knowledge and skill in all literature and wisdom; and Daniel had understanding in visions and dreams" (Dan. 1:17).

After the three years, they were all brought before Nebuchadnezzar. "And the king communed with them; and among them all was found none like Daniel, Hananiah, Mishael and Azariah; therefore, stood they before the king. And in all matters of wisdom and understanding, about which the king examined them, he found them ten times better than all the magicians and astrologers who were in all his realm" (Dan. 1:20).

Nebuchadnezzar had some troubling dreams and called in his astrologers, magicians, sorcerers and Chaldeans (an Assyrian group) to give him their meaning but they were not able to interpret it. So the Chaldeans in the Syriac language said to tell them the dream and they'd interpret it. "The king answered and said to the Chaldeans, 'My decision is firm: if you do not make known the dream to me, and its interpretation, you shall be cut in pieces, and your houses shall be made an ash heap'" (Dan. 2:5).

They were unable to tell the king what his troubling dream was nor its interpretation. So the king became frustrated and in his fury commanded that all the "wise men" be slain. "So the decree went out and they began killing the wise men; and they sought Daniel and his companions to kill them" (Dan 2:13).

Daniel went to the king and requested time to tell him the dream and its interpretation and the king granted his request. Daniel returned to his house and informed his companions asking them to ask God for his mercies. So God gave Daniel the dream with its interpretation and he went to the king and told him that what he'd dreamt was of a terrible image. "This image's head was of fine gold, its chest and arms of silver, its belly and thighs of bronze, Its legs of iron, its feet partly of iron and partly of clay" (Dan. 2:32).

Daniel told him a stone was cut out of a mountain without hands, and struck the image in its feet of iron and clay which caused the image to crumble and fall and be blown away like chaff. And the stone that struck it grew into a great mountain which filled the earth. The gold head was the king's kingdom or Babylon, another, the silver breast and arms, would follow that was inferior, and another, his belly and thighs of brass that would rule the earth, then another of iron which will subdue all things.

But the clay mixed with the iron showed that it would be divided and have the strength of the iron but as iron and clay do not mix neither will the kingdom. Iron mixed with clay are a picture of civil government mixed with religion. A kingdom would be established by God which would stand for ever. "And in the days of these kings the

God of heaven will set up a kingdom, which shall never be destroyed: and the kingdom shall not be left to other people, it shall break in pieces and consume all these kingdoms, and it shall stand forever" (Dan. 2:44).

The kingdoms represented here are Babylon, the head; Medes and Persians, the breast and arms; Greece, the belly and thighs and Rome, the legs of iron with the feet part of iron and part of clay; Rome's political-papal kingdom.

An image was constructed by Nebuchadnezzar which represented the political religious structure of Babylon. He had all the political authorities present for the dedication of the image. Upon the dedication it was declared that there would be the sound of instruments and all kinds of music, "that at the time you hear the sound of the horn, flute harp, lyre and psaltery, in symphony with all kinds of music, you shall fall down and worship the gold image that King Nebuchadnezzar has set up" (Dan. 3:5).

The story of Shadrach (Hananiah) Meshach (Mishael) and Abednego (Azariah) is a profound one, as these men refused to be intimidated and bow to the king's idolatrous image. They were committed to Yahweh and entrusted their lives to him even though their refusal meant they would be thrown into a "fiery furnace." They informed Nebuchadnezzar that whether their God delivered them from the furnace or not they would not serve nor bow down to his image.

The furnace was made to burn seven times more in its heat because the king was infuriated with their stance. However, after being bound and cast into the furnace (the flames so intense that those who had hold of them to throw them in were consumed) Nebuchadnezzar witnessed a fourth man in the furnace and not one of the four were being burned. "Look! he answered, I see four men loose, walking in the midst of the fire; and they are not hurt, and the form of the fourth is like the Son of God" (Dan. 3:25).

This example is comparative to the image of the beast in Revelation 13, which the majority of the people of the earth will unwittingly bow and adhere to. But God's people will refuse to worship it.

This is a wonderful picture for us to understand that we, with confidence in our heavenly father, should stand strong and not bow down or submit ourselves to a religious structure or our governments which exalt themselves against the God of heaven.

"Nebuchadnezzar the king made an image of gold, whose height was sixty cubits, and its width six cubits: He set it up in the plain of Dura, in the province of Babylon" (Dan. 3:1).

Babylon was a glorious kingdom, and Nebuchadnezzar shined in its glory (gold head) but although inferior to Babylon, the Medes and Persians defeated it. (Silver breast and arms) Greece rose up and defeated the Medo-Persian kingdom and conquered throughout the earth and became a powerful kingdom (brass belly and thighs). The Romans rose up in power defeating the Greeks and went out to conquer with an iron fist.

The Medes, ruled by Darius, who was a contemporary to Cyrus the Great of Persia, rose up and conquered Babylon about 460 BC. Thus, they now controlled Judah (Dan. 9).

God stirred up the heart of Cyrus, king of Persia, and he was stirred in his spirit to make a proclamation throughout his kingdom saying:

"Thus says Cyrus king of Persia: All the kingdoms of the earth the Lord God of heaven has given me. And He has commanded me to build Him a house at Jerusalem which is in Judah. Who is among you of all his people? May the Lord his God be with him, and let him go up!" (2 Chron. 36:23)

Those called out, that were stirred in their hearts and willing hearted were only about 42,000 out of over a million. Again "many are called but few are chosen."

The captivity of Babylon and being called out to rebuild the temple is more than just a historical account for Israel; it in fact is a foreshadowing of the Christian church. The prophets all gave warning messages and were ignored. Some were killed for prophesying the doom that was about to befall them. The prophets continued to declare, however, a new covenant to come, but after the second temple was built things changed. There was no longer an ark of the covenant in the temple; therefore, the high priests were not able to enter in on the Day of Atonement and sprinkle the sacrificial blood of the lamb on the mercy seat. Therefore, their means of atonement was also changed. Soon after these events the prophets fell silent.

The accounts of the rebuilding of the temple can be read in the books of Ezra and Nehemiah. Just as Gabriel had told Daniel, the walls were built in troubling times. There was much opposition from the nations to their rebuilding, and they actually engaged in battle while doing the building.

We read of Cyrus, king of Persia, allowing the Jews to rebuild and knew it was of God and was revealed to Daniel by Gabriel that the command would go forth. After Cyrus, Ahasuerus, thought to be father of Darius, became king and endeavored to stop the rebuilding of Jerusalem. The Hebrews, still in captivity had many exiled to Persia and lived in Shushan, the capital of Persia. They faced extermination in about 456 BC at the hands of grand vizier Haman. The king at that time was the above-mentioned Ahasuerus, also known as Xerxes. He favored a young Hebrew woman and made her queen of Persia. This may have encouraged the continuation of the building because Ahasuerus gave attention to the decree of Cyrus and relented with regard to the construction. It is not certain which Ahasuerus (Xerxes) was king; however, the time line points to a time short of Nehemiah, around 455 BC. The *Jewish Encyclopedia* recognizes this king to be the same king to support Cyrus' decree.

Esther, whose name by birth was Hadassah, was raised by her uncle, Mordecai, who had been carried away captive to Babylon and brought Hadassah with him as she had no parents. In Persia she was called Esther (meaning star) which is a variance of the goddess Ishtar; however, interestingly Esther means "hidden" in Hebrew. She indeed was hidden because no one new she was a Jew. The book of Esther is a beautiful account of how God used her to deliver the Hebrews from being slain by Haman, a man who held the position of vizier by Ahasuerus.

Persecution of the Jews rose up by means of Haman. Everyone gave him reverence and bowed before him at the gate except Mordecai, Esther's uncle, who would not bow to Haman, because he was considered by the Persians to be a deity. Haman became infuriated with him and reported to the king that the Jews in the kingdom were diverse and would not keep the king's laws. Because of this he received authority to destroy the Jews. Haman sent out letters with the king's seal concerning the upcoming destruction of all Jews throughout Persia and by throwing lots (pur) elected when it would be. However, Mordecai reported this to Esther and pressed upon her to use her position to save their people and said to her: "Yet who knows whether you have come to the kingdom for such a time as this?" (Esther 4:14)

With the persuasion of Mordecai, Esther promised to intercede, called for a fast and prayer all knowing that no one was to approach the king without being summoned as it was punishable with death. But to save her people she took her life into her hands saying: "if I perish, I perish" (Esther 4:16). She attired herself appropriately and approached the king. She found favor from him and the king held out his scepter to her. She then got permission to have a banquet where upon she invited Haman, this in order to learn of him. She again had a banquet and invited Haman who was pleased with this acknowledgment and bragged to his family but complained concerning Mordecai. His wife suggested he had Mordecai executed in order to rid him of the apparent insult and aggravation. Haman took the suggestion and built a gallows at his home site to hang Mordecai on.

The king, being restless one night and unable to sleep, decided to read, and he read the account of Mordecai reporting those who were conspiring to kill the king and therefore spared the kings life. The king prior to this was unaware of Mordecai's action and because of this he decided to honor Mordecai which only added fuel to the fire of resentment Haman had toward him and he became all the more anxious to kill all the Jews.

Esther however, had another banquet and at this time intervened and exposed her identity to the king and pleaded for the lives of her people. The king agreed and put forth a decree that no Jew would be slain. Also because Esther exposed Haman to be the one determined to exterminate her people, Haman, knowing the king would turn against him, fell upon Esther's bed to plead for his life. When Ahasuerus saw this he said: "Will he also assault the queen while I am in the house?" (Esther 7:8) He then had Haman hung on the gallows intended for

Mordecai and his ten sons hanged on the same gallows at Esther's request

There was a victory feast celebrated throughout the kingdom with the Jews and this initiated the feast of Purim, a celebration of deliverance called Purim which was the name for casting of lots that Haman did to decide which day he would slaughter the Jews. It fell on the thirteenth and fourteenth days of Adar. The Jewish community continues its celebration of deliverance today.

The Persians kept administrative control over Judah until the rise of Greece with Alexander the Great. Alexander conquered the entire civilized world. He arrived in Israel during the reign of the high priest Simon, known as "Simon the Just" in about 329 BC.

Alexander had been taught and influenced in religion by Aristotle, who gave him a respect toward a God, whether Zeus or Yahweh, the God of Israel. He therefore, contrary to his fierce reputation, gave two choices to Simon. One, to fight, which because of his army and reputation they were greatly intimidated, and the other to accommodate him and become a royal vassal. With this he would allow them to remain autonomous.

The people and Simon knew they could not defeat Alexander's army and therefore agreed to accommodate him and became vassals. They were so relieved of this outcome of their home not being razed to the ground as had been other nations, that the Jews instituted a method of collecting tax to pay Alexander which ultimately led to becoming a corrupt system of taxation.

Alexander died at the early age of twenty-nine, and his kingdom then divided to Seleucus in the north and Ptolemy in the south. Israel was in the middle. Seleucus and Ptolemy could not agree on their boundary lines and eventually the king of the Seleucids, Antiochus Epiphanes, invaded Jerusalem defiling the temple by even sacrificing a pig on the altar.

To reclaim Jerusalem and the temple, a man named Judas Maccabees arranged an army and with the help of God they defeated the Seleucids in a courageous battle. The temple was cleansed and re-dedicated and a miracle of oil for the lamps took place that is celebrated at Hanukkah.

In about 63 BC Rome rose to power, replacing the Seleucids as a great power and Judah became a province of Rome whom they now had to pay tribute to. Herod was appointed king of Judah by Rome and he remodeled the temple of Solomon. He was a great admirer of the Greco-Roman culture and was a pawn in the hands of Rome. He was given almost complete autonomy by Rome and ruled Judah until 4 BC After the death of Herod, Judah came under direct administration of Rome.

Thus far we see that Israel had been governed and under the dominion of six different kingdoms; the first being Egypt, then Assyria, Babylon, the Medo-Persian empire, the Greeks and now the Roman empire. Each was a head over Israel. They all represented a civil-religious authority and they all collected service and or tribute money from Israel. They were all powerful world dominating empires represented as beasts in the visions of Daniel and the apostle John.

The battles promulgated from these beasts were fought with bloody violence and with great losses sustained. They were fought with no less vigor, violence, losses and grievances than they are today.

CHAPTER 6

A NEW DAY DAWNING

There were many occurrences of individuals who were called out, separated and commissioned by God in the Old Testament or Old Covenant. We can read of Samson, Samuel, Elijah, Jeremiah, and many others who were willing to be a spokesperson and even endanger their lives for God.

They all were subject to the authority of the nations, but they made their stand with the God of Abraham, Isaac, and Jacob and God commissioned them toward his great plan to redeem mankind, giving them great prophetic visions and through them worked many miracles. They are all worthy to be read, studied, and learned from in order to learn, know and gain an intimate relationship with our heavenly Father.

A new day and a new covenant was being prepared, and through this covenant multitudes of the nations around the globe would turn to the God of Abraham, fulfilling the promise that he would become the father of many nations.

There are at least three hundred prophecies of the Messiah which reveal his birth and the location of his birth, his place of residence, reputation, ministry, his death and his resurrection. The following are just a few of the most familiar.

Malachi 3:1, "Behold, I send my messenger, and he will prepare the way before Me, and the Lord, whom you seek, will suddenly come to His temple, even the messenger of the covenant, in whom you delight. Behold, He is coming, says the Lord of hosts."

Isaiah 7:14, "Therefore the Lord Himself will give you a sign; Behold, the virgin shall conceive, and bear a Son, and shall call His name Immanuel."

Isaiah 53:3, "He is despised and rejected by men; a Man of sorrows, and acquainted with grief: and we hid, as it were, our faces from Him; He was despised, and we did not esteem Him."

MESSIANIC PROPHECY FULFILLED

"There was in the days of Herod, the king of Judea, a certain priest named Zacharias, of the division of Abijah. His wife was of the daughters of Aaron, and her name was Elizabeth. And they were both righteous before God, walking in all the commandments and ordinances of the Lord blameless. But they had no child, because Elizabeth was barren, and they both well advanced in years" (Luke 1:5–7).

Zechariah had the responsibility to burn incense in the temple. He entered into the temple to perform the order of his course and an angel of the Lord appeared unto him, standing on the right side of the altar of incense.

"But the angel said to him, 'Do not be afraid, Zacharias for your prayer is heard; and your wife Elizabeth will bear you a son, and you shall call his name John. And you will have joy and gladness, and many will rejoice at his birth for he will be great in the sight of the Lord, and shall drink neither wine nor strong drink. He will also be filled with the Holy Spirit, even from his mother's womb. And he will turn many of the children of Israel to the Lord their God. He will also go before Him in the spirit and power of Elijah, to turn the hearts of the fathers to the children, and the disobedient to the wisdom of the just, to make ready a people prepared for the Lord'" (Luke 1:13–17)

"As it is written in the prophets, Behold I send my messenger before Your face, who will prepare Your way before You,' "The voice of one crying in the wilderness, Prepare the way of the Lord, make His paths straight" (Mark 1:2, 3; Ref: Mal. 3:1; Isa. 40:3)

The angel appeared to Mary and told her that she would bear a son and his name would be Yeshua (Jesus). "And, behold you will conceive in your womb, and bring forth a Son, and shall call his name Jesus. He will be great, and will be called the Son of the Highest; and the Lord God will give Him the throne of His father David. And He will reign over the house of Jacob forever, and of His kingdom there will be no end" (Luke 1:31–33).

Mary, a virgin asked how this was possible and the angel answered and said: "The Holy Spirit shall come upon thee, and the power of the Highest shall overshadow thee; therefore, also that holy thing which shall be born of thee, shall be called the Son of God" Luke 1:35).

Jesus was born in Bethlehem, fulfilling Micah 5:2, "But thou, Bethlehem Ephrata, though thou be little among the thousands of Judah, yet out of thee shall he come forth unto me that is to be ruler in Israel; whose goings forth have been from of old, from everlasting."

Judah became a province of Rome and Judah, with all of Israel, were governed by Rome. The tax structure had become even more corrupt than during Alexander's reign and the publicans (tax collectors) were frowned on by the general populace especially the common people. Rome selected the leaders of Judah who would do their bidding. Herod also known as Herod the Great, was made a client king, which meant that as long as he paid tribute and chose Rome's side in any uprising Rome may have had, he'd be given almost total autonomy over the internal affairs of his country.

The Jews were financially exhausted from paying tribute and were equally tired of having Rome as their authority in all of their concerns. Their service to God had become corrupt and was at the time of Christ nothing more than another political religious system built on traditions set forth by the Pharisees, and Sadducees, with the influence of the Romans. The Sadducees were particularly accommodating to Rome and held wealthy positions as well as positions of the Sanhedrin. They were primarily interested in political rather than the religious aspects of their country whereas, the Pharisees were more inclined to religion but made many oral laws claiming them to be adhered to as the word of God. They held fewer positions in the Sanhedrin and the two groups were rivals in both religious and political matters.

Herod the Great was an admirer of the Roman and Greek cultures and had buildings constructed in their fashion. He also remodeled the second temple, expanding it with Roman/Greek influence. It thus became known as "Herod's Temple" but was in reality the second temple added onto.

Herod the Great had a reputation of being a tyrant, primarily because he set out to have anyone killed who threatened his throne. He had relatives of the previous Hasmonean dynasty executed, including his wife, who was a daughter of a Hasmonean king. He created a line of nobility which had their loyalty solely to himself. The high priests were appointed by Herod and he made certain that they had no connection to the Hasmonean dynasty.

Because of this, upon his death there was a void of power. Therefore, after Herod's death, Rome divided his kingdom among his three sons—Judea to Archelaus, Galilee to Herod Antipas and Jordan to Phillip and Jerusalem was under direct administration of Rome.

When Herod heard of Christ's birth and that he was to be king of the Jews, he set out to kill him. Because he did not know Jesus' precise location and date of birth, he ordered the murder of every infant age two and under. This fulfilled Jeremiah's prophecy: "Thus says the Lord; A voice was heard in Ramah, lamentation, and bitter weeping, Rachel weeping for her children refusing to be comforted for her children, because they are no more" (Jer. 31:15).

Joseph was warned by an angel of the Lord that Herod sought to kill Jesus and to go to Egypt until he was called out. He did as he was instructed, and after Herod's death an angel of the Lord appeared to him in a dream and told him it was safe to return to Israel. Joseph learned that Herod's son, Archelaus, was ruling in his place. He feared to return there and instead went into Galilee to the city Nazarene, which fulfilled the prophecy, "There shall come forth a rod from the stem of Jesse, and a Branch shall grow out of his roots" (Isa.11:1).

Jesus lived with his family and was subject to his parents. He grew up increasing in wisdom, stature and the favor of God. When he was close to thirty years old he set out to accomplish his mission in Israel that God had sent him for and he first went to John the Baptist to be baptized in order to fulfill all righteousness.

After this, he was compelled by the Spirit to remove himself into a wilderness area. There he would combat the enemy. The temptation of Christ can be contrasted with that of Adam. The devil presents his oration using the word of God, but perverts it to his advantage and tempts Christ with the desires of the flesh. We see the craftiness of the devil here, but Jesus was not deceived and rebuked him using the written word of God.

In this story, Jesus was tempted with the lust of the eyes, the desires of the flesh and the pride of life. All these attributes are of the flesh and averse to our Father. He was victorious over the flesh he took on from being born as a man. What Adam failed to do, Jesus was victorious over! He left in the power and strength of the Spirit to accomplish his mission.

When Christ began his ministry, he called out certain men to follow him. He had many disciples and even sent seventy out to preach the good news of the gospel, but twelve he separated for the purpose of becoming apostles (meaning "sent out ones") and taking the gospel to all the world of that day. All had to have willing hearts and a strong desire toward truth and their God. Christ and his disciples operated in opposition to the religious system and the governmental system. This indeed took conviction and bravery.

It was no small feat and only a few select would be up for the job. They would follow their Messiah, learning truths that had been buried in the civil-religious systems and traditions of men for hundreds of years. They were courageous to step out and declare the gospel knowing full well that the religious and political leaders would not be approving and possibly they would find their own lives at risk. They faced opposition not only from the authorities but from their own families. Is it any wonder that Christ said; "many will be called but few will be chosen?

In the Gospels you can read the teachings of Christ, the opposition he and the disciples faced, and the many miracles he performed. Judas Iscariot, one of the twelve, betrayed Christ by leading the authorities to him for a payment of thirty pieces of silver. He was unable to uphold his position as a follower of Jesus and face the opposition. He apparently felt under pressure and the enticement of payment to reveal Christ's whereabouts for capture caused him to cave in. With Christ in custody, Judas sees his condemnation repents himself and brings back the silver. When they would not receive the money he threw the silver in the temple and not able to bare what he'd done took his own life by hanging himself. The priests not able to take blood money used it to buy the potter's field to bury stranger's. This event fulfilled the prophecy; "And the LORD said to me, 'Throw it to the potter-that princely price they set on me. So I took the thirty pieces of silver and threw them into the house of the LORD for the potter (Zech. 11:13, 12).

Not everyone is able to function contrary to popular beliefs or speak truths contrary to the political authorities. Judas witnessed Christ telling the Pharisees they were hypocrites and correcting their practiced religious traditions they placed on men as doctrines from God. To stand against a religious political system would require strong convictions, confidence and intestinal fortitude. Christ targeted the core of corruption within their religion and government. He was accused of blasphemy, was despised by all authority and rejected on every side. Even the miracles he performed came under scrutiny.

Also, the Sanhedrin was under the influence of Rome's domination and did not want to rock the boat. Even though their countrymen suffered under Rome, they themselves faired quite well. They tried to trap Jesus in religious issues and tested his allegiance to Rome.

The leaders were blind to who he was and were hypnotized by the power and posterity of the religious political system of the Roman world. They expected the Messiah would come to them in great pomp and set up an all-powerful kingdom replicating the kingdoms of men. Jesus didn't fit the image they'd built up in their minds and they didn't recognize their own scriptures which prophesied of him.

On one occasion, Jesus spoke with a Samaritan woman who asked where the authorized place of worship was located.

"Jesus said to her, 'Woman, believe Me, the hour is coming, when you will neither on this mountain, nor in Jerusalem, worship the Father. You worship what you do not know: we know what we worship: for salvation is of the Jews. But the hour is coming, and now is, when the true worshipers will worship the Father in spirit and in truth; for the Father is seeking such to worship Him. God is a Spirit: and those who worship Him must worship in spirit and in truth'" (John 4:21–24)

The message Christ was conveying was that true worshipers are not united by a religious-political structure, established as a dictator of what their relationship with the Father would be. Nor would they be governed as to where they should assemble to worship the Father. The true believers would not look toward Samaria, Jerusalem, Mecca, Rome or any place established by man. They would assemble themselves according the dictates of their spirit and look solely toward the Father, worshipping him in spirit and in truth.

Jesus' ministry was in direct opposition to the civil-religious systems of not simply that day and time, but all the beast systems prior and all the beast systems to follow. Man's faith and confidence is grounded in man's presentation of God through an organization that receives their authority from the government or state they reside in. When Jesus taught and preached or even healed, he was frequently and sternly questioned: "by what authority do you do these things, or who gave you this authority?" His authority did not come from Rome nor did it come from the Sanhedrin, rather his authority came from his heavenly Father.

It is understood that when you are an ambassador for a country or even a company, you are operating in the name of that country or company. Your authority comes from them. Everything you present will be what you have been authorized to do or say. So it was with Christ, as many times he expressed that he came to do the will of the Father, or the words I speak are from my Father. When you operate your faith in the name of anything besides Jesus, you are not operating in his name or by his authority but you are operating in the name of your organization. This is very unpopular to tell people but it is also the truth.

Every Jesuit is sent out by the authority of the Roman Catholic Church. Every Mormon who knocks on your door was sent out in the name and authority of the Latter-Day Saints and its headquarters. So it is with every organization existing. You are married in a church by a pastor who upon finishing the vows will announce "by the authority of the (church he represents) and the authority of the (state he practices in) I now pronounce you man and wife."

When I was a young child, I was baptized into a denominational church. Notice I say "into a church," not into Jesus. This put my name in a book as a "member" of that organization. It did not put me in the Book of Life or into The Body of Christ, and to this day I am sure to be found in the records of their archives.

Neither Christ nor his apostles ever taught that they came to build a denomination and with it a name in which to function under. "Nor is there salvation in any other: for there is no other name under heaven given among men by which we must be saved." (Acts 4:12) "Is Christ divided? Was Paul crucified for you? Or were you baptized in the name of Paul?" (1 Cor. 1:13) From the beginning of time, mankind has wanted to establish a name for itself and build a tower that would reach to the heaven's. Jesus said "I am the way, the truth and the life. No one comes to the father except through me" (John 14:6). He also said: "Most assuredly, I say to you, I am the door of the sheep. All who ever came before Me are thieves and robbers, but the sheep did not hear them." (John 10:7–8)

Jesus was addressing the Pharisees here in John 10. Those who held positions and served a religion that had become corrupt and established by man under the authority of Rome. He was telling them they would not enter into God's kingdom through the system to which they held allegiance.

Christ was taken by the authorities, questioned, beaten profusely and then, because the Jews could not perform the task of execution, the Roman government was compelled to perform the execution via crucifixion. This all happened during the Passover, and Jesus fulfilled the events of the Lord's Passover as the Lamb of God slain for the sins of the world. The Jews did not kill Jesus neither did the Romans. The world's human populace was responsible.

We all know the beautiful story of Christ's resurrection. The historian Josephus inserted Christ's resurrection in his account of the Jews being in an uproar against Pilate for a decision he'd made regarding a current of water to be brought to Jerusalem. Of the resulting great number slain, Josephus writes:

Now, there was about this time Jesus, a wise man, if it be lawful to call him a man, for he was a doer of wonderful works-a teacher of such men as receive the truth with pleasure. He drew over to him both many of the Jews, and many of the Gentiles. He was (the) Christ and when Pilate, at the suggestion of the principal men amongst us, had condemned him to the cross, those that loved him at the first did not forsake him, for he appeared to them alive again the third day, as the divine prophets had foretold these and ten thousand other wonderful things concerning him; and the tribe of Christians, so named from him, are not extinct at this day.

Most think Jesus Christ was crucified on Friday and rose on Sunday morning. This is a teaching that came through the Roman Catholic Church in order to maintain a semblance to the sun god worship. Jesus in fact was crucified on Wednesday morning at 9:00 and died that afternoon. He spent Wednesday night, Thursday, Thursday night, Friday, and Friday night and Saturday in the tomb. He rose Saturday before the Sabbath had ended. Jesus was Lord of the Sabbath, and he rose on the Sabbath, not on our Sunday morning. The women who went to the tomb did in fact go to the tomb Sunday before dawn however, he'd already risen and the tomb was found empty. In reading the account in Luke 24 there is no place it states that Christ resurrected when or after the sun rose.

With today's technology and using the Biblical calendar, we are able to trace time back and correctly discern the day and time of his crucifixion which gives us the accurate day and time of his resurrection. We also need to remember that the Hebrew day begins at sundown. Therefore, the "first day of the week", which we refer to as Sunday, began at about 6:00 p.m. on what we refer to as Saturday evening.[1]

Nowhere does the Bible tell us that he had just risen prior to their arrival; simply that the tomb or sepulcher was found empty, for he'd already risen. Thus, Jesus fulfilled every event and time frame of the Lord's Passover.

The book of Acts reports some of the persecution of the apostles because they were found to be opposed to the religious-politics of their day and were considered a threat in turning people to, what was referred to as "the way," and to Christ. In Acts 7 we read of Stephen

---

1   The Astronomically and Agriculturally Corrected Biblical Hebrew Calendar, https://www.youtube.com/watch?v=9ZH1IOuqpGw

being stoned to death. He was the first to be martyred. Prior to this, they had already experienced imprisonment, and after this you find James executed by the then-reigning Herod. Besides imprisonment, they had received beatings and their lives were continually threatened on every side.

When the gospel was taken to the Gentiles, the church was now made up of both Jews and Gentiles. There were some confusing ideas on what was expected from the Gentiles, because all of the proselytes to the Jewish faith before them had to be circumcised. The question in those days was not, can a Jew become a Christian? but rather, can a gentile become a Christian? Why? Because Jesus or Yeshua was a Jew and all the Scriptures came from them, Jesus was the Son of the God of Abraham, Isaac, and Jacob, and there were many other factors such as his upbringing, clothing, food eaten et cetera that were and are strictly in relationship to the Jews. Therefore, this concerned the Jewish converts if a Gentile didn't adhere to the circumcision, the sign which set Jews apart from the nations. That issue was quickly resolved and the Gentiles were welcomed with open arms by the church. They were One in Christ.

But being one in Christ was about to change with the development of a new civil-religious system. In 1 Corinthians 1:12 and13 Paul dealt with that issue when he said: "Now I say this, that each of you says, I am of Paul, or I am of Apollos; or I am of Cephas; or I am of Christ. Is Christ divided? Was Paul crucified for you? Or were ye baptized in the name of Paul?" This same issue exists today and has existed throughout the entire church age.

In 2 Thessalonians 2:3 Paul tells them concerning the Lord's coming not to be shaken in mind, or troubled, neither by spirit, nor by word, or letter, "Let no one deceive you by any means; for that day will not come, unless the falling away comes first, and the man of sin is revealed, the son of perdition." So we ask ourselves, when did the church fall away? Who is this son of perdition?

In 2 Peter 2:1 it says: "But there were also false prophets among the people, even as there will be false teachers among you, who will secretly bring in destructive heresies, even denying the Lord who bought them, and bring on themselves swift destruction." So who were these false prophets and when did they arrive?

In Acts 20:29–31 Paul states: "For I know this, that after my departure savage wolves will come in among you, not sparing the flock. Also from among yourselves men will rise up, speaking perverse things, to draw away the disciples after themselves. Therefore watch, and remember, that for three years I did not cease to warn everyone night and day with tears." Who were these grievous wolves and when did they appear?

These things happened before all the apostles had passed on. It is apparent that they knew what was going to happen to the church. They explicitly warned the believers, and Paul writes he warned them for three years with tears.

In 3 John 1:9 he writes: "I wrote to the church, but Diotrephes, who loves to have the pre-eminence among them, does not receive us." What??? This was John the apostle whom Jesus loved! How could he and his company possibly not be received? Except that a man named Diotrephes wanted to be in control, to be head of the church.

Even though the church was already falling into the ways of men and darkness, there were still those who were holding fast to the faith and loved the Lord with all their heart. A great many were the Jews as the gospel was first delivered to them and the church was born in Jerusalem with thousands added daily. God left the corners of the field for the gentiles and they were grafted in with them to become partakers of the inheritance. However, the church became primarily all gentile as it began to fall away from the truths once delivered.

CHAPTER 7

THE GREAT REVOLT AND THE DIASPORA

While the church was busy being established and falling away, those still in Jerusalem who hadn't accepted their Messiah were busy protesting Rome's dictatorship and taxation. Herod Agrippa I, great-grandson of Herod the Great who ruled at the time of the Christ's birth, was the last of the Herodians to rule in Jerusalem. He was born Marcus Julius Agrippa in honor of the Roman statesman Marcus Vipsanius Agrippa. Obviously he had a close relationship with Rome and he had his territory expanded and was given autonomy over his territory. He was responsible for killing James in Acts 12 and intending to kill Peter, he had taken him prisoner. Peter was delivered the night before he was to face Herod by an angel of the Lord. Subsequently, Herod took the lives of the prison guards for not preventing his escape.

The Jews had been rising up in revolt against Rome, yet Emperor Nero wasn't very concerned about the revolt and went about his business. Later, after he'd made some misjudgments and experienced some defeats in battles he became distraught and committed suicide, on June 9, 66.

Josephus writes in his work *The War of the Jews* of a group called Zealots, founded by Judas of Galilee also known as Judas of Gamala to rise up against Quirinius' tax reform, shortly after the Roman Empire declared what had most recently been the tetrarchy of Herod Archelaus to be a Roman province and that they "agree in all other things with the Pharisaic notions; but they have an inviolable attachment to liberty, and say that God is to be their only Ruler and Lord." Hezekiah, father of Judas the Galilean, had an organized band of so- called "robbers" to make war against the Idumean (Edomite) Herod, and also during the reign of Herod if not before, as the system of religious and political murders practiced by the Zealots was in existence during his reign.

Simon the Zealot, sometimes referred to as Simon the Canaanite, was one of the apostles chosen by Jesus. "And when it was day, he called his disciples to himself; and from them He chose twelve, whom He also named apostles: Simon, whom He also named Peter, and Andrew his brother; James and John; Phillip and Bartholomew; Matthew and Thomas; James the son of Alpheus, and Simon called the Zealot, Judas the son of James, and Judas Iscariot who also became a traitor." (Luke 6:13–16).

This passage from our Bible speaks loudly of how God sees the heart of man and not just our appearance, also how we are forgiven regardless of our life's choices and transgressions. Jesus was not interested in the politics of Simon nor his zeal to fight Rome for the sake of his religion. Rather he saw in Simon's heart a misdirected love for the Father and called him out.

Battles between the Zealots and the Sanhedrin, the high court which was comprised of Sadducees, Pharisees and Scribes, were taking place within cities throughout Judea.

Because the Sanhedrin operated under the authority of Rome, they, for the most part, were not interested in revolting against them. However, the Zealots were of the belief that paying taxes to Rome was an offense to God and their faith as God was to be king and rule, not Rome.

The "Great Revolt" began around AD 66, with the Greek and Jewish religious tensions and escalated with the anti-taxation protests, leading to attacks against Roman citizens. The Jews were rebelling not just against Rome, but especially against Gessius Florus, the Roman Procurator of Judea.

An organized group of Jews had been protesting against a pagan sacrifice in front of a Caesarean synagogue that was deliberately set on fire. Gessius Florus arrested them and took money from the temple treasury. He then sent his troops to raid the markets in Jerusalem and 3,600 Jewish men, women and children were slaughtered. Thus the Jews around Judea took up arms against the Romans with the Zealots leading.

The Zealots took control over the revolt. But the Jews with their leaders wanted to maintain peace with the Romans. The response by the Romans was to plunder the temple and execute about 6,000 Jews of Jerusalem, and this resulted in a full on rebellion. The Roman garrison of Judea was swiftly overrun with rebels, and the pro-Roman king, Agrippa, along with the Roman officials, fled from Jerusalem.

Herod Agrippa II, the seventh and last Herodian king of Chalcis (located in southern Lebanon) and tetrarch of southern Syria, was made by Rome, a supervisor over the temple of Jerusalem. When he heard the news he sent two thousand riders to help out the Jewish leaders from the rebels. The riders were driven out and archives were set on fire, seemingly to encourage the people to engage in the rebellion. With the rebellion getting out of control, the Syrian legate, Cestius Gallus, brought in the Twelfth Legion of the Syrian army to snuff out the rebellion and bring order. The Syrian army was however, ambushed and defeated by the rebels losing four hundred of their men at the Battle of Beth Heron. Six thousand Romans were massacred and the legions' standard or aquila was lost. This was a shocking defeat to the leadership of Rome.

When a Sicarii leader, Menahem ben Yehuda, attempted to take control of the city but failed he was executed. The peasant leader, Simon bar Giora along with the rest of the Sicarii were expelled by the new government and Ananus ben Ananus, the high priest, began reinforcing the city.

Nero, after hearing the report on the Twelfth Legion and the Roman defeat, sent General Titus Flavius Vespasian, a very skilled military strategist, to end the rebellion. Thus Vespasian was selected to diminish the rebellion in the Judea province and his son Titus was second in command with him. They were given four legions and were assisted by king Agrippa with forces. Around 67, Vespasian invaded Galilee and the Romans determined to eradicate the rebel's strongholds and to punish the population.

Vespasian and Titus took over the greater part of the Jewish strongholds within a few months and later overran the Jodapatha after a forty-seven-day siege. He began his attack at Galilee with three of his legions and wiped out the Jewish forces. Jerusalem was yet defended by a strong rebel force and so was avoided. Because of this attack thousands of refugees and Zealot rebels were driven into Judea causing political conflict in Jerusalem.

Simon Bar Giora with fifteen thousand troops under his command were requested by the Sadducees to stand up against the Zealots and they took control of a great portion of the city. Internal strife had erupted across Jerusalem and the Romans were intent to have it ceased.

Confrontation erupted between the Sadducees and Zealots into bloody violence. Edomites entered the city and took up side with the Zealots and Ananus ben Ananus was killed with his faction receiving severe casualties. Simon Bar Giora was then invited by the Sadducees to return to Jerusalem with his fifteen thousand troops he was commanding to fight against the Zealots. He successfully took control of much of the city. John of Giscala commanded the Northern Revolt and Eleazar ben Simon. With Bar-Giora taking so much control there grew bitter fighting between those of John and Eleazar with those of Bar-Giora and continued until around 69.

Due to civil war and political upheaval in Rome a pause in military operations ensued. Vespasian had been called back to Rome and there made Emperor around the year 69, succeeding Nero. Because Vespasian was absent the Jerusalem problem had passed to the responsibility of his son Titus and he'd marched his legions down the coast and inward toward Jerusalem. By the year 68, Jerusalem became under siege. Jerusalem was a difficult city to take captive being heavily fortified. The city was walled on three sides with the north side the only open, and it had high towers, walls, and heavy fortifications. Titus, because of this, took eighty thousand soldiers to the borders. After laying a two-week siege they had control of the first wall and in another five days brought down the second wall where upon the legions marched in. The Jews however, had the advantage of knowing the cities layout and its streets so managed to inflict severe blows to the Romans.

Titus built a five-mile wall sealing off the city and ordered anyone touching it to be killed. It wasn't long before the Jews walled inside ran out of supplies and soon were plagued with disease and starvation. There were corpses filling the city and hurled over the walls. Civil confrontations developed with individuals being robbed for any food they might possess. Even the dead were searched, for if a mere crumb might be found. The stench of dead bloated bodies permeated the air and the Jews were growing weaker in body and in mind with each passing day. Unspeakable insane behaviors were a consequence among them. Yet anyone who thought to surrender was at risk to be killed. Josephus wrote in *The War of the Jews*,

> [T]hey (Jews) returned to their former madness, and separated one from another, and fought it out; and they did everything that the besiegers could desire them to do. For they never suffered from the Romans anything worse than they made each other suffer; nor was there any misery endured by the city which, after what these men did, could be esteemed new. It was most of all unhappy before it was overthrown; and those that took it did it a kindness. For I venture to say that the sedition destroyed the city, and the Romans destroyed the sedition. This was a much harder thing to do than to destroy the walls. So that we may justly ascribe our misfortunes to our own people.

Josephus continues,

> But the rage of the Idumeans was not satiated by these slaughters; but they now betook themselves to the city, (Jerusalem) and plundered every house, and slew every one they met; and for the other multitude, they esteemed it needless to go on with killing them, but they sought for the high priests, and the generality went with the greatest zeal against them; and as soon as they caught them they slew them, and then standing upon their dead bodies, in way of jest, upbraided Ananus with his kindness to the people, and Jesus (not Christ) with his speech made to them from the wall. Nay, they proceeded to that degree of impiety, as to cast away their dead bodies without burial, were condemned and crucified, and buried them before the going down of the sun. I should not mistake if I said that the death of Ananus was the beginning of the destruction of the city, and that from this very day may be dated the overthrow of her wall, and the ruin of her affairs, whereon they saw their high priest, and the procurer of their preservation, slain in the midst of their city.

Titus added to the food shortage by allowing Jews arriving for Passover to enter the city and then not allowing them exit. He set up battering rams to the third wall and breached it as well as the second wall and then went for the Fortress of Antonia north of the temple mount. This attempt was not successful however. The Romans were drawn into street fighting with the Zealots who retreated to the temple.

After approximately a month, the Roman soldiers had reached the temple. Titus then offered to spare the temple if the rebels would come out and fight but he was refused. Instead they set fire to parts of the temple in order to disallow entrance by the Romans. The Romans therefore added fuel to the fires to bring the entirety down and the temple was engulfed in flames, battered and destroyed, it was brought to the ground. Titus did not want the temple destroyed as he'd had a goal to seize it and then make it a dedicated temple to the Roman Emperor and Roman pantheon.

There was a most brutal seven-month siege and the Zealot infighting persisted. The accounts recorded by Josephus that took place within the walls of Jerusalem during this siege are the most horrific in the course of mankind. The Romans finally breached the defenses of the now extremely weakened forces of the Jews and gained their victory around 70 AD In the process the legions were literally climbing and stepping over dead bodies in pursuit of the enemy. Many of the dead were thrown over the wall into the Kidron Valley. By September 7, the Romans had complete control and many of the Jews escaped through underground tunnels but were hunted by the Romans and either killed or taken captive into slavery. By September 7 the Romans had complete control. Josephus reports 1.1 million Jews were slain, multitudes were taken into slavery and yet multitudes again were dispersed. Titus went back to Rome arriving with a greeting of triumph. In honor of his great victory an arch was erected commemorating the triumphal event.

The Arch of Titus stands today with carvings on it depicting some of the spoils taken from Jerusalem and brought to Rome. Among the sacred artifacts, the two silver trumpets, the table of showbread, and the menorah. Titus himself is depicted riding an eagle on his way to become a god. There are several different goddesses pictured giving him tribute and one placing a crown wreath upon him as well. The inscription reads:

SENATVS

POPVLVSQUE ROMANVS

DIVO TITO DIVI VESPASIAN F

VESPASIANO AUGUSTO

"The Senate and people of Rome (dedicate this) to the deified Titus Vespasian Augustus, son of the deified Vespasian." This is the arch of Titus: a tribute to a man who was a hero, an emperor, and a god of Rome."

The siege of Jerusalem with its destruction and the dispersion of the Jews not only impacted the Jews over the past two thousand years, but is of great significance to all believers in understanding God's plan of redemption for both Jew and Gentile. The disciples, with exception to those such as Stephen and James who'd been martyred, witnessed the destruction of the temple and the slaughter, enslaving and dispersion of their Jewish brethren including members of their own families.

The church was not ignorant to what was about to befall Jerusalem as Christ had given them prior warning. "Then Jesus went out and departed from the temple, and His disciples came to him to show him the buildings of the temple. And Jesus said to them, 'Do you not see all these things? Assuredly, I say to you, not one stone shall be left here upon another, that shall not be thrown down."

Now as He sat on the Mount of Olives, the disciples came to Him privately, saying, 'Tell us, when will these things be? And what will be the sign of Your coming, and of the end of the age'" (Matt. 24:1–3)?

The end of the "age" they spoke of here was the end of the age of the world they were living in. *Age* is from the Greek word *aion* and the "end" here is from the Greek word *suntelies* which means "entire completion." The disciples were therefore asking Jesus when the completion of the age or world they were in would come. Jesus told them to take heed that no man deceives them for there would be many coming in his name saying that they are Christ.

History records that during the time of Christ there were numerous individuals who were claiming to be the Messiah. This of course contributed to the extensive questioning the Sanhedrin imposed upon Jesus as they were accustomed to being confronted with false Christs and having to solve those cases however, they had never been confronted with anyone who possessed the powers and wisdom that Jesus possessed nor the followers. He presented a much different case for them and one that could not be easily resolved. They were intimidated by his knowledge, wisdom and miracles and resented him furiously. The events that followed soon after Christ's crucifixion were exactly as he foretold. History repeats itself and we are seeing these same events today.

"And you will hear of wars and rumors of wars. See that you are not troubled; for all these things must come to pass, but the end is not yet" (Matt. 24:6).

There were many wars fought in Judea and outside Judea before the final destruction. The wars inside Judea were fought with fury and those outside with equal fury. Rome had invaded Britain beginning in 40 AD and finally defeated it in 47 AD under emperor Claudius Caesar. Thrace of Greece, Noricum of Austria, Pamphylia of Asia Minor, Lycia of now Turkey, and Mauretania, now known as Morocco of northern Africa, and of course, Judea all engaged in war with Rome and were all annexed between 40 and 54 AD. Within Rome itself there were violent and bloody civil wars taking place which not only rocked the foundations of Rome but made the entire Roman world unstable.

When Vespasian returned to Rome, he went to defeat the enemy but he was unaware until his arrival that he would be engaging his troops to fight his own countrymen. It was through his victory however, that he won the position of emperor as there were others racing for the crown as well.

"For nation will rise against nation, and kingdom against kingdom. And there will be famines, pestilences, and earthquakes in various places. All these are the beginnings of sorrows." (Matt. 24:7, 8)

Indeed, Jerusalem was riddled with famine and disease as they fought against Rome before its destruction but it was not only contributed to by the horrific wars within the city but the earthquakes as well.

The first earthquake to take place is recorded in Matthew 27:51, which resulted in the veil of the temple being torn from top to bottom and happened when Christ was crucified. Afterwards there was "a great earthquake that shook the foundation of the prison house" (Acts 16:26).

Tacitus, a first-century historian, describes the conditions in 51 AD "This year witnessed many prodigy's signs or omens . . . including repeated earthquakes."

Josephus records an earthquake in Judea with such a magnitude that "the constitution of the universe was confounded for the destruction of men." He also wrote that earthquakes were a "common calamity" and that God himself had brought them about for a special purpose. There were earthquakes in Crete, Smyrna, Miletus, Chios, Samos, Laodecia, Hierapolis, Colossae, Campania, Rome and Judea. All of these were inhabited by Jews. Paul had started churches in Colossae and Hierapolis however, these cities along with Laodechia were destroyed. Laodecia was rebuilt soon after but Colossae and Hierapolis were not. Paul's letters pre-dated their destruction which was in approximately 61 AD.

The earthquake of Hierapolis was so severe that the emperor in order to relieve the people, remitted tribute taxes for five years. These earthquake disasters are recorded by Tacitus. Also Philostratus states; "there was also in the same reign as Crete", and "there were others at Smyrna, Miletus, Chios and Samos; in all which places the Jews had settled". Tacitus also records that "In the reign of Nero there was an earthquake at Laodicea."[2]

Also recorded by Eusebius and Orosius who add that Hierapolis, Colossae and Laodicea were overthrown by earthquakes. The earthquake at Campania in the reign of Caligula (Gaius Julius Caesar Augustus Germanicus - not Gaius Julius Caesar) which are spoken of by both Tacitus and Seneca, and another in Rome in the reign of Galba was spoken of by Suetonius, "to all which may be added those which happened on that dreadful night." These devastating events added to the already ignited fury and brought further stress to the Roman administrators.

At the time the Idumeans (Edomites) were excluded from Jerusalem before the siege began, Josephus states in *The War of the Jews*: "A heavy storm during the night violent winds arose, accompanied with

---

2   The tragic earthquake of AD 60, http://religiouslyincorrect.com/Articles/ TriCityAreaEarthquake.shtml.

the most excessive rains, with constant lightnings, most tremendous thunderings and with dreadful roarings of earthquakes. It seemed (continues he) as if the system of the world had been confounded for the destruction of mankind and one might well conjecture that these were signs of no common events."

"Then they will deliver you up to tribulation and kill you, and you will be hated by all nations for My name's sake" (Matt. 24:9).

Stephen, as previously mentioned, was the first to be killed (Acts 8:54-60), followed by James, the brother of John (Acts 12:2). The gospel continued to be preached in spite of the opposition, but eventually all but the apostle John were killed by the authorities of the political-religious systems. All of these events were taking place while the wars within Judea were taking place. The Lord's body of believers were not ignorant to the fact that Jerusalem would suffer destruction as they had been forewarned by Christ and had removed themselves, selling all they had and giving to those who had need (Acts 2:45). They were in fact, so well informed they didn't wait until Jerusalem was under seize.

Historian Eusebius writes: "the members of the Jerusalem church by means of an oracle, given by revelation to acceptable persons there, were ordered to leave the city before the war began and settle in a town called Peraea called Pella." Whether this statement is accurate or not, the Christian community did not wait until they were fenced in. Once the city was encamped around by Roman soldiers and the walls were built, no one was allowed to leave. The New Testament epistles are a clear indication they had not stayed in Jerusalem but left and spread the gospel of Christ.

The popular belief of Matthew 24 is that is the Lord describing the end of the (our) world. However, Jesus was answering the disciples question regarding the destruction of the temple and the end of their age. They had no thought of a world two thousand years beyond them nor were they aware of the size of the world. The US, Canada or South America were non-existent. Their question and their answer pertained to them. In Matthew 24:34 Jesus says, "Assuredly I say to you, (the disciples) this generation (theirs) will by no means pass away, till all these things take place." Indeed, all those things did take place before that generation had passed. The prophet Daniel in Daniel 9 wrote of this desolation and of desolations as well as abominations. There has been since 70 AD an "overspreading of abominations."

"Then he shall confirm a covenant with many for one week; But in the middle of the week he shall bring an end to sacrifice and offering. And on the wing of abominations shall be one who makes desolate, even until the consummation, which is determined is poured out on the desolate" (Dan. 9:27) The Septuagint reads: "and at the end of the time an end shall be put to the desolation." We are still in the desolate time but the end of the desolation is knocking at the door.

The events that transpired, earthquakes, wars and rumors of wars, nations rising up et cetera, are definitely an example for our time and are happening as part of the prophecy, but where our focus needs to be is on the events playing out with, and around, Jerusalem and the church. The desolations that Daniel wrote of have not ended yet. Jerusalem has continually suffered abominations. Moses wrote the words of the Lord regarding the consequences of their turning away. One in particular was: "For a fire is kindled in mine anger, and shall burn unto the lowest hell, and shall consume the earth with her increase, and set on fire the foundations of the mountains."

"I will heap disasters on them; I will spend My arrows on them. They shall be wasted with hunger, devoured by pestilence and bitter destruction; I will also send against them the teeth of beasts, with the poison of serpents of the dust" (Deut. 32:22–24).

Paul wrote: "For I do not desire, brethren, that you should be ignorant of this mystery, lest you should be wise in your own opinion, that blindness in part has happened to Israel until the fullness of the Gentiles has come in" (Rom. 11:25). The Lord, in speaking of what was to befall Jerusalem says, "And they will fall by the edge of the sword, and be led away captive into all nations. And Jerusalem will be trampled by the Gentiles, until the times of the Gentiles are fulfilled" (Luke 21:24).

The Jews have been in the lowest hell and have not yet fully emerged as they still face threats of destruction; however, God has gathered them back and has restored them as a nation and is restoring them to himself as we witness the veil being lifted and more and more discovering their Messiah.

All but the completion of this statement of Christ, "until the times of the Gentiles be fulfilled" has happened. Today we recognize that the latter statement concerning the Jews began its fulfillment in 1948 and is drawing closer to completion. There are more Jews now turning to the Lord than there are Gentiles, which is a great reason for rejoicing because as Paul states, "For if their being cast away is the reconciling of the world, what will their acceptance be but life from the dead?" (Rom. 11:15)

CHAPTER 8

A ONE-WORLD MANMADE RELIGION

After Titus defeated Jerusalem a strong contempt toward the Jews begin to develop and because the early church was first Jews and Christ had been a Jew a contempt toward the Christians also developed. They were considered at the time, another sect of Judaism. Although they did not present an immediate threat, they were considered exclusive in matters of religion and with the adherents increasing they could not be ignored. The Jews had been exiled, taken into slavery, and dispersed. The Jews living among the Romans begin to experience persecution as they would not give allegiance to Rome and its gods, and so were an object of disobedience to the sovereignty of Rome and Caesar.

The Christians likewise would not pay respect to the gods of Rome and so fell to the same persecutions and condemnations. Notably the more severe persecution came prior to Jerusalem's destruction, at around 64, when Nero was still emperor. He was known for barbarous atrocities and his temper. It is recorded that Nero himself, ordered his soldiers to set Rome on fire and then went up to the tower of Macainus and played his harp, sang the burning of Troy and declared he wished the ruin of all things before his death. He later blamed the Christians and punished them in a most horrendous manner. In particular, he clothed them in wax, fastened them to axletrees, set them on fire and then used them to illuminate the gardens. He also dressed them in animal hide and tormented the dogs in such a manner that they were mauled to death. On occasion they would suffer being beaten, burnt or placed in the Colosseum for sport to be eaten alive by lions or other wild animals. In spite of the persecutions they continued to flourish and were a thorn in the side of Rome. It was during this time that the apostles Peter and Paul were martyred.

In 81, Domitian, who was known for his cruelty, commanded the lineage of David to be killed. These events were sporadic; however, the possibility of becoming a victim to the torments was a daily threat for almost 300 years from the beginning of the church. Many remained true to the faith first delivered to them, but only for a space of time. False teachers had already come into the church and were turning the assemblies away from the truth. "For certain men have crept in unnoticed, who long ago were marked out for this condemnation, ungodly men, who turn the grace of our God into lewdness and deny the only Lord God, and our Lord Jesus Christ" (Jude 4).

Others succeeding Domitian continued the persecution, some with great severity. At Mount Ararat many were crowned with thorns, crucified and had spears thrust in their sides in mock of Christ's execution. Some were forced to walk over thorns, nails and other sharp objects with their already wounded feet while some were beaten and scourged so badly their sinews and veins were exposed. After the excruciating tortures, they were then put to death in the most horrid ways imaginable.

The apostle John some time during the ninth decade was boiled in oil while in Asia (modern-day Turkey) but somehow survived and was exiled to Patmos, where he wrote the revelations he'd received from Christ.

By 304, the persecution had reached Spain. There was an order for two of the Christian's leading overseers, Valerius and Vincent, to be taken and imprisoned. They banished Valerius but Vincent was racked and his limbs were dislocated and his flesh torn with hooks. He was laid on a gridiron which had fire under it and spikes which ran through him. Miraculously, he survived these tortures and thrown into a prison which was strewn with flints and broken glass, where he died and his body thrown into a river.

There was chaos throughout the Roman Empire. During the reign of Diocletian, there were four emperors who jointly governed the empire. After his reign in approximately 305 those emperors competed against each other to become the one single emperor. Thus the tetrarchy collapsed and civil war again broke out.

Constantine and Maxentius became contenders for the throne and Constantine determined to remove Maxentius. The night before the battle he claimed to have had a vision or dream in which he saw "the Christian symbol," the cross. He further claimed that the vision was accompanied with a voice promising him victory if he used this symbol. Another version is that the voice said "in this sign you shall conquer" Neither story would adhere to the teachings of Christ as he didn't teach his followers to engage in bloody warfare.

Constantine decided to confront Maxentius at Milvian Bridge where he would have access to the city. He was successful in defeating Maxentius and pushed his troops into the Tiber. Afterwards, Maxentius was pushed into the river as well and drowned.

Constantine now entered Rome as the victor and the Senate immediately declared him to be emperor. Maxentius was fished out of the river by Constantine's troops and they cut off his head then paraded it through the streets of Rome. Constantine credited his victory to the Christian god, although none of this was in the nature of Christ. After Constantine gained control he legalized Christianity. This in turn would advance his popularity and authority over the populace.

This victory resulted in Constantine's control of the Western Roman Empire and opened the door for Christianity to rule the empire. He set in motion a plan to build his own version of the Christian church. He issued an edict of toleration to stop the persecution of the "true believers of Christ" around 313 so that for a period of time the church had relief. With Constantine issuing his edict to no longer persecute Christians, the church now found relief and resulted in Christianity not only being legal but evolving into the state religion. In order to fit Christianity into Rome's mythical religion of polytheism and govern over both meant there had to be a uniting of the two, or in this case the many.

Rome, while conquering nations, would bring back the skills of architecture, science, medicine and religion they encountered. For example, they inherited the idea of a pontiff and a maximus pontiff from the Egyptians, who were so strong in their gods and superstition they made all their architecture revolve around their gods to honor them. Their architects were required to be educated as priests as well as in the skills of architecture. Rome needed to build a bridge over the Tiber and employed the skills of Egypt's bridge builders, considered the best at the time, who were called pontiffs. The definition of pontiff meaning "bridge-builder." The head supervisor or head pontiff was called "pontiff maximus," and they were all priests. Thus the idea of having a pontiff and pontiff maximus was incorporated into Rome's religion.

The position of the emperor and title was usurped with the "highest" in the command of bishops and became referred to as pope. This change in identity has been attributed to Tertullian during the second century by applying the term "pontiff maximus (supreme pontiff or pope) to the head of the Catholic church. However, he used the term in a sarcastic manner to Callixtus I because he believed him to be abusing his power in promoting it unilaterally. In effect he was actually calling him a bullying pompous father. Also, the title Pontifex Maximus was given to the Empire's priesthood, who were known as the Pontifical College.

The persecutions administered by the pagan authorities on the Christians and Jews was making a shifting from the Roman Catholic Christian authorities to the non-conformist Christians and Jews.

Bishop Basil opposed Arianism, and this brought to him a vengeance from the Arian bishop of Constantinople. Bishop Basil was also opposed to paganism. The emperor, Julian, sent to him representatives with threats of racks, and made promises to persuade him however, he remained firm in his convictions and spent a period in prison subjected to torments.

By accident the emperor had gone to Ancyra where the bishop was imprisoned and so decided to interrogate him himself. Julian proceeded to exercise all his abilities to alter Basil's persuasion yet found it futile. Basil remained firm to his faith and even delivered a prophetic announcement regarding Julian's death and declared to him that he should be tormented in the other life. This so enraged the emperor that he ordered that "Basil should be torn every day in seven different parts, until his skin and flesh were entirely mangled." Basil died from this brutal punishment on June 28, 362.

Others during this same year suffered similar barbarous punishments such as Donatus, bishop of Arezzo and Gordian, a Roman magistrate. and a commander in chief of the Roman forces in Egypt, Artemius, who was a known Christian was first denied his commission, then his estate, and last he was beheaded.

The Roman church continued in discourse and positional combat. It also experienced up rivals which frequently led to violence and bestial behavior. On one occasion Cyril a bishop of Alexandria ordained one Proterius a priest. After Cyril died a vehement enemy of his and his family, Discorus, occupied the see of Alexandria. The Chalcedon council condemned him because he supported Eutyches whom they opposed and made Proterius bishop of the see. A division of interests resulted and an insurrection. The Eutyches supporters decided to inflict their vengeance on Proterius and he fled to the church seeking sanctuary. However, on "good Friday" of 457 a large mass rushed him and brutally murdered him. Then drug his body through the streets, cut it to pieces and burnt it, afterward they scattered the ashes in the air.

These types of incidents existed to a point of common occurrence, either by the occasion of Christian against Christian whether clergy or laity, or the occasion of Christian against pagan . . . or vice versa. The Christian faith was bathed with bloody violence and truth was obscured and shadowed by erroneous monarchial doctrine from its high clergy. The violent acts were not limited to the lesser members of church but this demonic perversity reached out to the papacy that fathered it.

Council of Nicaea and Initiation the Trinity

Constantine convened the Council of Nicaea in 325 for political and religious reasons, in order to resolve a dispute over the doctrine of God. Constantine himself neither knew nor cared about the matter being disputed but he was very eager to bring an end to the controversy and unity to the empire. Hosius, an influential man in the court, suggested if those representing the entire church met, there may be harmony reached, and this appealed to Constantine. The issue at hand was two differing views of God. Arius, a priest in Alexandria, Egypt, taught that Christ must have a beginning because He was the Son of God and therefore, God, being his father, must be older. Athanasius, a deacon in Alexandria, opposed him with a Trinitarians view that the Father, Son, and Holy Spirit were one but at the same time distinct from one another. The decision reached was by and large arbitrary. Constantine was not actually a Christian and un equipped to reach any conclusive decision.

Constantine presided over the Nicene Council, guiding the discussions, and proposed the formula expressing the relationship of Christ to God. The creed was issued and though many were against the creed, all but two signed, being intimidated by the emperor.

The council, with the emperor's approval, rejected the view of Arius, which was a minority view and accepted that of Athanasius, also a minority view. The church had to, from this point forward, endorse a belief held by only a minority of those attending the council. The groundwork for the Trinity was laid three centuries after Christ's resurrection. This did not end the controversy. and at times there were bloody violent battles in the aftermath. Noted historian Will Durant states, "Probably there were more Christians slaughtered by Christians in these two years (342-3) than by all the persecutions of Christians by pagans in the history of Rome. [3]

Shortly following, the issue of the nature of the Holy Spirit arose. Added to Athanasius' creed was, "We believe in the Holy Spirit." Confusion as to whether the Holy Spirit was a synonym for God or something different was bringing disagreement. Men trained in Greek philosophy who were overseers or bishops such as Basil of Caesarea, his brother Gregory of Nyssa, and another Gregory of Nazianzus thought it not logical or intellectual but more of paradigm that confounded reason.

Disputes continued, and finally another council was arranged: The Council of Constantinople. In 381, about 44 years after the death of Constantine, Emperor Theodosius the Great convened this council in order to bring a solution to the dispute. Gregory of Nazianzus had

---

3   *The Story of Civilization*, Vol. 4: The Age of Faith, 1950 p. 8.

reached the position of archbishop of Constantinople and therefore presided over the council and pressed his view on the others, which was that the Spirit was consubstantial with the Father or in other words, the persons are of the same being as in substance. Gregory fell ill and died and Nectarius, a senator of the city, was selected to preside, and although he was not yet a baptized Christian, he appeared to have knowledge on theology. It was necessary that he be initiated into the faith before he could be baptized and consecrated. So it was the teachings of the three Cappadocian theologians that opened the door for the Council of Constantinople to affirm the divinity of the Holy Spirit though it had not been stated clearly prior nor clear in the scriptures.[4] The council took upon them the statement "We believe in one God, the Father Almighty, Maker of heaven and earth, and of all things visible and invisible, and in one Lord Jesus Christ, the only-begotten Son of God, begotten of the Father before all ages . . . and we believe in the Holy Spirit, the Lord and Giver of life, who proceeds from the Father, who with the Father and the Son together is worshipped and glorified, who spoke by the prophets . . . in one holy, catholic and apostolic Church." This became known as the Nicene-Constantinopolitan Creed. The Trinity became the official teaching concerning the nature of God through this declaration. Theodosius now would not tolerate any opposing views and issued an edict which read: "We now order that all churches are to be handed over to the bishops who profess Father, Son and Holy Spirit of a single majesty, of the same glory, of one splendor, who establish no difference by sacrilegious separation, but (who affirm) the order of the Trinity by recognizing the Persons and uniting the Godhead." And another, "Let us believe the one deity of the Father, the Son and the Holy Spirit, in equal majesty and in a holy Trinity. We authorize the followers of this law to assume the title of Catholic Christians; but as for the others, since, in our judgement, they are foolish madmen, we decree that they shall be branded with the ignominious name of heretics, and shall not presume to give their conventicles (assemblies) the name of churches. "They will suffer in the first place the chastisement of the divine condemnation, and the second the punishment which our authority, in accordance with the

---

4   *The Harper Collins Encyclopedia of Catholicism,* "God" p. 568.

will of Heaven, shall decide to inflict"[5] This was the setting in which the doctrine of the Trinity was established.[6]

Contrary to what is professed of the Trinity doctrine set in place by the founders and fathers of Catholicism, the *New Catholic Encyclopedia* states: "The majority of the New Testament texts reveal God's Spirit as something, not someone; this is especially seen in the parallelism between the spirit and the power of God."

Although Constantine had issued the edict of "toleration," the Roman Catholic Church was not installed as the official state religion until 380 with the edict of Thessalonica by emperors Gratian, Theodosius and Valentinan II.

The doctrine of the Nicolaitans (Rev. 2:4,15) was a healthy infant and developing with rapidity. The word *Nicolaitans* is a compound of three Greek words. *Nikos*: a conquest, victory, triumph, *Laos*: people (laity), *Ton*: a long "a" or tan by English contraction. The definition thus rendered to conquer the people or within the church to conquer or control the laity.

The Jews had already been expelled from Jerusalem in 312, and the Christians ruled Israel for the next three hundred years. They made it illegal for Jews to live in Jerusalem, and persecution of the Jews became the action of the authorities with Constantine's rule. Laws were placed in the church forbidding Christians to have Saturday for a day of worship and Sunday, the sun-god day became the rule. Anyone caught keeping the Sabbath faced severe punishment. Constantine's hatred toward the Jews filtered throughout the kingdom and the church. From now on Jews would not turn to their Messiah through faith and revelation rather they would receive threats to except the faith of Rome or suffer the consequences. There would be forced baptism with noncompliance resulting in death.

Jews paid a high tax, were not allowed to operate a business. Synagogues were burned down, and Jews were considered outcasts, were spat upon, had stones thrown at them, and constantly lived under the threat of execution unless they converted to the church of Rome.

---

5   *Documents of the Christian Church*, Henry Bettenson, editor 1967 p. 22.

6   Another reliable source is Karen Armstrong's book *A History of God*, New York: Ballantine Books (August 9, 1994).

Also, any Christian who did not accept the church as their supreme authority and become a member would face the same punishments. The sixth head of the Beast, Rome, was alive and well with a new mask.

The entire gospel became corrupted; truth was lost and replaced with false doctrines designed to control the people. "Let no one deceive you by any means; for that day will not come, unless the falling away comes first . . . For the mystery of lawlessness is already at work; only He who now restrains will do so until He is taken out of the way" (2 Thess. 2:3, 7).

The apostles were aware of what was going to happen and warned the assemblies. "Therefore, brethren, stand fast and hold the traditions which you were taught, whether by word or our epistle" (2 Thess. 2:15).

"But know this, that in the last day's perilous times will come. For men will be lovers of themselves, lovers of money, boasters, proud, blasphemers, disobedient to parents, unthankful, unholy, unloving, unforgiving, slanderers, without self-control, brutal, despisers of good, Traitors, headstrong, haughty, lovers of pleasure rather than lovers of God: having a form of godliness, but denying its power. And from such people turn away!" (2 Tim. 3:1–5)

Most take this to mean our generation however, Paul was talking to his generation. The last days began two thousand years ago. For example: There are seven days in a week, with Saturday and Sunday being called, "the week-end" or end of the week or the last days of the week. "But, beloved, do not forget this one thing, that with the Lord one day is as a thousand years, and a thousand years as one day" (2 Peter 3:8).

The end times also began two thousand years ago. With our English, we don't always understand the meaning of certain words. For example: *End* in the 1611 King James New Testament is translated from eleven different Greek words with varying implications. Other translations also frequently use the word end in place of what would be a better understood word.

With this we can understand that when the end is spoken of, a person needs to determine if it is the finality or if it is the beginning of the end to finality. A wonderful Jewish teacher, Michael Rood, explains it using a dog's tail for an analogy. His tail is at the end however, that is where the end begins and the final end is at the tip of the tail. For example, when the disciples asked Jesus in Matthew 24:3, "Tell us when these things shall be and what will be the sign of thy coming, and of the *end* of the world?" The word *end* was taken from the Greek word *scholazo*, so they were therefore asking when Jerusalem would become vacant. In Matt 24:6 Jesus said: "And you shall hear of wars and rumors of wars: see that ye not be troubled: for all these things must come to pass, but the *end* is not yet." Here the Greek word *telos* was used, so Jesus was telling them the point aimed at was not yet. Following through with the correct definitions, we can see that Jesus revealed what was to happen to their generation and age but reminding them that they are not going to face the final point of all things.

It is important to bear in mind that biblical incidents occur around biblical geography and people. The events surrounding prophecy are two fold in as much as it is applied to those being spoken to and the age as well as the nation of those spoken to, yet equally important biblical events are re-occurring and expand into the dimension of the future.

Constantine's ambition to have a religion for his empire that would identify obsequiousness to the deity and have loyalty to the emperor made Christianity a perfect fit because with it he would be patronized. Prior, Christians saw Christ as the "good Shepherd" as was Mithras and Apollo. However, the Christians did not look upon the crucifixion event as an image or idol.

Constantine's hatred toward the Jews dictated his decision to require all Christians to worship on Sun-day as the legal Sabbath and anyone found engaging the (Sabbath) Saturday for worship would face punishment. Sun-day, because that was the traditional day of their sun-gods, was synchronized into the church by re-arranging the written events from the gospels and epistles This of course, pleased the pagans because they themselves did not want to alter their traditions.

Although their numbers were yet small, with the imperial efforts to develop their state religion and have obeisance from its people the numbers were raked in. But there was still opposition from the persecutions and penalties that were suffered from various church groups. This of course, was greatly disturbing to Constantine and he determined to solve the problem by calling upon a "universal" or catholic faith. Because the churches already regarded themselves as universal, they maneuvered for preferment. Therefore, Constantine structured the church on the imperial army. Bishops would rule districts corresponding to the military dioceses and would impose discipline. Other clerics of a lesser position would, through a chain of command, report to his local pontiff or "Staff Officers" and wearing the clothing of presbyters or deacons would control funds and allocations.

The Christian community was disturbed with so many pagan temples and shrines dedicated to the false gods and their worship that remained throughout the city, and protested vehemently.

Constantine appeased the Christian community by confiscating the treasures of the ancient pagan temples and refusal to fund the shrines. He also had fabulous cathedrals built that were tax exempt and excluded the clergy from paying taxes and exempt from public obligations. Known as the Privilegia Ecclesiastics, this in itself made it very appealing to become a part of the clergy and many sought out positions. As well as being excluded from taxes and public obligations, they were even removed from the jurisdiction of normal courts of law. Thus, there were innumerable converts with very little religious incentive. This resulted in rivalries. Constantine's sons, who by birth would rule, murdered each other, and Julian, his nephew, took the throne, but because he detested the church doctrine, reversed many of the policies.

Constantine prohibited assemblies of those called heretics and confiscated their public property to the use of the revenue or the church. Those aimed at were partisan to Paul of Samosata, who were passionate in prophecy, the Novatians, who adamantly rejected "temporal effect of repentance, and those considered Gnostic." Extreme measures were taken and vigorous persecution in order to exterminate these assemblies.

Saint Augustine (354–430 AD) claimed error has no rights and justified punishment in severity by quoting Luke 14:16–23. He also referred to Paul being blinded by Christ in order to make him see the true light. He excused the church because, according to him, unbelievers persecuted out of cruelty whereas believers persecuted out of love. Any war to preserve or restore unity to the church was a just war.

The first execution for heresy was in 385, under Emperor Maximus, by the request of the Spanish bishops. The accused was the bishop of Avila, Priscillian, who was charged with witchcraft; however, the apparent truth was that he agreed with some of the opinions of "gnostics" and therefore was exterminated.

Heresy was classified as any denial of some essential doctrine, or any deviation from the orthodox line and by the fifth century there were over one hundred statutes regarding heresy. For the next thousand years it was agreed effectively by all theologians that heretics be persecuted. The reasons for persecution reached ludicrous dimensions. In 1051, at Goslar, Germany, Christians who had elected not to kill chickens were executed for committing an act of heresy.

CHAPTER 9

Holy Days: More Lies Embraced by the Church

There were other changes still to be grafted into the Christian faith. The Saturnalia holiday, a week-long festivity of lawlessness, was celebrated in December from the 17th to 25th. The courts of Rome were closed and the law dictated that no one was punished for the injury of people or the damaging of property. The authorities from each community chose an enemy to Rome who would be representative of the "Lord Misrule." They were required by force to indulge in food and pleasure through the week, and on December 25 the Romans then viciously murdered them, man or woman, in order to destroy the forces of darkness. The historian Lucian writes of his observance in a dialogue called Saturnalia that: "widespread intoxication, going from house to house while singing naked, rape, and other sexual license and consuming human shaped biscuits."[7] Stephen Nissenbaum, a history professor at the University of Massachusetts, Amherst wrote, "In return for ensuring massive observance of the anniversary of the Savior's birth by assigning it to this resonant date, the Church for its part tacitly agreed to allow the holiday to be celebrated more or less the way it had always been."[8] The earliest Christmas holidays were celebrated by drinking, sexual indulgence, and singing naked in the streets.

The irony is that the word *Christmas* comes from "Christ mass" or the mass of Christ. Rather than referring to the birth of Christ, it actually means the death of Christ. In the *World Book Encyclopedia*, the word Christmas is explained to come from the phrase *Cristes Maesse*, an early English phrase meaning "Mass of Christ." The *Catholic*

---

7   Simple to Remember – The History of Christmas, http://www.simpletoremember.com/vitals/Christmas_TheRealStory.htm.

8   Stephen Nissenbaum, *The Battle for Christmas*, Vintage, 1997.

*Encyclop*edia states: "In Christian law, the supreme sacrifice is that of the Mass." Also, "The supreme act of worship consists essentially in an offering of a worthy victim to God, the offering made by a proper person, as a priest, the destruction of the victim." The Latin word for victim is *hostia*, from which the word *host* is derived. What is really going on is a celebration of Christ's death. When you greet someone with the phrase "Merry Christmas" you are actually saying merry death of Christ.

Saturnalia had been imported in the fourth century in order to bring in the masses of pagans. The church leaders were able to bring in large numbers to conversion with the promise of keeping Saturnalia. There were other compromises reached by giving the pagan gods and goddesses reverence by incorporating positions of Saints, thereby they would still maintain their gods and their customs.

The Venerable Bede's, *Historia Ecclesiastica Gentis Anglorum* contains a letter from Pope Gregory I to Mellitus, arguing that conversions were easier if people were allowed to retain the outward forms of their traditions, while claiming that the traditions were in honor of the Christian God, "to the end that, whilst some gratifications are outwardly permitted them, they may the more easily consent to the inward consolations of the grace of God."

The Christians were not successful in altering the customs and in 1466 some of the perversity was re-constituted by the Catholic church when Pope Paul II forced Jews to race naked through the streets of the city, in order to amuse the people. One eyewitness account is: "Before they were to run, the Jews were richly fed, so as to make the race more difficult for them and at the same time more amusing for spectators. They ran . . . amid Rome's taunting shrieks and peals of laughter, while the Holy Father stood upon a richly ornamented balcony and laughed heartily."[9]

During the Saturnalia carnival in the eighteenth and nineteenth centuries, the rabbis of the Roman ghetto were made to wear clown outfits and march through the city streets while being pelted with objects and jeered at by the crowds. The rabbis in 1836 finally sent a petition to Pope Gregory XVI begging him to end the annual abuse.

---

9   A History of Israel, in the *Jerome Biblical Commentary* p. 1247.

His response was: "It is not opportune to make any innovation." Dec 25, 1881 the church leaders created, among the Polish groups, an Antisemitic phobic frenzy which led to riots. In Warsaw 12 Jews were brutally murdered and Jewish women raped. Large numbers were maimed and much property was destroyed.[10] ()

Further, Saturnalia originated from the date Tammuz, the Babylonian name for the earlier-mentioned Horus, was born to Semiramis, December 25th. In this story, Tammuz was killed in his fortieth year in a hunting accident by being gored to death by a boar. Also, in accordance with Babylon's story, Nimrod, his so called father, had become a son god after his death. Semiramis still, like the Egyptian story, had found Nimrod cut into pieces and reassembled him with the exception of his genitalia she was unable to find.

After his ascension to sun-god, Semiramis became pregnant with the rays of the sun and Tammuz was thus born. The sun-god worshipers set aside forty days, a day for each year, to lament over him and would deny themselves some type of pleasure that he might receive their pleasure. This transferred into the forty-day lent given to the church.

The prophet Ezekiel wrote concerning this: "So He brought me to the door of the north gate of the Lord's house; and to my dismay, women were sitting there weeping for Tammuz. Then He said to me, Have you seen *this*, O son of man? Turn again, you will see greater abominations than these. So He brought me into the inner court of the Lord's house; and there, at the door of the temple of the Lord, between the porch and the altar, were about twenty-five men, with their backs toward the temple of the Lord and their faces toward the east, and they were worshiping the sun toward the east" (Ezek. 8:14–16).

After Semiramis died, Tammuz was favored by the other gods and was noted as the "mother of god" and "queen of heaven" she being sent back by the gods, returned to the earth as the fertility goddess called Ashtarte (Ishtar) or in English Easter. She arrived to earth in a giant egg, a symbol of fertility, and proved her divinity when she changed a bird into a rabbit that would lay eggs. To further the obscenity of this day, priests of this religion would get virgins pregnant on the altar of

---

10   David I. Kertzer, *The Popes Against the Jews: The Vatican's Role in The Rise of Modern Anti-Semitism*, Alfred A. Knopf p. 74.

the fertility goddess at the Easter sunrise. A year afterward, when the babies had reached the age of three months, they would be sacrificed in front of the sanctuary and eggs would be dyed in the blood of those infants.

Because Tammuz was killed by a boar, they celebrated Astarte's Sun-day with the slaughter of a boar by the priests, and all gathered in would eat the meat (ham). This was done each year to avenge the death of Tammuz. The word mass by definition means to sacrifice or re-sacrifice. The service of re-sacrificing Christ is done every day throughout the year multiple times around the world.

The word *Christmas* or Christ-mass is considered the "High Mass" of the year and Easter also holds a "High Mass" for followers. Yet both have their roots and were birthed from the practice of worshiping false gods that most of the Christian world bought into. The gods and goddesses of other nations were acknowledged and adopted by Rome and in order to appease the multitudes that held to the traditions of their mythology they were synchronized into the church. Thereby maintaining peace, adding to the numbers of the state religion, increasing the wealth of the church and becoming stronger.

There are many other hidden things within the Christian churches that originate from the adoption of Babylonian religious practices and none of the churches are exempt. For example: In ancient Chaldea or Babylon the symbol of the god Tammuz the initial T (Tau) was used. In order to assist in convincing the pagans to adopt the new state religion they were permitted to keep pagan signs and symbols. Hence to simply lower the cross piece of the letter would allow them to retain their symbol and be accepted and also equally accepted by the Christians as a symbol of the implement of crucifixion for which there is much speculation do to the original Greek usage of the word to actually mean stake or pole.

Eighteenth-century Bible Translator Dr. E. W. Bullinger writes, "crosses were used as symbols of the Babylonian Sun-god . . .. It should be stated that Constantine was a sun-god worshiper . . . The evidence is thus complete, that the Lord was put to death upon an upright stake, and not on two pieces of timber placed at any angle."[11]

---

11   (E. W. Bullinger, *The Companion Bible*, p. 162.

To impress the assemblage, the church of Rome elected to place an image of Christ hanging from the cross to maintain a focus on the crucifixion. Later the Protestants chose to remove the image because they were compelled to view his resurrection rather than his crucifixion. The first-century believers used no symbols. The second-century believers also refrained from using symbols, with the exception of agreement to mark their underground meetings with a fish to allow other believers to locate their assemblage.

A quote from Plato, who embraced Orphic (entrancing cult of Orpheus) and mystery doctrines, to the Republic II (362e) in his reference to a "just" man also demonstrates why early Christians and others had displayed a strong disfavor toward such a symbol. "What they will say is this, that such being his disposition the just man will have to endure the lash, the rack, chains, the branding iron in his eyes, and finally, after every extremity of suffering, he will be crucified."

It is worthy to note that the cross with an image on it did not exist until the sixth century. The term *crucifix* comes from the Latin "cruci fixus" and means fixed to a cross.

As years passed with the entourage of popes, there were days set aside to honor various individuals who'd been proclaimed saints and various days marking events considered holy events and today, when the Catholic calendar is viewed, every day has a holy recognition assigned to it. The clergy are obliged to celebrate these days; however, the laity is bound only to their "high mass" days. Other alterations eventually were made throughout the city. The statue of Jupiter was given to be Saint Peter, Venus became the Virgin Mary and the adoption of "mother-child" worship was initiated. The accomplishment of unification of the former religion with the new Christian faith became an easy transformation making it acceptable to all, making it possible to increase the number of devotees to the system being formed.

There were some who still hungered for truth and the purity of the gospel and were determined to bring it to the forefront. The foundation of this intent was laid by the well-known French reformer Beregarius in about 1000, who preached the written gospel to his listeners and converted many souls to his doctrinal view. Other priests followed his lead, and by 1147 the numbers were enough for concern to the church of Rome.

Peter Waldo who resided in Lyons was strongly opposed to the popery and taught congregants strictly from scripture. His followers were called Waldenses or Waldoys. Pope Alexander III learned of the opposition from the bishop of Lyons and excommunicated Waldo and his fellow believers of scriptural doctrine and further commanded the bishop to exterminate them. Thus began papal death sentencing for any opposing the church and its doctrine.

There still remained other Waldenses whom the pope had sought out and encouraged to return to the church. Pope Innocent III in 1198–1216 authorized monks as inquisitors to deliver the non-conformist to the courts. A trial was never given and they were pronounced guilty through mere accusation. This did not alleviate the problem so it was determined to send monks to the Waldenses to preach and thereby regain their loyalty. Dominic was among those chosen and was very zealous for the cause and the papacy.

Pope Innocent III found the Dominicans and the Franciscans to be most like his other adherents with dedication and compliance to the church of Rome. He therefore, gave them exclusive license to preside over other courts representing "His Holiness." They were given the authority to excommunicate or sentence to death anyone they considered a heretic even with very little proof of heresy. They made crusades against heretics and partnered with princes to join their crusades with their own forces.

He formed an order in France instituting the Dominican Friars which has continued since as the principal inquisitors of the worlds inquisitions with Dominic canonized so his authority would receive respect. This order was forceful and merciless. If one was observed giving a drink to an imprisoned Waldenses they were charged as a heretic. If even at his or her death a person was found to be a Waldenses their property was confiscated, the heir defrauded and some were sent to the Holy Land while the Dominicans took the possession of all their property. Upon return of the heir the Dominicans conveniently knew nothing about it.

Successor Pope Honorus III approved of this order and it flourished in strength and acceptance and were used by popes for hunting out heretics of the church. In 1233, Pope Gregory IX established the inquisition for the purpose of combating heresy and it gained much force throughout Western and Central Europe.

The first mass murder of Jews took place in France about 1288 where they burned them at the stake.

Other popes followed suit and courts of inquisition were set up in various countries but the Spanish Inquisition became the most feared.

Frederic II, king of Germany and crowned emperor of Sicily, claimed himself a friend and protector of the inquisitors and increased their power further also putting forth an edict that all heretics who remained obstinate were to be burned and those who repented were to be imprisoned for life. The reach of determinant heresy comprised all that was spoken, written against any creeds or traditions of the church, those who did not read the bible in Latin, the Talmud of the Jews, magicians and because their unity had dissolved into opposition, the "Alcoran (full text of Koran) of the Mohammad."

By 1481, the Dominican Inquisitors (friars) were embraced and well established in Spain. The cruelty was unequaled and so horrid that even Spain's kings learned to dread and respect the inquisitors. They were the most powerful and exercised their power to the fullest. The dread of them was so intense that even those who held different opinions kept them concealed to avoid the horrid outcome.

A prisoner was not permitted to see the face of his or her accuser, and once condemned and imprisoned they were tortured with severity, sent to the galleys or put to death. However, the torture imposed upon those deemed heretics as administered with such severity rarely did one survive and if they did they were maimed and suffered as a life-long cripple. They were tied with ropes and stretched until limbs were torn from their sockets, some ropes were deliberately made thin so to cut through the flesh, they were bound with chains and drawn with pulleys and afterward the limbs that were torn free of their sockets would be re-set by a surgeon only so they could undergo the barbaric torture again. There were many devised measures of inflicting brutal pain upon the accused but hardly a one ever denounced their position of faith.

The Jews, being the primary target, were encouraged through threats and forced baptism to convert. Forced baptism however, was not considered a legal holy sacrament if one was physically forced, but if one submitted by threat of death or torture to be baptized, it was then recognized as such. Many Jews converted to Christianity to avoid the inquisitors and many yet fled the country. By the sixteenth century, the primary target turned to the Protestants.

The number of heretical accusations has never been established but is estimated to be in the vicinity of 150,000 who were accused and tried for heresy. The number of executions were also never established but are estimated at approximately 31,912 burned at the stake. There are exaggerations to the accounts and there are denials to the accounts. The truth no doubt is somewhere in the middle but whatever the accuracy, even one such act of brutality hardly portrays the nature of our Father and God of Abraham nor His son and savior Jesus Christ. It is absurd and unimaginable to think a person professing to be born from above could engage in such outrageous claims that their actions were in accordance with their creator.

None of this is descriptive of a "church" or of called-out believers that comes within the slightest degree of what Jesus the Messiah of Israel and Savior of the world began as his true church and "body." Sadly, what it is descriptive of is a powerful, controlling, political, demonic religious beast with roots in ancient paganism and tentacles creeping through and around the earth fastening itself like a leech and sucking the life out of the deceived and ignorant.

CHAPTER 10

Protestant Reformation and Counter-Reformation

The Protestant Reformation occurred primarily in the sixteenth century; however, it had begun centuries earlier with various individuals and groups who refused to bow to Rome. The Protestant movement was initially intended to reform the Roman Catholic Church, but with the heated resistance they met, it necessitated a turn in direction.

Most of the Protestant movement is attributed to Martin Luther, a German Augustinian monk. Because of the practices of indulgences (the paying of money to release punishments for sin) in order to raise money to construct Rome's Basilica of Saint Peter, and other practices, he wrote 95 theses and posted it on the church door in Wittenberg. This was actually a common practice to open a debate. However, his theses were an unwelcome challenge. Luther believed from scripture in justification by faith only.

He especially withstood the indulgences, stating in thesis 82, "Why does not the pope, whose wealth is greater than the riches of Crassus (extremely wealthy land owner in Rome, owning buildings and property to the extent of being accused of owning the city, also heavily involved with the politics) build the basilica of St Peter with his own money rather than with the money of poor believers?"

The pope wrote a letter of condemnation and declared Luther to be in conflict with the teachings of the church. Luther would not change his position, and in 1520 Pope Leo X issued a papal bull giving Luther 120 days to recant in Rome. He did not recant, and there were further papacy issuances against him including those from

91

various church authorities. Luther remained steadfast and firm to his convictions and he gained many adherents.

Martin Luther, although his reputation excels, was not the only voice to sound. There were a number who preceded him with proclamations of disagreements. John Wycliffe (1330–1384) had already launched an attack on the veneration of saints, pilgrimages, the selling of indulgences, the doctrine of transubstantiation, and even the low standards of the priests, both moral and intellectual. He disputed the supreme and ultimate authority of the popes and declared the people obliged to interpret scripture for themselves.

John Huss, a Bohemian priest, was in 1410 excommunicated as a heretic and burned at the stake in 1415 for his adherence to the Wycliffe doctrines and translating some of his declarations into Czechoslovakian. He also believed Christ to be the true head of the church.

In 1523 and during the Lutheranism advancement in Europe, Pope Clement VII became the second pope from Florence's powerful and wealthy Medici family. He kept his loyalty to the papacy and the Medici and aligned himself with Charles V, king of Spain and also the Holy Roman Emperor. This presented a problem, as France and Spain were at war, and the confrontations and warring in Italy between France and Charles V caused Clement to break his alliance with Charles V. His alliance went to France and Venice as they were all Roman Catholic and he felt Clement V had gained too much power in Italy. The result was devastating.

On May 6, 1527, a large army broke through the walls of Rome and into the city. Charles V had sent them but they were no longer controlled by him. They reached Rome in a ragged, hungry, barefoot, and financially broke condition. The Roman and Swiss guards defending the city were exterminated and the raucous army pillaged and burned with ferocity all around them. Orphanages and hospitals were invaded and those occupying within were slaughtered. The savagery targeted women including nuns who were taken to the brothels.

Priests were also included in the molestation. Looting took place in financial institutions and the wealthy were beaten until they relented to turn over every cent they had. Tortures were inflicted such as ripping out of fingernails, and children being thrown from upstairs windows.

Churches were invaded and divested of contents. There were valuable manuscripts used for the horses bedding while libraries and archives burned. Parading in papal garments were inebriated soldiers strutting as exemplars of holy rites. Even tombs were plundered. There were vast multiples murdered, two thousand bodies floating in the Tiber and another ten thousand yet to receive interment. The corpses that were piled in the city became an organ buffet for rats and stray dogs, which relieved the bloating but didn't relieve the putrid emitting odor.

The French force was driven back and Pope Clement, with his flight to safety nearly failing, managed to find refuge at the Castle of Saint Angelo in Rome, but as prisoner. There he could only view from the towers the wretchedness and desolation enacting below him accompanied with the screams of his people being ruthlessly butchered in the city. Daunting and remorseful he is reported to have asserted, "Why did you take me from the womb? Would that I had been consumed."

He remained a prisoner at the Castle of Saint Angelo until after six months' residency he purchased his freedom from some imperial officers and managed an escape disguised as a peddler. Upon his return the next year, October 1528, he found the city ravaged and devoid of people.

When the news of the barbarous invasion was dispersed throughout Europe, the Protestants, characteristically, interpreted it to be divine retribution and even had agreement from some of the Catholics. Cardinal Cajetan, who opposed Luther at Augsburg, wrote, "We who should have been the salt of the earth decayed until we were good for nothing. Everyone is convinced that all this has happened as a judgment of God on the great tyranny and disorders of the papal court."

John Calvin, a French theologian, had to flee persecution and in 1536 settled in Geneva where he instituted the Presbyterian-style government which birthed the Presbyterian Church. Calvin also held concern about the contacts France was having with Islam, which he believed only brought "filthiness and defilement." He opposed those who wanted separation of church and state, describing them as "libertines" and considered them questioning the authority of God.

John Knox embraced the Calvinistic views of the Presbyter acting government and imposed it upon Scotland to be the national religion of Scotland as a Calvinistic Protestant religion called Presbyterianism.

Civil war hit France by 1562. A group called Huguenots (French Protestants) were targeted when an aristocratic, Francois de Guise observed them having a religious ceremony in the town of Vassy. He was so intensely angered he directed men to set fire to their church and more than eighty Huguenots were killed, with many others wounded.

England, in the interim of these events, had its tumults. Henry VIII became king at age eighteen in the year 1509. He was a loyal adherent to Catholicism and commonly practiced brutal suppression of the Protestant section. He'd married Catherine of Aragon, aunt of King Charles V of Spain, who had not borne him a surviving son. He was now forty-two years of age and had been married to Catherine for twenty-four years. Catherine bore six children, but only one little girl, Mary, survived and she was now too old to bare more children. Because he was desperate to have the Tudor name continued he needed a son to succeed his throne. He had become infatuated with Anne Boleyn, one of Catherine's ladies-in-waiting. Henry was determined to have his marriage to Catherine annulled and marry Anne, who was only twenty years old and could therefore, he presumed, give him his heir. He only needed to be granted permission from the pope, Clement VII, who refused his permission.

Henry sent a message to the pope contending his marriage to Catherine was not authoritative since she had prior been married to his brother Arthur. Arthur had died and left Catherine a widow when she married Henry. In the interim, Catherine had learned of her husband's intentions and made appeal to her nephew Charles who, not wanting his aunt to lose position as queen, warned the pope that he would be extremely angry should he grant permission for a divorce.

Pope Clement was in a vice, because whichever decision he made one of these two powerful men would be displeased and so he procrastinated on his decision until in January 1533 when Henry discovered Anne Boleyn was pregnant.

Henry made arrangements to marry Anne immediately so the child would not be born illegitimate. King Charles V of Spain made threat then to invade England should marriage to Anne occur, but Henry ignored the threat. Anne gave birth to a daughter, Elizabeth, and the advocates of Catherine proclaimed it to be an act of God to punish Henry for illegally marrying Anne.

In March of 1534, the pope declared Henry's marriage to Anne invalid and Henry responded that the pope's authority in England ceased and by November an act was passed by Parliament declaring Henry VIII was head of the Church of England. However, the pope excommunicated Henry from the Catholic Church.

Church income transferred from the pope to Henry, and payment from landowners to the pope were made illegal. England broke from the Catholic Church and became independent from the pope in 1534 when Parliament passed the "Act of Supremacy". Henry became the supreme head on earth of the church of England.

William Tyndale translated the Bible into English, which the Roman Church considered heresy. Out of fear for his life he fled but was arrested in the Netherlands, he agreed with the doctrine of Luther's justification by faith and he'd also taken a stance on Henry's marriages and was tied to a stake, but because of his popularity, he was strangled to death before being burned so not to suffer too much. Witnesses reported that he had regained conscience before he died and said, "Oh Lord, open the King of England's eyes."

Pope Paul III succeeded Clement VII in 1534 and rescinded Henry's title as "Defender of the Faith" but England declared the title remained valid. Pope Paul had no power in England and was helpless while the Roman Catholic property in England transferred ownership and were sold. The Roman priests had to swear an oath to convert to Henry's church or terminate their position. Those who refused had their sustenance confiscated and were removed of their status. If they objected and caused political upheaval they were executed.

Pope Paul III put forth an "inquisition" created to bring resistance to the advancement of Protestantism. In France the Protestant movement was quickly spreading within community of lawyers and some nobility. The Catholic inquisition stepped in to defend the predominance of the church and the clergymen. Protestant churches experienced onslaught and in Meaux, France fourteen Protestant members were burned to death.

Massacres increased with Pope Paul and his inquisition, which included not only Protestants but Catholics whom he decided to be erroneous in their convictions. A group of Roman Catholics who were referred to as Spiritualists fell into this category and came under attack. They included in their group some elderly members and Michelangelo with Vittoria Colonna (the famous woman of letters), a close friend to Michelangelo.

In 1535, Thomas More, an old friend of Henry's was beheaded by him because he refused to sign the document making Henry head of the church. Henry had Catholics and Protestants executed for their opposition on his marriage or head of the church.

Pope Paul IV passed a law which kept Jews in secluded areas and were made to remain indoors at night. The men were forced to wear a yellow hat and the women a yellow veil or shawl to mark them as Jews. They remained in ghettoes for 315 years.

There were uprisings and condemnations involving punishments of persecution taking place throughout various areas of Europe. More broke away from the Catholic Church, primarily because of enlightenment with the education they were now receiving from reading the scriptures.

Johannes Gutenberg had invented the press and introduced it to Europe in 1439. This brought literacy to the common people however, translating the bible into colloquial languages or even helping with the printing was heresy to the Roman Church. In Europe, women were buried alive and men burned alive for committing this offense. A Paris printer was actually burned on a heap of his own books.

Other persecutions took place by not only the Catholics but the Lutherans and Calvinists alike. The precursors to the Baptist called Anabaptists believed in adult baptism rather than infant baptism or christening; they wanted social reform and were against killing, including capital punishment, and would not serve in the army. Their leaders were targeted for punishment to stamp out the movement.

Burned at the stake was Thomas Munzer, and Feliz Manz was drowned because he was an Anabaptist. Drowning was a way of mocking their belief in baptism and became a popular method of execution. One of the more severe recorded was Michael Sattler who had his tongue cut out, and then tortured with burning hot pincers before being burned alive.

At one point in the 1530s an entire town became Anabaptist, which brought the Protestants and Catholics together to take down the town. The leaders were tortured in like manner as Michael Sattler but their bodies were hung in cages outside of a church where they remained for a number of years.

Queen Mary of England and Ireland (1553–1558) known as "Bloody Mary" for slaying as many as 280 individuals whom she considered heretics, had persecuted John Rogers, a Catholic priest, when he converted to Protestantism and assisted in the translations of William Tyndale's English Bible. He was burned at the stake in 1555 and was the first in a series of executions carried out by the hand of the Queen.

In 1562, after thirty years of conflict French Protestants called Huguenots were slaughtered by Catholics at Sens, Burgundy. The Saint Bartholomew's Day Massacre, one of the worst atrocities of history took place ten years later in Paris on August 24, 1572 and literally thousands of Huguenots were inhumanly slaughtered by Catholic mobs. In turn, reports of slaughtering attacks were inflicted upon some Catholic priests and even Catholic children cut to pieces by the Huguenots. The disgraces that ran rampant throughout this so-called "reformation" were, to say the least, born of hell.

Alleged reports of priests being dismembered and dissected alive were not uncommon, though its believed they are exaggerated. Either way, the atrocity existed, and although such atrocities committed by the Protestants were uncommon, they display the fact that the lowest depravities exist, are evident, and manifest themselves without regard or prejudice in any one person or group so that none are exempt from the corruption of evil.

The Saint Bartholomew Massacre was designed to rid France of its Protestant movement with one catastrophic attack. The king plotted a marriage between his sister and the head of the Protestant army, Henry of Navarre. The scheme was that in honor of their marriage a magnificent festivity lasting four days would be celebrated. At the end of the four days, just prior to dawn when all were recouping at home asleep, the soldiers would be signaled to advance on all Protestant homes forcing entry. The chief Protestant Leader Admiral Coligny was seized and killed, his body thrown out of a window to the street where he was then beheaded and his head sent to the pope. His arms and genitals were cut off and his body then dragged three days through the streets to then be hung by the heels outside the city for viewing. Within those three days over ten thousand Protestants were slaughtered making a literal streaming of blood through the streets running into the river where they threw the bodies.

The frenzy spread and another eight thousand slaughtered were added to the number throughout the country. Few Protestants escaped, and even their own, if they were not in total submission to the pope, were added to the slain. Persons residing outside of France were favorable to these slaughters and King Phillip II of Spain and Pope Gregory XIII were pleased by this attack. The hatred for Protestants intensified, slaughtering was incited and a reported total of 30,000 Protestants were annihilated.

Ireland was reeling with treachery emulating Saint Bartholomew. October 23, 1641 (the day of the feast of Ignatius Loyola, founder of Jesuit Order), a planned revolt of the country was initiated to kill all Protestants at one time. The Protestants would be unsuspecting through acts of kindness rendering them completely off guard. Like Saint Bartholomew, the attack took place in the dawn hours and every Protestant located was murdered. Age, gender, lack of mobility nor illness were considered for mercy. They were taken by surprise after living in a safe, peaceful manner for years and were totally unprepared for their defense. Family, friends and neighbors contributed to their slaughters.

Vile behavior, such as women being stripped to the waist and tied to posts who would then have their breasts sheared off, leaving them to hang and bleed to death. Pregnant women were bound to tree branches and the unborn child cut out to be fed to the dogs and husbands forced to watch. All of Europe had the hell of religion unleashed upon it. "I saw the woman drunk with the blood of the saints and with the blood of the martyrs of Jesus" (Rev. 17:6). Unfortunately, it didn't end here with history, but hell masquerading as faith marches on.

European settlers were finally driven to escape the plagues of the religious wars into British North America; however, the idea of uniformity of religion within a society traveled with them and both Protestants and Catholics, believing to exercise the one true religion, held the belief that civil authorities were obliged to force conformity upon citizens for the sake of salvation. Those that refused to conform were considered heretics and could be executed. The determining factor of which faith the conformity was directed was dependent on the majority in the political arena. Thus there were times that Catholics persecuted Protestants and other times the Protestants persecuted the Catholics and still at other times both Catholics and Protestants would persecute a contrary religion.

In 1689, England renounced religious persecution, yet it continued with vehemence throughout the European continent, leaving behind a bloody trail of disgrace.

An edict was issued on October 31, 1731 by Archbishop Leopold von Firmian of Salzburg, Austria, to expel some 20,000 Lutherans and many, who were given only eight days to leave, froze to death while seeking safety from the blistering winter elements. Those who had wealth were granted a full three months to dispose of their property before leaving. They migrated into London, then over to Georgia and some to the Netherlands and East Prussia.

Ireland played out its part in Christian religious wars in 1641 when approximately 100,000 Protestants were murdered by the Catholics at the bridge over the River Bann. They were held as prisoners and endured torture until finally being taken to the bridge where they were stripped and forced into the water. Any that survived the plunge were shot.

Many Protestants fled the hot beds of persecution during the seventeenth century, establishing themselves in colonial settlements such as Virginia. The *Mayflower* left England on September 16, 1620 with more than one hundred men, women, and children aboard to settle in the Virginia Colony. These groups, known as Pilgrims, wanted to separate themselves from the Church of England so they could practice their faith by the dictates of conscience. Others, like the Puritans, had wanted to purify or reform the Anglican Church, but instead they met persecution and left England to practice religious freedom without threat of persecution.

Religious warfare had become a bloody, violent gore. Numerous killings were being enacted on the premise that God was on their side. The idea of a new world free of political and religious conflict became extremely attractive.

The purpose of eradicating the control of the pope, or an authoritative dictating church over the individual soul in order to achieve a personal relationship with the Lord was commendable of the Protestants. However, they, being accustomed to organization embodied the structure of clergy and laity and aspired to have acknowledgment, approval and license from the state. This was attainable in some sovereign territories however; it was irremediable in others.

The sixteenth through nineteenth centuries would, through the pains of endurance and persistence, establish the recognizance and legalization of Protestantism throughout Europe and the Americas. Springing up would be a variety of denominations, beginning with the Lutherans, Calvinists, Anbaptists, Methodists, Presbyterians, and so on, all lawfully able to practice their faith.

Contrary to the teachings of Christ and his apostles, there would be denominations or divisions resulting that would forever hinder the growth of the Body of Christ. Today there are over six hundred different denominations. They are by definition of denomination, fractions or divisions. The apostle Paul wrote, "Now I plead with you, brethren, by the name of our Lord Jesus Christ, that you all speak the same thing, and that there be no divisions among you, but that you be perfectly joined together in the same mind and in the same judgment" (1 Cor. 1:10).

The Roman Catholic Church was experiencing anxiety and insecurity of power with the loss of devotees. The spirit of supreme authority and desire to subdue the world was unconscionable and the pope being apprehensive of losing control, loyalty and power as well as monetary support determined to combat the situation. Reconciliation between Protestants and Catholics grew more and more hopeless. The Roman Catholic Church wanted to regain its universal power and adherence to its supremacy in the world. Measures to bring the "lost flocks" back to the church, gain their loyalty to the church and the ultimate authority of the pope became a fervor of priority.

CHAPTER 11

Jesuits - "The Society of Jesus" - A Strong Delusion

The Roman Catholic Church was an extension of the Roman Empire and its politics. It became an army dressed up in religious armor with the purpose and intent of ruling the world. It was the Roman Empire hidden behind new attire. As a government maintains various branches to it's military, so the church needed its military branches. The initiation of the Jesuit order would fill a great portion of the political-military operations needed. They would become the CIA of the Roman Church. They would involve themselves in the politics, banking, commerce, education, health, and every facet of a nation while cloaking a solemn religious order. The Vatican would prosper in power and wealth and expand in the world because of this order, or then again it would be consumed by this order.

Ignatius of Loyola, founder of the "Society of Jesus" was a Spanish Basque born Don Inigo Lopez de Recalde at the Castle of Loyola in 1491. He later changed his name to Ignatius in order to make it "Roman." He was transformed by Catholicism into a monk-soldier and his youth was spotted with criminal activities and the police reported him as being "treacherous, brutal, vindictive." His secretary, Polanco, whom he took into his confidence, referred to him as "An unruly and conceited soldier. He led a disorderly life as far as women, gambling and duels were concerned."

He engaged himself as a combatant defending Pampeluna against the French, commanded by Count de Foix. During the siege he was struck by a bullet which broke his leg. He was taken to the castle of Loyola and underwent surgery with no anesthesia which had to be endured a second time. In order to right the errors of the first surgery his leg was re-broken and re-set, again with no anesthesia and this left him with a limp.

While recovering, he read the books available at Loyola which were *The Life of Christ* and *The Life of the Saints.* His suffering ordeal caused him to be overly empathetic to the martyrdoms he read about and he spent hours dreaming and entrancing himself into a mystical imaginary life. This all led to his teachings on the practice of mysticism which later would be required study for all the aspiring Jesuits.

The "Society of Jesus" was actually formed in 1534. The construct was drawn up in the chapel of Notre Dame de Montmartre when Ignatius was forty-four years old. Their first mission vowed by Ignatius and his companions was to go to the Holy Land. There they would engage in converting those he referred to as infidels. Not being yet accepted by the pope, they involved themselves in missionary works. This Jesuit society would become the embodiment of a "wolf in sheep's clothing."

In 1540, a draft of the society's constitution was presented and approved by Paul III of Rome. The Jesuits made themselves troops at the pope's disposal and gave him their unquestioned obedience. As his new order they began in teaching, preaching confessionals and other ecclesiastical functions. They broke into political actions in 1546 when the pope for representation as "pontifical theologians at the Council of Trent, selected Laynez and Salmeron for the purpose.

The Jesuits continued with employment to the council and proved themselves as valuable personates to the pope by defeating their opponents. Laynez in his deliverance to thwart the opposition declared the infallibility of the pope with such impressive vigor it remained to be considered a tangible proclamation and three centuries later it was announced official by the Vatican Council. Paul III gave recognition to this "new order" in a Bull of Authorization as "Regimen Ecclesiae Militantis."

By the time Ignatius had died in 1556, his "sons of Loyola" had spread into India, China, Japan, throughout Germany, Portugal, Spain, France, Italy. Ireland and even into England. About two years after Laynez became general of the "Congregation." He was given the power to impose his views and declarations to the "Order" as he so determined.

Francesco Borja, great grandson of Pope Alexander VI and Duke of Gandia, became acquainted with Loyola in 1546. He involved himself with the operations of the order with Ignatius and assisted in the Jesuits missions to the East. He later assisted in the slave port and plantation of Rio de Janeiro by Emanuel Nobrega. and Joseph Anchieta, both senior Jesuits with Jesuit militia. In his announcement to join the Jesuits in 1554, he was made Cardinal Francis Borja.

Pope Paul IV was reigning during the time of Ignatius' death and was one of the greatest enemies of Pope Alexander VI and thus nominated Diego Laynez as Superior General. Pope Paul IV died in 1559 and was succeeded by Pope Pius IV. Laynez made himself securely from reach by aligning himself close to both.

A failed conspiracy to murder Pius IV caused Benedetto Accolti and other papal family members to be sought out and Benedetto was tortured and murdered for the alleged scheme. Borja responded and killed Pius IV, and within a few days Superior General Laynez received the same and died. Borja then was soon elected unanimously as the Superior General.

Borja, with great enthusiasm, strengthened even further the power of the Jesuit Order, it becoming the greater of any other in the Catholic Church. The "Congregation" was divided to Italy. Germany, France, Spain, England, and America then was divided again into provinces, gaining power and recognition. They were not subject to the authority of the bishops and were given rights to preach, say mass, distribute the sacrament, all without consult. Marriages were withheld; however, they could give absolution, change, or cancel vows.

Internally they could absolve punishment on other members and absolve their sins including heresy or fraudulent apostolic writings. To the extreme they were able to absolve injury to others, bigamy, murders and assassinations if they were not publicly known. Expanding their influence and power even further, Gregory XIII gave them permit to banking and commerce.

In 1562, the Council of Trent ended with the Holy See enjoying more power as a result of the Jesuit's crafty abilities. With this the playing field went from the church to politics and war. However, they remained masked as the missionary teachers, charity workers, preachers, et cetera, they were first viewed to be. Their efforts to transform souls to Christ became in fact, efforts to bring the world under control of the papacy. One very effective way to conquer the world leaders was to be directors and educators of the children in order to seize the future.

Well masked with the face of missionary teachers, colleges and schools were constructed within nations around the globe where Jesuit teachers were assigned the task of supplying a secular education compounded with instruction to cultivate loyal adherents and supporters of the church which in turn would secure their future dominance.

They needed to counter the educational movement of the Protestants, and tapping their power they accessed the Vatican archives and devoted themselves to a stratagem to the Protestant intellectuals. The order engaged in promoting their education and recruited many. With it came an assurance of higher education and a higher status of recruits making it a desirable education throughout the Catholic realm. They were fast known as an order dedicated to the excellence in education in the Catholic countries. However, in truth the original intent was a military structure.

To further counter the Protestants' advancement required involving security of trade routes. With the already obtained power to conduct commerce and banking, by Gregory XIII the Jesuits moved to purchase the port of Nagasaki from General Acquaviva, a Japanese warlord. They made it one of the most profitable trading ports of the world and gave them control in the taxing of imports.

They engaged in developing slave trade from Africa to South America for the gold mines by the initiation of Peter Claver S. J., who became known as one of the worst slave masters in history and the patron saint of slaves.

Countries such as Spain and Portugal were infuriated with the encroachment the Jesuits made on trade control and profits from slavery and began armament of the Jesuit enemies. And although the initial intent of the Jesuits' engaging in trade was to hinder the Protestant trade, the Catholic nations grew even more angry from losses. Even so, it became the issue of educational control that would lead them to disband.

The Protestant nations took the lead in commerce and industry as well as education, and the Catholic nations slipped behind in wealth and prosperity. By 1758, the Jesuits were expelled from Portugal by the Marquis of Pombal, and following suit was King Louis XV of France in 1764.

By 1769, the Jesuits had grown to such a magnitude of unpopularity and because various nations wanted them expelled a Papal Bull to disband them by Clement XIII was prepared as he feared the church itself might be expelled. But the night before it was to be delivered, General Lorenzo Ricci had the Pope murdered.

Clement XIV succeeded as pope and was effective in the disbandment of the Jesuits with a Papal Bull in July of 1773 and their churches were seized and assets confiscated through a series of raids. General Ricci was arrested and taken prisoner to Castel Sant'Angelo in Rome but his long arm had Pope Clement XIV assassinated on September 22, 1774 while still in prison where he spent the remainder of his years.

But because a Papal Bull cannot override a former one unless it was defective, the Papal Bull of Clement XIV was of no legal effect and the Jesuits could not actually be disbanded, not legally, not ever! They and their granted power were to remain untouchable. Clement XIV had shaken the order, even setting it back, but his suppression had no legal standing and even the imprisonment of General Ricci had no effect to the abolishment of the Jesuit Order except in those countries where the Papal Bull had been publicized and acted upon.

Fortunately for the Jesuits, they remained a legal acknowledged order in Prussia under Frederick of Prussia and in Russia under Catherine II because of their value to education and therefore some of the priests continued teaching in the Jesuit Colleges.

Because of their legal acceptance in these two countries the Jesuit Fathers decided to call for a "General Congregation" in White Russia where they would elect a Vicar to replace Ricci. Stanislaus Czerniewicz was elected as he was in that province, a leading Jesuit and Rector at the Polostsk College. He died in 1785 and another "Congregation of

White Russia" was called and they elected Gabriel Lenkiewicz as Vicar General who had been to Czerniewicz a close confidant and worked with him on matters concerning the continuing survival of the Jesuits.

Lenkiewicz would use his position to bring vengeance to the imperialist of Europe who assisted in weakening of the Jesuit influence and power. King Louis XVI of France wanted a change to improve living conditions and decided to raise the living standard of France and diminish the hunger plaguing the poor. He thought to do this would be through taxation of Noble families and the Catholic Church as well. To accomplish this, he summoned an Assembly of Notables who were dominate in Parliament and thus avoid the Parliament and receive approval from the assembly itself.

This, of course, infuriated the bishops of the Catholic Church who before had never been taxed, and they countered by calling in the Jesuits from Russia to undermine the King and his plans.

The Jesuits moved in with propaganda exploiting the king's intentions of avoiding Parliament and printed material which were anti-monarch and declared the king was working against the common people as the Parliament was elected by a third of the common people. They instigated disorder and created brawls. Claiming it was the people who wanted to see change, not the king and the tumultuous end was a new Constitution to the which France would act as constitutional monarch to provide democracy and political freedom for the first time in mainland Europe.

Pope Pius VI responded by ordering Leopold II, Holy Roman Emperor of Austria to ambush his brother-in-law. The Jacobite's who were controlled by the Jesuits, apprehended the king and the next two years was experienced by the "reign of terror" and over forty thousand people were executed, the majority of those without trial.

The consequence of this revolt was more than re-establishing the Jesuit Order it created a monstrosity of conceited self confidence in the Jesuit power and it instigated the audacity to apprehend the Pope and the vast wealth of the Catholic Church.

La Fayette was coerced and taken by the Jesuits to America with his large gold reserves while he was presumed to be imprisoned in Belgium for five years. The stolen gold was then placed in the then

Bank of New York, founded 1784, and now Bank of the Manhattan Co. (JP Morgan Chase Bank).

The Jesuits invested their time in re-capturing their status with carefully thought out plans. Antoine Christophe Saliceti, a Jesuit agent, directed a number of his years to developing Napoleon Bonaparte and in Paris of 1795 Napoleon defeated counter-revolutionary royalties and the regime leader, Paul Barras promoted him for his accomplishments.

Napoleon later married Josephine de Beauharnais, and was given by assurance of agent Saliceti the command of the French Army of Italy in March of 1796 where he was then ordered to invade Italy for the purpose of capturing the Pope of Rome.

Pope Pius VI signed with Napoleon the Treaty of Tolentino, his own peace treaty, which imposed surrender on the Papal side. Therefore, Napoleon could not arrest the pope and so the murder of French brigadier-general Mathurin-Leonard Duphot in Rome was planned and implemented through means of a riot. Blame fell to the papal forces and French General Berthier marched into Rome proclaiming a Roman Republic and demanded of the pope the renunciation of his temporal authority which he refused and so the arrest of Pope Pius VI was executed.

Prior to the pope's arrest the Jesuits via Switzerland formed the private banks "Darier Hentsch & Cie and Lombard Odier Darier Hentsch to maintain all of the gold, treasure and contracts confiscated during the escapade. After the arrest the agents of General Lenkiewicz S. J. reviewed all treasury notes, and the location of gold and treasure the Vatican held and sent it to the private banks in Switzerland. For recompense the bank funded Napoleon through his conquests. General Gabriel Lenkiewicz S. J. died in November 1798, and Father Franz Xavier Kareu was chosen to be Vicar General.

Pope Pius VI died in prison in August of 1799 and Cardinal Count Barnaba Chiaramonti succeeded him, but not until March 14, 1800. He began with a good report between himself and Napoleon but by 1808 he too was taken prisoner only this time the Jesuits were not responsible but Napoleon himself took the pope captive.

Napoleon suffered a tremendous blow when he attempted to rise up against Russia's refusal to blockade trade with Great Britain because it was hurting Russia's economy. Napoleon's failed invasion weakened his power and Tadeusz Brzozowski, a Jesuit leader, drew up an agreement with Pope Pius VII where he met him in prison, to completely restore the Jesuit Order and granting lands and rights in Asia. In return the popes safe release would be arranged and Napoleon would be taken prisoner. The Jesuits also would re-instate their loyalty to the pope and the pope would regain control of the Papal territories and some funds of the church would be returned to the Vatican. Napoleon was taken prisoner in April of 1814 and the Society of Jesus was restored on August 14, 1814 with a Papal letter, "Solicit Udine Omnium Ecclesiarum".

This restoring of the Jesuit Order would bring to them acceptance throughout the world. They would have liberty to move freely amongst the nations involving themselves in the politics, banking, commerce, education, food and drug, medical industry and every fabric of a nation's economy and development. Every nation determined advantageous to reach the goal of a one world order would be infiltrated and controlled at the highest level. They would instigate conditions, perceptions and attitudes to the end of creating wars between nations in order to manipulate the end result in their favor. Should they fail in their objective they simply would create a new avenue of operation but they would never cease in their mission to reel in the world under the control of a one-world government.

Put into practice by the Jesuit Order is the demonstrable fact that if you can control the economy, you can control the world. The Federal Reserve of the Rothschild's out of England would become the most powerful banking system developed with the purpose of manipulating and controlling the world economy of which the vast majority are ignorant too this reality.

One important target would be the United States of America. The Federal Reserve would accommodate their resources and give them the monetary control needed for supplying the power of subduing the country while veiled in good works for the eye of the public. This camouflage exceeds the discernment of the vast majority to the extent that most unwittingly, would raise up a defense to their cause to remain existent within the nation for the many good deeds rendered by the Jesuit Order.

CONSTANTINE THE GRREAT-DECLARED THE FIRST CHRISTIAN EMPEROR

TORMENT(

(*) VISION OF TORMEI

When the evidence did not allow a definitive
conclusion to be reached, but there were indications of
heresy and the accused refused to confess, then the
sentence of torment was pronounced.

This sentence was in no way the punishment that the
Court pronounced against the defendant but rather
the way to obtain the truth about the accusation.
While torture had often been used to mend the ways
of the heretic, it is true that it was only used as a last
resort before the obstinacy of the accused. As such
the inquisitions were neither particularly imaginative
nor especially cruel, but were limited in general to
adopting the kinds of torture used more commonly in
civil courts. The civil courts, however, used extremely
cruel forms of torture at times.

The sentence of torment was always delivered "in
compliance with the law, a clear conscience and careful
judgement by the judges". As the regulations in Spain

prevente
once, th
only to l
the torn
were ne
forced o
to ratify
ending t

Often th
torment
observir
obtain a
obtain a
Howeve
whateve
knew ab

MODEL TORMENT SEN

"Christi nomine invocato.

*With reference to the documents and merits of the process, indications and suspicions
that result thereof, we should condemn the defendant and sentence the accused to be
subject to torment, in which we order that he be held incarcerated for as long as
deemed righteous to that during this period he state the truth for which others have
borne witness and of which he is accused. If during the aforementioned torment he
deceases or is injured, bleeds, a limb is mutilated, it will be his own fault and
responsibility, and not ours, due to his reticence in uttering the truth. We hereby
pronounce and order the undertaking of this sentence, in writing."*

Order that w
declares that
institutions.

Torture Chamber. Public Domain

Pope Francis: World Government Must Rule U.S. 'For Their Own Good'

0 900

Share

∶

Pope Francis told the Italian newspaper La Repubblica that the United States of America has *"a distorted vision of the world"* and Americans must be ruled by a world government, as soon as possible, *"for their own good."*

The Pope made the observation in an interview with La Repubblica reporter Eugenio Scalfari.

"Last Thursday, I got a call from Pope Francis," Scalfari reported. *"It was about noon, and I was at the newspaper when my phone rang."*

He said Pope Francis had been watching Putin and Trump at the G20 and had become agitated. The Pope demanded to see him at four that afternoon, according to a Google translation of the Italian report.

"Pope Francis told me to be very concerned about the meeting of the G20," Scalfari wrote.

As translated into English by Agence France Presse, which picked up the story, the Pope said *"I am afraid there are very dangerous alliances between powers who have a distorted view of the world: America and Russia, China and North Korea, Russia and Assad in the war in Syria."*

Protestants] deem it their duty to keep the Sunday holy. Why? Because the Catholic Church tells them to do so. They have no other reason...

1 58,437

Share

.
.

"Most Christians assume that Sunday is the biblically approved day of worship. The Catholic Church protests that it transferred Christian worship from the biblical Sabbath (Saturday) to Sunday, and that to try to argue that the change was made in the Bible is both dishonest and a denial of Catholic authority. If Protestantism wants to base its teachings only on the Bible, it should worship on Saturday." — Rome's Challenge immaculateheart.com/maryonline Dec 2003.

"Is not every Christian obliged to sanctify Sunday and to abstain on that day from unnecessary servile work? Is not the observance of this law among the most prominent of our sacred duties? But you may read the Bible from Genesis to Revelation, and you will not find a single line authorizing the sanctification of Sunday. The Scriptures enforce the religious observance of Saturday, a day which we never sanctify." — James Cardinal Gibbons, The Faith of Our Fathers (1917 edition), p. 72-73 (16th Edition, p 111; 88th Edition, p. 89).

"For example, nowhere in the Bible do we find that Christ or the Apostles ordered that the Sabbath be changed from Saturday to Sunday. We have the commandment of God given to Moses to keep holy the Sabbath day, that is the 7th day of the week, Saturday. Today most Christians keep Sunday because it has been revealed to us by the [Roman Catholic] church outside the Bible." — Catholic Virginian, October 3, 1947, p. 9, article "To Tell You the Truth."

Who Made Sunday Holy?

"Written by the finger of God on two tables of stone, this Divine code (ten commandments) was received from the Almighty by Moses amid the thunders of Mount Sinai…Christ resumed these Commandments in the double precept of charity–love of God and of the neighbour; He proclaimed them as binding under the New Law in Matthew 19 and in the Sermon on the Mount (Matthew 5)…The (Catholic) Church, on the other hand, after changing the day of rest from the Jewish Sabbath, or seventh day of the week, to the first, made the Third Commandment refer to Sunday as the day to be kept holy as the Lord's Day…He (God) claims one day out of the seven as a memorial to Himself, and this must be kept holy…" — The Catholic Encyclopaedia, vol. 4, "The Ten Commandments", 1908 edition by Robert Appleton Company; and 1999 Online edition by Kevin Knight, Imprimatur, John M. Farley, Archbishop of New York.

During the reign of the Papal Church of Rome, tens of millions of Christians were persecuted and killed because they refused to bow to the "authority" of the Papal Church. This reign of terror lasted 1260 years and was prophesied in Daniel 7 and Revelation 13. This will happen again when the mark of the Beast (Roman Catholic Church) is enforced. Below are quotes from history describing the most awful persecution at the hands of the Roman Catholic Church. These quotes are not to cause upset, but to EXPOSE the Papal Church for what it really is.

The above image is of a statue of Ignatius Loyola, the founder of the Jesuit order. In it you can see Loyola holding the Jesuit Constitution while trampling underfoot a Christian holding a Bible. And this statue resides at the Vatican TODAY! This isn't just a statue that tells us about history. It is a statue in HONOR of what the Roman Catholic Church did to all those faithful Bible believing Christians. And that evil spirit still resides in the Catholic Church.

"On August 24, 1527, Roman Catholics in France, by prearranged plan, under Jesuit influence, murdered 70,000 Protestants within the space of two months. The Pope rejoiced when he heard the news of the successful outcome." (Western Watchman, Nov.21, 1912 (Catholic)

"There was no village of the Vaudois valleys but had its martyrs. The Waldenses were burned; they were cast into damp and horrid dungeons; they were smothered in crowds in mountain caverns, mothers and babes, and old men and women together; they were sent out into exile in the winter night, unclothed and unfed, to climb the snowy mountains; they were hurled over the rocks; their houses and lands were taken from them; their children were stolen to be indoctrinated with the religion which they

abhorred. Rapacious individuals were sent among them to strip them of their property, to persecute and exterminate them. Thousands of heretics or Waldenses, old men, women and children, were hung, quartered, broken upon the wheel, or burned alive and their property confiscated for the benefit of the king, and Holy See." (Thompson – The Papacy and the Civil Power)

"That the Church of Rome has shed <u>more innocent blood than any other institution that has ever existed among mankind,</u> will be questioned by no Protestant who has a competent knowledge of history . . . It is impossible to form a complete conception of the multitude of her victims, and it is quite certain that no powers of imagination can adequately realize their sufferings." (W. E. H. Lecky, History of the Rise and Influence of the Spirit of Rationalism in Europe, vol. 2, p. 32, 1910 edition)

TEMPLE MOUNT MASS HELD IN UPPER ROOM

CHAPTER 12

The United States Falls Into The Hands Of The Jesuit Institute, Its Controlled "Federal Reserve" And "IRS" System

Our first president, whom we call "The Father of our Country," George Washington, wrote to the Rev. G. W. Snyder on October 24, 1798: "It was not my intention to doubt that, the Doctrines of the Illuminati, and principles of Jacobinism had not spread in the United States. On the contrary, no one is more truly satisfied of this fact than I am."[12]

When Napoleon was taken prisoner on April 6, 1814, he was exiled to Elba (a Mediterranean island off the coast of Italy). He escaped and sailed to the French mainland where upon his return Austrian, British, Prussian and Russian allies formed a coalition preparing for war. Napoleon defeated the allies before they could engage their attack.

In June of 1815 Napoleon marched his forces into Belgium. Encamped there, were British and Prussian troops. The "Battle of Ligny" was fought on June 16, where the Prussians were defeated, but the entire Prussian army wasn't destroyed.

On June 18, 1815 Napoleon led his army of 72,000 troops against the British 68,000 troops who were positioned near the village of Waterloo. Napoleon waited until midday to command his attack because it had rained heavily the night prior and he wanted to allow the saturated soggy ground time to dry out. This became his error in judgement as it gave time for Blucher's (Prussian commander) remaining 30,000 troops to march in and join the battle.

---

12   George Washington, *Writings of Washington*, pp. 452–453.

The phrase "met his Waterloo" is derived from Napoleons defeat at Waterloo. This defeat now ended France's domination in Europe and the British now had expanded its gain of world control.

In the sixteenth century, England had established the world's first central banking system, and developed a monopoly controlling every segment of men's functions in the world. They were unsurpassed in commerce and trade and had control over every aspect of merchandising throughout the globe and every aspect of how the world functioned.

As previously mentioned Rome, before King Henry VIII applied for a divorce from Catherine of Aragon, had been captured by the Imperialists under Emperor Charles V and the pope taken prisoner from there on. Most of the gold and silver was taken to Switzerland and put in a private bank. Afterwards there was a strengthening in the Roman Catholic universities throughout Europe and the Jesuits were heavily involved in education.

The bank of Rome reorganized and began to open branches throughout European cities. Venice in 1587, Wisselbank in Amsterdam, 1609, Hamburg in 1619, Nuremberg in 1621, Rotterdam in 1635, and finally in 1694 the Bank of England which became the first "World Central Bank".

Previously England had outlawed usury and had no dealings with the bank of Rome. A Parliamentary act by Henry VIII stated that none could take above 20 per cent on lent money but was repealed because the word of God forbade usury. King Edward VI outlawed usury with a Parliamentary decree and stood in opposition to moneylenders. However, the moneylenders pressed on until the anti-usury law was repealed in 1571.

This became the gate entrance to the establishment of the Bank of England which was incorporated July 27, 1694 as a private joint-stock association holding a capital of 1.2 million euros. Its capital was loaned to the government and in return it received the right to issue notes with a monopoly on England's corporate banking. Only the principal was lent so interest continued to accumulate by compound interest. The loans could never then be repaid and that would give the moneylenders complete total control of the government and the people.

England had the largest portion of land in the American colonies, but because the Protestant Christians hated usury and money lending, it was lost with the moneylenders' greed. The Protestants were poor, and having no gold or silver, they issued non-interest-bearing paper notes. They worked hard and rapidly advanced in industry, commerce and wealth.

The moneylenders, of course, lusted for the developed wealth of the colonies and made their first attempt in 1765 to impose usury with the Stamp Act. Payment was required of various taxes to be made in specie or coin. Because the colonies had no coin to make payment they were obliged to borrow from the bank. This initiated the American war for Independence.

Benjamin Franklin is thought to have stated that the Revolution was caused by the Bank of England.

The Bank of England after the Revolutionary War still had a strong grip on the country. In 1791 was the chartering of the First Bank of the US, which was only to last for twenty years. In 1811, Congress refused to renew the charter and thus what became known as the War of 1812 was declared. General Jackson refused to renew the charter of the second bank, and it finally dissolved by 1836 which liberated the people from the Bank of England or in effect the Bank of Rome. But this only lasted until the Civil War of 1861.

America did not have a central bank, and the Jesuits needed to have another in America to supply them with a continuous flow of money which would provide for their wars and scheming plots in countries around the globe.

President Lincoln needed financing for the Civil War and made inquiry to solicit the bankers; however, they required 28 percent on usury, which Lincoln refused. To dodge the bankers, he issued $450,000,000 in Greenbacks (US notes) which were non usury paying notes backed by the nations credit. His direction was to close off the Bank of Rome from its financial degradation and influence in the US.

This infuriated the bankers, and so John Wilkes Booth became his assassin. He shot President Lincoln at Ford's Theater in Washington, DC, while the president and his wife, Mary Todd Lincoln, were watching the play *Our American Cousin* on Good Friday, April 14, 1865.

John W. Booth was a well-known theater actor. Although not born into a Roman Catholic family, he chose to convert to Catholicism in 1860 and was initiated into the Knights of the Golden Circle (Catholic organization of the laity). This organization was persuaded to slavery and devoted to maintaining slavery within the circle of land that borders the Caribbean Sea known as the "Golden Circle" whereby they chose their name.

They modeled their seal, a cross, to resemble that of the Knights of Malta (an order designed to fight against "heretics," companion and alliance to the Jesuit Order). Following is an excerpt from *The Great Conspiracy*, published in 1866, it quotes a handwritten letter from John W. Booth. The recipient of the letter is unknown but suspected to be a Jesuit ally of his and reads as follows: (return letters were signed only as "Veritas")

"Dear Sir: The K.G.C. had a meeting; I was initiated...They tell me that Lincoln, the damn chickenhearted nigger lover, will perhaps be inaugurated, but I most heartily wish, 'That never shall sun that morrow see'. . . . One thing is very clear to my mind, the South must take some decisive step. She must throw a bomb-shell into the enemy's hand that shall spread terror and consternation wherever it goes. You know what I mean, so don't be surprised.

Sincerely yours,

John Wilkes Booth."[13]

Four years later in 1869, John Sherman, an Ohio senator who was the head of the Senate Finance Committee, while traveling to Paris France for a monetary conference stopped in London where he received the red carpet treatment from Baron Rothschild and the upper echelon of society.

During Sherman's stay, he dined privately with the Baron and the two conversed on money issues. Their conversation is recorded in *A Tale of two Nations* by William Harvey as:

---

13   *The Great Conspiracy*, Philadelphia, Barclay & co. [c.1866].

"Five thousand pounds each year," went on the baron quietly, "placed in your hands, and supplemented by sums which you would consider necessary, I am satisfied would produce the conditions in the public mind desired. No accounting, you understand, would be required, absolute reliance to be placed in your wisdom and ability."[14]

Senator Sherman, having received these enormous bribes, returned to Ohio and introduced the bill to demonetize silver. With these large sums of money, he readily convinced members of Congress and the bill was passed. The result was the US was on gold standard and thus the nations of the world all went on gold standard.

Just a few short years later, in 1873 silver as coinage was abated via the Bank of England alias the Bank of Rome. Great Britain was one of the few exceptions of nations with free coinage of silver and gold. Any one was free to bring bullion to the government mint in order to have it coined into money, which was free to do and silver was equaled as gold. This was an excellent if not perfect monetary system of the world. But with silver being removed from coinage gold only was the standard and the result was a Great Depression.

The entire world economic system was disabled. The system of gold being measured to silver and silver to gold was at that time proportioned at 15 to 1. Money now was reduced in the world by half and the bond holders doubled their wealth. The stage was set to establish the Federal Reserve Bank by Rockefeller. By 1907 there was alarm and insecurity running ramped throughout the nation which led to the acceptance of the Rockefeller Federal Reserve paper, debt and usury monetary system.

In 1912 banker Bernard Baruch brought Woodrow Wilson to the Democratic headquarters and there a scheme was devised by which the Rockefeller-JP Morgan bankers would financially and politically support Wilson's campaign for presidency and in return Wilson would support the Federal Reserve fraud and push for the first time in history of the nation a progressive income tax on its citizens. Rockefeller and JP Morgan supported both sides of the election in order to ensure Wilson's election and poured money into the Progressive party of Teddy Roosevelt and with William Howard Taft, a Republican Party

---

14   William Harvey, *A Tale of Two Nations*, Nabu Press, 2012, p. 51.

candidate, and Senator Robert Lafollette's National Republican Progressive League supported Roosevelt over Taft, which caused a splitting of the Republican Party and resulted in the election of Woodrow Wilson of the Democratic Party.

After his election in 1913 Wilson signed the Federal Reserve Act and the Revenue Act of 1913 which brought the American people into bondage of the Federal Reserve and the IRS both unconstitutional and both illegal. However, in order to bring the appearance of legitimacy and make them binding Wilson through pressing congress, put in place the sixteenth and seventeenth amendments. He also, contrary to his campaign agenda took us into WWI and later on the League of Nations.

Wilson apparently later regretted his actions and is believed to have written in his diary,

"I am a most unhappy man. I have unwittingly ruined my country. A great industrial nation is controlled by its system of credit. . . all our activities are in the hands of a few men. We have come to be one of the worst ruled, one of the most completely controlled and dominated Governments in the civilized world, no longer a Government by free opinion, no longer a Government by conviction and the vote of the majority, but a Government by the opinion and duress of a small group of dominate men."

Today there are many Americans who have come to this knowledge and want to repeal the sixteenth and seventeenth amendments.

CHAPTER 13

The Affiliate Societies

Every nation of the world is ruled by one or more of the "secret societies" belonging to the Roman Catholic Church either directly or indirectly and affiliated with the Jesuit order, the society of societies.

The fact that there are secret societies undermining the structure of the US has not been unknown to our presidential leaders. Woodrow Wilson wrote in his book, *The New Freedom*, "Some of the biggest men in the United States, in the field of commerce and manufacture, are afraid of something. They know that there is a power somewhere so organized, so subtle, so watchful, so interlocked, so complete, so pervasive that they had better not speak above their breath when they speak in condemnation of it."[15]

Some of our leaders have unwittingly been participants of these societies. George W. Bush wrote in his autobiography: "My senior year I joined Skull and Bones, a secret society, so secret I can't say anything more."[16]

Originally Ignatius Loyola referred to his newly created order as "Los Alumbrados" which translates to The Illuminati. Ignatius had been a sympathizer of an already existing group, not an order, practicing mysticism and perversities in Spain. Los Alumbrados began around 1527. but because of their strange and contradictory behaviors were made an illegal sect and Ignatius at one time was arrested as a sympathizer. He practiced and taught mind altering with mystical spiritualism considered illuminating (*alumbrados* - lighting) but

---

15   Woodrow Wilson, *The New Freedom*, p. 5.
16   George W. Bush, et al, *A Charge to Keep*, Morrow, p. 47.

referred to his order as The Society of Jesus or Jesuits and thus there was no stigmatism from the name.

The "order" of the Illuminati was founded on May 1, 1776 at the Jesuit University of Ingolstadt in Bavaria. Jesuit Adam Weishaupt being the founder was educated by the Jesuits. Because Clement XIV's Bull of Extinction was not in force in Germany there was no resistance to the Jesuits and its order prospered at the Ingolstadt University. From here Weishaupt would establish the Illuminati, join the Grand Orient Masonic Lodge and thus unite the Cabalistic, Masonic, Jewish House of Rothschild with the wealth of the Society of Jesus (Jesuits).

The Jesuits leaders operate within the high positions of the Illuminati and through them control is maintained over the Knights of Columbus, Knights of Malta, Knights Templar in the U.S. and the Roman Catholic's secret order of Opus Dei, also created by the Jesuits. There is an illusory conflict devised to conceal the controlling of both sides.

Britain, France, Italy and the US are strongholds for the Illuminati and Jesuits with their many universities. The US alone houses twenty-eight Jesuit Universities. Weishaupt taught Roman Catholic Canon Law at Ingolstadt university and embraced the tenor of the Jesuits and with conspirators undertook the establishment of them throughout Europe. The, behind the scenes leader, actually being Mayer Amachel Rothschild. Agents were stationed within various factions of society to achieve their goal and would create dissensions that would require a "change" to be made. (The French and American Revolutions are both examples of concealed operations masked with the idea of freedom for the people but in fact the Rothschilds and the Georgetown University Jesuit leaders with their associates were the masterminds.)

The Jesuits and Rothschilds being organized with one another are committed to ruling the people through means of divisions and wars by deceptive controlling of politics, finances, religions and creating internal strife while operating both sides of the parties.

A quote from Weishaupt after infiltrating the Freemasons, was:

"The great strength of our Order lies in its concealment; let it never appear in any place in its own name, but always covered by another name, and another occupation. None is fitter than the three lower degrees of Freemasonry; the public is accustomed to it, expects little from it, and therefore takes little notice of it."

The Oaths taken by Knights of Columbus, Knights of Malta and Rhodes Scholars and not to exclude the very secret Skull and Bones are based on the Jesuit Oath. The following is an excerpt of the "Extreme" oath which is taken primarily by the high degree Jesuit.

The Extreme Oath of The Jesuits

1.

<<"I, ________________________ now, in the presence of Almighty God, the Blessed Virgin Mary, the blessed Michael the Archangel, the blessed St. John the Baptist, the holy Apostles St. Peter and St. Paul and all the saints and sacred hosts of heaven, and to you, **my ghostly father, the Superior General of the Society of Jesus**, founded by St. Ignatius Loyola in the Pontificate of Paul the Third, and continued to the present, do by the womb of the virgin, the matrix of God, and the rod of Jesus Christ, declare and swear, that the holiness *the Pope is Christ's Vicegerent* and is the true and only head of the Catholic or Universal Church throughout the earth; and that by virtue of the keys of binding and loosing, given to his Holiness by my Savior, Jesus Christ, **he hath power to depose heretical kings, princes, states, commonwealths and governments, all being illegal without his sacred confirmation and that they may safely be destroyed.** Therefore, to the utmost of my power I shall and will defend this doctrine of his Holiness' right and custom against all usurpers of the heretical or Protestant authority whatever, especially the Lutheran of German, Holland, Denmark, Sweden, Norway, and the now pretended authority and churches of England and Scotland, and branches of the same now established in Ireland and on *the Continent of America* and elsewhere; and all adherents in regard that they be usurped and heretical, opposing the sacred Mother Church of Rome. **I do now renounce and disown any allegiance as due to any heretical king, prince or state named Protestants or Liberals, or obedience to any of the laws, magistrates or officers.**

I do further declare that the doctrine of the churches of England and Scotland, of the Calvinists, Huguenots and others of the name

Protestants or Liberals to be damnable and they themselves damned who will not forsake the same.

I do further declare, that I will help, assist, and advise all or any of his Holiness' agents in any place wherever I shall be, in Switzerland, Germany, Holland, Denmark, Sweden, Norway, England, Ireland or America, or in any other Kingdom or territory I shall come to, and **do my uttermost to extirpate the heretical Protestants of Liberals' doctrines and to destroy all their pretended powers, regal or otherwise.>> End of Excerpt**

The oath of a Catholic Priest (*Provided by John Lyons, ex-Catholic priest, via a tract circulated in Glenside, Pa.*)

"I do declare from my heart, without mental reservation. that the Pope is Christ's vicar-general and is the true and only head of the Universal Church throughout the world, and that by virtue of the Keys of binding and loosing given to his Holiness by Jesus Christ, **he has power to depose heretical kings, princes, states, commonwealths and governments, all being illegal without his sacred Confirmation, and that they may safely be destroyed.** Therefore, to the utmost of my power, I will defend this doctrine and his Holiness, rights and customs against all usurpers of the Protestant authority whatsoever, especially against the now pretended authority of the Church of England and all adherents, in regard that they may be usurped and heretical, opposing the Sacred Mother, the Church of Rome.

I do renounce and disown any allegiance as due to any Protestant king, prince, or state, or obedience to any of their inferior officers. I do further declare the doctrine of the Church of England, of the Calvinist, Huguenots, and other Protestants, to be damnable and those to be damned who will not forsake the same.

I do further declare that I will help, assist, and advise, all or any of his Holiness' agents, in any place wherever I shall be, and to do my utmost to extirpate the Protestant doctrine and **to destroy all their pretended power, regal or otherwise.** I do further promise and declare that, notwithstanding, I may be permitted by dispensation to assume any heretical religion for the propagation of the Mother Church's interest, to keep secret and private all her agents' counsels as they entrust to me, and not to divulge, directly or indirectly, by word, writing, or circumstances whatsoever, but to execute all which shall be proposed given in charge, discovered unto me by you my most Reverend Lord and Bishop."

The Jesuits wear many hats. They are not all long robed priests. There are many "plain clothed" called the "short robes" who work in banks, schools, colleges, in ministries; even posing as a protestant minister or pastor (the end justifies the means), as lawyers, doctors of medicine or psychology, writers, journalists, counselors, theologian's scientists and everyday white collar and blue collar jobs, as missionaries and in political positions all over the world.

They are renowned teachers throughout the world and in the U.S. they not only have the twenty-eight universities afore mentioned but there are fifty Jesuit high schools and seventy primary and secondary schools. From the universities they can choose candidates for primary positions. The schools serve to educate and to indoctrinate the students so that by forming the thinking behavior of the next generation that will follow their agenda.

THE SINKING OF THE TITANIC

Again, America since the early 1830s did not have a central bank and the Jesuits were desperate to have a reservoir of money they could draw from to support their schemes and wars around the world. One of the worst schemes developed to achieve this was in the sinking of the *Titanic*. There are many reports that attest to this murderous plot. One in particular by Bill Hughes, *The Secret Terrorists*, expresses it as follows:

In 1910, seven men met on Jekyll Island just off the coast of Georgia to establish a central bank, which they called the Federal Reserve Bank. These men were Nelson Aldrich and Frank Vanderlip, both representing the Rockefeller financial empire; Henry Davison, Charles Norton, and Benjamin Strong, representing J. P. Morgan; and Paul Warburg, representing the Rothschild banking dynasty of Europe. We have already seen that the Rothschilds were the banking agents for the papacy's Jesuits, holding "the key to the wealth of the Roman Catholic Church."[17]

---

17   Bill Hughes, *The Secret Terrorists*, Truth Triumphant (2002).

The Morgans were friendly competitors with the Rothschilds and became socially close to them, Morgan's London-based firm was saved from financial ruin in 1857 by the Bank of England over which the Rothschilds held great influence. Thereafter, Morgan appears to have served as a Rothschild financial agent and went to great length to appear totally American.

His (Rockefeller's) entry into the field was not welcomed by Morgan and they became fierce competitors. Eventually, they decided to minimize their competition by entering into joint ventures. In the end, they worked together to create a national banking cartel called the Federal Reserve System.[18]

These three financial families, the Rothschilds, Morgans, and Rockefellers all do the bidding of the Jesuit Order because of Jesuit infiltration in their organizations. They do whatever is necessary to destroy constitutional liberty in America and to bring the pope to world domination. As we look back over the twentieth century, we see how successful the Jesuits have been. They have continued to squander the wealth of America and continually attack its great constitution and civil liberties. Daily, the power of the pope in Vatican City increases. One day they will achieve total power again.

The building of the *Titanic* began in 1909 at a shipyard in Belfast, the capitol of Northern Ireland. Belfast was a Protestant haven and was hated by the Jesuits. World War I began just a few years later. The *Titanic* was one of a fleet of ships owned by the White Star Line, an international shipping company.

Banking was not the only business in which Morgan had a strong financial interest. Using his control over the nation's railroads as financial leverage, he had created an international shipping trust which included Germany's two largest lines plus one of the two in England, the White Star Lines.[19]

There were a number of very rich and powerful men who made it abundantly clear that they were not in favor of the Federal Reserve System. J. P. Morgan was ordered by the Jesuits to build the *Titanic*. This "unsinkable" ship would serve as the death ship for those who

---

18   G. Edward Griffin, *The Creature from Jekyll Island,* American Opinion.
19   Ibid, p. 246.

opposed the Jesuits' plan for a Federal Reserve system. These rich and powerful men would have been able to block the establishment of the Federal Reserve, and their power and fortunes had to be taken out of their hands. They had to be destroyed by a means so preposterous that no one would suspect that they were murdered, and no one would suspect the Jesuits. The *Titanic* was the vehicle of their destruction. In order to further shield the papacy and the Jesuits from suspicion, many Irish, French, and Italian Roman Catholics immigrating to the New World were aboard. They were people who were expendable. Protestants from Belfast who wanted to immigrate to the United States were also invited on board.

Even the faithful and good Roman Catholic people were betrayed by the Jesuits. Irish, French and Italian Roman Catholics aboard Titanic ship perished in the middle of the cold water of the Atlantic Ocean.

All the wealthy and powerful men the Jesuits wanted to get rid of were invited to take the cruise. Three of the richest and most important of these were Benjamin Guggenheim, Isador Strauss, the head of Macy's Department Stores, and John Jacob Astor, probably the wealthiest man in the world. Their total wealth, at that time, using dollar values of their day was more that $500 million. Today that amount of money would be worth nearly $11 billion. These three men were coaxed and encouraged to board the floating palace. They had to be destroyed because the Jesuits knew they would use their wealth and influence to oppose a Federal Reserve Bank as well as the various wars that were being planned.

Edward Smith was a Jesuit tempore Co-Adjutor. This means that he was not a priest, but he was a Jesuit of the short robe. Jesuits are not necessarily priests. Those who are not priests serve the order through their profession. Anyone could be a Jesuit, and their identity would not be known. Edward Smith served the Jesuit Order in his profession as a sea captain.

Many interesting points about the *Titanic* are discussed in a videotape made by *National Geographic* in 1986, entitled *The Secrets of the Titanic*. When the *Titanic* departed from Southern England on April 10, 1912, Francis Browne, the Jesuit master of Edward Smith, boarded the *Titanic*. This man was the most powerful Jesuit in all of

Ireland and answered directly to the general of the Jesuit Order in Rome. The videotape declares:

A vacationing priest, Father Francis Browne, caught these poignant snapshots of his fellow passenger, most of them on a voyage to eternity. The next day Titanic made her last stop off the coast of Queenstown, Ireland. Here tenders brought out the last passengers; mostly Irish immigrants headed for new homes in America. And here, the lucky Father Browne disembarked. . ... Father Browne caught Captain Smith peering down from Titanic's bridge, poised on the brink of destiny.

Here is Jesuit treachery at its finest. The Provincial Father Francis Browne boards *Titanic*, photographs the victims, most assuredly briefs the Captain concerning his oath as a Jesuit, and the following morning bids him farewell.[20]

Browne went over with Edward Smith one last time exactly what he was supposed to do in the North Atlantic waters. The Jesuit General told Francis Browne what was to happen; Browne then tells Smith and the rest is history. Edward Smith believed that the Jesuit General . . .. is the god of the (Jesuit) society, and nothing but his electric touch can galvanize their dead corpses into life and action. Until he speaks, they are like serpents coiled up in their wintry graves, lifeless and inactive; but the moment he gives the word of command, each member springs instantaneously to his feet, leaving unfinished whatsoever may have engaged him, ready to assail whomsoever he may require to be assailed, and to strike wheresoever he shall direct a blow to be stricken.[21]

Edward Smith was given an order to sink the *Titanic*, and that is exactly what he did. By the command of God, (the Jesuit General) it is lawful to murder the innocent, to rob, to commit all lewdness, because he (the pope) is Lord of life, and death, and of all things; and thus to fulfill his mandate is our duty.[22]

There is no record in history of an association whose organization has stood for three hundred years unchanged and unaltered by all the assaults of men and time, and which has exercised such an immense

20   Eric Phelps, *Vatican Assassins*, Halcyon Unified Services, p. 427.
21   R.W. Thompson, *The Footprints of the Jesuits*, Hunt and Eaton, pp. 72, 73.
22   W.C. Brownlee, *Secret Instructions of the Jesuits*, American and Foreign Christian Union, p. 143.

influence over the destinies of mankind. "The ends justify the means," is his favorite maxim; and as his only end, as we have shown, is the order, at its biding the Jesuit is ready to commit any crime whatsoever.[23]

Let us remember the oath that every person takes to become a part of the Jesuit Order:

"I should regard myself as a dead body without will or intelligence, as a little crucifix which is turned about unresistingly at the will of him who holds it as a staff in the hands of an old man, who uses it as he requires it, and as it suits him best.[24]

When a person takes the Jesuit Oath, he is bound to his master until the day that he dies. Edward Smith had become a man without will or intelligence. He would commit any crime the Order wanted him to commit. Edward Smith had been required for martyrdom. On board the *Titanic* that night, Edward Smith knew his duty. He was under oath. The ship had been built for the enemies of the Jesuits. After three days at sea with only one pair of glasses for the bridge, Edward Smith propelled the *Titanic* full speed ahead, twenty-two knots, on a moonless dark night through a gigantic ice field nearly eighty square miles in area. Edward Smith did this despite at least eight telegrams warning him to be more cautious because he was going too fast.

Did Edward Smith need one caution? No, he had been traveling those waters for twenty-six years. He knew there were icebergs in that area. But eight cautions did not stop this man who was under the Jesuit oath, and under orders to destroy the Titanic.

The absurdity of warning veteran Captain Edward Smith repeatedly on Titanic's tragic night to slow down is nothing short of preposterous. The fact that smith never listened or heeded the warnings is insane. He had been given orders from his god in the Vatican, and nothing would turn him from his course.

The encyclopedias paint a very tragic picture of Smith in his last hours. When it came time to give the order to load and lower the life boats, Smith wavered and one of his aids had to approach him for the order to be given. Smith's legendary skills of leadership seem to have

---

23   G.B. Nicolini, *The History of the Jesuits*, Henry G. Bohn, pp. 495, 496, emphasis added.

24   R. W. Thompson, *The Footprints of the Jesuits*, p. 54.

left him; he was curiously indecisive and unusually cautious on that fatal night. Are these words to describe a legendary sea captain with 26 years of experience, or are these words to describe a man who was struggling in his mind whether he should do his duty as a sea captain or obey his master who told him to sink the ship?

John Jacob Astor's wife got into a life boat and was saved, while John Jacob Astor perished in the waters of the North Atlantic. There were not enough lifeboats and many of them were only half full with only women and children. To prevent nearby freighters from responding with help, the distress flares were white when they should have been red. White flares to passing freighters state that everybody was having a party.

One of the greatest tragedies of the twentieth century, the sinking of the *Titanic*, lies at the door of the Jesuit Order. The unsinkable ship, the floating palace was created to be the tomb for the wealthy, who opposed the Federal Reserve System. By April, 1912, all opposition to the Federal Reserve was eliminated. In December of 1913, the Federal Reserve System came into being in the United States. Eight months later, the Jesuits had sufficient funding through the Federal Reserve bank to begin World War I.

The Father Browne photograph collection contains the sole of *Titanic* photographs taken during the *Titanic* passage from Southampton to Ireland. From 1911 to 1916, Frank Browne studied theology at Milltown Park, Dublin. It was during this period that his uncle Robert (Bishop of Cloyne) sent him an unusual present: a ticket for the first legs of the maiden voyage of the *Titanic*, sailing from Southampton to Cherbourg and then on the Queenstown (Cobh), County Cork, Ireland.

While on board, an American millionaire offered to pay his way for the rest of the voyage to New York. On being appraised on this suggestion, Frank's Jesuit Superior General cabled Queenstown saying, succinctly - "GET OFF THAT SHIP PROVINCIAL." (Right! Because, Fr. Francis a. Browne is the Provincial Superior of the Jesuits in Ireland and off that ship, because the Jesuits and he himself will sink the *Titanic* deliberately as planned.)

After the tragedy Frank Browne's photographs appeared on the front pages of newspapers around the world. He had taken the last picture of Captain Smith and the only man ever taken into the Marconi room.

According to Thomas Schauf:

Dear American:

Pursuant to your request, I will attempt to clear up questions you have about the Federal Reserve Bank (FED). I spent much time researching the FED and these are the shocking and revealing conclusion:

THE FEDERAL RESERVE BANK is a Private Company.

Who actually owns the Federal Reserve central Banks? The ownership of the 12 Central Banks, a very well-kept secret, has been reveled:

ROTHSCHILD BANK OF LONDON

WARBURG BANK OF HAMBURG

ROTHSCHILD BANK OF BERLIN

LEHMAN BROTHERS OF NEW YORK

LAZARD BROTHERS OF PARIS

KUHN LOEB BANK OF NEW YORK

ISRAEL MOSES SEIF BANKS OF ITALY (Zionist Jew)

GOLDMAN-SACHS OF NEW YORK

WARBURG BANK OF AMSTERDAM

CHASE MANHATTAN BANK OF NEW YORK

Please, keep in mind as per world history. The House of Rothschild is the banker and key guardian of the Vatican Treasury (Wealth) under the Black Papacy "The Jesuit Superior General." Honest and reliable world historian knew it long time ago.

The world banks are an international cooperative. There are 188 countries who belong to this banking system. The expression "all roads lead to Rome" could also be all money leads to Rome. With the world banks controlling the worlds money the world's revenue flows through them primarily in the form of taxation. Within the US, the IRS imposes an unconstitutional income tax upon its citizens. Whistleblower and former Lawyer/Senior Council to the World Bank, Karen Hudes explained in one of her news interviews that when taxable income is calculated at the end of the tax year and an individual finds they have not paid their share they must send payment to the IRS for the amount owed. This money goes to the Fed, who sends it on to the Bank of London (England) who then divides it. Forty percent is given to the banks and 60 percent is sent on to the mother branch; the Vatican Bank of Rome.

The taxes are imposed and collected the same as they were imposed and collected from Israel during the time of Christ. The nations of the world pay tax money to Rome through these banks. The churches of Rome pay their tithes, offerings and penance. The universities and schools pay their tuition and then there are the hospitals, clubs and "mercy causes or charities" plus other vast means of revenue from politics, industrial, production, factories and such, of which Rome is involved within the nations around the world. There are also the many trades, businesses and stocks that are owned by the Vatican. The amount the Vatican holds is in the billions but it won't even assist to lift its own nation out of poverty?

For the purpose of clarification, it is important to remember that Rome itself is simply a city and there are wonderful people and Christians residing there. Rome is not despised nor its citizens. Most importantly the Catholics trapped in this system are precious victims to this system. The reference is to a system known as Babylon which has its beginning with Nimrod and the tower of Babel. It is called "Universal" and its goal is to live up to its name. It is a beast that is spread throughout the entire world. It is part of the image Nebuchadnezzar saw in his dream which was revealed to Daniel. It is a massive ancient system with many godly people trapped in its web who are unaware they are, or they don't know how to escape it and may be so entangled they even fear to try. The people trapped in this system are not just Catholics but are all who serve a manmade system. The Protestants are in that system, they are her daughters and the apple doesn't fall far from the tree.

"So they worshipped the dragon who gave authority to the beast; and they worshipped the beast; saying; Who is like the beast? Who is able to make war with him? (Rev. 13:4)

Indeed, who is able to make war with this huge monstrosity? Thanks to our heavenly Father, we are not called to make war with the beast but we are called to avoid its mark. Six - man's number. Man's religions, man's civil governments, and man's monetary systems may be the significance to consider as that is the element of a beast system.

"Here is wisdom, let him who has understanding calculate the number of the beast, for it is the number of (a - was not in the original text) man. With just a little research you find that it should read: it is the number of man: and his (the beasts-man's) number is 666" (Rev. 13:18).

Holding the purse strings of the world's monetary systems is an avenue of certainty for controlling and manipulating the world into your chosen destiny. Situations resulting in conflict between nations can be created. Propaganda on both sides can be circulated to arouse tension and reason for war. Within nations divisions between the civilians can be created in order to bring internal strife resulting in the necessity to create new laws and policing for control of the masses. Politicians can be manipulated through financing and opposition can be cleverly and mysteriously removed with infallible cover-up.

On January 22, 1870 a letter was written by the Illuminati leader Guiseppe Mazzini to Albert Pike who was a 33-degree Freemason reading:

We must allow all of the federations to continue just as they are, with their systems, their central authorities and diverse modes of correspondence between high grades of the same rite, organized as they are at present, but we must create a super rite, which will remain unknown, to which we will call those Masons of high degree whom we shall select. With regard to our brothers in Masonry, these men must be pledged to the strictest secrecy. Through this supreme rite, we will govern all Freemasonry which will become the one International Center, the more powerful because it's direction will be unknown.

A response by Albert Pike was sent to the Illuminati leader Mazzini on August 15, 1871, in which he revealed his plans to create world chaos which would make a "New World Order" necessary. It would be accomplished with three major "world wars". His letter reads as follows:

> *We shall unleash the nihilist and the atheists, and we shall provoke a formidable social cataclysm which in its horror will show clearly to the nations the effect of absolute atheism, origin of savagery and the most bloody turmoil. Then everywhere, the citizens, obliged to defend themselves against the minority of revolutionaries, will exterminate those destroyers of civilization, and the multitude, disillusioned with Christianity . . . will receive the pure light through the universal manifestation of the pure doctrine of Lucifer . . . the destruction of Christianity and atheism. Both conquered and exterminated at the same time.* (this letter was for a short time displayed at the British Museum Library in London and was copied by William Guy Carr, who was a former Intelligence Officer in the Royal Canadian Navy)

Pikes and Mazzini's intents for the three world wars are defined in "threeworldwars.com" as:

The Fist World War: To overthrow the power of the Czars in Orthodox Russia and bring about an atheistic communist state.

The Second World War: To originate between Great Britain and Germany. To strengthen communism as antitheses to Judeo-Christian culture and bring about a Zionist State in Israel.

The Third World War: A Middle Eastern War involving Judaism and Islam and spreading internationally. (This is being accomplished today)

Researcher Dr. Dennis L. Cuddy states:

Mazzini, with Pike, developed a plan for three world wars so that eventually every nation would be willing to surrender its national sovereignty to a world government. The first war was to end the Czarist regime in Russia, and the second war was to allow the Soviet Union to control Europe. The third war was to be in the Middle East between Muslims and Jews and would result in Armageddon.

God in the past used the evil men of nations such as Pharaoh of Egypt and Nebuchadnezzar of Babylon to fulfill his will as written in the prophecy's and today he continues to use men and women to accomplish his will.

World War II, with the atrocities against the Jewish people, literally pressured them to migrate back to Israel and the United States under President Harry S. Truman who played a major role in assisting the Jews to have their homeland restored to them.

It was midnight on May 14, 1948, that the Provisional Government of Israel proclaimed the new State of Israel. On that same date the United States, represented by President Truman, recognized the provisional Jewish government as de facto authority of the new Jewish state (de jure recognition was extended on January 31). The US delegates to the United Nations and the leading State Department officials were distempered over the fact that Truman released his recognition statement to the press without notifying them first. (On May 15, 1948, the Arab responded with Arab armies invading Israel and the first Arab-Israeli war began.)

A nation was born in one Day-May 15, 1948. "Who has heard such a thing? Who has seen such things? Shall the earth be made to give birth in one day? Or shall a nation be born at once?" (Isaiah 66:8).

As planned, the Rothschilds' hold Israel's purse strings, and with a democratic form of government the Pharisaic rulers are undistinguished.

A third world war is in the making which will result in the New World Order. The chaos created in the middle east is only a portion of the scale needed. More chaos between nations is being created through the governments of China, Russia, Japan, Africa, United States, Great Britain, Mexico, Australia and other nations around the globe. A New World Order will be the only possible solution.

CHAPTER 14

The 30-Year Jesuit Civil War

Count Wladimir Ledochowski, Jesuit Superior General, by 1941 had reached supremacy heights. He was 75 years of age when he instigated an assault against the Catholic National Socialism over Catholic National Communism. Fr. Himmler S. J. who was the new Grand Inquisitor of the Roman Catholic Church was pressured for the assault.

Fr Himmler S. J., Fr Joseph Stalin S. J. and Catholic Adolf Hitler were relentless in their accomplishments of control and were involved together in a number of military and scientific fronts until the Nazi Russian invasion. The finger of accusation fell to the pawn Hitler who was blamed as being "drunk" with power and invaded Russia because of his extreme hatred, toward Russians. However, in comparison to Himmler and his large tortuous armies Hitler was simply another soldier.

It was Himmler who was the right man for the job and Himmler was highly persuaded by Ledochowski. Yet, Stalin apparently was painted a different picture of purpose and when Hitler invaded in 1941 Stalin, against all other judgment to protect his power, refused his generals to engage completely and then having them executed repeated the extremity until almost reaching Moscow. But by December of 1941 the Jesuit controlled Soviets had overcome the German Army. And the Jesuits shifted their power from Germany, France and Italy to America.

Fr Himmler S. J. a German devotee, in seeing the fraud of Wladimir Ledochowski would be infuriated. On December 13, 1942 Ledochowski met sudden death which most assuredly was the by the hand of Himmler's assassinates for the ruin of the German, Swiss, French Illuminati Jesuits.

This feat created the Jesuit Civil War and hindered them from convening a General Congregation until the war ended. As a result, the Jesuits would have the permission to elect their Superior. Vicar General Norbert de Boyne couldn't be made Superior General. This then gave the American Jesuits under Fr. Edmund Walsh S. J. the liberty to advance their programs in America and their other international goals

Represented by the faction of the Illuminati guard were the German, Swiss, French and Itallian Jesuits and the now murdered betrayer, Fr Ledochowski S. J., representing the other faction the new guard aka the "New World Order" is headed up by the American-Canadian and English including Australian Jesuits. These were at war with each other and between these two holding neutral positions were such provinces as the Netherlands and Spain who were still engaging in their battle for survival against the Vatican supported Opus Dei Mari (Spanish Satanic devotion cult) reception.

At the end of World War II, in 1946 Europe and American Jesuits finally elected a new Superior General, Jean Baptiste Janssens of Belgium, who presided from 1946 to 1964. After his death the division between North America Jesuits and those of Europe broadened in philosophy and approaches.

Pedro Arrupe S. J. was elected in 1965 as Superior General and resided until 1983. There was a decline in numbers and academic standards as the Nihilist principles made their impressions. A partial agreement of suspension was made in 1972 when the office of President of Jesuit Conference of the United States and office of President of Jesuit Conference of European Provincials were formed by having an avenue to equally converse. Thus a complete truce was attained.

When Pedro Arrupe S. J. died, Peter Hans Kolvenbach, a Dutch, was elected Superior General from 1983-2008. At this point the Jesuit Order was depleted in its illustrious fame, particularly in the United States. The Jesuit Order in the U.S. seemingly became insignificant and it was at this time in 2008 Peter Hans Kolvenbach resigned as Superior General. He became a "visitor" which meant his attention was reawakening the spirituality of the Order and its exponents. To aid this accomplishment, he engaged in speaking at various universities throughout the country where he encouraged his audience to commit to the future Jesuit Order vision of spiritualism and globalism.

With the formation of the Federal Reserve Bank in the US, the funds for World War I were now available.

By 1914, the Jesuits were now ready to begin their vengeance: the second thirty years' war, on Europe. Russia, China and Japan having banished THE COMPANY "forever" from their shores. The order would use the Federal Reserve Bank, "their financial Frankenstein," to pay for it. The "Fed" was given the exclusive privilege to create credit with no collateral, that is, "out of thin air." Like the Bolshevik Revolution - also financed by the Fed - the Jesuits would use their Masonic Jewish Zionists such as Paul Warburg (yearning to rebuild Solomon's Temple) as the visible leaders of the Fed. This would enable the Order to justify American Anti-Jewish fury at the later date in the person of the ex-Basillian (secret Jesuit) radio-priest, Charles E. Coughlin, "the father of hate radio." Being the personal friend of J. Edgar Hoover and FDR, he would blame the Jews for the Order's Great Depression and the New Deal, calling it "the Jew Deal."

The Jesuits credit was extended to the American Congress, controlled by the Jesuits Council on Foreign Relations, to build a vast war machine with which to fight the Jesuits second thirty years' war. This Jesuit war machine became Fourteenth Amendment America's "Military Industrial Complex."[25]

The Jesuits waited from 1913 to 1929 to make a virtual monopoly out of their "Frankenstein Fed." the Great Depression put all the smaller banks out of business and made the Federal Reserve Bank "lord of all." And who caused the Great Depression? According to FDR's son-in-law, Curtis Dall, it was the Knight of Malta, Joseph P. Kennedy. We read:

"The feeling around the Street, in succeeding months, was that there were, in particular, three large short-sellers of stock, allegedly, Tom Bragg. Ben Smith and Joe Kennedy... Of the three mentioned well-known short-sellers, Joe Kennedy was allegedly the most important, the most powerful and the most successful. This service . . . made him

---

25   Phelps, *Vatican Assassins*, p. 463.

invaluable. . .Was Joe Kennedy carefully selected by world money leaders to sell short?"[26]

The Pacific Institute with their extensive research supplies us with reputable facts and events of our major wars.

The Serbians, who are Orthodox Christians, have, because of religious convictions, been in opposition to the Catholic Church, who since 1054 has been waging war against the Orthodox Christians. The Catholic Croatians had for fifty years prior to World War I displayed an intense hatred for the Serbians who were rivals to Rome and therefore needed to be annihilated. Sarajevo, the capital of Bosnia was predominately Serbian. In 1914 Archduke Francis Ferdinand who was heir to the Austria-Hungarian throne, and his wife were assassinated while riding in an open carriage. With this the foundation of a war to follow was laid.

Pope Pius X held a strong hatred for Orthodox Christians and consistently provoked Francis Joseph of Austria-Hungary to discipline the Serbians. On July 26, 1914 after the Sarajevo murders, Baron Ritter, a Bavarian representative at the Holy See informed his government by writing: "The Pope approves of Austria's harsh treatment of Serbia. He has no great opinion of the armies of Russia and France in the event of a war with Germany. The Cardinal Secretary of State does not see when Austria could make war if she does not decide to do so now. . . ." There, in true colours, is the Vicar of Christ (the pope), the gentle apostle of peace, the Holy Pontiff whom pious authors represent as having died of sorrow at seeing the outbreak of war.[27]

The pope clearly perceived that with Austria-Hungary crushing the Serbians, the Orthodox Christians of Russia would rise to defend their brothers in faith. With this, Germany, France and others would enter into the conflict and a major war would result. This was welcoming to the papacy as Russia, being primarily Orthodox, and the papacy wanted them abolished around the globe.

The Jesuits were exceptionally pleased to have Russia engaged because almost100 years earlier in 1816, Alexander I, the Russian Emperor, had expelled the Jesuits from Russia due to their political invasions and other maneuvers hindering the nation's welfare and

26   Ibid.

27   Edmund Paris, *The Vatican Against Europe*, The Wickliffe Press, p. 14.

stability. He issued a royal decree expelling them from Saint Petersburg and Moscow and again in 1820 he completely excluded them from Russia. Coincidently, only five years later, Alexander was poisoned to death and the czars were under attack by the Jesuits.

Alexander II had progressed well with his great reforms and had attached his signature to a Constitution to be adopted by Russia. The next day a bomb was thrown at his carriage, which killed and wounded a number of Cossacks, who accompanied the carriage. The emperor, in deep sympathy, left the carriage to look at the dying men, when a second bomb blew him to pieces.[28]

The last czar and his entire family was murdered in 1917, meaning that there would never again be an emperor of disapproval from the Romanoff House rule Russia or shelter the Orthodox Christians. The Jesuits would now have their vengeance. The demolishing of the assemblage of czars guaranteed the demolishing of the Orthodox Church.

Russian revolutionaries were financed and Lenin, Trotsky and Stalin were all aided by the Jesuits.

The instruments of this new alliance between the Soviets and the Vatican were to be the Jesuits, described as the hereditary enemies of the Orthodox Church. Reportedly, there were large numbers of representatives of the Jesuit Order in Moscow during the Revolution.[29]

Among the 1,766,188 victims up to the beginning of 1922, figures obtained from the Soviet documents, nearly five thousand were priests, teachers, nuns and others of the Orthodox Church. Nearly 100,000 Lutherans banished. Whole villages were wiped out. Thousands of churches of the different branches have been demolished and the work of destruction goes on.[30]

William Franklin Sands, a director of the Federal Reserve Bank of New York, had just contributed $1,000,000 to the Bolsheviks.[31]

---

28   Arno Gaebelien, *Conflict of the Ages*, The Exhorters, p. 85.

29   James Zatko, *Descent into Darkness*, University of Notre Dame Press, p. 111.

30   Ibid, pp. 103–106.

31   Anthony Sutton, *Wall Street and the Bolshevik Revolution*, Veritas Publishing, pp. 133–134.

The Jesuit in America assigned the task of taking over the American banking system and getting the Federal Reserve established was Jacob Schiff. He had come with orders from the Rothschilds to accomplish control over the American banking at the turn of the century.

By the turn of the century, 1900, Schiff had mastery of the entire banking fraternity on Wall Street.[32]) Now Schiff with his control of the Federal Reserve Bank, the financing of the Communist Revolution was cinched.

In the February 3, 1949, issue of the *New York Journal American*, Schiff's grandson, John, was quoted by columnist Cholly Knickerbocker as saying that his grandfather (Jacob Schiff) had given about twenty million dollars for the triumph of Communism in "Russia. [33]

Pacific Institute explains: In today's money, that twenty million would be $420 million, money essentially stolen from the American people through the Federal Reserve Bank.

Jacob Schiff was in control of the entire banking fraternity and was financing a government whose avowed principles are the direct antithesis of the United States Constitution. Schiff pretended to be an American capitalist. He was living in America, but his sole objective was that of the papacy: the ultimate destruction of America.

Also vengeance toward Germany came with the war. Germany was the mother land of the Lutherans and gave opposition to the Jesuits and the papacy in the 1850's and 70's. Germany aka Prussia during this time had military victories led by Chancellor Otto von Bismark, over Austria and France which were controlled by the Jesuits. Otto von Bismark had made the Jesuit Order illegal with the Kulturkampf law in 1872. Germany became the country affected the worse with the Treaty of Versailles which literally sacked Germany. Clemenceau, a French later stated to the press "We have guaranteed another war" when asked what the leaders had given to the world from the treaty.

With the war came exhaustion, grieving for those killed and everyone wanted to see the end of the war. This paved the way for Woodrow Wilson to initiate the League of Nations for purpose of ensuring peace and have it readily excepted without close examination

32   Myron Fagan, *The Illuminati and the Council on Foreign Relations*, taped
      lecture.
33   Griffin, Ibid.

to the resulting factors. Which included a one world government. However, Senator Henry Cabot Lodge Sr. thwarted the attempt of the United States from joining the League of Nations which hindered the Jesuit scheme for a single government through which they could control the world. Therefore, another World War would be necessary in order to subdue the nations.

Woodrow Wilson made himself subject to Colonel Edward Mandell House. He stated:

"Mr. House is my second personality. He is my independent self. His thoughts and mine are one."[34]

In Mandell House's time of service, he performed presidential tasks such as conducting foreign affairs and administrative diplomacy. George Vierick says in *The Strangest Friendship in History* that while Wilson was running for re-election in 1916 on a platform of "because he kept us out of war," House was negotiating a secret agreement with England and France, on behalf of Woodrow Wilson, that America would enter the war immediately after the election. House was also intimate with the power centers of money and power in Europe. House had close contacts with both J. P. Morgan and the old banking families of Europe.[35]

Woodrow Wilson was controlled by House, and House was a Jesuit committed to their purpose. Manipulating Wilson is what created the League of Nations which the Jesuits wanted. But the United States did not join so the goal of another war was in effect and this one would be so devastating that for the desire for relief of war from the masses, it would create the United Nations to ensure peace.

And so it was that World War II indeed became the most devastating war in history. There were hundreds of thousands who died during the war. And sadly the vast majority have no idea why or what brought in the war. President Roosevelt admitted, "In politics, nothing happens by accident. If it happens, you can bet it was planned that way." Wars are painstakingly planned and enforced by top government officials. If you want a traffic light at an intersection and your city

---

34   Charles Seymour, *The Intimate Papers of Colonel House*, vol. 1, Houghton Mifflin, pp. 114, 115.

35   Griffin, p. 239.

doesn't put one in because they don't see reason for it, the solution to get the city into action is to create an accident which would lead to installing the traffic light.

Popes and their Jesuitical agents have been and are the instigators of wars, and while the world is having real pain, Rome is having champagne.[36]

The pope was just as much a part of the Second World War as was Hitler and Catholic Mussolini and therefore just as guilty of the murder of six million Jews. In fact, popes have been in or instigated most, if not all, the European wars down through the centuries.[37]

One may say quite specifically that in 1914, the Roman Church started the series of hellish wars; It was then that the tribute of blood which she has always taken from the peoples began to swell into a veritable torrent.[38]

In the memoirs of the German Kaiser Wilhelm, the Kaiser tells of his visit to the Jesuits' great friend, Pope Pius X (1903–14). Here are the Kaiser's own words:

"The Pope said to me on this occasion that Germany must become the sword of the Catholic Church. I remarked to him that the old Roman Empire of the German nation no longer existed; but he stuck to his words.[39]

Ambassador to the pope in Berlin, Mgr. Pacelli and Franz von Papen, the pope's confidant chamberlain, solicited a uniting with Rome for purpose of abolishing the Weimar Republic. Although the German Catholics opposed Nazism because the pope was partial to Hitler full rights were voted to Hitler on January 30, 1933 and after this, Italy made a concordat. The German Episcopate swore allegiance to the Fuhrer and Catholic Youth Organizations combined with those of the Nazis.[40]

---

36   Jeremiah J. Crowley (former Catholic priest), *Romanism: A Menace to the Nation*, Menace Publishing, p. 144.

37   F. Paul Peterson, *Peter's Tomb Recently Discovered in Jerusalem*, p. 63 - quoted in: *Is Alberto for Real*, Sidney Hunter, Chick Publications, p. 41.

38   Paris, p. 48.

39   *The Kaiser's Memoirs*, by Wilhelm II, translated by Thomas R. Ybarra, New York, 1922, p. 221.

40   Paris, p. 15.

Hitler was aided by the Vatican in gaining power and to seize his hold on all of Germany by instructing the Catholic Party of Germany to vote for Nazis. This made a majority vote for Hitler and gave him the right to form a government by 1933. The Vatican also gave orders to the Catholic Reichstag Parliament members to give support to the legislation giving Hitler power of dictatorial rule and he could by this power destroy German Communism.

The whole Vatican-Hitler bargain had been conducted in secret before Hitler became Chancellor of Germany in January 1933. In June of the same year, Hitler and the Vatican signed a Concordat, under terms of which the church swore allegiance to the Nazi regime.... Soon afterward, Catholic Franz von Papen, the second in command to Hitler, put the essence of the Hitler Vatican alliance very succinctly in these words: "The Third Reich," he said, "is the first power which not only recognizes, but puts into practice, the high principles of the Papacy."[41]

Even Hitler said he was helped by the Jesuit counter - Reformation to continue his war. (We) have witnessed Catholicism's open support of every step taken by Nazi-Fascism to impose authoritarian regimes upon all peoples.[42]

The German Catholic political party (Zentrum) and Catholic von Papen were responsible for bringing Hitler to power in 1933 and so Hitler patterned his Third Reich to that of the corrupt papacy. He engaged himself and became their puppet while they supported him.

Immense sums of money belonging to our national bank depositors have been given to Germany on no collateral security whatever . . . Billions upon billions of our money has been pumped into Germany by the Federal Reserve Board and the Federal Reserve Banks... On April 27, 1932, the Federal Reserve outfit sent $750,000, belonging to American bank depositors, in gold to Germany. A week later, another $300,000 in gold was shipped to Germany in the same way. About the middle of May $12,000,000 in gold was shipped to Germany by the

---

41   Avro Manhattan, *The Vatican Moscow Washington Alliance*, Ozark Books, - quoted in Sydney Hunter, Is Alberto for Real, Chick Publications, pp. 42–43.

42   Leo H Lehman, *Behind the Dictators*, Agora Publishing, pp. 36–39.

Federal Reserve banks. Almost every week there is a shipment of gold to Germany.[43]

Remember, the Federal Reserve Bank is controlled by the Jesuits and Hitler was a tool in the hand of the Jesuits. The Fed is not owned by the Americans. The Americans would not have financed this war.

Other events were playing out between Rome, Spain and General Francisco Franco. At the turn of the twentieth century, Spain was teetering from a Roman Catholic monarchy and the move toward a republican government. The teeter-totter continued until the 1930's when babies' bodies were discovered under Spain's convents. The examinations of doctors revealed that they had died from suffocation. It was learned that priests and nuns engaged in sexual activities and when the most inconvenient baby was born unwanted by the church they were exterminated at birth.

This incited the people to make laws which diminished the papacy's power.

Alberto Rivera, ex-Jesuit exclaims, "In 1936 the new Spanish inquisition exploded. It was called "The Spanish Civil War secretly orchestrated in the Vatican."

The pope excommunicated the heads of the Spanish republic and declared war between the Holy See and Madrid. Under the banner of the Vatican the Muslim forces invaded the Canary Islands and then attacked southern Spain. When the inquisition accomplished its goals, Spain was in ruins, bleeding and beaten, but safely back in the hands of the Vatican. General Franco eventually became the Roman Catholic dictator of Spain. Franco's government was recognized August 3, 1937, by the Vatican, just twenty months before the civil war ended."[44]

When Franco marched on Madrid, nearing the close of the late civil war in Spain, when he was reinstating the Catholic government and overthrowing the people's government the Protestants had set up a few years before, he said, "I have four columns of soldiers with me, I

---

43   H. S. Kenan, *The Federal Reserve Bank*, The Noontide Press, 1966, p 158.

44   Jack Chick, Alberto pts. 1, 3, 6, Chick publications, pp. 12, 21, 28, 29.

also have a fifth column in the city of Madrid who will betray the city into my hands when I get there."[45]

War was initiated on March 31, 1934 with the signing of the Pact of Rome and the oath to support Mussolini and Hitler. Then in 1937 the Vatican gave legal acceptance to the government of Franco in Spain who received military support from Nazi Germany.

Mussolini was revered by Rome's Jesuits as they possessed in him "the man of providence" who restored the Vatican City back to the papacy in 1929.

Pius XI opinions:

"Mussolini is making rapid headway and, with elemental strength, will conquer all in his path. Mussolini is a wonderful man-Do you hear me? -a wonderful man. . .. The future is his."[46]

For today Rome considers the Fascist regime the nearest to its dogmas and interest. We have not merely the Reverend (Jesuit) Father Coughlin praising Mussolini's Italy as a Christian democracy," but Civilta Cattolica, house organ of the Jesuits, says quite frankly, "Fascism is the regime that corresponds most closely to the concepts of the Church of Rome."[47]

There had been negotiations between Italy, Mussolini, and the agents of the papacy held in secrecy which brought about the Lateran Treaty uniting the Papacy with Fascism with an affirmative vote from Catholic priest Don Sturzo - chief of the Catholic Group. With it came the seduction of Ethiopia and the assault against Albania.

Mussolini, like Hitler, had put into practice the papacy politics and like Hitler performed to their command. We learn, too the US President Franklin Roosevelt performed for Rome.

[Cardinal] Spellman was offered an unprecedented opportunity by Roosevelt that would necessitate leaving his archdiocese for months on end . . .. The astounding proposal Roosevelt put forth was that Spellman act as a clandestine agent for him in the four corners of the world. It would be the archbishop's job to contact chiefs of state in

45   Albert Garner, *The Devil's Masterpiece: The Mystery of Iniquity*, Blessed Hope Foundation, pp. 70, 71.

46   Ibid. p. 69.

47   Pierre Van Paassen, *Days of our Years*, Hillman-Curl, p. 465.

the Middle East, Europe, Asia, and Africa. He would carry messages for the President . . . and act as Roosevelt's eyes and ears. . . . The President offered him an opportunity to wield more power than any other American religious figure had ever had. Spellman would move as an equal among the greatest figures on the world political stage . . . But few people were certain about what the archbishop did during his far-flung travels. His clandestine work raised questions at home about the role of a religious figure involved deeply in governmental affairs.[48]

Spellman, while committed to Pope Pius XII, was used by Roosevelt as his agent.

Roosevelt and Eisenhower approved of the forced repatriation of some six million (Orthodox Christian) people back to Russia, many of whom were tortured or killed after they reached their destination. Two Russians who have written about this abominable decision by these American leaders are Nikolai Tolstoy and Alexander Solzhenitsyn. The Americans called this repatriation "Operation Keelhaul," after the naval form of torture where the prisoner is hauled under the keel of a ship by a rope tied to the prisoner's body, to be severely cut by the barnacles on the bottom of the ship.

These six million individuals were not only soldiers who had fought on the side of the Germans against the Russians, but they were women and children as well . . . .. Even though it was Churchill and Roosevelt who made the incredible decision to send millions of anti-Communist Russians back to certain death, it was General Dwight Eisenhower who enforced "Operation Keelhaul," with no apparent pangs of conscience.[49]

Roosevelt had carried out the Jesuit intent of annihilating as many as possible Orthodox Christians. They intended to demolish Serbia's Orthodox Christians during World War One and succeeded in diminishing millions of Russian Orthodox Christians by end of World War Two with aid of Roosevelt, Eisenhower, and Churchill.

Jesuit General, Count Halke von Ledochowski, was disposed to organize, on the common basis of anti-communism, a certain degree of collaboration between the German Secret Service and the Jesuit Order.

---

48   John Cooney, *The American Pope*, Times Books, pp. 124, 125.
49   Ralph Epperson, *The Unseen Hand*, Publius Press, p. 301.

Von Ledochowski considered the forthcoming bellicose settling of accounts between Russian and Germany as inevitable...And the Baseler Nachrichten (March 27, 1942) did not hesitate to write: "One of the questions arising from German activity in Russian which is of supreme importance to the Vatican, is the question of the evangelization of Russia."

This is confirmed by Father Duclos himself in a book covered by the Imprimatur, "During the summer of 1941, Hitler appealed to all Christian forces . . . (he) authorized Catholic missionaries to go to the new eastern territories . . . . Nor has it been forgotten that, in France, Cardinal Baudrillart and Mgr. Mayol de Luppe recruited the L. V. F. For the crusade against Russia."[50]

Russian Orthodox Christians were being annihilated by the papacy and in the interim Yugoslavia was suffering its massacres. Many written accounts of World War Two's horrific traumas have been unfolded in books such as *Convert . . . or Die!* By Edmond Paris, *The Vatican's Holocaust* by Avro Manhattan, and *Ravening Wolves* by Monica Farrell, detailing the Utashi-Catholic Actionists led by monks and priests and even nuns.

The mass expulsion or forced conversion of the Orthodox Christians to Roman Catholicism was on the agenda. All measures, aiming at the elimination of Serbdom in Croatia were carried out under the slogan enunciated by one of the Croatian ministers: "We shall massacre the first third of the Serbs, expel the second third from the country and force the final third to accept the Catholic faith, whereby they will be absorbed by the Catholic element."[51]

In the late 1990s, the papacy was still attempting to eliminate Orthodox Christians in Serbia. It engaged the US as the scapegoat brute to bomb Serbia. And in actuality the pope and his church are responsible for the Balkan's slaughter, yet they are trying Slobodan Milosevic for war crimes.

Another outcome for the Second World War for the Jesuits was to through the severity of inhumane tortures against the Jews it would <u>force them into</u> Palestine. The Balfour Declaration was signed which

50   Paris, pp. 240, 241.

51   Lazo M. Kostich, *Holocaust in the Independent State of Croatia*, Liberty, p. 18.

enabled the Jews to go back to Palestine yet many were so established that they hadn't any desire or reason to return. Besides the territory was still nothing but a desolation. The Holocaust with its persecutions gave the Jesuits what they sought and the Jews soon longed to return home which many did.

The Jews return to their homeland, which has not yet completed, is a fulfillment of prophecy. Just as God used Pharaoh, Sannacherib, Nebuchadnezzar, Titus, and others to fulfill his word so he continues to use those who are so inclined to bring about his plans.

In May of 1948, Israel was declared to be a sovereign nation, and not surprisingly, Jesuit Cardinal Francis Spellman had been the deciding factor in the acceptance of Israel as a sovereign state.

Behind the Zionist banner there was to be found the ancient Messianic hope for the coming of a global theocracy, as predicted by all the seers and prophets of Zion. It was to be a theocracy in which Jehovah, not Christ, was to be king.

The specter of the creation of such a theocracy has haunted the inner chambers of the Catholic church from her earliest inception, and still is a dominant fear. In Vatican eyes, therefore, the millenarian yearning for a global Hebrew theocracy, represents a deadly threat to the eschatological teachings of the Catholic church. When translated into concrete political terms, such a view spells not only rivalry, but implacable enmity.[52]

Although the Jews returning to their homeland was achieved by the will of God and in his divine timing, those who determined the process believe themselves to be the grand masters of the event. They are unaware that they were as Pharaoh, raised up to accomplish his will.

The result for the Jews since being granted sovereignty in 1948 has been nothing but continuous battles with the Muslim nations surrounding them. The Jesuits goal for Israel is to create such horrific tormenting conditions throughout the middle east with bloodshed and loss of lives that there will be an urgency felt for peace.

The First World War failed in bringing in a world-governing entity for the Jesuits however, the second world war made it possible with the

---

52   Manhattan, pp. 169–170.

development of the United Nations in 1945. For the war weary people of the world this was an answer for peace because the United Nations was to act as a peace keeper. It has not kept peace. Even though it asserts that peace is the objective for its existence there are currently more than eighty wars around the globe. Instead, it has been a tool of suppression such as exercised in the quash of Rhodesia by UN forces.

Japan became a target of World War II because of the 1639 exclusion of Catholics. Originally during the latter part of the sixteenth-century trade with foreign nations were welcomed by the Japanese and as well the Catholic missionaries were welcomed. Because the Catholics would not tolerate the difference of faith, severe bloody persecutions arose. Japan issued an edict refusing to allow the entrance of foreigners and for two hundred years Japans ports were closed to Jesuit missionaries, whose intent had been to conquer Japan for the pope. The Jesuits sought their revenge and during the last half of the 1800s Japan suffered military blows until finally with World War II the bombing of Hiroshima and Nagasaki incapacitated her.

CHAPTER 15

Assassination of Yet Another President

Less than twenty years after World War II ended, the first Catholic president, John F. Kennedy, was elected chief and commander of the armed forces of the United States of America. He was supposed to be a loyal pawn for the Vatican Jesuits; however, he displayed a mind of his own, and this would cost him his life.

Most, whether they lived during the 1963 murder of Kennedy or not, have heard the reports. Kennedy was shot, sitting in the back of an open motorcade next to his wife Jackie in Dealy Plaza in downtown Dallas Texas, Friday November 22, 1963 at 12:30 p.m. Soon after, he lay dead at the Parkland Memorial Hospital.

From the day this event played out until the present there has been much doubt and speculation over why he was shot and who actually shot him. There were basically two main reasons why Kennedy was assassinated. These reasons are involved with the Vietnam War, and the Federal Reserve Bank.

President Kennedy sent two aides to Vietnam, McNamara and Taylor, who gathered intelligence that convinced him that the United States needed to withdraw from Vietnam. Their memo to the president was entitled, Report of McNamara-Taylor Mission to South Vietnam.

With this report in hand, President Kennedy had what he wanted. It contained the essence of decisions he had to make. He had to get re-elected to finish programs set in motion during his first term; he had to get Americans out of Vietnam. (Col. L. Fletcher Prouty, JFK: The CIA, Vietnam, and The Plot to Assassinate John F. Kennedy, Carol Publishing Group, p 264)

Fletcher Prouty explains, "On November 22, 1963, the government of the United States was taken over by the superpower group that wanted an escalation of the warfare in Indochina, and a continuing military buildup for generations to come."[53]

While Kennedy was reducing America's involvement in Southeast Asia his murder was being planned out by this "superpower group". But the question is who was the group and why did they want America in South Vietnam?

Avro Manhattan, a British journalist employed for years by the British Broadcasting Company who has engaged in lengthy research and written upwards of fifteen books regarding the Roman Catholic Church's participation in world affairs, gives us from his book, *Vietnam: Why Did We Go? The political and military origin of the war of Vietnam has been described with millions of written and spoken words. Yet, nothing has been said about one of the most significant forces which contributed to its promotion, namely, the role played by religion, which in this case, means the part played by the Catholic Church, and by her diplomatic counterpart, the Vatican. Their active participation is not mere speculation. It is an historical fact as concrete as the presence of the US, or the massive guerilla resistance of Asian communism. The activities of the last two have been scrutinized by thousands of books, but the former has never been assessed, not even in a summarized form. The Catholic Church must be considered as a main promoter in the origin, escalation and prosecution of the Vietnamese conflict. From the very beginning this religious motivation helped set in motion the avalanche that was to cause endless agonies in the Asiatic and American continents.*

The price paid was immense: thousands of billions of dollars; the mass dislocation of entire populations; political anarchy; military devastation on an unprecedented scale; the disgrace upon the civilized world; the loss of thousands upon thousands of young Asian and American lives. Last but not least, the wounding, mutilation, and death of hundreds of thousands of men, women, and children. The tragedy of Vietnam will go down in history as one of the most pernicious deeds of the contemporary alliance between politics and organized religion.

---

53   Ibid. p. 264

Factors of a political, ideological, economic, and military nature played no mean role in the unfolding of the war, but the religion of the Catholic Church was one of its main instigators. From the beginning her role has been minimized when not obliterated altogether. Concrete facts however, cannot be wiped away so easily, and it is these which we shall now scrutinize, even if briefly.[54]

Avro Manhattan, world authority on Vatican politics, has blown the cover on the real reason our boys suffered and died in Vietnam. He traces their death to the Vatican's passionate desire to make Asia Roman Catholic. Vatican agents hatched and plotted the Vietnam War. American soldiers were serving the Vatican in their desperate struggle to survive the jungles, the hell of warfare, pain, death and destruction. It was all engineered by . . . her Jesuits.[55])

Avro Manhattan reveals that the Vatican wanted to create for itself a power base in Southeast Asia in order to subdue all of Southeast Asia and then all of Asia and so it was for this reason the war in Vietnam was fought. Another excerpt from his books states:

Ho Chi Minh began before World War Two to maneuver for a communist Vietnam. He received help from the US against the Japanese but used that aid to consolidate his hold on the highlands of Tonkin. In August, 1945 he marched into Hanoi and set up the provisional government of the Democratic Republic of Vietnam. A master strategist, he cooperated in the transplanting of nearly a million Catholic North Vietnamese into the South...After the election of Pope John the XXIII in 1958 and the turn of the Vatican from the Cold War toward cooperation with Marxism, Ho Chi Minh made a secret deal with Pope John which eventually led to full control of the country by the North.[56]

President Ngo Dinh Diem of South Vietnam was a practicing Catholic who ruled South Vietnam with an iron fist. He was a genuine believer in the evil of Communism and the uniqueness of the Catholic Church. He had originally been planted in the presidency by Cardinal Spellman and Pope Pius the XII. He transformed the presidency into

---

54   Avro Manhattan, *Vietnam: Why Did We Go?* Chick Publications, 1984, p. 13.

55   Ibid. p. 3.

56   Ibid. p. 177.

a virtual Catholic dictatorship, ruthlessly crushing his religious and political opponents. Many Buddhist monks committed suicide by fire, burning themselves alive in protest against his religious persecutions. His discriminatory persecution of non-Catholics, particularly Buddhists, caused the disruption of the government and mass desertions in the army. This eventually led to U.S. military intervention in South Vietnam. In this terrorization he was aided by his two Catholic brothers, the Chief of the Secret Police and the Archbishop of Hue.[57]

The instigator who brought America into the combat was none other than archbishop of New York, Cardinal Francis Spellman. He was active in persuading the US to select Diem and support him as president of South Vietnam. He was made Vicar General of the US Armed Forces and called the GIs the "Soldiers of Christ" (meaning soldiers for the Catholic Church) in his frequent visits to the Vietnam war front.[58]

Conducting themselves in their customary manner of playing both sides, the Vatican controlled Diem in the South and at the same time was making bargains in secrecy and advising Ho Chi Minh in the North. In this way regardless of the outcome the Vatican would have its victorious control over Vietnam. When Kennedy attempted to end the bloody brutal warring the disapproving Jesuits responded by having him permanently removed.

The following occurred the day after Kennedy's assassination:

At 8:30 a.m., Saturday, the 23rd of November 1963, the limousine carrying CIA director John McCone pulled into the White House grounds. . . . He was also there to transact one piece of business prior to becoming involved in all the details entailed in a presidential transition - the signing of National Security Memorandum 278, a classified document which immediately reversed John Kennedy's decision to de-escalate the war in Vietnam. The effect of Memorandum 278 would give the Central Intelligence Agency carte blanche to proceed with a full-scale war in the Far East. . . . In effect, as of November 23, 1963, the Far East would replace Cuba as the thorn in America's side. It would

---

57   Ibid. p. 56.
58   Ibid. p. 71.

also create a whole new source of narcotics for the Mafia's worldwide markets.[59]

America stopping its participation in the Vietnam war was countermanded the day after Kennedy's assassination and the papacy's Vietnam plan forwarded.

Robert Morrow further explains that another reason the Jesuits needed the war to continue was the billions of dollars to gain in the international drug trade. The Jesuits had been involved in the Far East drug trade for the previous four centuries and were not willing to let this occasion slip them regardless of the countless lives it took.

Since the original Jesuit mission had established itself in Beijing in 1601, the Society of Jesus (the Jesuits) had held the key to the Far East Trade-including the drug trade.[60]

Our administration out of Washington, being controlled by the Jesuits, wanted the Vietnam War to continue. The Jesuits wanted to have a Catholic power in Southeast Asia and continue their Far East four hundred years of controlling the international drug market and Kennedy was a hindrance that needed to be exterminated.

A statement JFK made which encouraged his demise:

"There exists in this country a plot to enslave every man woman and child. Before I leave this high and noble office, I intend to expose this plot."

President John F. Kennedy - seven days before he was assassinated.

The other reason to exterminate Kennedy was his intention to eliminate the Federal Reserve. When Kennedy called for a return of America's currency to the gold standard, and the dismantling of the Federal Reserve System - he actually minted non-debt money that does not bear the mark of the Federal Reserve; when he dared to actually exercise the leadership authority granted to him by the US Constitution . . . Kennedy prepared his own death warrant. It was time for him to

---

59   Robert Morrow, *First Hand Knowledge*, Shapolsky Publishers, p. 249.

60   Assorted authors, Dope, Inc.: The Book that Drove Kissinger Crazy, Executive Intelligence Review, p 117.

go.[61] The Federal Reserve System was created by the Jesuits for their monetary gain and Kennedy wanted it eliminated.

According to the US Constitution, Congress is supposed to coin money which if it did there would not be hundreds of billions of dollars in interest being paid every year to the bankers for the national debt on money created out of thin air. It was for this reason that Kennedy began to issue US government money, free of debt, in place of the Federal Reserve dollars we use. Had he succeeded, the US would not be facing the financial dilemma it does now. However, it is necessary to break the financial backbones of the nations in order to usher in the need of a one world currency for a one world government and this is the ultimate goal.

Note: Kennedy was raised Catholic, yet expendable as he held to his commitment vowed to his country and he was not a Jesuit.

"Finally, let all with such artfulness gain the ascendance over princes, noblemen and the magistrates of every place that they may be ready at our beck and call, even to sacrifice their nearest relatives and most intimate friends when we say it is for our interest and our advantage."[62]

Cardinal Francis Spellman of New York was the military vicar of the American Armed Forces in Vietnam. He was also the unofficial link between the pope and John Foster Dulles, the US Secretary of State and therefore the Secretary's brother, Alan, who was the head of the CIA.[63]

So the Jesuits, with the Roman Catholic Church and Cardinal Spellman, had their influence and were able to manipulate John Foster Dulles, Secretary of State, and his brother Alan, head of the CIA. Cardinal Francis Spellman, head Cardinal of New York, controlled both of those offices along with the FBI.

The Catholic Church in the USA financially can stand up to all the giant trusts of America. Politically, she looms ever larger in the

---

61 Colonel James Gritz, *Called to Serve: Profiles in Conspiracy from John F. Kenney to George Bush*, Lazarus Publishing, pp. 511–512.

62 W. C. Brownlee, *Secret Instructions of the Jesuits*, American and Foreign Christian Union, p. 47.

63 Avro Manhattan, *Murder in the Vatican*, Ozark Books, pp. 35–36.

White House, in the Senate and in the Congress. She is a force in the Pentagon, a secret agent in the FBI and the most subtly intangible prime mover of the S.S. wheel within a wheel: The Central Intelligence Agency.[64]

"The woman was arrayed in purple and scarlet, and adorned with gold and precious stones and pearls, having in her hand a golden cup full of abominations and filthiness of her fornication" (Rev. 17:4).

An excerpt from Jean Hill, who was a witness to the Kennedy murder, wrote a book entitled *JFK: The Last Dissenting Witness*. She stated that in conversing with a friend of hers, J. B., one of the policemen in the motorcade with Kennedy, that he told her the following:

"Well while Kennedy was busy shaking hands with all the well-wishers at the airport, Johnson's Secret Service people came over to the motorcycle cops and gave us a bunch of instructions. The darnedest thing was they told us the parade route through Dealy Plaza was being changed." "Changed? How," Jean Hill asks. "It was originally supposed to go straight down Main Street." J. B. Said, "but they said for us to disregard that. Instead we were told to make the little jog on Houston and cut over to Elm." Jean felt her mouth drop open. "If you'd stayed on Main Street, Kennedy might've been completely out of range of whoever was shooting at him. My 'shooter' behind the wooden fence definitely wouldn't have had much chance to hit him from there." J.B. stared at her with a straight face. "Maybe that's why they changed the route," he said bluntly. "But that's not all. They also ordered us into the craziest escort formation I've ever seen. Ordinarily, you bracket the car with four motorcycles, one on each fender. But this time they told the four of us assigned to the president's car there'd be no forward escorts. We were to stay well to the back and not let ourselves get ahead of the car's rear wheels under any circumstances. I'd never heard of a formation like that much less ridden in one, but they said they wanted to let the crowds have an 'unrestricted view' of the president. Well, I guess somebody got an unrestricted view of him all right."[65]

---

64   Ibid. p. 271.

65   Jean Hill, *JFK: The Last Dissenting Witness*, Pelican Publishing, p. 113.

"What are you talking about?" Jean asked innocently. "I don't understand." "My friends in the motorcade say he started ducking down in the car a good 30 or 40 seconds before the first shots were fired. I'd say that's just a little peculiar, wouldn't you?" "Oh, come on, J. B." Jean Hill said, thinking he had to be joking. "They obviously weren't serious, were they?" "As far as I know they were dead serious." J. B. Said. "One of them told Maguire that he saw Johnson duck down even before the car turned onto Houston Street, and he sure as __wasn't laughing when he said it." "Well, maybe Johnson just dropped something on the floor and bent over to pick it up. I mean there can be a simple explanation." "Maybe so." J. B. said. "I don't claim to know what his reasons were but this guy said it sure looked like he was expecting bullets to be flying. When I heard it, it made me start wondering about a whole lot of other stuff too."[66]

Interestingly, in Texas if a person dies in the state the law prohibits them from being taken out without an autopsy. The doctors at Parkland Memorial Hospital in Dallas released Kennedy's body without the autopsy, but at gunpoint. Due to the evidence of more than one bullet killing J. F. Kennedy and many that would have been discovered had an autopsy been performed. The concocted Warren Commission report could not have been released and patsy Lee Harvey Oswald would have been shown to not be the only shooter. In fact, the rifle that Oswald had was not capable of delivering the deadly blow that was claimed it had. So the autopsy was not allowed in Texas and the body of President Kennedy was flown to DC for a pretend federal autopsy. The Jesuit cover-up and lies were kept intact.

Three days after the assassination, Carl Renas, head of security at the Dearborn Division of the Ford Motor Company, drives the limousine, helicopters hovering overhead, from Washington to Cincinnati. In doing so, he noticed several bullet holes, the most notable being the one in the windshield's chrome molding strip, which he said was clearly" a primary strike," and "not a fragment." The limousine was taken by Renas to Hess and Eisenhart of Cincinnati where the chrome

---

66   Ibid. pp. 114–116.

molding was replaced. The Secret Service told Renas to "keep your mouth shut."[67]

The man in charge of the Dearborn Division of the Ford Motor Company, Lee Iacocca, chose to send Carl Renas to go to Washington, DC to get the motorcade car Kennedy was in because he was head of security. Iacocca remained head of the Dearborn Division until becoming President of Ford Motor Company in 1970. He was involved in the cover-up of Kennedy's assassination because he concealed evidence.

In Lee Iacocca's autobiography, he states:

"It took me a number of years to fully understand why I had to make a good confession to a priest before I went to Holy Communion, but in my teens I began to appreciate the importance of this most misunderstood right of the Catholic Church. In later years, I found myself completely refreshed after confession. I even began to attend weekend retreats where the Jesuits in face-to-face examinations of conscience made me come to grips with how I was conducting my life."[68]

Years later Iacocca became president of Chrysler, and in financial need went to Congress for assistance. Because he'd displayed obedient servitude to the Jesuits, another Catholic obedient to the Jesuits, Speaker of the House, Thomas" Tip" O'Neill flexed his power and got Lee Iacocca all the money he needed.

These are only a few who knew or were involved. Those who witnessed the assassination and those who knew the circumstances around it have conveniently died untimely deaths. Jean Hill reports that she has experienced several attempts on her and her children's life.

Jim Marrs, author of *Crossfire: The Plot That Killed Kennedy*, wrote: "In the three-year period which followed the murder of President Kennedy and Lee Harvey Oswald, 18 material witnesses died - six by gunfire, three in motor accidents, two by suicide, one from a cut throat, one from a karate chop to the neck, five from natural causes."...A mathematician hired by the London Sunday Times in February of

---

67   Charles Crenshaw, *JFK: Conspiracy of Silence*, Penguin Books USA, p. 106.

68   *Iacocca: An Autobiography*, Bantam Books, p. 8.

1967 concluded that the odds of the number of witnesses involved in the assassination of John F. Kennedy dying between November 22, 1963 and that date were 100,000 trillion to one . . . . In the time period ranging from November 22, 1963 to August 1993 over 115 witnesses have died or fallen victim to death by strange circumstances, suicides or murder.[69]

Lee Harvey Oswald was murdered by Jack Ruby, aka Jacob Rubenstein, who operated strip clubs and dance halls in Dallas, Texas. He also had ties with the Mafia and a cordial relationship with a number of Dallas Police Officers, which involved favors for leniency in the monitoring of his businesses. He on November 24, 1963, without restriction, hindrance or resistance entered the downtown police station basement, while Oswald was being escorted by department authorities to a more "secure jail," and emerged from a crowd of press and lunged toward Oswald, shooting him with a close range shot to the upper left side of his abdomen with a .38 revolver. The pistol Ruby used was reported to have been given to him by a Dallas police officer at some time prior.

Jack Ruby pled his innocence on the grounds that he was so grief-stricken with Kennedy's murder that he suffered "psychomotor epilepsy" and shot Oswald unconsciously. He was found guilty of "murder with malice" and sentenced to die. However, in October of 1966 the Texas Court of Appeals reversed the decision on the grounds of improper admission of testimony and that Ruby couldn't have had a fair trial in Dallas at the time.

Ruby died in 1967 of lung cancer while in a Dallas hospital awaiting a new trial. Suggestions are that there was a double conspiracy and Ruby was hired to kill Oswald so he didn't have a chance to talk. If true, then Jack Ruby's payoff took care of his family after his death. Ruby knew he had a short time to live and thus had nothing to lose. Oswald declared his innocence to the shooting that killed President Kennedy and on at least one occasion exclaimed: "I'm a patsy!"

Thomas Jefferson warned that a paragon of conduct seen in our leaders should be interpreted as a conspiracy when he wrote: "Single

---

69   Craig Roberts and John Armstrong, *JFK: The Dead Witnesses*, Consolidated Press, p. 3.

acts of tyranny may be ascribed to the accidental opinion of a day; but a series of oppressions, begun at a distinguished period and pursued unalterably through every change of ministers, too plainly prove a deliberate, systematical plan of reducing us to slavery."[70]

---

70   The Works of Thomas Jefferson, Vol. 1, p.130.

CHAPTER 16

What About the Protestants?

The Protestants have down through the years, pointed their finger to the Catholic Church for all its faults, deceptions, and violence, while viewing themselves to be, at least pure of heart and intent. Each sect and denomination prides themselves to be "the way" and sits confident in their doctrine.

They believe they have washed themselves clean through the blood of Christ and are on their way to heaven. They love to tell the story of Martin Luther and his brave stance against the church with his 95 theses. Many sermons are fervently preached in Martin Luther's honor. He is given great credit for the initiating of the Protestant Reformation and how it all began. Martin Luther and others such as Tyndale, Wycliffe, and other reformers are mentors and laid a path for Protestants to follow as an example of faith. However, upon closer examination it might tell us different and not to follow too closely.

Many centuries of Catholic indoctrination had not been so easily eradicated by these men. Ideas, doctrines, and views handed down from their mother church were deeply embedded into the minds and the emotional makeup of the masses. And these ideas did not vanish simply because a reformation was born. The Protestants had been impregnated with many corrupt doctrines, including the spirit of anti-Semitism. This spirit of hate would create a holocaust of the greatest magnitude in the history of the world.

Martin Luther took a drastic turn from his position of charity or love to a position of absolute hatred directed toward the Jew. Because he had already been accepted and established in the minds of the

Protestants of Europe, he had their ear. When Hitler came on the scene he read and embraced Luther's thoughts, ideas and statements.

The multitudes of Protestants had been exposed for centuries to the demeaning treatment and remarks of the Jewish people and had been so conditioned that Hitler's anti-Semitic approach made no impression of ill will toward the Jews. Their conscience was seared and made numb.

Hitler quoted Martin Luther's writings and statements and implemented his opinions and ideas. It was easy for Hitler to advance in his corrupt extermination of the Jews; the people were already mentally brain washed with the poison and conditioned to accept it.

Initially, Martin Luther had respected the Jews and defended them. He condemned anti-Semitism and made public speeches and wrote articles on their behalf. The following is an essay "That Jesus Christ was Born a Jew" by Martin Luther in 1523.

If I had been a Jew and had seen such dolts and blockheads govern and teach the Christian faith, I would sooner have become a hog than a Christian. They have dealt with the Jews as if they were dogs rather than human beings; they have done little else than deride them and seize their property. When they baptize them they show them nothing of Christian doctrine or life, but only subject them to popishness and mockery...If the apostles, who also were Jews, had dealt with us Gentiles as we Gentiles deal with the Jews, there would never have been a Christian among the Gentiles...When we are inclined to boast of our position (as Christians) we should remember that we are but Gentiles, while the Jews are of the lineage of Christ. We are aliens and in-laws; they are blood relatives, cousins, and brothers of our Lord. Therefore, if one is to boast of flesh and blood the Jews are actually nearer to Christ than we are . . . If we really want to help them, we must be guided in our dealings with them not by papal law but by the law of Christian love. We must receive them cordially, and permit them to trade and work with us, that they may have occasion and opportunity to associate with us, hear out Christian teaching, and witness our Christian life. If some of them should prove stiff-necked, what of it? After all, we ourselves are not all good Christians either.

Luther had made unsuccessful attempts to convert the Jews of Germany, and he became agitated, embarrassed, then furious and ultimately obsessed with their destruction. He began campaigning against the Jews in Saxony, Brandenburg, and Silesia. Following his campaign in Saxony, the Elector of Saxony, John Frederick, issued a mandate prohibiting Jews from conducting business, inhabiting or even to pass through his province.

Luther wrote books condemning the Jews and said that whoever would help the Jews was doomed to perdition and other Lutheran pastors who read his material adopted his views.

Robert Michael, a European History Professor, writes that a Lutheran pastor in Hochfelden gave a sermon arguing that his parishioners should murder Jews, "They are our public enemies. They do not stop blaspheming our Lord Christ, calling the Virgin Mary a whore, Christ, a bastard, and us changelings or abortions. If they could kill us all, they would gladly do it. They do it often, especially those who pose as physicians-though sometimes they help-for the devil helps to finish it in the end. They can also practice medicine as in French Switzerland. They administer poison to someone from which he could die in an hour, a month, a year, ten or twenty years. They are able to practice this art."

This type of preaching infected the minds of the people and helped to pave the way for the rise and acceptance of Hitler and the Nazi's move to annihilate the Jews.

In 1543, Luther wrote and published *On the Jews and Their Lies*. Within its contents were harsh statements such as:

Jews are a base, whoring people, that is, no people of God, and their boast of lineage, circumcision, and law must be accounted as filth. They are full of the devil's feces . . . which they wallow in like swine. The synagogue was a defiled bride, yes, an incorrigible whore and an evil slut. . . . Their synagogues and schools should be set on fire, their prayer books destroyed, rabbis forbidden to preach, homes razed, and property and money confiscated. They should be shown no mercy or kindness, afforded no legal protection, and these poisonous envenomed worms should be drafted into forced labor or expelled for all time. We are at fault for not slaying them.

Martin Luther even attacked the prophet Jeremiah in his writings: "Jeremiah you wretched heretic, you seducer and false prophet." Other outrageous statements and claims were made by Martin Luther in which he says, "Jewish history was assailed by much heresy, and Christ the logos swept away the Jewish heresy and goes on to do so as it still does daily before our eyes." Also. He says, "Jewish Prayer is blasphemous and a lie, and vilifies Jews in general as being spiritually blind and surely possessed by all devils."

In *Christian History* magazine, an article was written on Martin Luther in their 39th issue, 1993 published by *Christianity Today* are quotes of Luther which has influenced not only the Lutheran churches but all Protestant churches.

"Set fire to their synagogues and schools, Jewish houses should be razed and destroyed, and Jewish prayer books and Talmudic writings, in which such idolatry, lies, curing, and blasphemy are taught, (should) be taken from them. Their rabbis (should) be forbidden to teach on pain of loss of life and limb."

Luther counseled government officials and clergy to implement these actions. Luther met criticism over this and his friends begged him to stop his anti-Semitic apprises. In spite of this, Luther continued in his assertions in various literatures. He fabricated lies making statements such as: Jews killed Christian babies, declared them dogs, said they murdered Christ over and over by stabbing the Eucharist hosts and even accused them of poisoning wells.

He encouraged the safe conduct on the highways to be completely abolished for Jews and that all cash, treasure, silver and gold be taken from them. He said "What Jews can do is have a flail, an ax, a hole, a spade put into their hands so young, strong Jews and Jewesses could earn their bread in the sweat of their brow." He set the stage for the Holocaust in feeding his poison into the people and into the state authorities. He was their pattern, their blue print excepted as one of, if not the, greatest reformers and moralists in Christian history.

Martin Luther had become so obsessed (or was it possessed) in his Jewish hatred that his last breathing words, spewed out upon his death bed was: "We are at fault for not slaying them!"

Christianity played a prominent role in the Holocaust, as Hitler drew from the already planted hatred toward the Jews and was able to gain much popularity and support with his quotes of Luther. He took from his ideas as his own wretched approach to the demise of the Jews and advancement of Nazism. World War II added another ugly mark on the face of Christianity and admittedly it is to its shame.

There are some today who still deny or will not admit these facts, but it is difficult to deny or hide what are documented, historical facts on record. Lucy Dawidowicz, an American historian, in her book, writes, "both Luther and Hitler were obsessed by the demonologies universe inhabited by Jews, with Hitler asserting that the later Luther, the author of On the Jews and Their Lies was the "real Luther." She states that: "the line of anti-Semitic descent from Luther to Hitler is easy to draw."

The *Volkischer Beobachter*, a German, newspaper, on August 25,1933 quoted Hitler's education minister, Bernhard Rust, as saying, "Since Martin Luther closed his eyes, no such son of our people has appeared again. It has been decided that we shall be the first to witness his reappearance . . . I think the time is past when one may not say the names of Hitler and Luther in the same breath. They belong together; they are of the same old stamp."

A leader of the Protestant League, Fahrenhorst, called Luther "the first German spiritual Fuhrer who spoke to all Germans regardless of clan or confession." Also in a letter to Hitler, Fahrenhorst said that "his old fighters were mostly Protestants and that it was precisely in the Protestant regions of our Fatherland in which Nazism found its greatest strength." He invited Hitler to become the official patron of the Luthertag, a Luther Day festivity.

It seems ironic that Protestants supported Hitler and his Nazism when he himself is noted as a Catholic and all historic indication points to the Catholic Jesuit maneuvers for the war. But we need to remember that all sides are played in the political arena keeping the truth disguised and hidden and the masses confused.

God used the Second World War to inspire the Jews to return to their homeland. Multitudes of European Jewish people returned and Israel was established as a state in 1948. This became a wonderful miracle. There has never in history been a people who were cast from their land without becoming a diminished people. Yet after 2,000 years, the Jews not only survived as a people but returned to the land from which they were cast from. This is none other than the work of our Lord.

Changes within the church world and the major nations of the world also emerged from the war. Today the Protestant churches are heavily involved in various movements, societies, clubs, and politics. They are a part of the ecumenical movement, the World Council of Churches (WCC), the National Council of Churches (NCC), and the New World Order (NWO). Many pastors, ministers, and members of churches belong to the Masons and or Freemasons and many embrace and practice within their congregations the New Age form of worship which envelops all religions of the world.

Although it is true that the church first fell into "darkness" by the aid of Catholicism it is equally true that the gospel of Christ was already suffering distortion some 200 years before Constantine and the idea of his universalism (Catholicism) with one man as head was introduced. The apostles warned the early believers that the church was entering into darkness. In order to make a point I will again quote verses of warnings.

In talking to the elders of the church of Ephesus Paul said: "Therefor take heed to yourselves and to all the flock, among which the Holy Spirit has made you overseers, to shepherd the church of God, which He purchased with His own blood."

"For I know this, that after my departure savage wolves will come in among you, not sparing the flock."

"Also from among yourselves men will rise up, speaking perverse things, to draw away the disciples after themselves."

"Therefore watch, and remember, that for three years I did not cease to warn everyone night and day with tears" (Acts 20:28–30).

Paul stated here that he knows that the people are going to be drawn away. he states that it will be men of their own selves, drawing away disciples after themselves. How easy it must have been to deceive and subvert truth with the stolen waters and secret bread (Prov. 9:17) when you have people you have been worshiping with, praying with, sharing meals with et cetera, who love and trust you.

"But I fear, lest somehow, as the serpent deceived Eve by his craftiness, so your minds may be corrupted from the simplicity that is in Christ. For if he who comes preaches another Jesus whom we have not preached, or if you receive a different spirit, which you have not received, or a different gospel, which you have not accepted, you may well put up with it" (2 Cor. 11:3, 4).

Here Paul declares if the Corinthian believers receive and accept another gospel, spirit or another Jesus, you might well put up with it. In other words, you are ideally putting up with it or might as well give your permission to the doctrine.

The apostle John was the only apostle who died at an old age. His life was preserved until the end of the first century. It is estimated that he was 95 years of age when the Lord took him. He, when still a young man, walked with Christ and heard first hand his teachings. He experienced the love of Christ in a profound way and gained the reputation as the "apostle of love". The Lord kept John as witness and speaker for the things to come upon the church and the nations. John, before being exiled to Patmos Isle, was the overseer of the seven churches of Asia which Christ addressed. Jesus revealed himself to John and told him to write the things he's seen, the things that are, and the things which take place after this (Rev. 1:19). He was to write them unto the angels of the seven churches of Asia.

Jesus addressed and prophesied both the problems and the righteousness of the churches. He made it clear that he was aware of those things that were right and good amongst them but to most warned them of where they had fallen and that they must repent and to the others to hold to the faith.

The accounts are all given in Revelation 2 and 3. Ephesus was told they had left their first love and to repent from where they have fallen. Smyrna was told some would be cast into prison, have tribulation and to remain faithful. Pergamos was told that He (Christ) had a few things against them because they held the doctrine of Balaam and also the doctrines of the Nicolaitans, which He hates, they were warned to repent. Thyatira had Jezebel and her teachings and were warned that those that kept her doctrines would be destroyed, those that did not to hold fast till he comes. Sardis was told that what they had was ready to die and their works were not perfect. Philadelphia was one that they had a little strength, kept His word, and not denied His name. Philadelphia and Smyrna were the only churches that Christ had given encouragement to and told to hold on to what they had. Laodicea was neither hot nor cold in their faith but were lukewarm or indifferent because of "being increased in goods" having a lofty attitude. Christ said He would spew them from His mouth because they were lukewarm.

There are many ideas pertaining to these churches. Some consider that Yeshua was addressing primarily the Jews because of His references to them and because Constantine usurped authority over that area of the world making it Catholic. Others that He was addressing only those churches and what would become of them. Some consider that the change in the spiritual condition of the church down through the centuries are represented. While others consider the message to be for all believers at all times. I tend to hold to the latter.

All seven churches were located in what is now known as Turkey. When John wrote Revelation, that area was a province of Rome known as Byzantium. Constantine made it the Roman capital called Constantinople and it became the nerve center of the Roman Empire. He erected a column in Constantinople and enclosed its base with a statue of Athena and baskets said to have held the bread Christ fed his disciples. Asia was a blend of Christianity and paganism.

Rome introduced a vast number of legal opinions that were sometimes contradictory. In 528, the emperor Justinian appointed a commission of ten men who classified the Roman emperors' written constitution into 4,652 laws. (And many of us say the 613 that God gave Israel were too numerous to keep; it is estimated the US, combining federal and state, has over 2,000,000)

Within the context of these laws were sound civil laws; however, the criminal laws were barbaric in nature. The Christian jurists made crimes of heresy and seduction. So-called heretics were barred from holding office and denied their inheritance. One sentenced for seducing was automatically executed and his victim if she consented. If her chaperone encouraged the union, molten lead was poured in her mouth. Even though this legal system of Justinian was cruel it became the model for most of Europe's legal systems.

The Byzantines considered themselves to be the chosen people of God and their emperor was considered to rule by divine right. Mysticism flourished with monasticism and by the fifth century they spread into Western Europe. There were monks living in cities, caves, deserts and remote islands who influenced the ideas of the empire.

In the interim, barbarian leaders Alaric, Attila, Clovis, and Theodoric attacked Italy and other areas throughout the Roman Empire and demolished the ruling class and the Byzantine Empire rose to power. It remained in control of the empire for over one thousand years. There was constant rivalry between the eastern and western churches, a constant struggle for power within the empire and a decline in commerce and trade weakening the empire. However, what brought them down was the Muslim Ottoman Empire. Rome had been competing with Constantinople for rights over the people and that the Byzantine Empire should be subject to the Roman See's divinely chosen primacy. With the Ottoman Empire conquering, growing more powerful and expanding, the competition became obsolete and the Muslim faith gradually swallowed Catholicism and any form of Christianity.

The seven churches became non-existent. Ephesus had been all but completely annihilated by an earthquake, others were lost through battles or deserted. Christ's prophetic warnings came to pass and their candlesticks were indeed removed. But still there has always been a remnant that will not bow down and these became the woman which had a place prepared for her in the wilderness.

The first split from the Roman Catholic Church was in 1054 when the Eastern Orthodox Church split off. Then of course in the sixteenth century the Protestant split. The Protestants then splintered into many varied denominations.

The word *ecumenical* comes from the Greek word *oikoumene*, meaning "the inhabited earth." The ecumenical movement has ancient roots, but its maturity began in the twentieth century and flowed over into the politics of nations across the world.

Serbia, during World War II, was considered a friend and ally to the United States. Serbia had delayed Russia's invasion by Hitler for five weeks, which ultimately spared the world. Hitler had prepared to invade the Soviet Union with the largest force in the world's history during spring of 1941. The invasion was being supported with supplies of oil by Rockefeller's Standard Oil Company and trucks by Ford Motor Company. But the Serbia constraint altered the advance. Yugoslavia sided with the allies, infuriating Hitler, and he responded by the invasion and bombing of the country.

The Ecumenical Movement

In 1958, the Jesuits initiated the ecumenical movement within the United States and other countries around the world. However, before they could accomplish this they needed to remove their opposition. That opposition was none other than Pope Pius XII who had declared "war to the death with all of Rome's enemies" and would *never* except the ecumenical movement. Pope Pius XII died a sudden death by poisoning and was replaced with Pope John XXIII, who commenced the Vatican Council II, aka, the ecumenical movement.

The Latin Mass was halted and the claim that there is no salvation outside of the Church of Rome was dismissed and any and all religions would be received in heaven as long as they exercised sincerity. The Vatican II Council's doctrine of ecumenism includes sincere Communists to Muslims, atheists to all Christian faiths, Jews, and every "sincere" faith, even witchcraft. Ecumenism does not embrace the teachings of Christ. "I am the way, the truth and the life. No one comes to the father except through Me" (John 14:6). It is appealing because it does embrace a civil humanistic behavior to those who have beliefs, social, religious or political that differ from one another.

Christ himself taught us to love our neighbor and even our enemies. He never taught us to war against them or force them through severe punishments to submit to our doctrine. But what does that have to do with the fact that there is only one way and that way is through Jesus (Yeshua)? Isn't it simply the way one ought to conduct themselves in societies regardless of the other?

So why, after hundreds of years of wars, opposition, and persecution should there be a change of heart? Because it isn't a change of heart but rather a change of method. With the Vatican II Council, the Catholic Church no longer refers the Protestants as heretics, but they are referred to as "separated brethren," which to most Protestants is accepted as an expression of unity. Nonetheless, the primary goal in ecumenism is to gather in the "lost sheep" or "separated brethren" under one principle: the pope. The primary goal of the Protestant is to become "one in Christ." Therefore, ecumenism is welcomed as a path to the almighty.

Great is the deception of the ecumenical movement. With the Vatican II Council, there were hundreds of monasteries closed and the monks were instructed that they should join the United States military and the United States government. Multitudes of nunneries were also shut down and the nuns were instructed to become teachers within the public-school systems, even though the public-school systems had previously been condemned by the "Syllabus of Errors" identified by Pope Pius IX.

Today, because of the ecumenical movement, Yugoslavia again in 1999 was attacked just like Hitler attacked. but this time by the Pentagon. "Operation Allied Force" killed anything and everything that moved in Serbia. Most being women and children. The bombing from "Operation Allied Force" lasted from March 24 until June 10. It was a massacre carried out by our own Pentagon because the press painted them as monsters and accused them of committing atrocities against the Kosovo Albanians.

There were hospitals and embassies of foreign countries bombed, which, according to international law, is an act of war against that country. Adding to this military episode, the Pentagon bombed the Chinese embassy in Belgrade on May 7, 1999, causing the death of four diplomats.

What was the reason for this massacre? Serbia's resistance to NATO (North Atlantic Treaty Organization) aggression or the NWO (New World Order) imperialism.

After this, Iraq, a former ally was targeted. Created by the British in 1920 after the defeat of the Ottoman Empire, the United

States maintained a good rapport with Iraq. That was only until the establishment of Israel as a state in 1948.

It was on January 16, 1943 that Iraq declared war on not only Germany, but Italy and Japan. The signing of this declaration was done by the Foreign Minister Abdul llah Hafidh. In Washington, Iraqi minister Ali Jawdat officially informed Secretary of State Cordell Hull. Among the grounds cited for the action in a long communication to the Department of State were Germany's interference in the domestic affairs of Iraq and its fomenting of rebellion against the government. Six days later, Iraq adhered to the Declaration of the United Nations, January 1, 1942, in a notification to Secretary Hull. Iraq was the thirtieth nation to do so.[71]

The main reason Iraq was attacked was their refusal to acknowledge and accept the state of Israel. This rejection was inconvenient to the Jesuits who, remember, control the Pentagon and they turned Iraq into a literal hell on earth.

May 11, 1949, Flushing Meadows, New York. The UN General Assembly voted to admit Israel to the United Nations as the fifty-ninth member. Iraq was one of six Arab nations that walked out in protest immediately after the balloting.[72]

Bob Woodward a Washington insider and investigator sheds light in his book *Plan of Attack*,

> *As Tim leads a team of CIA operatives in northern Iraq, Bush's war cabinet searches for a casus belli, a reason for attacking Iraq that the world community will accept. Saddam is unpopular and feared even in the Muslim world, having massacred minority Kurds and Shiites in Iraq and thumbed his nose at the U.N. by expelling inspectors who verified that he destroyed all weapons of mass destruction (WMD) developed and used in the past. Cheney mentally links Saddam's WMD capability with al-Qaeda's track record for terrorism, and, despite the CIA's evidence, turns it into a fact. Bush buys into the syllogism and elevates his rhetoric, proclaiming an "Axis of Evil" exists among Iraq, Iran, and North Korea. Congress, as it had in*

---

71   Henry E. Mattox, *A Chronology of United States-Iraqi Relations*, 1920–2006 p. 25.

72   Ibid. p. 32.

1991, authorizes use of force against Iraq and Bush's conservative base demands swift action. Propriety and international pressure demand the U.S. make an effort at finding a diplomatic solution, however, and Powell is tasked with presenting the case before the Security Council, resulting in Resolution 1441. The two-stage process begins with the return of U.N. inspectors to Iraq to determine if Saddam has complied with previous demands. If he hasn't, there must be debate with the U.N.'s response. Cheney is chagrined and Bush's patience wears out. Tim, meanwhile, has succeeded in penetrating Saddam's security and military organizations, allowing Franks' final plan to be swifter and more effective.[73]

Excerpts from Bob Woodward's *Plan of Attack* record the following:

"The war on terrorism is going O.K.; we are hunting down al Qaeda one-by-one," Bush began. "The biggest threat, however, is Saddam Hussein and his weapons of mass destruction. He can blow up Israel and that would trigger an international conflict.[74]

Bush had 18 more House members to the Cabinet Room on Thursday, September 26. He opened by saying the last thing he wanted was to put troops in harm's way "Believe me, I don't like hugging the widows."

Launching into a familiar indictment of the Iraqi leader, he said, "Saddam Hussein is a terrible guy who is teaming up with al Qaeda. He tortures his own people and hates Israel."[75]

"If I decide to deal militarily with the situation in Iraq, it will mean the end of the current regime-nothing short of that." The president said he wanted to create a new Iraqi government that represented all the different religious and ethnic factions of Iraq. "The main goal is not really the return of inspectors to Iraq, but to make sure that Iraq has no weapons of mass destruction that could pose a threat to the kingdom and/or to Israel." Bush added that when he made up his mind on the military option, he would contact the crown prince prior to his final decision.[76]

---

73   Bob Woodward, *Plan of Attack* - his summary of his book.

74   Ibid, p. 186.

75   Ibid, p. 188.

76   Ibid. p. 230.

There were many bogus Jews who had in fact both financed and fought for Hitler. But when Hitler began losing the war. The Jesuit general ordered the Nazis to cast some of those same bogus Jews into concentration camps to create a superb propaganda for the founding of the state of Israel.

Remember, the Jesuits want the Jews all in one place for easy annihilation. Our Heavenly Father however, has other plans.

"Behold, the day of the LORD (Yahweh) is coming, and your spoil will be divided in your midst."

"For I will gather all the nations to battle against Jerusalem; the city shall be taken, the houses rifled, and the women ravished. Half of the city shall go into captivity, but the remnant of the people shall not be cut off from the city,'

"Then the LORD (Yahweh) will go forth, and fight against those nations, as He fights in the day of battle."

"And in that day His feet will stand on the Mount of Olives, which faces Jerusalem on the east, and the Mount of Olives shall be split in two from east and to west, making a very large valley; Half of the mountain shall move toward the north, and half of it toward the south."

"Then you shall flee through My mountain valley, for the mountain valley shall reach to Azal. Yes, you shall flee, as you fled from the earthquake in the days of Uzziah king of Judah. Thus the LORD (Yahweh) my God (Elohim) will come, and all the saints with You" (Zech. 14:1–5).

Ecumenism is a subject of disagreement. There are two major bodies considered. The World Council of Churches and the National Council of Churches. The purpose of the Ecumenical Movement is to bring all denominations, cults, and such together as a one world religion. The motto of the first Ecumenical Assembly that was held in Amsterdam in 1948 was "One World One Church." This became an excepted term to define and represent the ecumenical goal. One of the major issues the WCC labors over is of all religious organizations and all ideologies and the relationship they have with the churches.

Though not a member, the Roman Catholic Church maintains an intimate relationship with the WCC. In the Ecumenical Vatican Council of 1962–1965, they revised their liturgy in an attempt to bring their "separated brethren" back to their fold.

Booklets are being distributed to Catholic laymen on "ecumenical etiquette." Each year millions of leaflets, "Week of Prayer for Christian Unity" are distributed. Catholics and Protestants are having joint communion services. They undertake joint projects for social activities, and even have joint folk-singing programs. One of the biggest drives toward unity is the amalgamation of Catholic and Protestant seminaries. For the first time in history Roman Catholic churches are joining the church councils of Americas cities. The leaders of World Council and the leaders of Rome are working together for a union of these two bodies. No fewer than thirty-nine representatives of Protestant churches have been received by the pope. The Archbishop of Canterbury was the first Anglican primate to visit a pope in four hundred years. Official Roman Catholic documents are beginning to use the term *church* to describe Protestant churches. A Lutheran professor has urged all Protestants to reunite with Roman Catholicism, which he described as their "ecclesiastical homeland."[77]

With the ecumenical movement ushering in a World Church, it will bring with it the acceptance of the pope as its head. In 1972, Michael Ramsey preached at Saint Patrick's Cathedral in Manhattan. Terence Cardinal Cooke and Archbishop Iakovos of the Greek Church of North and South America attended the service. In Ramsey's message he said, "I can foresee the day when all Christians might accept the pope as presiding bishop. Perspectives change, and we must give the bag a good shake and see what happens."

The popular evangelical Billy Graham was quoted in a German newspaper as saying, "that it would be a great tragedy if the ecumenical policies of the late Pope John were reversed. Pope John brought an entirely new era to the world. It would be a great tragedy if the cardinals elect a pope who would react against the policies of Pope John and bring back the walls between the Christian faiths."

---

77   *The Ecumenical Movement* by H. Duncan.

From all appearances, we are living in the last days and prophecy tells us that there will be a joining of churches under the headship of one man. "And in that day seven women shall take hold of one man, saying, we will eat our own food, and wear our own apparel: only let us be called by your name, to take away our reproach" (Isa. 4:1).

Let's take a close look at this. Women in the Bible represent churches. The number seven represents completion. So you have all (complete) the churches taking hold of one man (leader). Food represents doctrine and apparel is their covering. Therefore, they want to keep their doctrine and the covering which comes from their organizational government but be called by his name. In other words, take on his nature and operate with his authority. Why? To take away their reproach.

The shame of leaving their "mother church" and receive favor from men and the nations. This is none other than the woman of Revelation 17. "Mystery Babylon, the Great, the Mother of Harlots and Abominations of the Earth." This is a difficult saying. No one wants to admit that they are, metaphorically speaking, a harlot . . . or the mother of harlots.

From its beginning the papacy has taken great, and frequently brutal measures to establish its kingdom in the world. The pope is considered the "Vicar of Christ" and to be infallible. The popes are not successors to the Apostle Peter as they claim. They are actually successors to Constantine. They have followed his example, which is for the purpose of establishing their own kingdom, and hundreds of thousands have been brutally massacred. Still many continued to resist with protestation the church of Rome and spread the truth in God's word, making their attempt of reformation.

With the numbers of those resisting heretics growing, a Counter-Reformation became necessary, and the Jesuits arrived on the scene at the right time. They were commissioned by the pope to end the Protestant Reformation by any means available.

The Jesuit Constitution of 1540 states,

Let whoever desires to fight under the sacred banner of the Cross, and to serve only God and the Roman pontiff, His vicar on earth, after a solemn vow of perpetual chastity, let him keep in mind that he is part of a society, instituted for the purpose of perfecting souls in life and in Christian doctrine, for the propagation of the faith...Let all members know, and let it be not only at the beginning of their profession, but let them think over it daily as long as they live, that the society as a whole, and each of them, owes obedience to our most holy lord, the pope, and the other Roman pontiffs, his successors, and to fight with faithful obedience for God.

The Jesuit today may not be torturing and murdering Protestants or anyone else if they do not convert to Catholicism, yet the objective remains. The determination to bring the lost brethren back has not changed but rather the methods used to accomplish this has. In today's world, with the exception of groups such as the Islamic Isis and such, torturing and murdering is no longer tolerated. So, what action or method is used today?

The method today is the Jesuit spirituality. The Jesuits have been consistent with their influence using their mystical prayer practice and the "spiritual exercises" initiated and taught by Ignatius Loyola.

We further have today the "Eucharist Evangelization" to draw people to the Eucharist Christ. A Jesuit priest, Anthony De Mello, has written *Sadhana, A way to God.* He embraces the Hindu mysticism and has written, "To silence the mind is an extremely difficult task. How hard it is to keep the mind from thinking, thinking, thinking, forever thinking, forever producing thoughts in a never-ending stream. Our Hindu masters in India have a saying: one thorn is removed by another. By this they mean that you will be wise to use one thought to rid yourself of all the other thoughts that crowd into your mind. One thought, one image, one phrase or sentence or word that your mind can be made to fasten on.2

An excerpt from, Ray Yungen, in his book *A Time of Departing*, 3 explains that Sadhana, "is very open in its acknowledgment of Eastern mysticism as an enrichment to Christian spirituality."

It doesn't take a long search to find De Mello within the evangelical/Protestant camp. In fact, Richard Foster, one of the pioneers of the evangelical spiritual formation (contemplative) movement wrote the introduction to one of De Mello's books, *The Sacrament of the Present Moment.* In *A Glimpse of Jesus*, popular contemplative author Brennan

Manning quotes De Mello. Amazon shows that De Mello's book, *The Sacrament of the Present Moment* is cited in 82 books, some of which are written by some of evangelicalism's most popular authors, including John Ortberg, Richard Foster, Jan Johnson, Philip Yancey, and Calvin Miller. Incidentally, all these are contemplative advocates.

Another example of Jesuit influence in the evangelical/Protestant church is the *Be Still* DVD, where Richard Foster quotes eighteenth-century Jesuit priest Jean Nicholas Grou as saying, "O Divine Master, teach me this mute language which says so much." This "mute language" Grou speaks of is the mystical "silence" practiced by contemplatives and mystics throughout all religions.

Leonard Sweet is a major component of the new progressive Christianity. In his book *Quantum Spirituality*, he writes, "Mysticism, once cast to the sidelines of the Christian tradition, is now situated in postmodernist culture near the center."

In recent years there has been a "new age" movement within the Protestant churches which promotes a "new age" form of worship. The music is slanted toward ecumenism with melody and lyrics. It is difficult to hear the lyrics on most of the faster beats however, on the slower beats one can hear the message of "uniting" in the lyrics. The spirit is conveyed through music and can be extremely influential.

As long as Protestants and/or evangelicals engage in mysticism practice through song praise and prayer, ultimately, through method of thought control, the goal of the Jesuits will be accomplished.

With this "new age" movement comes the acceptance of secular designed worship as well. We can see that even within Pentecostal denominations such as Assemblies of God. You find the music worship being conducted with a secular presentation resembling a rock band performance. Although it is primarily engaged in by the youth, the adults condone and also participate with them. When asked the reason for condoning this behavior, the pastor or other clergy respond with an exclamation that is hardly acceptable. Usually it's "this is what they want and if we don't have what they want, they will leave. We need to please the people." This type of remark is based on the idea of the greater the numbers, the greater the money.

The New Age movement is one of the largest religions of the world. Their belief is that in order to enter into an age of "enlightenment" (age of Aquarius), the world needs to become "vibrationally sympathetic," which means that the population masses need to engage in *mystical* prayer. They are receptive to all forms of mystic religions in order to seek and find God.

Ecumenism on the surface would appear to be a great accomplishment for mankind. The idea of everyone coming together in unity is very appealing. It could change the entire mind of the planet. Wars would end, famine would end and we would all finally be one - "brethren" with a common goal. "Peace on earth and goodwill toward men." Sounds heavenly, except they would not be one in Christ. They would be one with the woman (church) riding the beast of religious civil governments.

The National and World Council of Churches, already sit on the back of government. The message is one of peace and unity. There are over 560 million people, and counting, that are represented by the WCC and at least 349, and counting, Anglican, Orthodox and other Protestant denominations that hold membership in about 110 nations and territories around the globe. Under the pretense of "The Kingdom of God" they are actually promoting socialism and communism.

The WCC was founded in Amsterdam with 147 denominations in 1948. It had as its members both Protestant and Orthodox. Today their headquarters is located in Geneva Switzerland. Their main purpose is to bring all churches into a unity of one faith and one Eucharistic fellowship called Ecumenisms. A One-World Religion

The doctrinal bases of the WCC states: "The World Council of Churches is a fellowship of Churches which confess the Lord Jesus Christ as God and Savior according to the scriptures and therefore seek to fulfill together their common calling to the glory of the one God, Father, Son and Holy Spirit." Not an objectionable statement yet further it states: "Since the World Council of Churches is not itself a church, it passes no judgment upon the sincerity with which member churches accept the basis."[78] In other words, regardless of your sincerity,

---

78   "The Truth About the World Council of Churches" by L'isbeth Noelle Roth, http://www.apfn.org/apfn/WCC.htm.

beliefs, or stance you can sign the WCC basis. You can be an excepted member even if you practice devil worship and slaughter animals! That hardly represents a unity in Christ. But note, they can eat their own food and wear their own apparel.

Jesus said, "I am the way, the truth and the life: no one comes to the Father, but through Me" (John 14:6).

"Every kingdom divided against itself is brought to "desolation; and a house divided against a house falls" (Luke 11:17).

And Paul states, "Do not be unequally yoked together with unbelievers. For what fellowship has righteousness with lawlessness? And what communion (partnership) has light with darkness? And what accord (trough for cattle) has Christ with Belial? (worthless, as an epithet of Satan) Or what part has a that believer with an unbeliever? And what agreement has the temple of God with idols? For you are the temple of the living God; As God has said, I Will Dwell in them, and walk among them. I will be their God, and they shall be My people. Therefore, come out from among them, and be separate, says the Lord, do not touch what is unclean, and I will receive you. I will be a father to you, and you shall be my sons and daughters, says the Lord Almighty" (2 Cor. 6:14–18).

In close scrutiny one cannot see how through ecumenisms you can reach the Father as it is not the way through Christ. But its members are unequally yoked and divided so that eventually it will have to crumble. They are open to receive any religion and/or cult that agrees with their purpose even if they disagree with the Word of God or do not believe in His Son.

Within the WCC are both pacifists and revolutionaries who try to alter the thinking of the other through their influence. Also, one hears frequent attacks on Western Imperialism and on Capitalism yet infrequently is there any remarks of criticism of Socialism or Communism. Again, you will hear attacks on non-communist dictatorships but not on communist dictatorships. The voice of conservatives is rarely heard and when heard they are never released as official statements to the world governments. According to Pastor Marion H. Reynolds, editor, *Foundation* magazine, Fundamental

Evangelistic Association, any Evangelicals within the WCC are there to be used as window dressing to hide the WCC apostasy.

The Salvation Army, the Irish Presbyterian Church, and a Lutheran Church in Germany suspended membership in protest to an $85,000 grant to a communist guerrilla group known as the Patriotic Front of Zimbabwe. This Front has bragged about murdering missionaries and shooting down a commercial airplane. The WCC charged the news media for misrepresentation that falsified the situation. If that were the case, then why did these organizations feel the need to suspend membership? The WCC Central Committee supported its PCR (Program to Combat Racism) Commission saying, "Although the adverse image and understanding of the PCR needs to be changed, the content and thrust of the PCR itself should not be changed."

Again, according to Pastor Marion H. Reynolds, over $3 million has been given to radical groups around the world and though the claim that all the monies come from gifts to fund designated, the PCR could not operate without the administrative offices and support of the WCC.

The commitment the WCC has to the creation of a "new society" socialistic in nature and function. A 1969 quote from the WCC General Secretary, Dr. Philip Potter, in the WCC Central Committee directive states: "We call upon the churches to move beyond charity, grants and traditional programming to relevant and sacrificial action leading to new relationships of dignity and justice among all men and to become the agents for the radical reconstruction of society." And clarifying what this means he stated: "But the conflict has become intense when it has been perceived that a radical change of economic, social and political structures are needed and not the mere prudential transfer of resources and technologies."

And in another WCC document it is stated: "In the developed countries it means changes in the production structure and employment policies which will only be possible through a certain socialization of decisions that have been taken autonomously on the basis of interests of the private sector."

The tension within the WCC has increased with the acceptance of homosexuality, acceptance of gays and lesbians for ordination and ordination of women.

The Roman Catholic Church works closely with the WCC, and although not a member, it has for about forty years cooperated with it. They commission and send observers to every meeting, assembly, and conference. The Vatican's Pontifical Council for Promoting Christian Unity nominates twelve members to the WCC's Faith and Order Commission as full members.

The WCC and the United Nations are closely tied together. It is the voice of the WCC which resonates in the ear of the U.N. not the individual believers and churches that may oppose the actions of the UN. The WCC stands behind disarmament and against US national security! To embrace the WCC's program for disarmament and its stance against military strength or militarism and the arms race would leave the US defenseless. But this is inconsistent with their insistence on national sovereignty and security for many new nations and governments formed through communist revolutions.

Today the WCC is careful with its terminology. Instead of using the alarming term "One Church" they say "conciliar fellowship" and "unity in reconciled diversity" or trying to "relate the right kind of diversity to the right kind of unity."

The WCC operates in opposition to the Word of God by ignoring the scriptures. The following is a quote from Marion H. Reynolds Jr., "At the very heart of the whole matter is the failure of the world council of churches to accept the Bible as the authoritative, infallible, inerrant, eternal, unchangeable Word of God. Note the following: "In the WCC we experience both the possibility for common confession of faith and worship together and also the obstacles to Christian unity. We are agreed in giving vital place in our thinking to Bible study and worship; we are able to worship our one Lord in the very different way of the churches represented among us. yet we are also aware of problems concerning the authority of the bible remaining unsolved among us and of the fact that we are yet part of one Eucharistic fellowship. It is not surprising therefore that there is controversy among Christians about the meditative use (rather than simply the intellectual study) of the holy books of other faiths and about the question of common worship between those of different faiths."

One speaker said, "The document on Hope coming out of Bangalore had succeeded in bringing out the fruitful tension between doctrinal unity and union in radical involvement in human hopes." But it has not settled the underlying question. "What is that underlying question? "The problem is no longer the problem of loving one another, but the problem of understanding the faith." The doctrinal basis of the WCC is an empty shell, a front to deceive the unwary. Only by accepting God's Word as our only, absolute and final authority can we enter into true unity with those who truly belong to Christ-and at the same time be fully separated from those who appear as angels of light but are in reality the servants of Satan."

Further revealed is the WCC's close relationship with the Roman Catholic Church. They now hold to the thought that we no longer attempt to convert souls from one another but rather seek unity and worship together.

The WCC denies they are pro-Communism yet they are one of the strongest allies of Communist nations. In the past they have worked with the National Council of Churches to bring the recognition of "Red China" by the US. Matt Costella of the Fundamental Evangelistic Association writes: WCC and NCC have a proven track record of leftist political and religious ideology and practice and are frequent yet sometimes subtle critics of capitalism and democracy. Bible believing Christians should have nothing to do with those churches, denominations and organizations that are a part of the WCC and or NCC.

Like many other organizations, until you take a close examination, the dogma and motive of the National Council of Churches (NCC) is not discernable. It was first founded as the Federal Council of Churches in 1908 at a convention which met at the Academy of Music in Philadelphia. By 1923 it had expanded its offices to New York City, Washington, DC, and Chicago.

It began with thirty-two ecumenical Protestant denominations, and in 1950 merged with other ecumenical Protestant denominations and changed their title to the National Council of Churches. It has a reputation of supporting radical causes and by admission in statements and actions are anti-Israel.

While accusing Christian Zionists of being the stumbling block of bringing peace to the Middle East, they refrain criticism of radical Islamist groups regardless of the number of brutal murders and be headings they commit.

The NCC has a history of supporting Communism. In February of 1968 at San Diego, California, the NCC held a General Assembly entitled "NCC Ministries and the Communist World." It was disclosed that $1,584,000 was given to Poland's Communist government through NCC's ministry which was identified as "Church World Service." Accordingly, it was received in the name of the Polish Ecumenical Council however, it was administered by the Communists for their purposes. Also from 1952 to 1967 there was given to the communist government of Yugoslavia food, clothing and other items which totaled over $40,000,000. All from the same source the "Church World Service." They paid to re-locate Brazilian Communists in Mexico in a "refugee program" as well.

Adding insult to injury, our US government, through a created organization called "Ocean Freight Refunds," donated over $23,000,000 between 1957–1960 to the NCC; yet oddly, the US government will not allow prayer in our schools!

The NCC exercises heavy involvement in politics. In fact, much more than in saving souls, so it would appear. During the 1968 General Assembly at San Diego the NCC placed demands on the U.S., which were to "stop the bombing of North Vietnam (as a prelude to seeking peace), avoid military actions against Communist China (as it appears to have a "legitimate" interest in Asia. Encourage the admission of Peking to the United Nations. Construe a means of cooperation between the US and the Communist countries of the Soviet Union, Eastern Europe, and Cuba. Also to give recognition to the Cuban government and the East German Republic. Further, they demanded removal of restrictions on imports from Communist countries and the US, including cultural exchanges.

The gospel of Marxist socialism had been planted and conceived in the seminaries and divinity schools, before the turn of the twentieth century, by the American theologians who had studied in both England and Germany then returned to America. They learned the method of conspiracy which had altered the spiritual and moral configuration of Europe. It was only a short time until there were conspirators developed in Americas clergies. One prominent Walter Rauschenbusch, who had graduated from Rochester Theological Seminary, was submerged in the Socialist principals of Luminism. Karl Marx, an atheist, said, "Luminism is really nothing else but Marxism." Rauschenbusch was both an Illuminist and a Marxist. He stated, "If ever socialism is to succeed, it cannot succeed in an irreligious country. It must start in the churches."

I remind you Ignatius Loyola is the father of Luminism and there are the Illuminati, the Jesuits, who work continually with conspiracy and embrace socialism/communism.

An excerpt from "The National Council of Churches, Apostasy" reads:

"By 1914 the Federal Council of Churches had become one of the major outlets in America for Marxist propaganda. On February tenth of that year a group of conspirators met in the home of millionaire industrialist Andrew Carnegie and laid plans for something called the Church Peace Union. Charles S. Macfarland (at the time General Secretary of the FCC) reveals that this group included only those religious leaders who were in some way connected with the Federal Council of Churches. This newly formed organization was the brainchild of top conspirator Andrew Carnegie, who used it to capture for the Insiders the controlling clique of the Federal Council by subsidizing the Church Peace Union to the tune of $2 million."[79]

"By 1935 Communist infiltration of religion in the United States was in full swing, presaging orders of the Seventh World Conference of the Comin tern at Moscow to maintain such subversion. On September 10, 1935, a Report on the FCC from the Office of Naval Intelligence was read into the Congressional Record, establishing that the Federal Council was one of several organizations which "give aid and comfort to the Communist movement and Party." Its leadership, the Intelligence Report revealed, "consists of a small radical group which dictates its

---

79   (Dr. R. J. Rushdoony, *Apostasy - The National Council of Churches.*

policy," and "it is always extremely active in any matter against national defense." In fact, the Chief of Naval Operations, Admiral William H. Standley, formally accused the FCC of collaborating with the Communists.

In a report that was issued in 1942 by the Commission to Study the Bases of a Just and Durable Peace, convention of the FCC called for "a world government of delegated powers. Complete abandonment of US isolationism. Strong immediate limitations on national sovereignty. International control of all armies and navies. A universal system of money. Worldwide freedom of immigration. Progressive elimination of all tariff and quota restrictions on world trade. A democratically controlled international bank. The chairman releasing this was John Foster Dulles, leader of the Federal Council of Churches.[80]

The summation of the FCC conference was:

"Many duties now performed by local and national governments can now be effectively carried out only by international authority. Individual nations . . . must give up their armed forces except for preservation of domestic order and allow the world to be policed by an international army and navy."[81]

The FCC was invited in 1945 to send delegates to the International Conference at San Francisco which founded the "United Nations." Alger Hiss a Communist agent, presided over this secret meeting and also served as a chairman of an important committee of the Federal Council of Churches, who bragged about their being the first to introduce the idea of a United Nations.

After the Federal Council of Churches gained new members and became the National Council of Churches, in 1954 the National Council of Churches pushed to terminate Bible reading in public schools. Through the years, the NCC submitted many proposals which were Communist in nature and received and collected monies for undermining agencies who gave aid to Communist Vietcong, and for promoting the Communists Vietnam Moratorium project.

It is incomprehensible that an organized group of Christian churches can sympathize with, yet alone, give monetary and political

80   Ibid.
81   Ibid.

support to communism. Communists are atheists! Trying to unite Christians and Communists is like trying to Unite God and Satan. They cannot mix!

What we are witnessing today is Protestantism within the NCC and the WCC being submerged into the Roman Church. It is not limited to the apostate Christianity. The Ecumenical Movement, aka, The New Age Movement is advancing on all the religions of the world and bringing them under the headship of the Roman Catholic Church. When they are all tied together along with the other "Abrahamic" religions, they will conclude the picture John saw in Revelations of "Mystery Babylon.

The "Beast" she rides on is none other than the civil governments or kingdoms and the waters are the peoples, tongues and nations. It cannot be ignored that the NCC, WCC, Ecumenicalism along with Roman Catholicism Judaism and every other ism, receive their authority from the governments they ride on like all the religions before them since the beginning.

This refers to any religion, because it is by permission of their government that they are allowed to operate. Not all the nations of the world permit Christian churches to function so many groups operate under ground. Some such as China keep their Christians in persecuted conditions however, they permit the religions of China to function openly.

The New World Order will slip in without resistance because it will seemingly be necessary for the achievement of peace. For example, on September 11, 1990, former president George Bush addressed the US Congress regarding the Persian Gulf War, and stated, "We stand at a unique and extraordinary moment. This crisis in the Persian Gulf, as grave as it is, also offers us a rare opportunity to move toward an historic period of cooperation. Out of these troubled times, our objective, a New World Order, can emerge. A hundred generations have searched for this elusive path to peace while a thousand wars raged across the span of human endeavor. Today, that New World Order is struggling to be born; a world quite different from the one we've known."

With the New World Order (NWO), all the religions come together and are permitted by the One World Government to operate.

According to many who have studied the subject of the New World Order, the nations to include as specific to a NWO or One World Government include: Australia and its areas, Central and South America, China (Taiwan Korea, and Mongolia), Japan, NAFTA (Canada, US, and Mexico), North Africa and the Middle East, Russia and Eastern Europe, South and Southeast Asia, Tropical Africa, and Western Europe or European Union.

This is a global picture of the church. "Mystery Babylon, the great, the mother of harlots and the abominations of the earth" (Rev. 17:5). She's committed fornication with the kings of the earth and she sits clothed in purple and scarlet, adorned with gold and precious stones and pearls. In her hand she holds a golden cup which is full of the abominations and the filthiness of her fornication and she is drunk with the blood of the saints and the blood of the martyrs of Jesus. She is the mother of Harlots, primarily the Protestants. Why? Because the Protestants were birthed by her and have committed the same fornication with the rulers or kings of the earth to receive authority to operate.

The WCC and the NCC take council with the UN and the UN receives council from them; they are in bed with each other.

Cities have been referred to as harlots because they had an idolatrous religious-political structure. Nahum had pronounced judgement on the city of Nineveh, calling her a harlot, "Because of the multitude of the harlotries of the seductive harlot, the mistress of sorceries, who sells nations through her harlotries, and families through her sorceries" (Nahum 3:4).

Isaiah speaks of Tyre, another ancient glorious and wealthy city, saying: "Now it shall come to pass in that day, that Tyre will be forgotten seventy years, according to the days of one king. At the end of seventy years it will happen to Tyre as in the song of a harlot" (Isa. 23:15).

Also, every time Israel or Jerusalem turned from Jehovah it was because of being enticed by these false religious systems and the Lord called them a harlot or in some translations a whore. "You also played the harlot with the Assyrians, because you were insatiable; indeed, you played the harlot with them and still were not satisfied" (Ezek. 16:28).

Protestant reformers have long held to the idea that the pope is the Antichrist and his church is the infamous whore or harlot of Babylon; however, it is a system of world churches who have their beginning and their roots winding back to Babylon and from Nimrod. How else will this one world religion be established?

Secreted in Protestantism

Another element amongst many of the Protestants is the involvement of a popular and considered renowned secret society known as Masons and Freemason's which outwardly appears as a sort of charity organization with high moral values but inwardly is full of the occult and deception.

There are Protestant churches whose Pastors are Masons and/or Freemasons. Generally, they have not exceeded about the third degree; however, some have. Most individuals are not aware of the deep cult side of Masonry. Neither are they aware that it is another arm of the Jesuits.

Masonry is a secret society and has its primary origin dating back to the 1600s however, some think it began as far back as the sixth century BC, the first being Buddha, who reformed the religion of Manous. This is not well substantiated however.

Albert Pike is the well-known Sovereign Grand Commander of the Scottish Rite's Southern Jurisdiction from 1859–1891. His commentaries and writings on the Masons have been both criticized and rehearsed throughout the years.

The original Masons were skilled stoneworkers from guilds in England and Scotland. Their buildings were magnificent, and much labor was involved. In construction, if there was the slightest variation in measurement it could easily become a fatal error. Secret signs were developed and taught to those who had mastered in the trade. This insured the contractor that he had the best skilled men working for him and eliminated error.

This lasted until the late 1500s, and then the availability of work ceased and that was the end of stoneworkers and their guilds. Apparently those of the wealthier who liked the secrecy of the signs also enjoyed the idea of a secret society. They joined the "Operative

Masons" and were accepted as Masons. Before long they changed it into what would be perceived as a gentlemen's club.

Rather than stonemasons in a guild, they were now philosophers in a fraternity. The Speculative Masons of today seen in Masonic Halls are said to have started in the Grand Lodge of England in 1717. This is plausible, as during this time the prominent of England all belonged to the Mason's as well as many not so prominent.

With all this said, no one actually knows the Masons' origin or it is kept secret. Why though, is it such a secret?

There are degrees in the Masons. They start as a Craft, Blue Lodge or Ancient Craft Mason. They enter as an Apprentice on initiation then go on to Fellow craft which is the second degree then to the Master Mason which is third degree. The process requires memorizing ritual words and body movements and other requirements are included.

Within the framework of the Masons secrecy are cultist symbols, oaths, and rituals, statements are made that are anti-Christian. It allows a union of all creeds and sects. They carry and wear the Triangle Eye: Sun and God, the Eye of Gold: The Sun of the Deity, the Sun Triangle and Star: God and Correct Knowledge, the Sun and Moon: Osiris and Isis, the Sun and Moon: also, Hermes-Mercury-Thoth and the Master of the Lodge.

- In Masonry the sun is viewed as Deity, once worshiped as a God.

- Represented in Masonry by a golden sun

- Represented in Masonry be a golden eye

- The sun and moon together are viewed as:

- The Master of the Lodge

- The god Thoth aka Hermes or Mercury

- The gods Osiris and Isis

- Represented in Masonry as gold and silver

- Represented in Masonry by the columns in front of Solomon's Temple, Jachin and Boaz

- Representing the generative and productive powers of nature

For a candidate of the twenty-fourth degree, they have a ritual Mourning of the Sun in which the nominee enters into the tabernacle and it is completely dark and completely silent to bring to mind death. He then hears the lamentations over the deaths of Osiris (Egypt), Kama (India), Mithra (Persia), Atys (Phrygia), and Tammuz (Phoenicia). Their deaths are symbolic of the temporary victory of darkness and evil over the light. The mythologies associated these deities speak of their death and resurrection. (Should a Christian be a Mason? By David W. Daniels)

"Brethren, enacting ancient drama, mourn Osiris, who is representative of the sun, of light, of life, of good and of beauty. They reflect upon the way the earth may again be gladdened by his presence. Attempts are made to bring life to the dead Osiris with the grip of the Apprentice, a symbol of science, and with the grip of the Fellowcraft, a symbol of logic."

The dogma's of the Masons explain Jesus as being a messiah; however, just another messiah in the line of messiah's.

There are many more rituals and as the degrees ascend they become more perverse in performance, even inviting demonic possession for the purpose of acquiring mental powers.

First, Second and even Third Degree Masons are normally unaware of the depth of cultism within this secret society however, they have been exposed enough to the realities that they are without excuse.

The Protestant does not "protest" a religious political structure, nor do they always recognize idolatry within the church. What the Protestants originally intended was to maintain their Catholicism only reformed. Initially Martin Luther had no intention of separating from the church of Rome. He actually thought he would reform the church however, because of the strong stance he took he was excommunicated.

While Protestants are quick to point out the various pagan practices of the Catholic faith, they fail to realize that they have many of the same pagan practices incorporated into their churches and order of worship. It has been said; "When the protestants left the Catholic church, they took everything with them except the pope". The exception generally being the obvious such as deifying the saints (who are the believers) and praying to them according to the office assigned them. For example, when traveling one prays to the saint of travel, Saint Christopher. Another obvious is the transubstantiation of the bread and wine into the literal body and blood of Christ or the statues erected in the sanctuary. It is the less obvious of things not searched out and taught which are clung to and practiced as a part of Christian faith and doctrine.

The Greco-Roman pagan practices incorporated into the Roman Catholic Church was displayed in the structure of their buildings and incorporated into the order of worship. When the reformation began with men like Luther and Calvin, they had been heavily indoctrinated with the Greco-Roman style of worship. They carried those ideas with them and it wasn't long before they had accumulated enough monetary support to erect buildings for worship which resembled that of the churches they'd come from. The Church of Rome was literally their blue print.

Ancient Judaism had the priests and the temple as well as their sacrificial system. Also the pagan religions had their temples and priests with their sacrifices. The popes designed their churches around these same functions. However, Jesus did away with temple worship and the people are now the temple of God, "Do you not know that you are the temple of God and that the Spirit of God dwells in you?" (1 Cor. 3:16)

Jesus also became the lamb of God sacrificed once and for all. "By that will we have been sanctified through the offering of the body of Jesus Christ once for all" (Heb. 10:10).

Jesus became our "high priest." "By a new and living way, which he consecrated for us, through the veil, that is, His flesh, "and having a high priest over the house of God,"

"let us draw near with a true heart in full assurance, of faith, having our hearts sprinkled from an evil conscience, and our bodies washed with pure water" (Heb. 10:20–22)

We are made priests of God. "And has made us kings and priests to His God and Father; to Him be glory and dominion for ever and ever. Amen" (Rev. 1:6).

Roman Catholic priests generally stood behind a pulpit located to the right from the altar table to give his sermon. The altar table was located in the center as a central focal point and where the Eucharist was performed. Luther made his change by moving the pulpit to the center and made preaching the central focus. Other Protestants initiated the same format but others replaced the altar table with a communion table.

Luther's primary change was changing the Latin spoken Eucharist into the people's language, changing the idea that the mass was Christ being sacrificed, allowed the congregation to partake in the bread and wine, making the sermon the main focus and instituting singing by the congregation. He kept the order of worship and because of a strong belief in ordained clergy he kept to the practice. He believed that those who preached had to be specifically trained the same as the Catholics believed.

The Anabaptists believed that all the members of the congregation should stand up and speak. The Lutheran's opposed this idea and used violence against them. Luther himself declared that they should be put to death. The Anabaptist however, were closer to the truth regarding all the believer's participation when they came together.

Paul wrote in his letters that the congregating believers made up the body of Christ and that every joint supplies. "But speaking the truth in love, may grow up in all things into Him, who is the head, Christ, from whom the whole body joined and knit together by what every joint supplies, according to the effective working by which every part does its share, causes growth of the body for the edifying of itself in love" (Eph. 4:15, 16).

The church that Jesus built had nothing to do with a structure or a building. His building was made up of believers - "living stones." "You also, as living stones, are being built up a spiritual house, a holy priesthood, to offer up spiritual sacrifices, acceptable to God through Jesus Christ. Therefore, it is also contained in the scripture, behold I lay in Zion a chief corner stone, elect, precious: and he who believes on him will by no means be put to shame" (1 Peter 2:5, 6).

The first Christians assembled together in homes. The idea of owning property and buildings never entered their mind until Constantine spread his fervor to institute church buildings. On May 11, 330, he dedicated his capital Constantinople and decked it with the treasures removed from the pagan temples. He further used their magic formulas for protecting crops and for healing diseases. He built the Church of the Apostles, comprising monuments of the twelve apostles surrounding a centrally located tomb which he had reserved for himself so to make himself the thirteenth apostle.

After Constantine's mother, Helena, returned from her journey to Jerusalem he began constructing his buildings around the Roman Empire like those of the pagan temples honoring their gods and named them after saints. His first church buildings were constructed over the cemeteries of the dead saints. The largest buildings were built over the tombs of those martyred because it was believed that they possessed powers that were those of the pagan gods. The most famous holy space is Saint Peter's on Vatican Hill, which is claimed to be over Peters tomb. There were many other buildings constructed claiming to be sitting over the sites of tombs such as the Church of the Holy Sepulcher in Jerusalem supposing to be over Christ's tomb.

The sixteenth-century reformers were primarily priests who'd left the Roman Church but took with them the concepts and style of church buildings and worship only making a few changes and minor adjustments. The Roman church buildings were magnificent works of art and designed to create an awe and were patterned after the basilicas. They held beautiful vibrant colored glass, walls were decorated with art work and went upward to high ceilings which graduated upward so also drawing the eyes upward, all creating the illusion of being in a heavenly holy atmosphere.

There were raised platforms or stages structured and seating was arranged so the audience could observe the performance. This design was adopted so it could separate a clergy from the laity. It was for the purpose of a hierarchy form of worship and is the same as the Nicolaitan's worship format. The Protestants maintain the same design, only usually more modestly structured.

The idea of steeples came from Egypt's obelisks and the tower of Babel, which held the idea of progressing to or reaching the heavens. Very few church buildings are constructed without some sort of steeple erected.

When reading the New Testament, we do not find that a church refers to a building or any structure. The believers comprised the church or the assembly. When Jesus prophesied the destruction of the temple he did not at any time make reference to it being replaced by church buildings. The early church believers understood that they were now the temple in which Jesus and the Father would make their abode. They did not "go to church" because they were the church. It was Clement Alexandria, toward the end of the second century, long after the apostles, who started using the phrase "go to church."

There were no special buildings that the believers assembled in for the first three centuries. The closest thing resembling a modern church structure was the house at Dura-Europos which was actually a home which had removed an interior wall to create a large living area.

The mainstream Protestant churches today all have a headquarters to "head" over all their buildings, clergy, and members. They operate much like a corporation operates and run on an elaborate budget. In the U.S. alone the churches to date, owns real estate valued at approximately $230 billion (50% of most church finances go to real-estate). Attached is a high cost of overhead and maintenance which amounts to about $7 billion annually and the income of the pastors and clergy amounts to about $48 billion annually. This all coming from the tithes and offerings of their congregations and this all for the purpose of creating great wealth and power for the organizations. The church today resembles that of the Laodiceans.

"I know your works, that you are neither cold nor hot: I could wish you were cold or hot. So then because you are lukewarm, and neither cold nor hot, I will vomit you out of My mouth. Because you say, I am rich, have become wealthy, and have need of nothing'- and do not know that you are wretched, miserable, poor, blind, and naked" (Rev. 3:15–17).

It is easy to see that a phenomenal burden of monetary responsibility is placed on the shoulders of the laity, pastors and other clergy members. This is a sharp contrast to the early churches "in home" gatherings where their offerings went to assist the needs of their brethren.

Satan would have us burdened and enslaved to a system. He would have us divided and in doctrinal conflict with one another. Saying "I am of Paul, or I am of Apollos, or I am of Cephas or I am of Christ. Is Christ divided? Was Paul crucified for you? Or were you baptized in the name of Paul?" (1 Cor. 1:12, 13).

There has been an inherent desire, almost agreed to acquire wealth and power with a famed name amongst church leaders which drives them to build and then build and then continue to build. But. . . ." unless the LORD builds the house, they labor in vain who build it; Unless the LORD guard the city, the watchman stays awake in vain" (Psalm 127:1).

Christ fulfilled the need for temple or building worship with himself sacrificed so that he became sacrifice for us once and for all and poured out the Father's Spirit writing his commandments in the fleshly tables of our hearts making us as believers his place of abode.

Why are we so compelled to enslave ourselves to the obligation and support of a religious system and most times not even examine it for its truths? A dear coworker of mine told me how when she was a child her family owned both cattle and sheep. When they had the cattle she learned to heard them in by rounding them all up which required assistance from their dog as they were not always willing to be herded and would sometimes go if able, in a different direction. When they had the sheep, she only needed to bring in one or two at most because when the others saw them going they would all follow without questioning. Sheep need a shepherd or they go astray. Our shepherd should be Christ or we will follow others without question.

"And when he brings out his own sheep, he goes before them; and the sheep follow him, for they know his voice. Yet they will by no means follow a stranger, but will flee from him, for they do not know the voice of strangers" (John 10:4, 5).

The Protestant churches have a close association with that of the Roman Church which has a close association with that of the Roman Empire. The structure of the leadership with the top-down or hierarchy system exists in every denomination including those who claim non-denomination.

The pastor of the Protestant church is viewed as the head of the church and holds the final authority over the assembly. The pastor is considered to have a special insight to understanding the Word and is responsible to distribute that understanding to the congregation. Most pastors have studied in seminaries where the theology of their denomination was taught to them and most have attended classes to learn the art of preaching. Very few have been taught solely by the Spirit of God even though that is how we are to be taught. John wrote to the believers:

"But the anointing which you have received from Him abides in you, and you do not need that anyone teach you; but as the same anointing teaches you concerning all things, and is true, and is not a lie, and just as it has taught you, you will abide in Him" (1 John 2: 27).

The formation of church leadership began after the death of the apostles. John was the last remaining apostle. Before he died he witnessed the hierarchy (doctrine of the Nicolaitans) being formed in the church and was given instructions by Christ to write to the churches regarding this error and that they should repent. Christ stated that he hated the doctrine of the Nicolaitans.

"Thus you also have those who hold the doctrine of the Nicolaitans, which thing I hate." (Rev. 2:15).

As mentioned before, the word *Nicolaitans* comes from the Greek *Nikos*, to conquer or subdue, and *Laos*, the people. which is where we get the word *laity* from. It literally means to be over the people. This exists in every congregation there is.

Within the early church there were elders (plural) who were overseers, meaning they concerned themselves with the needs of the people. They did not have some special office as with a plaque hanging over the door reading pastors office nor did they function alone but there were two or more attending at all times. They were mature in the things of the Lord and therefore were elders and servants of Christ for the church. Never did they have a position of being over the church. Peter wrote to the elders to "Shepherd the flock of God, which is among you, serving as overseers, not by compulsion but willingly; not for dishonest gain, but eagerly; nor as being lords over those entrusted to you, but being examples to the flock" (1 Peter 5:2, 3).

The assembly or church was to operate on an even plain where everyone was to supply what they had for the edifying of the whole body. Each individual has something to offer and one is not exalted over another.

"Let nothing be done through selfish ambition or conceit, but in lowliness of mind let each esteem others better than himself.

"Let each of you look out not only for his own interests, but also for the interests of others" (Phil. 2:3, 4).

The job of ministering is for the entire body, not one individual.

The churches today are modeled after Rome, lacking open worship, sharing, and having an open ministry. With all eyes fixed on the pulpit and the man behind it being the uttermost of importance the congregation becomes nothing more than an audience of spectators.

Even the custom of wearing your "Sunday go to meeting" or dressing up for church was not practiced by the early believers. This idea was created when the emperors would arrive unexpectedly to check on their churches and surprise the congregation. Therefore, it became necessary to look your best in case the emperor should show up unannounced. To day people say, they want to dress their best in case the Lord should come. What would they say if He asked them to sit on the grass?

Pastors have been greatly burdened with the responsibilities lain on them and the individual's spiritual growth has been greatly stunted for not being spiritually exercised. The man made religions we serve today are a far cry from the church that Jesus built. It would appear, where Christ came to set the captive free, the churches came to take the free captive.

Charles Elliott Newbold Jr. describes in his book the condition of individuals locked in and trying to break away from the church system. "Many who dare to leave one church go down the street hoping for a better "spiritual climate: only to find the same old whore in a brand new dress. Only the rules are slightly different. They go from church to church looking for that which is genuine only to find more phony religious facades; they go looking for Spirit and truth only to find more flesh and hypocrisy. Yet, they continue their search, because they are addicted to it. They bob up and down on their wooden horses unable to dismount because of the velocity of that carousel—the church system that perpetually spins round and round, going nowhere.

A few discerning persons are able to break away from the bondage of church, but often leave damaged and resentful. Some of these attend anonymous groups, seeking recovery from the religious abuses inflicted upon them by these religious systems of men's traditions.

Church, as we have come to experience it, permeates every aspect of our society. It is the only thing we have seen and known that supposedly represents Christ. In going after it, just as did Israel of old we have played the harlot and provoked the Lord to jealousy." (The Harlot Church System, by Charles Elliott Newbold Jr.)

Chapter 17

Heritage of Israel and The World's Present Threat

Jerusalem is a coveted territory. The powers that be will brutally kill, maim, persecute, and terrorize to obtain ownership. It is the most sacred place in the world with its history and antiquities. Jerusalem is the only city in the world that has suffered being besieged twenty-three times, attacked fifty-two times, captured and re-captured forty-four times and is still undergoing assaults. No city in the world would be still in existence. It is a testimony to us that its survival is supernatural.

The Roman Catholic Church throughout the Protestant uprisings during its early years was experiencing anxiety and insecurity of power with the loss of devotees. The spirit of supreme authority and desire to subdue the world was unconscionable and the pope being apprehensive of losing control as well as monetary support determined to combat the situation.

The Christian faith continued to expand; however, it was generally done through force. Anyone who held opposition to the emperor's state religion became the object of persecution. The largest target of persecution during the establishment of Rome's new religion fell to the Jews. Jerusalem was coveted by Rome because of its strategic location, history and extreme value.

According to a former Jesuit priest, Alberto Rivera, behind closed doors, decisions and schemes to accomplish ownership of this priceless territory were being planned. He left the church and became a protestor to it after learning some of it's dark history. His testimony has been naturally rebuked and, according to his family, his reputation attacked with fabricated false accusations. Interestingly however, there are many testimonials and literature written that support his claims.

Alberto Rivera states that while he was in service to Rome as a Jesuit priest, a Jesuit cardinal, Augustine Bea, revealed to him the desperate attempts to secure ownership of Jerusalem by the Roman church. They needed a plan and so it was determined to create a pawn of man-power to make Jerusalem a Roman Catholic city. The best "untapped source of manpower" for this task was no less the children of Ishmael. Alberto expresses: "The poor Arabs fell victim to one of the cleverest plans ever devised by the powers of darkness."

After Mr. Rivera begin disclosing to the public the information he'd learned, there were a number of attempts made on his life. He ultimately and mysteriously was found dead from food poisoning.

This is his story:

The Arabs initially brought gifts to the "House of God" and the Kaaba (sacred mosque of Mecca) overseers were pleased to receive them. Some people would bring their idols and in order to be inoffensive they would also be received. It is mentioned that the Jews viewed the Kaaba as an "outlying tabernacle of the Lord" with veneration until it became polluted with the idols. A tribal contention over Zamzam, a well, resulted in these pilgrimage treasures to be cast down the well and it was filled over with sand and lost. Years later Adb Al-Muttalib had a vision revealing to him where to find the well and its treasure. He because of this, became the hero of Mecca and was destined to be the grandfather of Muhammad.

Prior to this, Augustine was made bishop of North Africa and found success in bringing many of the Arabs to the Roman church, including some entire tribes converted to Catholicism. The idea of looking among them for an Arab prophet was hence conceived.

Muhammad's father had died from an illness and customarily, sons of great Arab families, in sacred places like Mecca were sent to be nursed and spend a portion of their childhood raised up with Bedouin tribes where they could be trained and avoid city plagues; thus Muhammad was sent there. His mother and also his grandmother died and Muhammad was with his uncle when a Catholic monk discovered his identity.

He was the ideal for the Arab prophet they sought, so putting the plan in motion he said: to whom? "Take your brother's son back to his country, and guard him against the Jews, for by God, if they see him and know of him that which I know, they will construe evil against him. Great things are in store for this brother's son of yours."

What the Catholic monk did ignited the fire for persecution of Jews by the followers of Muhammad. The church was desperate to have Jerusalem for its religious significance, and the only thing preventing them were her rightful owners, the Jews.

In the interim, Roman Catholicism was increasing in power and would not tolerate opposition. There were at the time Christians in North Africa who preached the gospel without endorsing or adhering to Roman Catholicism, but followed the scriptures only. Therefore, the Vatican needed a means to eliminate those believers along with the Jews. They employed some of their Roman Catholic converts to report information to the church leaders. Others they used in an underground spy network to continue controlling the masses who rejected Catholicism. Saint Augustine's monasteries were bases to seek out and destroy the biblical literature owned by the non-conforming Christians.

It necessitated creation of a "messiah" for the Arabs whom they could raise to be a great leader. One with a charisma they could train to unite all the non-Catholic Arabs to following him and creating a strong army that would succeed in the capture of Jerusalem for the pope. Alberto Rivera says that while in the Vatican briefing, Cardinal Bea told us this story: (quoted excerpt from his book *The Prophet* by Chick Publications)

A wealthy Arab lady who was a faithful follower of the pope played a tremendous part in this drama. She was a widow named Khadijah. She gave her wealth to the church and retired to a convent, but was given an assignment. She was to find a brilliant young man who could be used by the Vatican to create a new religion and become the messiah for the children of Ishmael. Khadijah had a cousin named Waraquah, who was also a very faithful Roman Catholic and the Vatican placed him in a critical role as Muhammad's advisor. He had tremendous influence on Muhammad.

Teachers were sent to young Muhammad and he had intensive training. Muhammad studied the works of Saint Augustine, which prepared him for his great calling. The Vatican had Catholic Arabs across North Africa spread the story of a great one who was about to rise up among the people and be the chosen one of their God. While Muhammad was being prepared, he was told that his enemies were the Jews and that the only true Christians were Roman Catholic. He was taught that others calling themselves Christians were actually wicked impostors and should be destroyed. Many Muslims believe this.

Muhammad began receiving supposedly divine revelations, and his wife's Catholic cousin Waraquah helped interpret them. From this came the Qu'ran. In the fifth year of Muhammad's mission, persecution came against his followers because they refused to worship the idols in the Kaaba.

Muhammad instructed some of them to flee to Abyssinia where Negus, the Roman Catholic king accepted them because Muhammad's views on the virgin Mary were so close to Roman Catholic doctrine. These Muslims received protection from Catholic kings because of Muhammad's revelations.

Muhammad later conquered Mecca and the Kaaba was cleared of idols. History proves that before Islam came into existence, the Sabeans in Arabia worshiped the moon-god who was married to the sun-god. They gave birth to three goddesses who were worshipped throughout the Arab world a "Daughters of Allah" An idol excavated at Hazor in Palestine in 1950's shows Allah sitting on a throne with the crescent moon on his chest.

Muhammad claimed he had a vision from Allah and was told "You are the messenger of Allah". He began his career as a prophet and he received many messages. By the time Muhammad died, the religion of Islam was exploding. The nomadic tribes were joining forces in the name of Allah and his prophet, Muhammad.

Some of Muhammad's writings were placed in the Qur'an, others were never published. They are now in the hands of high ranking holy men (Ayatollahs) in the Islamic faith. When Cardinal Bea shared with us in the Vatican, he said, these writings are guarded because they contain information that links the Vatican to the creation of Islam.

Both sides have so much information on each other that if exposed it could create such a scandal that it would be a disaster for both religions."

In their "holy" book, the Qur'an, Christ is regarded as only a prophet. If the pope was His representative on earth, then He also must be a prophet of God. This caused the followers of Muhammad to fear and respect the pope as another holy man.

The pope moved quickly and issued bulls granting the Arab generals permission to invade and conquer the nations of North Africa. The Vatican helped to finance the building of these massive Islamic armies in exchange for three favors: 1) Eliminate the Jews and Christians (true believers which they called infidels); 2) protect the Augustinian Monks and Roman Catholics; and 3) conquer Jerusalem for "His Holiness" in the Vatican.

The Islam nation grew and became a tremendous force of determination and power. Jews and true Christians were slaughtered, and Jerusalem fell into their hands. Roman Catholics were never attacked, nor were their shrines, during this time. When the pope asked for Jerusalem, he was surprised at his denial! The Arab generals had such military success that they could not be intimidated by the pope-nothing could stand in the way of their own plan to conquer and seize.

Under Waraquah's direction, Muhammad wrote that Abraham offered Ishmael as a sacrifice. The Bible says that Isaac was the sacrifice, but Muhammad removed Isaac's name and inserted Ishmael's name. As a result of this and Muhammad's vision, the faithful Muslims built a mosque, the Dome of the Rock, in Ishmael's honor on the site of the Jewish temple that was destroyed in 70 AD. This made Jerusalem the second most holy place in the Islam faith. How could they give such a sacred shrine to the pope without causing a revolt?

The pope realized that what they had created was out of control when he heard they were calling His Holiness an infidel. The Muslim generals were determined to conquer the world for Allah, and now they turned toward Europe. Islamic ambassadors approached the pope and asked for papal bulls to give them permission to invade European countries. The Vatican was outraged; war was inevitable. Temporal power and control of the world was considered the basic right of the pope. He wouldn't think of sharing it with those whom he considered heathens.

The pope raised up his armies and called them crusades to hold back the children of Ishmael from invading Catholic Europe. The crusades lasted centuries and Jerusalem slipped out of the pope's hands. Turkey fell and Spain and Portugal were invaded by Islamic forces. In Portugal, they called a mountain village "Fatima" in honor of Muhammad's daughter, never dreaming it would become world famous.

Years later when the Muslim armies were poised on the islands of Sardinia and Corsica to invade Italy, there was a serious problem. The Islamic generals realized they were too far extended. It was time for peace talks. One of the negotiators was Francis of Assisi. As a result, the Muslims were allowed to occupy Turkey in a Christian world, and the Catholics were allowed to occupy Lebanon in the Arab world. It was also agreed that the Muslims could build mosques in Catholic countries without interference as long as Roman Catholicism could flourish Arab countries.

Cardinal Bea told us in Vatican briefings that both the Muslims and Roman Catholics agreed to block and destroy the efforts of their common enemy, Bible-believing Christian missionaries. Through these concordats, Satan blocked the children of Ishmael from a knowledge of Scripture and the truth.

A light control was kept on Muslims from the Ayatollah down through the Islamic priests, nuns and monks. The Vatican also engineers a campaign of hatred between the Muslim Arabs and the Jews. Before this, they had co-existed peacefully. The Islamic community looks on the Bible-believing missionary as a devil who brings poison to the children of Allah. This explains years of ministry in those countries with little results.

The next plan was to control Islam. In 1910, Portugal was going Socialistic. Red flags were appearing and the Catholic Church was facing a major problem. Increasing numbers were against the church. The Jesuits wanted Russia involved, and the location of this vision at Fatima could play a key part in pulling Islam to the Mother Church.

In 1917, the Virgin appeared at Fatima. "The Mother of God" was a smashing success, playing to overflow crowds. As a result, the Socialists of Portugal suffered a major defeat.

Roman Catholics world-wide began praying for the conversion of Russia and the Jesuits invented the Novenas to Fatima which they could perform through North Africa, spreading good public relations to the Muslim world. The Arabs thought they were honoring the daughter of Muhammad, which is what the Jesuits wanted them to believe.

As a result of the vision of Fatima, Pope Pius XII ordered his Nazi army to crush Russia and the Orthodox religion and make Russia Roman Catholic. A few years after he lost World war II, Pope Pius XII startled the world with his phony dancing sun vision to keep Fatima in the news. It was great religious show biz and the world swallowed it. Not surprisingly, Pope Pius was the only one to see this vision.

As a result, a group of followers has grown into a Blue Army world-wide, totaling millions of faithful Roman Catholics ready to die for the blessed virgin. But we haven't seen anything yet. The Jesuits have their Virgin Mary scheduled to appear four or five times in China, Russia and a major appearance in the US."

Bishop Sheen states with regard to this in relation to Islam:

"Our Lady's appearances at Fatima marked the turning point in history of the world's 350 million Muslims. After the death of his daughter, Muhammad wrote that she "is the most holy of all women in Paradise, next to Mary." He believed that the Virgin Mary chose to be known as Our Lady of Fatima as a sign and a pledge that the Muslims who believe in Christ's virgin birth, will come to believe in His divinity. He further believes, that the pilgrim statues of Our Lady of Fatima were welcomed with enthusiasm by the Muslims of Africa, India, et cetera, and as a result, many Muslims are converting to Roman Catholicism."

The lust for Jerusalem between the Muslims and the Catholics with the Satanic compulsion to govern the world in its entirety knows no boundaries. The populace of the nations is expendable having no value for the cause. The numbers are unacceptable and serve only to create complexities. In fact, the population numbers make it hard to conquer. The fewer the numbers the easier, so deliberately creating famines, diseases, developed in labs - aka biological warfare, and inciting wars serve to reduce the numbers.

The pope has maintained a friendship relationship with the Muslims primarily out of necessity. In fact, Pope John Paul II was photographed kissing the Qu'ran after having audience with Patriarch Raphael I of Iraq, where he bowed to the book when it was presented to him, received it and kissed it. Sadly, many Protestant leaders and laity applauded this act as a gesture of peace through acceptance Today we have Pope Francis, the first *Jesuit* pope who has gained much recognition and advancement in the political arena.

The difficulty for the pope and the Vatican will be that Islam will not without fighting to the death alter their position on Jerusalem. They will ultimately ignore their secret history between them, the pope and the Vatican, and attempt to conquer it as well through their chaotic and violent military acts.

Recently the UN agreed to give $150 billion to Iran, cutting a deal which is supposed to prevent them from developing and becoming a nuclear power. $150 billion! Given! To a small nation which maintains its determination to see Israel and the United States wiped off the map and any other people who are considered non-Muslim infidels! Where does that money come from? There have been billions and billions over the last decades pumped into the hands of the worlds enemies yet we can't feed the poor. As the expression goes," What's wrong with this picture?"

Today the world is threatened by radical Muslims. Groups like ISIS are determined to eliminate the Jew and the Christian. There are Christians being beheaded and thrown into prisons. There are continual daily attacks on Israel and innocent people are desperately trying to escape the grips of their tormentors.

ISIS is another faction of the beast, another tentacle but it doesn't rule the world. It in itself is a beast system born from the religious-political Islam, born of Roman Catholicism which was born of the idolatrous nations that ruled before them.

NOTE: On March 14, 2013, "Day of Blood" and the birthday of Mithra, Jorge Mario Borgoglio (he took the name Francis because it sounds more Italian) was declared pope. He succeeded Pope John XIII.

This is a pivotal position for the Catholic Church as Pope Francis is a Jesuit Priest and the Jesuits are discouraged from becoming bishops and would never have been considered to become a pope.

Christ Received

In spite of opposition and severe persecution, many Muslims are turning to Christ. The reports, not heard on your local news broadcast, keep pouring in. One incident written in Chris Mitchell's book *Dateline Jerusalem*, is of an Iranian woman, Dina, who actually was serving in the Female Secret Police. She and her co-workers hunted out other women who for the least infractions violated Sharia Law. Dina began in secret watching *Iran Alive*, a Christian satellite program hosted by Hormoz Shariat. She was a tormentor to the programs staff through phone calls where she would ridicule and demean their belief shouting phrases like, "You Christians are going to hell."

Her life changed one night during a call when she confided to Hormoz that she and her mother had cancer and planned to kill themselves during his broadcast. Hormoz, calmed his distress and asked Dina to grant Jesus a week, and if at the end of the week nothing happened to commit their suicide. Dina accepted his "foolish" challenge and committed herself to call back in a week to carry out their suicide, "If you are brave enough to take my next call." Hormoz promised to accept her call but first requested that she would pray and accept Jesus as her Savior. With disinclination she accepted and prayed. Dina made her call one week later and in shock Hormoz took the call. Chris Mitchell's traveling companion who has received knowledge of the account Tom Doyle, recites the conversation:

"Welcome back, Dina. How are you?"

"Hormoz, last week I repeated the words you told me to say, but I didn't take them seriously. The TV host nodded into the camera as Dina continued. "But God did. Tonight my mother is with me again. She's standing here beside me!"

This time, it was Hormoz who struggled to hold back tears. "And?"

"I didn't want Jesus to be the answer. All week long, I thought of everything in my life that was negative. I was trying to feel depressed. But each time I tried to concentrate on my problems, I was flooded with peace. I would stop by the mirror, amazed at the smile on my face. As for my mother, she's well, Hormoz. She's well! And so am I! Jesus is everything you promised. Thank you, my friend."

There are heart breaking accounts of Muslims accepting Christ when knowingly they face a horrifying death for their stand such as Fatima Al-Mutairi also described in Chris Mitchell's book, *Dateline Jerusalem*.

Fatima was born to a prevalent Bedouin tribe which resided in the town that was named after Fatima, the fourth daughter of Muhammad. It was a religiously fervent community yet there was access to the Internet where Fatima began to listen to stories of Muslims turning to Jesus and devoting their lives to him. Tom Doyle says, Fatima's family expected nothing but absolute devotion to Islam.

Fatima conversed with others online and began reading the New Testament with fervency. Her understanding became enlightened and learning about this remarkable man called Jesus she embraced Him with deep gratitude and love.

Fatima privately started communicating in poetry about Jesus to others over the internet using a pen name "Rania." A day came when her brother discovered her poems and Christian communications. Fatima returned home to find her brother announcing to the family that she had committed herself to the "infidel" faith. For this she would face death. He verified his announcement by asking her "Are you a Jesus follower?"

Fatima confirmed by responding with "Yes. Yes, I am".

He confiscated her cell phone so she could not call for any help and locked her in her room. She waited for four hours knowing her impending doom. But while she waited wrote her last poem about Jesus on her computer and sent it out to her church online. A portion from Tom Doyle's account reads, "May the Lord Jesus guide you. O Muslims, and enlighten your hearts that you might love others. We do not worship the cross, and we are not insane. We worship the Lord Jesus, the light of the world."

And Messiah says: "Blessed are the persecuted." And we for the sake of Christ all things bear. What is it to you that we are infidels?

Enough. Your swords do not concern me, nor evil, nor disgrace. Your threats do not trouble me, and we are not afraid. And by God, I am unto death a Christian. Verily, I cry for what passed by, of a sad life. I was far from the Lord Jesus for many years. Oh History record and bear witness, Oh witnesses! We are Christians-in the path of Christ we tread.

Take from me this word, and note it well. You see Jesus is my Lord, and He is the Best of Protectors.

As to my last words, I pray to the Lord of the worlds. Jesus is the Messiah, the Light of clear Guidance. That He changes nations, and sets the scales of justice aright. And that He spread Love among you O, Muslims."

Within minutes after Fatima sent out her last poem her brother came into her room and severely beat her. He broke bones in her body, and broke open areas of her flesh then cut out her tongue. He then dragged her outside and set her on fire, burning her alive.

There are numerous other accounts of Muslims receiving dreams and visions of Christ and when they turn to him they know well that they have an imminent threat to their very lives, yet they are willing to lay it down for their Savior Jesus whom they love.

There are hundreds of Muslims and Jews daily getting their eyes opened to Yeshua, and when they do there is nothing that can prevent them from embracing Him.

"Who shall separate us from the love of Christ? Shall tribulation, or distress, or persecution, or famine, or nakedness, or peril, or sword? As it is written, For Your sake we are killed all day long; We are accounted as sheep for the slaughter. Yet, in all these things we are more than conquerors through Him who loved us. For I am persuaded, that neither death, nor life, nor angels, nor principalities, nor powers, nor things present, nor things to come, nor height, nor depth, nor any other created thing, shall be able to separate us from the love of God, which is in Christ Jesus our Lord" (Rom. 8:35–39).

CHAPTER 18

The Beast Manifested

Although the Protestant Reformers attempted with limited progress to break away from the grips of the beast system, its tentacles like a cancerous tumor grows throughout the world and the church. Most likely when the reformers came to America they did not have a full understanding of the enormity of the beast system, which they were trying to escape, nor how it would grow yet even more enormous throughout the years to come.

The book of Revelation reaches back through history to describe the beast. The mountains are the religious-political nations that have ruled the world. They form the beast. The heads give them their individual identity. They are the kingdoms. When the apostle John wrote Revelations, there were 6 heads on the beast already formed. He saw in his vision a 7th head to come.

The first beast John saw came up out of the sea.

"Then I stood on the sand of the sea. And I saw a beast rising up out of the sea, having seven heads and ten horns, and on his horns ten crowns, and on his heads a blasphemous name" (Rev. 13:1)

The sea are nations of people. (Rev. 17:15) The heads represent the authority or the kingdoms that "headed" or ruled over the world at that time. History tells us Egypt, Assyria, Babylon, Medes & Persians and Greece had come and gone and Rome was ruling at the time. And the seventh head was yet to come.

The ear marks of a nation being referred to as a beast in the Bible is their religious-political government and their rule "over the world." The empire that rose up after Rome in military strength was that of the

Ottoman Empire. During its days England had overspread the world not only militarily but economically as well. Although the Ottoman Empire grew and operated as a beast system during England's rise to power, it was not a "world" ruler. It therefore did not constitute as one of the heads.

Horns represent kings. The Bible is consistent, so if horns represent kings in one place they will represent kings in another.

"The ram which you saw, having the two horns - they are the kings of Media and Persia. And the male goat is the kingdom Greece. The large horn that is between its eyes is the first king" (Dan. 8:20, 21).

The crowns on the horns in Revelation 13 were most likely varied because they represented the legitimacy and glory given to them by the nation that each horn was assigned to and every nation had its own designed crown.

The beast had a "deadly wound."

"And I saw one of his heads as it had been mortally wounded, and his deadly wound was healed. And all the world marveled and followed the beast" (Rev. 13:3).

With the rise of the Ottoman Empire, Rome lost its position as a world ruler and for about 1,000 years there was no world ruler. The Ottoman Empire, while having a strong and fierce military and being a religious governmental force making it a beast, never gained dominion over the world. They never were a "head" on the beast. They did however govern over Jerusalem for 400 years. The Ottoman Empire (Islamic-Muslim) was another faction produced by the beast system.

The Church of England was only a little more than the already existing Catholic Church; the primary difference being that instead of the pope as its head, the king was its head. It was many years before the separation from Rome would come (it never became completely separated) and there were numerous executed for resisting the religious-politics of the king.

The Seventh Head

England rose up, becoming the seventh head of the beast. It was the only empire following the sixth head, Rome, to become a world governing political-religious empire." Five are fallen." Egypt, Assyria, Babylon, Medio-Persian and Greece Empires had fallen at the time of John's revelation. "One is." Rome, the sixth head, was the world ruler at the time. "And one, the seventh head, has not yet come." The only possible empire to become the seventh head would be that of England or Great Britain (Rev. 17:10).

The United Kingdom originated in the sixteenth century from the overseas possessions and trading posts established by England. The British Empire embodied and dominated colonies, protectorates, mandates and territories ruled by the United Kingdom. It grew into the largest empire in the history of mankind as the foremost global power. Before its demise it dominated 458 million people. Its expanse incorporated some 13 million square miles The phrase "the empire on which the sun never sets" described how the British Empire expanded around the globe so that the sun was always shining on one of its territories. It had developed a strong military and its navy called at that time, the "Navy Royal "was a fighting force unsurpassed by any.

England ruled the seas with its navy and engaged in vicious acts of piracy, drug importing, and slave trade. It became a tyrant and a great oppressor to the nations. The East India Company was developed and became a forerunner in trade.

The East India Company was formed in the early 1600s as an English and later British joint stock company in order to obtain trade with the East Indies but ended up trading primarily with India and China. It grew to be accountable for at least half of the world's trade particularly that of cotton, silk, indigo dye, salt, saltpeter, tea and opium.

The company ruled large areas of India and had its own private armies that exercised military power and assumed administrative functions. Wealthy English merchants and aristocrats controlled and owned the company's shares but the government had no shares and only indirect control.

The East India Company was responsible for killing and enslaving the people of India and also of terrorizing China. They in fact, poured opium into China, keeping the people in an immobilized condition and rendering them incapable of threat.

England united with Scotland in 1707 and the new sovereign state called Great Britain was formed. Great Britain ruled a worldwide empire, the largest ever recorded. On January 01,1800, Ireland united with Great Britain and the United Kingdom of Great Britain and Ireland was formed.

The East India Company eventually was disbanded by Queen Victoria after an Indian mutiny arose in 1877 over the harsh treatment and economic ruin inflicted upon the people and government. After this Queen Victoria became empress of India.

The East India House, located in London was formed as the headquarters of the East India Company. With the demise of the company the intelligence remained and within the East India House the roundtable was formed. This became the think tank where prominent figures hashed out their world views and ideas such as the new world order, population control, also a one world religion and economic system were hatched.

The East India House today is the Lloyd's Building. It continued its think tank when it was replaced with the title of the "Royal Institute of International Affairs." Since, it has come to be known as the Chatham House.

The inscription on the East India House is interesting, as it is an ancient limestone tablet that was inscribed by Nebuchadnezzar, king of Babylon sometime between 604–560 BC. It is now housed in the British Museum. The inscription reads:

I am Nebuchadnezzar, king of Babylon, the exalted prince, the favourite of the god.

Marduk, the beloved of the god Nabu, the arbiter, the possessor of wisdom, who reverences their lordship, the untiring governor who is constantly anxious for the maintenance of the shrines of Babylonia and Borsippa, the wise, the pious, the son of Nabopolasser, king of Babylon; To Marduk, my lord I make supplication; Oh eternal prince, lord of all being, guide in a straight path the king whom thou lovest and whose name thou hast proclaimed as was pleasing to thee. I am the prince, the favourite, the creature of thy hand. Thou hast created me and entrusted me with dominion over all people. According to thy favour lord, which thou dost bestow on all people, cause me to love thy exalted lordship. Create in my heart, the worship of your divinity, and grant whatever is pleasing to thee because thou hast my life; By thy command, merciful Marduk, may the temple I have built endure for all time and may I be satisfied with its splendour; in its midst may I attain old age, may I be sated with offspring; therein may I receive the heavy tribute of all mankind; from the horizon of heaven to the zenith, may I have no enemies; may my descendants live therein forever and rule over the people.

Great Britain suffered economic and personal damages during WWI. The United States originally refrained from entering the war, but after 128 Americans died when a German U-boat sank the British luxury liner, *Lusitania*, President Woodrow Wilson, with Secretary of State William Jennings Bryan, got Germany to agree to a policy of restricted submarine warfare. This meant that a targeted ship had to be signaled a warning before it was torpedoed.

Germany broke that agreement in 1917 and returned to their former method, attack without warning, and Great Britain feared the German subs would harm and hinder their trans-Atlantic supply lines. Americans were biased toward Great Britain, and with the manpower and industrial strength Great Britain had they wooed the US into the war as an ally. British intelligence had intercepted a German telegram to Mexico from Foreign Secretary Arthur Zimmerman attempting to bring Mexico into an ally relationship with Germany and create a war diversion on America's southwestern border. Great Britain, upon intercepting the telegram, immediately notified the United States.

This, with Germany's unrestricted sub warfare brought the United States into the war in April of 1917. The US, by the following year had enough soldiers in France to help England and France push back the Germans. By fall of 1918, the Americans were positioned with troops under command of General John J. "Black Jack" Pershing, flanking the German lines. The British and French troops held the German front in place and kept them from advancing.

With the involvement of the US, the British Empire maintained its position as the world ruler when the Meuse-Argonne Offensive forced Germany to surrender. The Paris Peace Conference ended WWI and The League of Nations was established on January 10, 1920 as a measure to maintain peace throughout the world.

But another world war was in the making, and the League of Nations was ineffective in its prevention. And when WWII arrived it completely crippled Great Britain's dominance and the massive British Empire was slain. It received a deadly wound.

Many religions teach that when the pope was imprisoned during Napoleon's era that this constituted the deadly wound of the beast. Then its wound was healed in the early 1900s when the pope and Vatican, with Mussolini's, aid, were released from their boundaries and given freedom to openly operate in the world. However, when you examine history, you learn that the Roman Catholic Church never had the world dominance that Great Britain had. The British Empire had control over the worlds banking system, trade, commerce and every function of man's mobility as did the kingdoms before it. The Catholic Church has never had that world control; however, it rides this system and enjoys a great deal of influence and persuasion.

The Eighth Head

After WWII, the world was crying out for peace. People were exhausted from the two wars and their impact to the point they were willing to give up their sovereignty for peace. The British Empire had been slain but came up again partnering with the United States. The United States and Great Britain determined together to create the United Nations which was supposed to maintain a world peace.

The League of Nations had failed to keep world peace, and in 1939 the Chatham House set up a western branch called the "Counsel on Foreign Relations" (CFR), the think-tank of the United States. The think tanks of the United States and England (Chatham House & CFR) came together to create the United Nations.

At its beginning, the UN had fifty-one member states; today it is 133. The Holy See never applied for membership, but on April 6, 1964 it was given the privilege to be a permanent observer of their work with a non-member status. She has the right to attend all sessions and has been able to influence the decisions of the UN General Assembly, Security Council, and Economic and Social Council.

In Revelation 13:11, another beast rises up out of the earth. The first beast and the second beast are the same. The first was raised up with its authority from the nations - the seas. The beast then rose up with authority from religion, and exercises all the authority of the first beast (Rev. 13:12). Authority, sometimes translated "power" is, in this passage, the Greek word *exousia* which is delegated authority or a legal right. It had all the authority (**legal** authority) of the first beast before it.

When the apostle John wrote the book of Revelation, the Roman Catholic Church had not been established. The beast was still in the sea (multitudes and nations), after the establishment of Catholicism along with the birth of Protestantism, the beast was firmly planted in the Earth. All the beasts of Revelation are the same but different in how they are established. It's like placing the same picture in a different frame.

This beast has the ability to bring down "fire from heaven." Reflecting back on our weapons technology and what we observe when we witness the explosions created in the skies we see fire come down from heaven. The bombings, including the bombing of Hiroshima and Nagasaki, the nuclear and laser technology used and other high-tech weaponry used today, couldn't have been described by the apostle John any better.

The beast out of the earth makes an image to the beast out of the sea. This word *image* is not an idol statue. It comes from the Greek word *eikon*, in English icon. There is an "icon" of this beast system in every aspect of man's existence and functions today. It is primarily manifested through the media.

The US and England are both considered Christian nations. They have "horns like a lamb"; they have an overlay that looks Christian, but they "speak as a dragon." They are a civil governing power. In 1945 many nations sailed to San Francisco and signed the charter to the United Nations. This created the eighth head on the beast. The UN governs the world, in economics, merchandise, trade, drugs, farming, energy, medical, and more. And it governs the wars.

In Revelation 17:3, a woman is riding the beast. All the religions of the world ride the back of their civil governments which rely on the

UN's blessing to exist and the religions of the word depend on this blessing as well. This is especially evident with the WCC, the NCC, and other organizations who counsels with the UN. The following is a reliable substantial quote.

> *The World Council of Churches and the United Nations continue their close ties. In fact, we might call them "blood brothers." There were repeated favorable references to all sorts of UN programs in the Central Committee Documents at Jamaica - The New International Economic Order, the New International Information Order, the World Health Organization, the World Court, UNESCO, etc, it was reported that "an intervention was made on behalf of the WCC in the Security Council debate on South Africa in March 1977." It was stated that they were seeking "to sensitize churches, inviting them to lobby with their governments . . . as well as to mark the 30th Anniversary of the Universal Declaration of Human Rights." The WCC issued a special document promoting the UN sponsored International Year of the Child, totally ignoring the fact that even though this appeal is made with the image of starving children in mind, the real thrust of this program is toward socialization of the child and the family. Individual believers and churches that are opposed to the philosophy and program of the UN should realize that it is not their voice which is heard in places of power and decision - it is the voice of the false prophets in the WCC that prevail and speak for you whether you like it or not.*[82]

"Here is the mind which has wisdom: The seven heads are seven mountains, on which the woman sits." Many Protestants have claimed this to be the Catholic Church of Rome because it has been claimed to sit on seven mountains. But Rome actually has no mountains. Rather, it has about eleven small hills at best.

"There are also seven kings. Five have fallen, one is, and the other has not yet come; and when he comes, he must continue a short time. The beast that was, and is not, is himself also the eighth, and is of the seven, and is going into perdition. The ten horns which you saw are ten kings who have received no kingdom as yet; but they receive authority for one hour as kings with the beast. These are of one mind, and they will give their power and authority to the beast" (Rev. 17:9–13)

82   Ibid.

The eighth head is "of" the seven. It is something that morphed onto the beast. The only empire that meets this description is Great Britain and its partner in the world, the United States. Together with a Christian exterior they create from their seats of authority, the two horns that look like a lamb. But they Speak as a Dragon "The Parliament of Man and the Federation of the World have already been hailed by the poet, and these mean a step much farther in advance of the proposed reunion of Britain and America . . . . I say that as surely as the sun in the heavens once shown upon Britain and America united, so surely is it one morning to rise, shine upon, and greet again the reunited state, "The–American Union."[83]

2016 brought in a new and reformed leadership to the United States and the world.

The Mark of the Beast

Most likely people today that feel the pull in their heart to seek a walk with God beyond the confines of religion are not aware that they are hearing the call to "Come out of her, my people, lest you share in her sins, and lest you receive of her plagues" (Rev. 18:4).

No one wants to receive the plagues generated by the harlot and no one wants to receive the "mark of the beast". Most however, don't perceive the beast or the harlot riding the beast. The mark of the beast has been defined as many different things. Sometimes it is said it would be a computer chip placed in the forehead and/or the hand. Others look for an identifying number printed on an ID card or a food ration card. Some have even suggested that everyone would be tattooed.

What, then, is the mark on the forehead? It is what is in your mind or where and what you give your thinking to. In short, who or what you serve. If you give your mind and thinking to the political-religious systems of the world than you have received that mark in your forehead, (not on your forehead). Also where you give your hand of fellowship and work is the mark in your hand (not on your hand). You have planted your roots in the earth and the earthly things of the world is where your commitment, your thinking and your energy is given. It <u>has precedence.</u>

83 Andrew Carnegie, *Triumphant Democracy* – quoted in *Brotherhood of Darkness* by Dr. Stanley Monteith.

The mark is not seen except by God. When God put a mark on Cain so he would not be slain, it wasn't a visible mark (Gen. 4:15). It meant that God noted him and designated him to be kept from being slain. He was set aside from that outcome. If your noted to serve the beast then you are marked, noted and designated for the outcome.

The number 6 represents mankind in the Bible. Man was created as were the beasts of the field on the sixth day. The governmental structures in every nation of the world is based on the civil-political-religious views of the nation. Every nation of the world has its civil authority, political authority and religious authority which governs it. These represent the three factors of mankind in the earth and these are man's mark (6) in the earth. Remember Jesus said: "I am the way, the truth and the life." When Christ walked the earth, he confronted the beast system of Roman-Israel and it was that system which crucified him.

Christ's authority came from his Father and the authority of his church should come from the Father, which in the beginning it did yet the churches today receive their authority from their nation or states. This is witnessed in various ways, for instance, when a minister marries a couple he will announce to the couple in the presence of an audience," By the power (legal authority) vested in me by the state of (name of state) and the (church name) I now pronounce you man and wife."

Many church leaders believe when they are baptizing it is necessary to say, I baptize you in the name of Jesus or for others, I baptize you in the name of the Father, the Son, and thee Holy Spirit. Both are erroneous perceptions. They are not *IN* the name of Jesus. Rather they are *IN* the name of their organization, their church and their state. To operate in a name means you have the authority of the individual or entity in which you operate.

The Apostle Peter said: "Repent, and be baptized everyone of you in the name of Jesus Christ for the forgiveness of your sins. And you will receive the gift of the Holy Spirit." (Acts 2: 38) He said this because he was operating by the authority which Christ had given him. He was operating *IN* Jesus name. He wasn't even telling them that he himself, was going to baptize them nor stating that the name had to be said. He was telling them to *repent*. That is to turn from their past, come out of that authority and enter Christ's authority through His baptism. It was Shavuot or Pentecost and the people were performing their mikvahs or baptisms and thus, understood what Peter was saying, Therefore, it is not what you are saying, it is whether you have the right or the power of attorney. Neither can you operate under two different authorities or heads. Therefore, if as a leader, you are baptizing by the authority of the state or church, then it doesn't matter what you say, you are not operating *IN* the name of Jesus. This is why Jesus was frequently required to explain where His authority came from. He always claimed His authority came from His Father. We should be no different.

CHAPTER 19

IT'S TIME FOR A CHANGE

The United States of America is the ruling entity of the world today. Therefore, if you change the United States, you change the world. *"So goes the Unites States; so, goes the world."*

Over the past twelve years we have seen unprecedented changes take place, not only to the United States but, to the entire world. These changes have been profoundly hazardous for the most part. The United States government no longer exists as founded. It operates like a third world country housing a tyrannical leadership. As a result, the nations of the world are crumbling to the point of non-recognition.

The excitement, education and beauty of experiencing different cultures and societies is being stripped away as the self-called elite disintegrates every culture and nation. Engaged in diminishing heritages, with the unique and accepted differences of societies and their own beliefs and their own histories in order to produce their imagined globalist agenda, the tower of Babel-one world government, a.k.a. New World Order. The beautiful variety of our world and the individuality of people are being raped, dismantled, sabotaged and eradicated by measure. "Change we can believe in". The 2007 campaign slogan of the selected and groomed Barack Hussein Obama for the 2008 United States presidential election. Considered the first black president. Yet in actuality, he is not a black American but rather a half white American and half Kenyan man but, the color of someone's skin is not a consideration nor a reason of most people to elect a person for such a position. He was however, the first Muslim president according to the evidence provided by his own books, his childhood education, his father and his occasional slip ups referring to himself as a Muslim.

In Obama's book, "Dreams of My Father", his grandfather, Hussein Onyango Obama, is stated to have converted to Islam. Also, that his father was a Muslim but became an atheist before he met his mother.

His stepfather, Lolo Soetoro, an Indonesian which thus far, is the largest Muslim country on earth, was Muslim. Obama stated that his stepfather did not practice his Muslim faith. However, both accounts: his father becoming an atheist and his stepfather being a Muslim in name only is suspiciously fictitious because it is not in accord with Islamic religious/political standards.

Obama attended an Islamic school in Indonesia. Dressed in the Islamic traditional clothing and engaged in the Islamic school study programs. Thus he was groomed to be a Muslim.

While Obama protested his involvement as a Muslim and publicly denied the faith, he was hiring Muslims into the political arena as well as propagandizing the Islamic faith during speeches by proclaiming things such as "Islam has been woven into the fabric of our country since it's founding." Then proceeded to exclaim how Muslim immigrants "came here and went to work as farmers and merchants and factory workers, helped to lay railroads and to build up America."

He boasted that the first Islamic center in New York City was founded in the 1890's and that America's first mosque, was established in 1929 in North Dakota. However, both events were well after the founding of our country.

He failed to mention of course, that the United States was embroiled into involvement with Islam. Attributing to this was the rapid increase of attacks by Muslim pirates upon unprovoking Americans. They captured the American sailors, sold them as slaves, or held them for ransom and looted the ships. This is documented in history as the Barbary Wars.

The Barbary States consisted of North African states of which the majority of those states supported and participated in acts of piracy which allowed them to exact tribute from lesser Atlantic powers. The Morocco kingdom maintained its independence but, Algiers, Tunis, and Tripoli held a partial allegiance to the Ottoman Empire.

The United States warred with Tripoli (1801–1805) and Algiers (1815–1816), albeit of those captured, tortured and held in the Barbary States, there were intervals where the United States paid tribute for their release.

Per The Heritage Foundation paper, Muslim pirates from the Barbary States (todays Morocco, Algeria, Tunisia, and Libya) began a short time after the 13 colonies declared independence from Britain in 1776 and continued for about forty years.

The *people* of Islam or Muslim's are simply just that, people, like anyone else. Many are kind warm hearted individuals who are pleasant to be with. Yet, like so many around the globe they are subjects and prisoners of a political religious system. A beast system.

So, why then is it an issue of importance that Obama was a Muslim and assigned many to strategic positions in our government? The answer is simple. Our constitution allows freedom of religion, freedom of speech etc. However, the hitch here is that in order to remain free there must be a total separation from non-freedom of religions, politics, and other non-free establishments and governments. Therefore, to have individuals who are not supportive of our national constitution and seek to change it to a system of tyrannical dictatorship are a direct threat to those freedoms. Whether a communist, socialist, globalist, Muslim, etc. their involvement in our politics, banking, education, policing or any state or federal position should not be condoned. It is foolish to allow an opposer to operate in sensitive categories where they have the ability to make alterations to the very fabric of our freedoms.

The moral decline, and varietal plagues and famines that this world suffers today with the globalist menu for repair began years ago however, it was the election of Barack Hussein Obama to presidency that put the illuminati, one world religion, one world government Globalist so called "elites" agenda in spot light view for those who are looking. Actually, the conspiracy to have a one world order is an ancient idealism that remained well hidden until now. But, the constitution of the United States and the freedoms our people enjoy are not conducive to the globalist mentality.

It is not contribeuted to Barack alone but many who superseded him. In fact, the forty first presidential seat was held by globalist;

President George H. W. Bush. His speech before congress on September 11, 1990 was the first time the world majority heard the phrase new world order. The following excerpt is a quote from his speech.

"We stand today at a unique and extraordinary moment. The crisis in the Persian Gulf, as grave as it is, also offers a rare opportunity to move toward an historic period of cooperation. Out of these troubled times, our fifth objective — *a new world order* — can emerge: a new era — freer from the threat of terror, stronger in the pursuit of justice, and more secure in the quest for peace. An era in which the nations of the world, East and West, North and South, can prosper and live in harmony."

What is he saying here? That the Persian Gulf crisis gave us excuse to launch their "fifth objective" which is a *new world order?* Not surprising as in their thinking; the end justifies the means.

The idea of a one world religion coupled with a one world political system has been around since the tower of Babel. However, man's idea of a political religious world government is not God's idea. It is in direct opposition of our Heavenly Father's gift of eternal life in *His* new world order.

George W. Bush, son of George H. W. Bush, was elected to the presidential office in 2000. On September 11. 2001, about eight months' after he took office, the twin towers, the world trade center in New York city, completed in 1973, were brought down. Supposedly by commercial jet aircraft being deliberately flown into them.

There was aircraft flown into them alright however, that was not what brought them collapsing straight down as though the very foundation was yanked away. According to some construction engineer experts and the building blue prints, those buildings could withstand far greater impact then that of a one hundred twenty-eight thousand pound, four hundred fifty mile per hour jet ripping into the side of them. because the buildings standing at one hundred and ten stories high were constructed to withstand not only the possibility of being hit by aircraft but also, with the wind conditions at that height they had the ability to sway. The collapse and manner in which they collapsed is questionable and arguable. There are opinions and support of both theory's.

Jet fuel ignites at about one hundred degrees Fahrenheit and combusts at around four hundred and ten degrees. It will burn between eight hundred and three thousand hundred degrees. Steel requires between twenty-two hundred and twenty-five hundred degrees Fahrenheit to melt. Therefore, it would be conceivable that the combustion of jet fuel would melt down the steel in the twin towers even though the steel was treated with Spray-Applied Fire-Resistant Material (SFRM). In addition, the plane was carrying an excessive amount of fuel. But the impact was at the ninety third and ninety ninth stories and heat rises. Therefore, it would appear that the fires would spread upward and there would be ample time to bring them under control before the heat would spread downward. Then again, metal is a good conductor of heat so whether horizontal or vertical the heat would spread. Of course, steel is not the best conductor of heat Copper and alumina are the best for conducting heat. Non the less, the heat could travel throughout the beams and weaken its steel structure if it could maintain high enough temperatures down all ninety-eight floors below. Hardly seems feasible and the majority of construction engineers consulted will testify to the impossibility of a structure like the twin towers to collapse the way they did without an explosive demolition.

In nineteen-forty-five a WW B25 Mitchell bomber flew into the one hundred two story empire state building, leaving an eighteen by twenty-foot hole. Eleven people were killed inside the building plus the three inside the plane. The building also had a steel beam skeleton but, the steel was thicker and it also had a strong core structure with girders every twelve feet at its core while the twin towers did not. This has been used to compare why the twin towers were destroyed however, the B25 weighed about twenty thousand pounds and was flying approximately two hundred miles per hour only the fuel load was a relatively lite load but in mass consideration it is not a contributing factor.

There were eye witnesses to the twin tower attack, including one police officer who stated that there were no windows on the plane. If so, then it was not a commercial jet. Also, there were many standing by who claim that prior to the collapse they heard numerous explosions like bombs were being detonated. The fact is, that happens to be the preferred method used by demolition crews for bringing down tall buildings. If bombs are strategically placed at the base of a structure and detonated it would cause an implosion and the building would then, collapse down into its footprint. F. (Ref. ImplosionWorld.com)

The belief that this attack was government orchestrated comes from these eyewitness accounts. Also, the understanding that some days prior the owner increased his insurance on the buildings would raise eyebrows and lend support to this opinion.

An excerpt from River City Readers on forensic evidence written by, Kathleen McCarthy states as follows:

"World Trade Center Towers

Jet fuel burns no hotter than 1,200 degrees. Consequently, the fires caused by the plane crashes could not possibly burn hot enough to melt the core steel structure of each floor, let alone to collapse the entire building(s). This dispels the official story that the steel trusses' joints melted from jet-fuel fires, "pancaking" the floors on top of one another - leaving completely ignored the question of what then happened to the 47-beam grid in the center of both towers.

Molten steel girders were found in the debris at Ground Zero. The damage to the steel itself was notable - deformed, twisted, but curiously not cracked. The only substance capable of creating the heat necessary to cause this kind of damage to steel is Thermite, which must first be detonated. Residue from nearby buildings that were in the path of the huge smoke/debris plumes created when the buildings collapsed was extensively tested, revealing that Thermite was abundantly present in the dust that covered Ground Zero and its surrounding blocks.

Film footage of the collapse of the twin towers, when played in slow motion, reveals a pattern of explosive bursts, called "squibs," preceding many of the floors' collapse as the buildings dropped straight down. This is precisely what occurs in planned building demolitions. The majority of the world's structural, mechanical, metallurgical, and chemical engineers, architects, and demolition experts agree that nothing but a planned demolition using strategically placed explosives could mimic the perfect straight-down free-fall that characterized the collapse of both towers. More important, planned demolitions require extensive analysis of the structure, and therefore must be planned months in advance.

When interviewed, countless witnesses - many of them survivors from the towers, including firefighters - claimed they heard and/or saw secondary explosions after the plane crashes. Some heard explosions in the basements of the buildings, some in the lobbies, others on various floors as they were escaping to safety. So many individual reports of explosions (including live news reports on-site), each independent of one another, were summarily removed from the media's coverage after 9/11.

The security company for the towers was Securacom, then operated by President George W. Bush's brother Marvin. A brand-new security system was installed just two weeks prior to 9/11, leaving security cameras inoperable throughout the buildings during that time, and access by large trucks was given between 3 and 5 a.m. the weekend before the 9/11 attacks, reported CIA asset and whistle-blower Susan Lindaur.

The Pentagon

Not a single body or body fragment, piece of luggage, or identifiable piece of the plane - including the fuselage, engines, wheels, wings, and seats - belonging to American Airlines Flight 77 was found at the Pentagon crash site. The official story claims that the fire from the crash "disintegrated" the plane, along with everyone and everything in it. Twenty minutes after the crash, the roof collapsed above the crash site, revealing all the floors, computers, desks, etc. completely intact around the plane's point of impact. Yet the 8,600 gallons of remaining jet fuel should have reduced the impact site to rubble, but there was very little heat or smoke damage to the structure adjacent to the impact site.

Various eyewitnesses claim it was a smaller aircraft that crashed into the Pentagon than the reported American Airlines Boeing 757. (Eyewitnesses who saw the second plane crash into the second World Trade Center tower made similar claims, saying it was gray in color with no windows or markings.) There were security cameras all around the impact site and throughout the Pentagon that could help confirm or deny such reports, but all cameras were immediately confiscated, and the FBI has only released five frames from a single camera's footage of that day. However, the date stamp on each frame is incorrect, showing 9/12/2001 at 17:37:19. There is no sign of an actual plane in these frames, only the explosions and fire created upon impact.

A Boeing 757 is nearly 125 feet from wingtip to wingtip, more than 155 feet from nose to tail, and almost 45 feet from the ground to the top of the tail. However, the actual hole in the Pentagon wall was only 65 feet wide. These dimensions do not remotely correspond, making it a physical impossibility for a Boeing 757 to have been the aircraft that crashed into the Pentagon. *National Geographic* attempted to explain the discrepancy using a computer simulation showing the aircraft›s wings breaking off before slamming into the building. This does not explain why, then, the wings weren›t found on the lawn outside the Pentagon where the plane hit. There are several versions of events of the attack on the Pentagon that demand to be sorted out.

Pilots and engineers affirm that it is aerodynamically impossible for a plane the size of a Boeing 757 to have made the necessary 270-degree turn into the Pentagon while maintaining flight speed and a distance of less than 20 feet from the ground before crashing into the building. Witnesses on the ground reported seeing a much smaller aircraft - possibly even a Global Hawk drone - flying into the Pentagon on 9/11, but certainly not a passenger airliner the size of a Boeing 757. A drone is a plausible explanation for the precision with which the plane hit the Pentagon, the lack of wreckage found at the site, and the smaller hole made in the Pentagon wall.

Every single defense protocol - including the Pentagon's own missile-defense system - that would normally have been deployed in a hijacking scenario (let alone the invasion of airspace around the building) failed on 9/11. The magnitude of this failure undermines the defense department to its core, yet this astonishing breach is all but ignored by the media cartel. NORAD failed to intercept the planes after it was notified of the hijackings. But prior to 9/11, NORAD had completed 67 successful interceptions, so clearly it had the proper training for such crises.

Air controllers along the flight paths of all four planes reported the hijackings, requesting military response to no avail. There was mass confusion about where planes were and weren't, evidenced by the recorded tapes of numerous air-control calls and conversations that day.

Military response was sluggish because all bases had new orders to stand down relative to hijackings unless approval came directly from the Pentagon, specifically Secretary of Defense Donald Rumsfeld, who could not be located the morning of 9/11. Coincidentally, three months before 9/11, the standard protocol for immediate military intervention in the event of a hijacking was replaced with a protocol that required permission from the Pentagon before taking any action. This short-lived protocol was reversed following 9/11. Interestingly, Rumsfeld was photographed carrying debris from the crash site at the Pentagon later that day.

Pennsylvania

No bodies or wreckage were found at the Pennsylvania crash site, just a barren hole in the ground. Yet a driver's license belonging to a flight attendant and a passport belonging to a hijacker were found near the site. The official story is that the plane disintegrated with all its occupants.

The cell-phone calls claimed to have been made from Flight 93 at 30,000 feet in the air prior to the crash were not possible because in 2001, the technology for such calls was not available.

Seven World Trade Center

A third building collapsed around 5 p.m. on 9/11. Seven World Trade Center, previously known as the Solomon Brothers Building but now more commonly referred to as WTC7, collapsed in exactly the same manner as the towers - straight-down free-fall as in a planned demolition. But no plane crashed into it.

WTC7 housed offices for the Secret Service, CIA, Department of Defense, IRS Regional Council, Federal Home Loan Bank, Securities & Exchange Commission, ITT Hartford Insurance Corporation, Standard Center Bank, American Express Bank International, Solomon Smith Barney, NAIC Securities, and Providence Financial Management.

No skyscraper made of steel had ever collapsed due to fire before the World Trade Center towers. Nor has any steel building been destroyed by fire since. Yet less than 30 minutes after the towers' collapse, the media cartel reported that the fire fed by the jet fuel "brought the buildings down." Those same reports just as quickly credited Osama bin Laden with the heinous crimes. Later, miraculously, a passport of one of the hijackers was found that had survived the inferno that brought down not one but two reinforced steel structures - confirming that al-Qaeda was behind the terrorist attacks. It begs the question why bin Laden was never charged with any crime associated with 9/11.

Money and Wars

Larry Silverstein exercised a $3.4-billion lease for the World Trade Center six weeks before 9/11. He negotiated his insurance coverage on the towers to include any damage from terrorist attacks. He was awarded $7 billion when the dust settled.

On September 10, 2001, Rumsfeld held a press conference to notify the public that the Pentagon "could not track $2.3 trillion in transactions." This missing money was never mentioned again after the events of 9/11."

After the attack president Bush determined to send intelligence and military to the middle east in order to flush out and destroy those believed to be responsible.

A new cabinet-level department of Homeland Security was developed and United States military forces were sent to Afghanistan to dismantle the Taliban created for the purpose of terrorism by Osama bin Laden whom they were to capture as well. The dismantling of the Taliban was successful however, Osama Bin Laden was not captured.

President Bush ordered reform of the military in order to fight the new enemy. He invaded Iraq on the conclusion that Iraqi president Saddam Hussein was a major threat to the United States. His former invasion of Kuwait which led to the Persian Gulf War that his father, George H. W. Bush administered when he was president, plus the reports of his brutality and abusive leadership gave reason, according to the Bush's, to hunt him out.

President George W. Bush addressed the U.S. stating; "Saddam Hussein and his weapons are a direct threat to this country, to our people, and to all free people…I believe Saddam Hussein is a threat to the American people. I believe he's a threat to the neighborhood in which he lives. And I've got good evidence to believe that. He has weapons of mass destruction…The American people know that Saddam Hussein has weapons of mass destruction."

Thus, on these premises a war was ensued. Yet, as we now know, these claims were untrue. There were no weapons of mass destruction and there was no threat to the United States. Rather it appears that the reason we engaged in this war was to help Israel.

Bush was elected a second term but during that term, Iraq was a disrupted country where rivals were killing American servicemen and American friendly Iraqis. These situations were wearying on the nation's citizens. People were turning on news programs and daily hearing about the loss of lives within Iraq.

Saddam Hussein was successfully captured. He was tried by an Iraqi court for crimes against humanity, namely the Dujail massacre (the killing of 148 Iraqi Shi'ites) and was executed on December 30, 2006.

All of the terrorist activity and military responses set the stage for Obama's campaign. Many embraced the idea of a change, a *fundamental change*. Impressionable individuals who lacked understanding of government tactics were easily persuaded in the direction of a *fundamental change* of the nation.

In many of Obama's speeches he reiterated that he wanted to make a *fundamental change* of the nation. This was a very dangerous and threatening statement that was not picked up on by many people. Fundamental is the very core or base of central importance. Therefore, what he was stating was that he intended to remove our constitution for our **constitution is our fundament**. A very dangerous *change* was in effect.

In order to accomplish such an enormous change, there has to be a removal of the leading nations. The United States must fall as well as its companion Great Britain and allies of the United Kingdom. There can be no single world governing power in existence. No country by itself can establish the world's monetary exchange, trading standards, international relationships, military operations or any type of world involvement nor moral standards such as the right to sovereignty.

That may seem fair and just but, the reality is a chaotic assemblage of differences will emerge which cannot be resolved. No one nation will want to relent their political position and their religious priority's. Nor should they. The world itself, is too large and inhabited to control. The globalists or illuminati are well aware of this and have developed a means to combat this opposition.

The Obama administration indeed brought about many changes. He, like so many before him, was selected, groomed, prepped and indoctrinated for the election. Not the first pawn for the globalist agenda, but one of the best. He had credentials that would be greatly advantageous. He was a man of color and that fact could be exploited for votes. He was younger than his opponents, and gained admiration of the younger votes by construct of speeches and gave away phones which for some sealed their vote to his favor. Forbes reports a young lady holding up a phone and exclaiming: "Keep Obama in president, you know! He gave us a phone, he's gonna do more."

His speech was articulate and he held a charismatic demeanor which captivated the youth and they were excited to be involved in a *change* and by a first *black* president! So, many votes poured in from deceived young and liberally indoctrinated voters.

Obama laid the foundation of the creation of Black Lives Matter. Which upon close examination, you find they are a terrorist group involved in the destruction of our nation from within. Antifa groups emerged from his administration having the same mind set as the BLM army's have. Michelle Obama, who well-nigh professes to despise this nation, encourages the destruction of those Caucasians who founded it. Yet, disregarding her contempt of our nation she chooses to stay, if only to see its demise.

Wonderful black people like Martin Luther King, Rosa Parks, Maya Angelou, James Baldwin and others who had an awareness of the globalist, illuminati, the one world political religious government, those subtle deceivers that infiltrated our nation such as George Soros, Klaus Schwab, Bill Gates, the Clintons, Obamas, Bidens and so many more, have had their names defamed, their race disgraced and demeaned through these Antifa and BLM deployed destroyers. Beyond that they make a display of their idiocracy by the foolish immature extremist dethroning our precious Aunt Jemima and honored Uncle Ben. But they allow us to pretend we still have our patriot Uncle Sam while our military is being plummeted with the same social nonsensical regurgitation and deliberately enervated.

After his departure from the White House, rumors erupted of his forming an army consisting of about thirty thousand (not to be confused with the thirty thousand deportees to Afghanistan) all youths whom he could deploy for chaos and destruction when politics didn't support the agenda of the globalist. Fact checkers like Snopes claim these rumors are unfounded however, if you are educated on who the fact checkers are and represent then you understand that they themselves are unreliable and extremely biased as they have been hired to mislead the news populace. Thus, it is yet to be learned if this is real or imagined.

There has been a multitude of lies and deceptions handed to the citizens of America and the world from all sides and all groups. Albeit, if you want to learn truth, the best place to go is out of this country. It is a fact that other nations know more truth and accurate information about the United States than its own citizens.

Succeeding Obama was supposed to be Hillary Clinton who had served in the Obama administration as secretary of defense. Even though she was directly responsible for the Benghazi tragedy which took place during this administration. She with her accomplices actually looked mothers and fathers in the eye and lied about the events leading to the attack on our embassy resulting in the death of their child. Knowing all the time that the attack was orchestrated in order to conceal the trafficking she was making of United States military weaponry to Syria out of Libya. (Ref. Town Hall Tip/Fox News May 8,2015)

Her loss came as a colossal surprise to the left. The anticipation was that the "fix" was in for her election. However, the quantity of votes for Donald J. Trump was not anticipated and unplanned for thus, he won the majority. Had he not won, our destruction would have been sooner.

After Donald Trump was elected violence broke out across the nation that was obviously instituted by an authority to the degree that charges were kept from people committing unacceptable criminal behavior such as crushing police vehicles by jumping up and down on them, smashing through store front windows, looting, starting dangerous fires, throwing explosive devices, injuring individuals, etc. These incidents do not need to be fact checked as it was captured on film and reported on news outlets here and abroad.

The Obama administration created an extreme liberal mentality and ideas such as the "all inclusive" movement has its roots within his administration. All globalists are extreme liberals but, it is only a mask they wear. The reality is there is no liberalism in their globalist agenda. Upon careful examination, one learns that globalism is a world governmental enslavement.

Hormonal Delusions

Transgenderism and the woke also has its roots in the liberal globalist agenda. This idea removes any discretion a company, a business or any organization would have in the decision of who would be an acceptable asset. The employees are coerced and forced to accept the "all inclusive" mentality. But any intelligent self-thinker understands to be all inclusive is a dangerous stance to take. It leaves you completely open and vulnerable to every invasive, deterioration and destruction imaginable.

These manufactured, funded and protected ideologies are presented to the most persuaded groups of our society for the purpose of re-indoctrination. Our public schools are subjects of target because if you can shape the mind of a child then when they are adults, they will process information and respond to that information in the manner designed by the indoctrinator.

The globalist agenda is also to reduce the world population. Not because, as they would tell you, it is advantageous to the stabilization of a healthy existence by less food consumption, water usage, energy consumption, less pollution and less opportunity to spread disease. This sounds good but, it is not the reality of their agenda. The reality is control. The world numbers are too many, to vast and spread out for control thus, because they cannot control the masses, they must eliminate them.

All of these agendas and more were set before the people and presented like a banquet of the best exquisite varieties of delicacies prepared for our national improvement if we should only swallow them down. Through our schools and educational system, the young were indoctrinated to accept their world view, policies and agenda. Through speeches, through the media, through entertainment, movies and music included. Many were wooed and swallowed the bait. Now we have a number of non-American thinkers trying to force everyone to drink their Kool-Aid. Right is left, up is down, male is female, dads are moms, moms are dads, wrong is right, captivity is freedom, peace is war and so it spins and weaves throughout our society until we are all drunken. Sadly, they themselves are so distorted and confused in their perception of the world around them that they cannot comprehend the differences between any of it.

A plan, or conspiracy if you wish, by the globalist for accomplishing the pursuit to reduce the human population was introduced. A simple and undetected means that would wipe out millions within a few years. A killer virus. Namely a COVID and bring in a pandemic. Frighten the multitudes around the world so they will be complicit in the scheme. Then introduce an inoculation created as a faux vaccine which would contain toxins that would cause death or injury either in a short time after the injection or a long time after the injection.

Also, to ensure those put in hospitals would not recover through proper medical treatment, a protocol treatment would be enforced upon hospitals and medical staff. Such as administering remdesivir and placing people on ventilators. Taking them off of fluids such as water and removing all nutrition. Incentive to carry out these procedures without protest would be the carrot of thousands of dollars earned by diagnosing the so-called virus. Thirty thousand dollars could be earned just for placing them on a ventilator. If they die all the more dollars would be granted. By the time they entered the hospital and died a handsome sum of around one hundred thirty thousand dollars would be earned from every dead person. If that wasn't enough incentive to join the evil scheme of lies and deception a threat to their career would be in place. Many lost their jobs for not complying. Many doctors lost their license because they would not comply to the rules set forth. Many have been put behind bars for speaking against the narrative and our bought-out media would support the narrative and spew forth falsehoods to lull the masses into compliance.

This hoax wasn't just brought to the United States but, every nation became the cesspool of the biggest lie ever perpetrated on an entire world.   Evidence supports that the so called COVID19 virus was actually created during the Obama administration in North Carolina at Fort Deitrick and in or around 2015 it was transported to the Wuhan Lab in China. There were no bats, penguins or any other animal involved only what was incorporated in the development of this man-made flu type virus.

The virus (if you want to call it a virus) actually was and is not as life threatening as the majority of our already existing flu virus'. But the fear and anxiety presented and promoted across the pharmaceutical supported media brought the people in like cattle herds lined up for the jab. The coup de gras to the COVID outbreak.

Major companies went along with the faux reports and unknowingly set demands on their employees to be inoculated with the, what was being termed as a vaccine for the COVID. or lose their jobs and positions. Dr's. were threatened that they would lose their license. A faux lockdown was instituted and many lost their livelihoods. Businesses were shut down and anyone who worked in the establishment that was not considered a necessity to function e.g., a grocery store, a hardware store or a medical establishment was ordered to close. Even church buildings for worshippers to gather in had their doors locked. And the whole affair was a test of human will and a cheap hoax executed on the entire planet! And we everyone failed the populace through ignorance and compliance. However, we passed the globalists construct and performed like the sheeple they anticipated. Sadly, many still are with blinders on following the globalist narrative. Like sleep walkers reaching out in the dark, they don't have a clue what they are engaged in.

These COVID jabs have been followed by death, and injury. Some immediately, some within a few days, some after a few months and the understanding of the medical science researchers some jabs are designed to effectively kill their host after a number of years. Up to seven. Of course, after a number of months it is unlikely that the injury or death of an inoculated individual would be traced to the inoculation. Thus, having the serum vials vary in content structural release decreases the suspicion of the harm being administered. Yet whether the vial content has a short-term or long-term impact period is of no consequence to the set goal. Each serum constructed has harmful components and is guaranteed to weaken the immune system to the degree that a normal flu will be impossible to recover from and ultimately kill you.

Of to date, many microbiologists have found unusual components within the blood of COVID inoculated recipients. Reports by individuals such as Pfizer's, previous to the COVID hoax, valued employee Karen Kingston and others have revealed on slides self-assembling circuitry, graphene and other metals, spiked proteins and a host of other damaging materials.

But, why the microscopic self-assembling circuit boards? The obvious it to have you wired into a WIFI type of messaging, control and or kill. If that isn't enough documentation for the book; Dr. Brian Ardis discovered snake venom from the Chinese Krait snake and Cobra.

The following is a quote from Dr. Ardis during an interview with broadcaster and host Mike Adams.

"they are using synthesized peptides and proteins from venoms of snakes and they are administering them and targeting them to certain people. Now the amazing thing about these 19 toxins found in cobra venom, is they are specifically sequenced to target specific organs, like the pancreas in the diabetic, like the heart in a heart disease patient, like the liver in a hepatitis patient." This makes the cause of death almost undetectable.

"This is the most original of all bioweapons ever!"

He goes on, *"I can't think of anything more evil than envenomating the entire world with snake venom and then injecting snake venom into your veins, and then using mRNA technology that they've been isolating from snake venom for years. That they know are unusually stable. More stable than any other mRNA that they've isolated from any other natural organism, for decades. In 2015, they took mRNA from cobra venom and krait venom and they actually wrapped the mRNA in nanoparticle hydrogel... and they made it even more stable. Then they actually added what is called 1 to those nanoparticle hydrogels, surrounding the mRNA of snake venom and it made even more stable and made it last even longer and easier to get inside your cells. Do you know what Dynabeads are? Magnetic metal nanoparticles!"*

"There isn't an aspect of Covid19, its symptoms as a disease or an infection none of the symptoms or side effects of [the antiviral] Remdesivir, none of the side effects or adverse advents, serious or minor, of the mRNA vaccines that cannot be linked to snake venom poisoning. All of it is related!"

So the mRNA 'vaccines' are instructing the body to manufacture snake venom in their own cells?

Alarmingly, people's bodies have become *"snake venom factories"* says Adams. *"That's exactly what's going on"* agrees Ardis. *"Since 2011, they've been taking mRNA from snake venom and figuring out how to inject it into the cells and into the DNA of cow's cells and they used venom mRNA to do it"*

"When they talk about replicating spike protein, no, no, you are replicating snake venom peptides or proteins, and it just continues to replicate throughout the body"

Does anyone feel like they are part of a sci-fi movie yet? We live in a fabricated world. We can't tell truth from fiction, right from wrong, male from female. We don't even understand the difference between flat and round any more. All facts are ignored and referred to as "conspiracy theories". A conspiracy is nothing more that a plan between two or more parties. Whether it is a theory or not is shown by the evidence.

Karen Kingston has presented more evidence than anyone person on the stage of truth tellers. She has worked relentlessly to bring to the public an education on the COVID subject. She does not open her mouth without documented facts to back her up. She is not alone but, because she was a former Pfizer employee, she is very credible in her knowledge of the pharmaceutical industry. She has displayed copies of literature, patents, and other documents which disclose the COVID inoculations as bioweapons. Therefore, everyone involved in the manufacturing and distribution of these bioweapons has committed an act of war and treason on their nations and the world.

With all the evidence presented it is reckless and foolish to suggest that these individuals and their supporters are conspiracy theorists. None the less the media will use their fallacious fact checkers and pound out the words, **conspiracy theory**. When in truth the conspiracy is no theory at all.

The MAGA Era

A Good Time to Release Their Biological Weapons

As mentioned previously, Hillary Clinton was chosen by the globalists to continue the agenda the Obama's and others were employed to accomplish. But our creator determined to decelerate their destructive ambitions with the unexpected multitudes of approval, and support of a non-politician. An astute sharp-witted businessman. A self-made billionaire who could relate to the working backbone of the country. As rough around the edges as any good old red neck country or street educated city slicker can be. A pull no punches, call them as he sees them kind of man but, with a transparent honest and caring heart for the citizens and country he loves.

Donald J Trump, with his economical savvy observed the intentional demise of his country and knew he possessed the intellect and experience to correct the hell-bent path it was on. He determined to "Make America Great Again". His aspirations became contagious and thousands heralded his message. They gathered at his rallies with snow balling effects. Gathering momentum and increasing in size up to and even beyond his election, the support for Trump and "MAGA" grew in phenomenal numbers. The majority of the citizen's wanted their country back. The salutation of USA, USA, USA, was a common epizeuxis resounding through every Trump rally.

Under the Trump administration, we became energy independent, the economy exploded and there was so much work available that employers were hunting for people to fill empty positions. Our military grew and strengthened. Our borders were made secure and an overdue, long time needed border wall was finally being constructed. The veteran's received increased and improved health care and so did everyone as the damaging repercussions of Obama Care were being resolved. Factories and manufacturing companies were returning to America and the "made in the USA" status was proudly returning. Gas and energy prices were affordable again as well as housing improvement and rates. Our farmers were being taken care of and able to produce as they should and America was respected by all other countries around the globe. The American people had a greater sense of pride in their nation and were more optimistic, confident and ambitious than ever. People were giving honor to God and country with deliberation and without pretense.

All of this prosperity and resolve of poor policy's, not just for the United States, but for the entire world was not what the globalists had bargained for. They needed to carry out their attack on the world population and create enough fear and havoc people would run for the faux protection of their elected authorities.

The time for re-election came. There was absolutely no doubt Trump would be elected back in office in 2020. The American people wanted to continue in prosperity, independence and security. They were regaining their relationship with God and placing value back into the family unit. We were a country in healing.

Donald Trump's polls showed that he was a shoo-in and his rallies were substantially bigger than the previous election rallies. But having Donald Trump in office for another four years could completely alleviate the globalists plans, so prior to the finish of his first term it was determined to unleash their bioweapon termed as COVID19.

This would force delay and with a little reinforcement put an end to everything he was trying to accomplish. They would surround him with individuals giving him false information on the development and components of their disease as well as the location of its source.

This information coming mostly from Anthony Fauci, physician-scientist and immunologist who had cleverly gained position as chief medical advisor to the president. He with others created and funded their virus which carried the same impact as a bad flu, but was propagandized as being worse than the black plague. Most deaths from their virus were a direct result of the protocol that Anthony Fauci insisted needed to be practiced by physicians and hospitals. Thereby ensuring that many would die.

Robert Malone created the inoculation they termed as the "vaccine" which is no vaccine at all but, upon reading the Pfizer patent, (serial number: 613066) one learns it is in actuality, a bioweapon that was created for harming, maiming and killing. The serum was created to vary so that the results would differ among the injected. The reason obviously being that if everyone were to have the same reaction it would reveal its intended harm.

Some people would die within a few days, some a few weeks and some months and others years. Auto immune disease, experiences of severe nerve damage, developed rare cancers and turbo cancers, increased diabetis, mental fog and inability's, strange clotting in the blood, myocarditis and many other crippling, killing, diseases and physical disabilities have been reported to VAERS (vaccine adverse event reporting system). The majority of vaccine adverse events has not been reported. In fact, it is suggested that less than six per cent of all adverse events are actually reported.

Because a treating physician is responsible to make the report and because many reactions are so far delayed from the time of inoculation and the physician's reputation is reflected in the administering of the inoculation, the majority of adverse events go unreported. Although at this point in time, VAERS because of the jab's unpopularity, is no longer eager to report the facts but hides them behind a lot of manipulated ambiguous data.

These bioweapon shots are what is termed a "slow kill". The term applied is because of the damage done to the immune system, causing people to fall ill of various diseases or not have the ability to fight off normal flus or colds and thus ends up losing their lives.

The main purpose of these created diseases and killing inoculations is to reduce the world population. One indisputable fact of the inoculations is the attack on the reproductive organs of both men and women. Disabling them to have children. And should an injected woman conceive, she will likely experience termination of her pregnancy either through natural abortion or the infant may not develop properly and dies in the womb or may be birthed full term with defects. A roulette scenario.

A now well-known film "Died Suddenly" brought to us by Stew Peters, gives good coverage and documentation on these adversities. They are reported and described by highly skilled and reputable biologists, scientists, immunologists, physicians and even morticians who have witnessed first-hand these events.

"Operation Warp Speed" was going to be the answer during Trump's administration. Even the military would be deployed if and as necessary to deliver these bioweapons masked as COVID 19 Vaccine's. Like Super-Man swooping in to save the day, Trump was going to cleanse the country of this threatening virus. He'd been deceived and convinced to initiate "warp speed". Any biologist would tell you it is impractical, unethical and not probable to create a vaccine at "warp speed". Impossible…not if you are not concerned for the outcome.

A collective sigh of relief went across the nation as everyone who took the bait lined up for their jab. And after learning that one wasn't enough, they obediently lined up for the second. Then it was soon reported that a booster had to be administered. Those who had not yet received any negative response to the first two injections submitted to this round of treatment as well.

The damages have been indescribably horrific and are ongoing. The evil instigators within our government knowing of the harm and deaths to come, made the pharmaceutical companies immune to liability. However, now more than three years into the inoculations, the immunity has finally lifted and Pfizer, for one, can be sued for damages. A small victory compared to the millions of directly related deaths. The vast majority either from hospital protocol abuse or the jab itself.

Many individuals have learned the intent and results of this inoculation and have now refused to submit themselves to the booster program. Also, many parents are learning that having their children subjected to the vaccine program requirements are placing their children at risk for damaging physical malfunctions i.e., autism, enlarged hearts, cancers etc. and therefore refusing the program for the safety of their children.

Although the deep state orchestrators brought fabricated accusations against president Trump and released a lab created bioweapon upon its citizens and the world during his administration, which resulted in resistance to the momentum of his accomplishments. Almost bringing them to a halt as they planned, his popularity did not waiver and they knew he would be re-elected to finish the rebuilding of our nation. For which to this day, those opposing our country's prosperity claim he is not rebuilding it, but rather he is destroying it.

We now have proof of events that transpired during the two thousand twenty presidential elections. It has been clearly demonstrated that the election of Donald Trump was altered through nefarious means in order to place Joe Biden in the White House (in leu of Hillary Clinton) who would be the face of Barrack Obama, the person who is in charge by proxy of the deep state operatives, both here and abroad, of our country. The person who has not left the White House although discharged. The person who said that he wanted to run the country from his own home and just be the mouthpiece of the installed individual playing president. He is Oz behind the curtain and he has been running his third term without our electing him. The nation is on the self-imploding path with economical failure and banks collapsing, the dollar value depleted in the world, energy deficiency and high cost, decreased farming and food shortage, weakened military and infrastructure, rise of severe illness coupled with rise of health cost, inefficient education with replaced history included etc. etc. All designed to destroy our country from within. It is called a "fundamental change". All of this is being in "warp speed" manipulated to make up for their lost four years with Trump and they had to insure he would not have eight years to improve and strengthen the country any further or their mission might fail.

Is it any wonder that the first thing Biden did was to shut down the Keystone pipeline? Which according to the Washington post cost the US economy over fifty-nine thousand jobs and more than nine and two-thirds billion dollars with one stroke of the pen. And since then, he has pulpited the commands of Obama and everything he has done has been to our deliberate demise. This could not occur if Trump had been placed in the White House, so his election had to be altered and prevented. Most say it is obvious we have imposters in the White House.

January six of two thousand twenty-one, there were thousands of individuals who gathered at the capital in Washington D.C. in order to display their objection to a stolen election. What began as a peaceful protest turned into chaos. The main stream media was reporting that the "mob" was an "insurrection". Kamala Harris even compared January six to Pearl Harbor. Apparently, she doesn't know our history very well.

Those of us who viewed the events objectively, realized that something did not look right nor did any of it make sense. What was being declared was not factual. It appeared another lie in the string of lies was being perpetrated upon America and the world.

It was witnessed to be police and FBI instigators in the crowd directing the people to become riotous. Four unarmed individuals were police targeted and killed by either shooting them or beating them to death. The footage being shown on the news was manipulated designed and presented with dropped film thread to look like the protesters broke into the capital. People in the crowd were made to look like they were out of control when in fact they were trying to escape being shelled on.

Many who were in attendance were followed up with arrests and to date are in prison on false and exaggerated charges. Some have been so severely beaten they have irreversible damage. One man is made blind in one eye from the beatings. They have been held in solitary confinement. In many cases not fed, not given water and left unable to clean themselves. These are people who were exercising their rights, not destroying statues, breaking storefront windows, looting, starting fires, stomping and jumping up and down on police cars, shooting, and knifing one another. These were not BLM, ANTIFA or other violent groups, yet they are being exposed to treatment worse than we would treat a violent pow, child rapist or murder convict.

Now with the twenty twenty-four elections, Trump again is ahead in the poles. And every imaginable fabricated and falsified charge is being brought against him in hopes to cause him to be disqualified. They even tried the fourteenth amendment for which doesn't apply to him as he has never been an officer. Everything thrown against hm has failed because it is all false and cannot be supported. But what has been successful, is keeping him in court so he can't campaign effectively. None the less, the majority of Americans are aware of what the left is doing and Trumps pole numbers are climbing.

People are being censored and, in some cases, even arrested if they speak contrary to the narratives of the left. New York has even recently passed a law that allows individuals who are considered a health risk for reasons such as not being Covid inoculated or any reason accepted when presented, will be forcibly removed from their place of dwelling and put into a camp. (New York GOV. Article forty-eight) There is no longer rule of law in our country under this present administration.

The Wars are on.

In 1949 the North Atlantic Treaty Organization was created primarily by the United States with Canada and other European nations which to date total about twenty-two. The purpose of NATO was to create an alliance of defense against the former Soviet Union. Otherwise known as Russia, Ukraine, Belarus, Moldov, Lithuania, Latvia, Estonia, Georgia, Armenia, Azerbaijan, Kazakhstan, Uzbekistan, Kyrgyzstan, Tajikistan, and Turkmenistan. The USSR existed from around nineteen twenty-two to nineteen ninety-one.

As I write this the USSR has not existed for thirty-two years, yet NATO remains. Not only does it remain, but it has expanded. In fact, within a little more than ten years, from nineteen ninety to early two thousand's, it distended itself three times adding the Czech Republic, then Hungary and Poland. It added more all from further east including some who were members of the dissolved Soviet republics of Estonia, Latvia and Lithuania and in two thousand-nine Albania and Croatia were included.

According to Vladimir Putin it was agreed in the nineteen nineties' that NATO was not to expand eastward and therefore, promise after promise has been broken. No one seems to know the truth of that agreement. Some say there was no such agreement while others say there was and unless we could actually see the accounts recorded of the meeting, we don't really know.

None the less, as previously mentioned, the USSR has not existed for better than thirty-two years and NATO was constructed for the purpose of resisting it. Resisting now something that no longer exists. So, the question is: why do we still have it? The answer you will be told is, in case the USSR should form again. What? After thirty-two years we are still dumping billions to fund this unnecessary organized group and paying in more to have it distended further.

The United States uses NATO as a measure of security with European nations. It is supposed to bring democracy with rule of law and individual liberty and ensure peaceful resolves to disputes for all of its members. So, the group since the dissolution of the USSR has transformed itself into its own military alliance and still remains a counter to Russia. Albeit, the NATO military ability and strength does not hold much compared to Russia's military.

Vladimer Putin attended the Bucharest summit meeting of two thousand-eight and spoke out against bringing Ukraine into NATO. It was made very clear that if NATO was parked on his doorstep, it would be crossing the line. Regardless and carelessly there has been a continuation of talks and proposals since to join Ukraine with NATO. It would appear and is even obvious that Russia had been provoked in its invasion of Ukraine.

Within just a few months after Russia launched its military inside Ukraine, on September twenty-two, the Nord Stream pipeline's both one and two were sabotaged. Both pipelines were installed in order to transport natural gas to Germany via the Baltic Sea by the Russian owned company Gazprom.

The following report is one of many that reveals the United States was privy at the least to Nord Stream's sabotage. The subsequent result of this destruction is that it not only blows hole in Russia's pocket book, but it has mercilessly left the German people suffering without energy.

"In June 2023, The Washington Post reported that the United States had intelligence of a Ukrainian plan to attack Nord Stream, and in November 2023 reported that Roman Chervinsky, a colonel in Ukraine's Special Operations Forces, had coordinated the Nord Stream pipeline attack."

Examining the actions of the United States it clearly has an interest in crippling the energy generated and supplied by not just other nations, but its own as well. Oil in today's world structure, is an absolute necessity. To be a major oil or gas supplier not only makes you a wealthy country, but also places you in a powerful bargaining position with both allies and adversaries. So, why has the United States put the blade to its throat?

As of the nineteen seventies the majority of wars are fought over a conflict in oil. Interestingly since the Liberian tanker, Argo Merchant ran aground at Nantucket Shoals when delivering oil for a winter supply to a Salem Massachusetts energy plant, we experience an average of six spills per year. Seems we need new captains.

The first recorded oil spill was more than one hundred years prior. In eighteen fifty-nine oils being transported by the Titusville, Pennsylvania oil company had an ocean accident resulting in its spill. Now, over one hundred years later, with better and stronger built ships we have a significant increase of damaging and costly oil spills plaguing the oceans.

The destruction of the Nord Stream pipeline did not hurt Russia as much as it hurt Germany and other recipients of its gas dependency. Why then, would you want to cripple your allies just to only slightly injure an opponent? The end justifies the means.

While in twenty twenty-two the Ukraine/Russia war was blazing and the United States was depleting its already depleted funds on Ukraine, which was well known in advance could and would not win , the Israeli invasion of Hamas was being planned.

Biden, shut down the Keystone and through various other measures, made us energy dependent on other countries because we don't produce quite enough to make us independent. He had the Nord Stream sabotaged leaving Europe energy crippled and through the orchestrated Ukraine/Russia conflict the grain and wheat supply across Europe, the middle east, Egypt/Africa and other areas of the world including the United States, has been greatly reduced if not altogether stopped.

On October seven, two thousand twenty-three, the day known as "the last great day" of Israel's "Feast of Tabernacles", the Palestinian terrorist group, Hamas, invaded Israel. They were allowed to enter through the heavily guarded Gaza border. They entered through fencing that was equipped with such highly developed, sensitive technology; not even a mouse could cross without alerting the IDF into action. Yet about four hundred Hamas soldiers entered without any resistance.

Once inside, they were able to, unhindered, continue on and attack the unsuspecting Israeli citizens. They were free to commit horrific, merciless assaults, killing and raping victims, even defenseless children were attacked and many Israelis were taken hostage.

The aftermath reports of the Israeli citizens were that there was no military intervention for six to eight, and some say twelve hours from the initial invasion. Even IDF soldiers have stated that it was impossible for Hamas to break through the border and that they were under stand down orders during the attack. Also reported is that a couple of weeks prior to the attack the Israeli government disarmed its people. Those in the Kubutz were always armed however, during the attack they were defenseless. Days later they were re-issued arms.

Why would the Hamas attack be a set-up? Possibly because Israel wants the oil the Palestinians are sitting on. A conference on trade and development held by the United Nations put out a paper in two thousand nineteen saying that there are oil and gas reserves in Palestinian land as well as waters and some of the east Mediterranean gas belonged to the Palestinians. This would give reason to develop excuse to remove them. With no Nord Stream operations, Europe's energy source would be primarily from the middle east. Saudi Arabia has been the largest exporter of oil and Russia was the second largest. Interestingly, since the Nord Stream destruction, China, India and Turkey are the major importers of Russian oil while Europe is practically receiving no oil from Russia.

The United States produces its own energy, yet not enough to meet the demand. This is of course, by design. There are exports of oil from the United States however, it exports the least of all exporters and still, for economic and crude grade reasons, it becomes necessary to import. The top five countries the United States imports oil from are: Canada, Saudi Arabia, Iraq and Columbia.

Owning and operating the worlds primary energy supply leads to large bargaining power. Also, the Suez Canal brings in more than nine billion dollars a year through trade and yet is limited in size. Therefore, it is desirable and feasible to open a wider more efficient canal through Gaza using the same water source. And it would become twice as profitable. Thus, the land must be unoccupied for this as well.

With the United States currently playing big brother to Israel, and the rest of the world watching, it puts the peoples in a precarious position because, so goes Israel, so goes the United States and so goes the United States, so goes the world. This is a fact. The repercussions from the leading nations turning on Israel will be planetary.

There were many false reports such as forty Israeli babies being beheaded by Hamas and their deliberately bombing hospitals etc., which were slanting the reality and views of the nations. Later these reports were found to be false and or misreported, but the corrections were not well broadcast thus, many still believe them to be real events.

Because mainstream media is controlled by Israeli globalists interest, the news will report every harm that comes to Israelis by Hamas. The atrocity's delivered to the Palestinians (the citizens; not Hamas) go unreported. The water, food, energy etc. being cut off leaving them so lacking in supplies that they don't even have anesthesia to administer for children who require operations from injuries sustained during bombing. At times even needed amputations and these children have no more to do with Hamas than our children do with the violent gangs in our own nation. But war has no mercy and all become victims.

The word Hamas in Hebrew means violence and in Arabic it means zeal. Indeed, they seem to have a zeal toward violence. There is no question that groups like Hamas, are perversely zealous, violent and intolerable. Yet, not all Palestinians are Hamas. The greater majority, in fact, have a lesser tolerance for Hamas than the nations around them because they have been caged in and unwilfully living with them.

Hamas cannot defeat Israel. But combined with allies such as Hezbollah and support from other middle east nations like Iran and Türkiye, Israel begins to look less challenging. The world is divided on whose side it supports however, within the Muslim nations, there is no question. They do not support Israel.

The United States shares in the Israeli cause. Congress and the president are controlled by Israeli globalists. Since president Carter, every president in office has signed their commitment to Israel and acceptance of the Noahide laws. Other nations such as Italy have done the same. The designed purpose of all the wars, the energy production and transport interference, the hindrance of food production as well as all the other nefarious government activities around the globe is for the purpose of ushering in the new world order which will require that all gentiles are under the Noahide laws.

A conference on trade and development held by the United Nations put out a paper in two thousand nineteen saying that there are oil and gas reserves in Palestinian land as well as waters and some of the east Mediterranean gas belonged to the Palestinians. This would give reason to develop excuse to remove them.

In the globalists mind, the worlds headquarters is supposed to be located in Jerusalem. From there the globalists elite will govern the world. This would, in their thinking, fulfill the prophecy which reads:

"For out of Zion the law shall go forth, and the word of the Lord from Jerusalem. (Micah 4:2)

All three Abrahamic religions would agree to this structure because of its biblical origin. But in actuality, it is simply the usual modus operandi of Satan imitating God. The true believer understands that the Lords plans are not the same as those of the globalist's religion. Indeed, *the law will go out from Zion, the word of the Lord from Jerusalem,* however it won't be through a globalists construct. Contrarily it will be from the believers or the body of Christ. Neither Jew nor Greek (gentile) but one new man (mature, fully grown, adult).

The globalists have a year two thousand and thirty maximum goal to accomplish their intent to usurp authority over the world and therefore perceive an urgency to act. They will stop at nothing.

CHAPTER 20

Last Call

Y2024

In the minds of most people, the United States is facing a make or break for our country with the election of a new president. Yet in actuality, Donald Trump was re-elected in twenty-twenty hands down. The proof is overwhelming; although the mainstream media will deny it and paint a different picture. The world is aware, but the blindsided of the United States swallow up the media's paid for narrating without any deep investigating of their own. Many rely instead on organizations such as "factcheck,org"; A construct of the Annenberg Public of Pennsylvania. But who checks the fact checkers?

The reality is our current administration was installed through deceptive measures. This is verifiable. Those sitting in the presidential and vice presential seats are imposters. Donald Trump was and is the last elected president of The United States of America. Whether he is re-installed in twenty-four or not, he is the last. The door is closing on the Gentile age. This beast system must collapse and falling with it is its rider "Mystery Babylon". A new day or a new age is on the rise for God's people and glorious changes will come, but not without hard travail.

The United States is the beast with two horns like a lamb, but speaks like a dragon that came up out of the earth exercising authority of the beast before him; Great Britain who is a partner and is closely related to the United States. (Revelations 13:11) It therefore plays crucial role in end time events for Christ's Body of believers, Israel, the religious, and the secular world. So goes the United States, so goes the world.

Trump has gone back on the campaign trail and has been accepted by the populace in spite of his poor record on the C19 inoculation. The media is performing its dog and pony show and jumping through the hoops of those who support them (the far-left globalists) and fabricating the popularity of Trump's opponents.

For the better half of twenty-four Biden was campaigning against Trump. But his public appearance and performance was suffering badly. His stuttering and inability to recall events made his campaign at best, imagined attainability. Those surrounding him with pretend favorability, claimed he was "sharp as a tack", had a wonderful memory, understood the issues of the country, understood the issues which the world faced and many more tongue in cheek statements about their selected candidate. But after a campaign debate between Trump and Biden on the twenty-fourth of June in Atlanta Georgia, Biden's performance was so sufferable that it was decided that he couldn't be redeemed and should resign. Kamala Harris, the vice president occupier, replaced him by default. Seemingly they were unable to obtain another candidate that would yield to the bidding of the man behind the curtain. With Harris they could capitalize on her skin tone and pretend she is from African descent also, that she manifests the female approach. Both of course, are lies. She is of east Indian from her mother and Jamaican from her father and neither were American citizens when she was born thus, she doesn't even qualify for the position of president. Regarding her representing the female population, it would have to be narrowed down to the few woke young girls who have just broken into voting age and lack understanding of the political arena. Not to dismiss the radical globalists women who are using her for a temporary stepping stone toward the annihilation of the United States. She is another means to sow destruction and division. She has no presidential capabilities and the world leaders of the nations will not by any means honor her. She is the ultimate dooms day for the country and selected for that purpose.

If they cannot rig the upcoming twenty twenty-four election as was done to the twenty-twenty election and get her installed, they have plans to release chaos, civil uprising, terrorist attacks and war within our country. WW111 will be in place, and already is, regardless of who becomes president. Also, the terrorists attacking will be in place accompanied with famine, water shortages black outs, gasoline shortage, diseases and severe manipulated weather modifications. Harris will rest through it and let what falls on the people fall, just like she has with the border crises. Trump will have many sleepless nights battling the collapse which will no doubt delay the inevitable, but the time is short and the things that will be, will be.

The globalists are so determined to reach their twenty-thirty goal for domination, that they will do anything it might require. Lives mean nothing for thy have no regard for life whether it be human animal or vegetable. They will uproot and destroy anyone or anything in their path to this dominance. They are compelled by evil and wallow in perversion.

Impression has it, that in desperation to remove their resistance an assassination attempt was made. On July thirteenth of twenty twenty-four in Butler, Pennsylvania, a Trump campaign rally was being held. A young man (Thomas Mathew Crooks) placed a ladder next to a building that was 430 feet away from the rally and climbed upon the roof while packing an AR15 rifle and proceeded to do a low crawl across the roof toward his target site. Although it was a clamorous metal roof and officers of the secret service were inside the building, he miraculously wasn't heard. Outside rally participants observed him and notified the secret service as well as local police of his presence and reported he appeared to have a gun. The officers made motions like an intent to respond, but did nothing to a prevent the suspects advancement. Recordings of individuals yelling, "there's a man on the roof; he's got a gun" and other warnings have since been revealed. Shots rang out, first hitting Donald Trump and burning through the top of his right ear, then following shots, one killing a spectator and other's injuring at least two others were seemingly from different guns and a different area.

The snipers, on an adjacent building 430 feet away had spotted Crooks twenty minutes before there were any gunfire. However, It has now been reported that his presence was known by the secret service for ninety-two minutes prior to the shooting. The secret service body guards, some able-bodied men, included some unskilled and untrained women who didn't have the body mass to cover Trump efficiently and one appeared to be so untrained with weapons that she struggled to holster her gun. The entire security was sloppy to say the least.

The investigation of circumstances is still ongoing as I write and many situations surrounding this event is coming forward and being disclosed. And the more it unravels, the more revealing it is of a leftist globalist attempt to assassinate Donald Trump. Not a lone gunman with a Trump phobia. Suspiciously, the authorities had Crooks body cremated without even his family being aware. This would suggest there was something about Crooks body they didn't want discovered. Some reports indicate that Iran was behind the assassination attempt. Which is a possibility, but if true, they were undeniably working with our globalist intelligence and will call for a deeper investigation of our Iranian supporters within.

Soon after that attempt, came the announcement that Joe Biden would drop from the campaign and shortly thereafter, he endorsed Kamala Harris to take his place. If Harris steps into the oval office, it will be by another arranged selection. The inevitable demise of our country and the world will happen with lock step speed. People will literally be fighting for their lives as food will be scarce, weapons will be confiscated, medical needs will be withheld, all rights and freedoms will be removed and non-compliers put into the already structured FEMA camps. Currently, we are seeing individuals put in jail for speaking against the government's narratives and operations. Yet that is what the first amendment is supposed to protect us from.

With Trump in office these inevitable events will be held at bay and it will give more time for preparation. But the plans to launch gladiatorial battles across our land, collapse the dollar, create famine and bring in more fabricated diseases with a multiplicity of other murderous maneuvers is ready for deployment upon announcement.

This third world war will bring Israel to its knees, collapse the beast system and usher in the millennial. So, while Christ's body of believers have nothing to fear the world on the other hand will be under judgement and many will perish. Yet many will be saved.

Yeshua/ Jesus is scheduled to return soon and will come for His body. Those who've believed, conquered and prepared themselves to rule and reign for this next thousand years. The seventh day from creation.

The events that are engineered around the globe have been surreptitiously orchestrated in the past, but are now blatant and full throttle in motion like the Big Boy locomotive, they are blasting through while mercilessly obliterating anyone who stands in their way.

DELVING FURTHER

Never before has there been such a time as this; A time to wake up and acknowledge your creator and accept His salvation through His Son, Yahushua Ha Mashiach/ Jesus the Christ is now. The time to leave a religious structure that is taking you to the grave is now.

Knowing that the beast system has through the centuries, been formed, is here and in full operation bringing us to the climax of our Father's plan, the question is; what now?

As previously pointed out, the Beast has been around since the beginning. A person could always be marked (noted) by giving their mind and their fellowship to a civil-religious man-made structure. Moses himself could have given over to the beast system of his day, but we are told in the book of Hebrews that he rejected the beast system of his day.

"By faith Moses, when he became of age, refused to be called the son of Pharoah's daughter,"

"choosing rather to suffer affliction with the people of God, than to enjoy the passing pleasures of sin"

"esteeming the reproach of Christ greater riches than the treasures of Egypt; for he looked to the reward".

"By faith he forsook Egypt, not fearing the wrath of the king; for he endured as seeing Him who is invisible." (Hebrews 11: 24-27)

Moses is probably the greatest example, next to Christ, of an individual who could have had everything given to him had he complied and sided with the civil-religious power he was living under. But he gave his heart, soul, mind, and commitment to the Lord and His people instead. He laid up his treasures in heaven with Christ and now has a crown of life eternal rather than the fading crown of mankind.

This is a choice that every believer has. It is easy to follow the system that is in place. Where you'll have no resistance, no persecutions, but rather you can live without threat and prosper by giving your mind, your labor and committing fellowship to a man made political-religious system.

"Enter by the narrow gate; for wide is the gate and broad is the way that leads to destruction, and there are many who go in by it. Because narrow is the gate and difficult is the way which leads to life, and there are few who find it" (Mathew 7:13)

If you see the majority accepting a particular path or a questionable doctrine, they are almost certainly entering a way to destruction and it is our responsibility to know the difference.

There are questionable doctrines saturating journalism and media communications today. We have to go beyond them and dig a little deeper to learn more of the truth.

Currently, the Christan world is has is convinced and has succumbed to the belief that it must rally in support of Israel. This belief that it is necessary to support the Israeli leaders in every decision they make and every action they take is a deception that was foisted upon the Christian people in early nineteen hundred with the creation of the Scofield Bible.

Theodore Herzi and the Rothchild's had gone to then residing pope Pius X and presented their idea of the Zionists and were rejected regarding the aiding of the Zionist takeover of Palestine. Thus, the support of the protestants became necessary. They hired a Christian theologian, Cyrus I. Scofield to convince protestants that the Jews must re-take the "promise land" in order to fulfill prophecy. The objective was to infiltrate the mind of the Christian world by using their own scriptures.

LORD ROTHSHILD - BALFOUR DECLARATION

The following is a speech given by Lord Rothchild on November 15, 2017

"It is a particular honour for my family that the letter containing the Balfour Declaration was addressed to my great Uncle Walter, the second Lord Rothschild.

In 1915 he had inherited the title from Nathaniel, his distinguished father, and with it the leadership of the family and British Jewry.

The letter was delivered to his home at Piccadilly and from there taken to him at his estate at Tring. Walter's great passion was zoology and his museum at Tring housed what was to become the finest private collection of natural history specimens ever made by one man.

The decision to address the Declaration to him was seen as surprising by some. For example, Nahum Sokolow remarked that the main reason for it being sent to Walter, rather than the Zionist Committee, was that the Zionists "had no address while Walter had a very fine one at 148 Piccadilly". The historian Cecil Roth described it as "incongruous". But Walter had been deeply involved in the Zionist movement. He had been introduced to Chaim Weizmann and the cause through his formidable Hungarian sister-in-law Rozika, a convinced Zionist, who had married his younger brother Charles.

Walter's commitment to Zionism was fired by his very first meeting with Weizmann. He became convinced that the future of the Jews lay in Zionism and dedicated himself to the cause. After the Declaration Weizmann wrote to him: "May I offer you our heartiest thanks in making this possible — I am sure that when the history of this time will be written it will be justifiably said that the name of the greatest House in Jewry was associated with the granting of the Magna Carta of Jewish liberties...."

Even if Walter's connection to the Zionist movement was somewhat unconventional, from another side of my family Baron Edmond de Rothschild played a significant if very different role in the years prior to the Declaration.

The Baron had been deeply involved in the resettling of Jews in Palestine following the dreadful pogroms of the 1880s in Russia. He was moved to support the early settlers by a number of factors, such as the increasing antisemitism and violence in the Pale of Settlement which made a refuge for Jews from pogroms and persecution imperative. But he was looking for more than a refuge. Above all he was inspired by the vision of the rebirth of the Jewish spirit in its ancient land. As he would later write to the early pioneers of Rishon LeZion: " I did not come to your aid because of your poverty and suffering for to be sure there were many other similar cases of distress in the world. I did it because I saw in you the realisers of the renaissance of Israel and of that ideal so dear to us all, the sacred goal of the return of Israel to its ancestral homeland."

In the spirit of this vision, Edmond was inspired to support not only the physical and economic needs of the fledgling communities but also the intellectual and spiritual dimension of their activity. For example, he saw the development of The Hebrew University as "a great event in the modern history of Judaism" and actively supported the revival of the Hebrew language. Indeed, Eliezer ben Yehuda, the father of modern Hebrew, dedicated his famous Hebrew dictionary to him.

For all of that, his relationship with the early settlers was complex.

Edmond had originally calculated that it would take between one and three years before the early settlements would achieve economic independence. Clearly that was not to be the case. And the difference of outlook between the Labour Zionist pioneers, concerned with basic challenges of security, epidemics and subsistence, and the Baron's more sophisticated ambitions, which included the manufacture not only of wine, but also, at various stages, of tobacco, silk and perfume to furnish the salons of Europe, were not without tensions — and often lively correspondence.

Fortunately, the relationship survived the frustrations in the years that followed and contributed to an unimaginable transformation. In 1867 Mark Twain had described Palestine as "a hopeless, dreary and heartbroken land". By the time Edmond made his last visit in 1925, it was altogether different. Speaking in the Great Synagogue of Tel Aviv he reminisced: "When I look back on the stretch of land where I began my work, I recall how Palestine appeared in those days: a rocky, barren land full of thorns. Today it seems to me I'm in a dream."

It is poignant that Edmond passed away on November 2nd, the anniversary of the Balfour Declaration. His activity in Palestine, and then Israel, was continued by his son James and James' wife Dorothy.

James and Dorothy both came to play a role in the parallel story of the diplomacy that led to the Declaration. James had grown up in France but left to study at Cambridge, in part because of the antisemitism he saw revealed by the Dreyfus affair. In England, he married Dorothy Pinto, a 17-year-old girl from an Anglo-Sephardi family, who would herself would play an important part in the story of the Declaration.

The story of how Chaim Weizmann, an immigrant chemist, came to England and through his charm and brilliance and passion — as well as his scientific contribution to the war effort — won over the British leadership is well known. Less well known is the story of how he gained the access that was crucial to this success.

Weizmann, not surprisingly, wanted to meet with Baron Edmond, or at least his son James, to recruit their support. In the event, Edmond was in France while James was convalescing from his war injuries, so it fell to the teenage Dorothy to meet him. It is not clear who was more charmed by whom but a relationship developed — he wrote to her no less than 33 times between 1914 and 1916 — and through Dorothy and James, as well as the wider family, the door to a significant circle of the British establishment was opened.

Their commitment to Palestine and then Israel was unswerving. James' parting gift was to give the Knesset building to the State of Israel. Dorothy decided to continue his work through the foundation, Yad Hanadiv, and it was her idea to offer the magnificent Supreme Court building.

This commitment to Israel of these two very different branches of the Rothschild family devolved to me through inheritance of the title and through Dorothy entrusting me with the chairmanship of the family foundation.

Today the foundation continues to support Israel as a healthy vibrant democratic society, committed to Jewish values and equal opportunity for the benefit of all its inhabitants. In carrying out its work, it recognises the potential of all individuals, religious and secular, Jewish and Arab, men and women, to bring about change — whether in the school system or academia, whether in the work place or the environment, continuing a legacy that goes back to the Balfour Declaration and before.

Today Yad Hanadiv employs some 40 people in Jerusalem and supports a wide range of good causes. In particular, over the last 15 years or so, we have been helping to build Israel's new National Library in Jerusalem, for the People of the Book, to link Jewish communities throughout the world for the first time, thanks to the internet and digitisation revolution and to serve all faiths.

As we celebrate the Balfour Declaration, we all surely recognise the remarkable human effort by ordinary and extraordinary individuals which led first to the Declaration and since then to a miraculous reality.

My family and I are proud to have played a role in this story. My hope is that our commitment and involvement in this historic and inspiring mission will continue in the years ahead."

Scofield constructed a reference bible which reformed the thinking of the protestant world to believe in the dispensation of the Jews to the promise land. A popular phrase he wrote:

"For a nation to commit the sin of ***anti-Semitism*** brings inevitable judgement".

This became embedded in the minds of Christianity. Believing Christians and particularly the evangelic assemblies have, through the Scofield biblical Israeli references, come to believe they must give unquestionable and noncritical support to Israel as commanded by God. When in reality, there is no such commandment nor even a suggestion to do so.

In nineteen hundred and nine the first publication of the Scofield reference bible was released and made such an impact on the Christian heads of church and state, for which the Rothchild's held great influential power, that by nineteen hundred and seventeen the Balfour declaration was issued as a public pledge by Britain to establish a national homeland for the Jews.

The Scofield bible had played a significant role in the acceptance and support of the nations to this cause. And the thinking of the Israel today as being the self-same Israel of the Old Testament has grown and established itself in the minds of the Christian. For some, it is to the extent that they are afraid of God's wrath should they find any fault with the behavior of Israel.

In nineteen eighty-four the New Scofield Study Bible was released with an additional commentary which reads; "For a nation to commit sin of anti-Semitism brings inevitable judgement" This and other similar influential messages has deterred the thinking of Christians all over the globe.

Individuals quote bible passages such as the following to support their stand with Israel.

"Pray for the peace of Jerusalem: May they prosper who love you."

"Peace be within your walls, Prosperity within your palaces."

"For the sake of my brethren and companion, I will now say, 'peace be within you."

"Because of the house of the LORD our God I will seek your good." (Psalms 122: 6-9)

These are good scriptures with a good message, but let us not forget they are the same scriptures Christ grew up learning. Yet He separated the hypocrites, vipers, and false teachers from the Judean with hearts that were true and never did He apply these scriptures to the corrupt Jerusalem system. In fact, there is no record that He ever mentioned these passages. Rather what He said to Jerusalem was quite contrary.

"O Jerusalem, Jerusalem the one who kills the prophets and stones those who are sent to her! How often I wanted to gather your children together, as a hen gathers her chicks under her wings, but you were not willing! See! Your house is left to you desolate, for I say to you, you shall see Me no more till you say, Blessed is He who comes in the name of the LORD" (Mathew 23: 37-39)

This is strong language stating the truth of how they kill God's people and His prophets. It is also a prophetic statement regarding the future of Jerusalem and it hasn't changed. Christ said Jerusalem would not see Him again until they say "Blessed is He that comes in the name of the LORD". (Jehovah)

To this day they not only deny Him, but on a whole, they despise him. It is not uncommon and even acceptable for Christians to be spat upon in Jerusalem. None the less their leaders will take advantage of the Christians commitment to Israel and use them for their own needs such as in war or aid etc. Imagine if the disciples of Christ were so dedicated to Israel, they rallied in support of His crucifixion. Yet in effect, that is what the Christian world is doing by supporting those who make themselves an enemy to God. Those who reject His Son and if He were here today, they would crucify Him again.

Jerusalem has played the whore to God. Throughout the bible you read over and over how the Israelites turned away from God and sought the gods of the nations around them. Israel lost its way, but a remnant received their Messiah, Yeshua, and are written in the Lambs Book of Life today. There will yet be more to receive revelation of Yeshua our Lord and His gift of eternal life.

The greatest ally of Israel today is the United States. This is appropriate to history as, unknown to many, it was Judeans from Spain who discovered the Americas with Columbus, frequently reported a Jew himself.

Although Columbus was raised in Italy, his mother practiced Judaism and kept Jewish literature and artifacts in the home. To this day many scholars believe He was in fact a Jew. But because the Jews were under persecution and being exiled from Spain, he did not reveal his identity. When he approached the Queen proposing his mission she granted him not only permission for exploratory sailing, but she also allowed Jews that were to be exiled to accompany him as crew. For which Columbus was well pleased.

With the discovery of America and the expulsion of Jews from other nations, many turned to the Americas for relocation. The first recorded Jews to come to America was in 1654 as refugees from Recife, Brazil and landed in New York, then called New Amsterdam. Although they were not signatories on the Constitution, Declaration of Independence and other major national documents of the day. None the less they were supporters with our founding fathers and were actively involved in the formation of the country as well as participating in the Revolutionary War etc. Since then, there has been German, Sephardic and even Ashkenazi Jews migrated to the United States.

The Judeo-Christian beliefs are a foundational part of our heritage and cannot be ignored. Therefore, it is a contributing factor and a strong force to United States consistent alignment with Israel. Unfortunately, this is reflective of a double standard as we have many different races who contributed to the founding of the country, yet we don't blindly align ourselves with their country of origin. Not to mention the fact that the land of Israel itself didn't exist at the founding of our country. Thus, it is a moot point

Regardless, of the afore mentioned fact, we have had many Jewish professors and instructors in our schools and colleges, a multitude of Jews holding congressional positions, and of course our infamous world banking cabal as well as our health industry. Through these establishments they are able to fenagle, persuade or dissuade to what they perceive is beneficial to their own interests and not necessarily to that of the nation. This complete with the foisted theology of Scofield's biblical approach and presuppositions of the Jew and their land creates "a three-strand cord not easily broken" between Israel, the United States, and the Evangelical world. And it is not a Godly arrangement.

Although, covertly ruled by outside factions, the United States of America is the ruling entity of the world today. Therefore, if you change the United States, you change the world. *"So goes the Unites States; so, goes the world."*

Over the past sixteen years we have seen unprecedented changes take place, not only to the United States but, to the entire world. These changes have been profoundly hazardous for the most part. The United States government no longer exists as founded. It operates like a third world country housing a tyrannical leadership. As a result, the nations of the world are crumbling to the point of non-recognition.

The excitement, education and beauty of experiencing different cultures and societies is being stripped away as the self-called elite disintegrates every culture and nation. Engaged in diminishing heritages, with the unique and accepted differences of societies and their own beliefs and their own fabricated histories in order to produce their imagined globalist agenda. None other than the tower of Babel-one world government, a.k.a. New World Order (globalist). The beautiful variety of our world and the individuality of people are being raped, dismantled, sabotaged and eradicated by measure.

For a brief four years of Trumps administration, the United States and the world began to establish peace and prosper. However, before this positive productive atmosphere could be established, it was dismantled by the installation of an unelected administration, destructive globalists with hired violent protestors staged to display destructive outrage and disrespect toward the Trump administration, the constitution, history and the tearing down off historical monuments and statues, the law and anyone that was not considered of color, All of this was allowed with no or very little repercussions. While at the same time spouting out "all inclusive". Seems they aren't so "all inclusive" unless it's their chosen groups of like-minded soldiers and pawns.

None the less, it will fall. The plan of a globalist regime will fail and the only new world order that will be coming in is the Kingdom of God. The globalists are a snake swallowing its own tail.

Europe has been invaded to its extinction and the same is happening to the United States while Israel is, through its brutal war crimes, creating enemies thus leading to its own destruction. Yet they have no clue it is a work of the Lord to bring the Beast of Great Britain and the United States down with the religious system that has been riding its back and enjoying its protection while gaining worldly wealth.

"For the LOVE of money is a root of all evil, for which some have strayed from the faith in their greediness, and pierced themselves through with many sorrows" (1 Timothy 6:10)

A sizable part of the wealth they gain comes from being pardoned from paying tax. Every religious organization enjoys a tax-exemption which is saving them hundreds and thousands of dollars to exist and operate each year by filing a 501c3 status. Whether part of the mainstream religions or a non-denominational organization. Or whether your assembly doesn't recognize organization to claim themselves a non-organization doesn't matter. If you're a group offering spiritual benefits or other humanitarian benefits, you can take advantage of this government exemption gift.

Once the 501c3 has been accepted it allows the government to observe your operations. It allows then to place restrictions and requirements. Most tolerable and sensible such as having ample parking, handicap access, two bathrooms and an emergency exit in the occupied buildings. Things like meeting health standards if you have an operating kitchen etc. These are all common-sense practices and are easy to agree to for the financial benefit received in exchange. However, what they've done is shaken hands in an agreement with the beast.

The churches are not forced to sign up to the 501c3 in order to be tax exempt, however when they claim tax exemption it automatically puts them in the same file cabinet as far as the government is concerned and they will be monitored with the rest.

Now they are not only told to have two bathrooms, but they are told what they cannot preach from the biblical word of God. They are told they must close their doors during a health crisis; whether a manufactured one or not. They are told to encourage their congregation to receive inoculations and not to sing during their meetings but keep masks on, once allowed to meet again, to also remain six feet apart. The pastors can even be arrested for non-compliance if they refuse these mandated requisites.

It is fair to apply the apostle Paul's statement even though his subject was not regarding taxes.

"A little leaven, leavens the whole lump". (Galatians 5; 9

Our Lord paid His taxes and taught His disciples to do the same "Then they sent to Him some of the Pharisees and the Herodians, to catch Him in His words. When they had come, they said to Him, 'Teacher, we know that You are true, and care about no one; for you do not regard the person of men, but teach the way of God in truth. Is it lawful to pay taxes to Ceasar, or not? Shall we pay, or shall we not pay?'

But He, knowing their hypocrisy, said to them, 'Why do you test Me? Bring me a denarius that I may see it.' So they brought it.

And Jesus answered and said to them, 'Render to Ceasar the things that are Cesar's, and to God the things that are God's." (Mark 12: 13-17)

The churches have leavened their entire lump in making this tax-exempt agreement with the beast. They have given authority to him by not remaining distant from him and allowing him to peer through their windows.

All the congregants of these assemblies claim a reimbursement at the end of each tax year for supporting their tax-exempt church. But the Lord never taught them to do so and in doing so, it allows the beast to scrutinize their spiritual involvement as well.

The church that Christ built didn't have a mortgage payment, didn't have utility costs, nor did it house over one hundred people under one roof. His church was meetings in homes. It was trying to stay free from government control of any sort. The offerings that people gave were to assist one another, not pay for a building. They were not and did not strap themselves down with these responsibilities until some three hundred years later when the church had already fallen into a church-state organization.

"No one can serve two masters; for either he will hate the one and love the other, or else he will be loyal to the one and despise the other. You cannot serve God and mammon". (money material wealth or promise of wealth)

There were distinguishable boundaries between your commitment to the Father and your commitment to gains. No one wants to sell their birthright for a bowl of porridge. Regardless of how hungry you are, it isn't worth a hand shake with the beast.

In times past it wasn't so dangerous to dance with the system. However today, it is extremely dangerous. We live in the age where people have abandoned all rationale. Our Heavenly Father is shaking the heavens and the earth and making a final call to anyone who will here His voice and come out of her. Come out of that religious system that is riding the beast system and anyone taking favors from the beast such as not paying taxes. is riding the system.

The Beast of Revelations is so enormous and so tangled with so many variables that it literally takes in the world. There is no nation on earth that isn't part of this Beast. Because, as brought out, every nation's government was developed on a manmade religious- political system making it a beast. Yet not necessarily the Beast. For example, the Hindu religion of India has nothing to do with Abraham or Christ and doesn't govern the world, so although they are a beast system, they are not the Beast of Revelations. However, it has its mind given to the Revelation Beast and maintains, for benefit, a hand shaking friend to it.

Another powerful entity is Satan which itself is a beast. As previously mentioned, the Bible refers to the Devil and Satan as the dragon (a beast) and that old serpent (a beast). So, we know they are the same and from the same source. (Genesis 3;1; Revelations 12;9) But have different features.

To understand the enormity of the beast system and what it is, it's necessary to examine the different sections incorporated into this system and identify them according to how they are used and identified in the Bible.

• Dragon = civil government (There are different English words used for the word translated *dragon*. Sometimes serpent, other times jackal, leviathan, sea serpent and other times it is in reference to a particular ruler such as Pharaoh)

• Great Red Dragon = a world ruling civil government

• Beast = a government of religion and politics (the Beast is a system)

• Woman = a church or religious organization (on occasion it is referencing a city)

• The Dragon gives the Beast its power or ability and authority to operate

• The Beast System governs the earth

The Woman rides the Beast (the civil-religious governments is what the church depends on to stay seated in its position) The church of Jesus Christ depends entirely upon Him and receive their authority from Him.

"These are the ones who were not defiled with women; for they are virgins. These are the ones who follow the Lamb wherever He goes. These were redeemed from among men, being first fruits to God and to the Lamb" (Rev. 14:4).

The church of Jesus Christ depends on the Holy Spirit to teach and lead them and will search the Word of God for truth and will not be deceived nor speak deceit.

"And in their mouth was found no deceit, for they are without fault before the throne of God" (Rev. 14:5).

The beast has been around since the beginning, gaining momentum, and now is so large it can't be seen and boggles the mind.

Five thousand years ago, an individual could take that mark by serving the religious-political system of their day such as Egypt. It is not new. The beast is an ancient creature created by the seas of people and manifests itself in man's religious-political imaginations. It infiltrates the entire earth and has been received as a familiar old friend. Without a spiritual eye. it is unrecognizable.

The majority believe their involvement in religion or politics classifies them as being a humanitarian and feel they are performing good deeds. Yet sadly, they are being deceived and reeled into the clutches of the beast system by serving an organization that serves this system.

It can be very difficult for a believer to examine themselves and to determine what is written in their forehead (where their mind is) and where their allegiance and commitments are. Also, to examine their doctrine and determine if they have believed or inherited false doctrine. However, if a person is honest with himself and with God, they can renew the mind through his Spirit and Word and have a closeness with Him they never imagined possible.

Please understand, every religious-political structure of any nation constitutes a beast system and what I have written is only a small part of how the beast operates in the world and how vicious it can be. There are thousands of other instances and examples documented however, I believe what I've shared here is enough to paint a clear picture for the reader to understand that whenever you have a marriage of civil authority with religious authority, they produce a beast.

The intent of the Beast-Government is to control and rule over the people of a land through man's inclinations, perspectives, incentives, lusts and greed. In other words, from bestial motives. God is not the driving force. Great Britain/United Kingdom and the United States/North America rose up together professing Christianity, they undeniably were motivated by power and greed. They each bore a Lambs horn, but ach spoke as a Dragon. It is these areas of the world that are now under attack, that have now become invaded and will now inevitably come to their demise. It had grown to enormous proportions and intimidated the world.

It should be avoided and not supported. Allegiance, devotion and all worship belong to our Heavenly Father and Christ His Son, whom the Father gave for our salvation. Jesus *only* is the Way, the Truth and the Life. The call continues going forth to "Come out of her my people". My advice to you dear reader is: Watch, Listen, Observe and don't walk, Run and run fast from any religious organization that bows down and receives its authority from the government. Don't shake hands with the Beast.

There is little time before our Savior returns for His bride whom will rule and reign with Him for the next thousand years. Many will not be prepared, but that doesn't mean they are lost. We have a merciful forgiving and patient heavenly Father. During that thousand years there will be many saved souls as this earth is restored back to righteousness.

"The LORD is merciful and gracious, slow to anger, and abounding in mercy. He will not always strive with us, nor will He keep His anger forever. He has not dealt with us according to our sins, nor punished us according to our iniquities." (Psalms 103: 8-9)

He will resurrect everyone who has encountered Him and knows Him. His desire is that none should perish.

IN CLOSING

The behavior of the Beast is manifested in varying degrees, methods and antithetical approaches to humanity. Through the sensitivities of religion, politics, agriculture, health, economics, education, transportation, resources, wars and more, it coerces, propagandizes, and strangleholds its subject into submission. The Beast does not reveal itself, but hides behind cloaks of humanitarian deeds. Deeds such as the Catholic church aiding the invaders under the guise of "doing good unto others" doctrine. When in reality the seated pope is also a globalist and working for the globalist agenda. Yet unquestionably the Vatican will not receive any immigrants and its walls remain high and heavily guarded.

This is not the end of the saga. The United States writes the final chapter to the last six thousand years. This twenty-four election will be the beginning of the collapse of the Beast that has controlled mankind from its inception. Stay far back, as the beast is going to buck hard to rid its rider. IT will collapse and it will be a tremendous earthshaking event as every element of men's structures disintegrate. But following is the seventh thousand-year reign that all of Christ's people ae looking forward to.

My prayer for this book is that anyone who reads it will obtain a clearer understanding of the Word of God, understand the beast (man's system in the world), and how it defies and exalts itself against our Heavenly Father. How it is determined to govern the people of this world. Even if it requires the perverse slaughters we have witnessed, and still do witness, in order to bring them into submission and under their control. For they who belong to this beast system, believe the means justifies the end and will do anything to achieve that goal. Further, that you are able to identify it and have the knowledge of how not to fall prey to it.

I also pray that through the reading of this book you obtain a closer walk with the Father and his precious Son, our Lord and Savior Yeshua Ha-Mashiach, Jesus the Messiah, our beloved.

May you forever experience the blessings our Father has and desires to give you.

Amen, Amen.

ENDNOTE REFERENCES

CHAPTER 6

1.The Astronomically and Agriculturally Corrected Biblical Hebrew Calendar, https://www.youtube.com/watch?v=9ZHIIOuqpGw

CHAPTER 7

The tragic earthquake of AD 60,

http://religiouslyincorrect.com/Articles/TriCityAreaEarthquake.shtml.

CHAPTER 8

1. The Story of Civilization, Vol. 4: The Age of Faith, 1950 p. 8

2. The Harper Collins Encyclopedia of Catholicism, "God" p. 568.

3. Documents of the Christian Church, Henery Bettenson, editor 1967 p. 22

4. Another reliable source is Karen Armstrong's book A History of God, New York: Ballantine Books (August 9, 1994).

5. Ibid.

6. Ibid.

CHAPTER 9

1. Simple To Remember – The History of Christmas, http://www.simpletoremember.com/vitals/Christmas_TheRealStory.htm.

2. Stephen Nissenbaum, The Battle for Christmas, Vintage 1997.

3. A History of Israel, In the Jerome Biblical Commentary p. 1247.

4. David I. Kertzer, The Popes Against the Jews: The Vatican's Role in The Rise of Modern Anti-Semitism, Alfred A. Knopf p. 74.

5. E. W. Bullinger, The Companion Bible p. 162.

CHAPTER 12

1. George Washington, Writings of Washington, pp. 452-453.

2. The Great Conspiracy, Philadelphia, Barclay & co. [c.1866].

3. William Harvey, A Tale of Two Nations, Nabu Press, 2012, p. 51.

CHAPTER 13

1. Woodrow Wilson, The New Freedom, p. 5.

2. George W. Bush, et al, A Charge to Keep, Morrow, p. 47.

3. Bill Hughes, The Secret Terrorists, Truth Triumphant (2002).

4. G. Edward Griffin, The Creature from Jekyll Island, American Opinion.

5. Ibid, p. 246.

6. Eric Phelps, Vatican Assassins, Halycon Unified Services, p. 427

7. R. W. Thompson, The Footprints of the Jesuits, Hunt and Eaton, pp. 72, 73.

8. W. C. Brownlee, Secret Instructions of the Jesuits, American and Foreign Christian Union, p. 143.

9. G. B. Nicolini, The History of the Jesuits, Henry G. Bohn, pp. 495, 496, emphasis added.

10. R. W. Thompson, The Footprints of the Jesuits p. 54.

CHAPTER 14

1. Eric Phelps, Vatican Assassins, p. 163.

2. Ibid.

3. Edmund Paris, The Vatican Against Europe, The Wickliffe Press, p. 14.

4. Arnold Gaebelien, Conflict of the Ages, The Exhorters, p. 85.

5. James Zatko, Descent into Darkness, University of Notre Dame Press, p. 111.

6. Ibid, pp. 103-106

7. Anthony Sutton, Wall Street and the Boshevik Revolution, Veritas Publishing, pp. 133-134.

8. Myron Fagan, The Illuminati and the Council on Foreign Relations, taped lecture.

9. Griffin, Ibid.

10. Charles Seymore, The Intimate Papers of Colonel House, vol. 1, Houghton Mifflin, pp. 114, 115.

11. Griffin, p. 239.

12. Jeremiah J. Crowley (former Catholic priest), Romanism: A Menace to the Nation, Menace Publishing, p 144.

13. F. Paul Peterson, Peter's Tomb Recently Discovered in Jerusalem, p. 63 – quoted in: Is Alberto for Real, Sidney Hunter, Chick Publications, p. 41.

14. Paris, p. 48.

15. The Kaiser's Memoirs, by Wilhelm II, translated by Thomas R. Ybarra, New York, 1922, p. 221.

16. Paris, p. 15.

17. Avro Manhattan, The Vatican Moscow Washington Alliance, Ozark Books – quoted in Sydney Hunter, Is Alberto for Real, Chick Publications, pp. 42-43.

18. Leo H. Lehman, Behind the Dictators, Agora Publishing. Pp. 36-39.

19. H. S. Kenan, The Federal Reserve Bank, The Noontide Press, 1966, p.158.

20. Jack Chick, Alberto pts. 1, 3, 6, Chick publications, pp. 12, 21, 28, 29.

21. Albert Garner, The Devil's Masterpiece: The Mystery of Iniquity, Blessed Hope Foundation, pp. 70, 71.

22. Ibid. p. 69.

23. Pierre Van Paassen, Days of our Years, Hillman-Curl, p. 465.

24. John Cooney, The American Pope, Times Books, pp. 124, 125.

25. Ralph Epperson, The Unseen Hand, Publius Press, p. 301.

26. Paris pp. 240, 241.

27. Lazo M. Kostich, Holocaust in the Independent State of Croatia, Liberty, p. 18.

28. Manhattan, pp. 169-170.

CHAPTER 15

1. Ibid p. 264

2. Avro Manhattan, Vietnam: Why Did We Go? Chick Publications, 1984, p. 13.

3. Ibid. p. 3.

4. Ibid p. 177.

5. Ibid p. 56.

6. Ibid p. 71.

7. Robert Morrow, First Hand Knowledge, Shapolsky Publisher's, p. 249.

8. Assorted authors, Dope, Inc. The Book that Drove Kissinger Crazy, Executive Intelligence Review, p. 117.

9. Colonel James Gritz, Called to Serve: Profiles in Conspiracy from John F. Kennedy to George Bush, Lazarus Publishing, pp. 511-512.

10. W. C, Brownlee, Secret Instructions of the Jesuits, American and Foreign Christian Union, p. 47.

11. Avro Manhattan, Murder in the Vatican, Ozark Books, pp. 35-36.

12. Ibid p. 271.

13. Jean Hill JFK: The Last Dissenting Witness, Pelican Publishing, p. 113.

14. Ibid. pp. 144-116.

15. Charles Crenshaw, JFK: Conspiracy of Silence, Penguin Books USA, p. 106.

16. Iacocca: An Autobiography, Bantam Books, p. 8.

17. Craig Roberts and John Armstrong, JFK: The Dead Witnesses, Consolidated Press, p. 3.

18. The Works of Thomas Jefferson, Vol. 1, p. 130.

CHAPTER 16

1. Henry E. Mattox, A Chronology of Unites States-Iraqi Relations, 1920-2006 p. 25.

2. Ibid. p. 32.

3. Bob Woodward, Plan of Attack – his summary of his book.

4. Ibid. p. 186.

5. Ibid. p. 188.

CHAPTER 17

1. Ibid. p. 230.

2. The Ecumenical Movement by H. Duncan.

3. "The Truth About the World Council of Churches" by L'isbeth Noelle Roth, http://www.apfn.org/apfn/WCC.htm.

4. Dr. R. J. Rushdoony, Apostasy – The National Council of Churches.

5. Ibid.

CHAPTER 18

1. Ibid.

2. Andrew Carnegie, Triumphant Democracy – quoted in Brotherhood of Darkness by Dr. Stanley Monteith

CHAPTER 19

1. Barrack Obama, Dreams of My Father p. 407.
2. Institute for Historic Review by Mark Weber
3. Implosionworld.com
4. The Karen Kingston Reports
5. Dr Ana Mihalcea
6. Dr. Brian Ardis
7. Dr. David Martin

CHAPTER 20

1. The Jewish Chronicles